Lavish praise for
KATE EMERSON
and

→ *Secrets of the Tudor Court* ←

"Emerson captures the pageantry and the politics of the Tudor court, portraying real-life characters who negotiated turbulent times, and giving historical-fiction fans a first-rate read."

—*Booklist*

"I love this series and conti
book. . . ."

"No one knows the unusual
Tudor court like Kate Emerson."

—Karen Harper, author of *The Irish Princess*

"Explores the tempestuous world of the Tudor court."

—*Publishers Weekly*

→ *By Royal Decree* ←

"Another captivating no
Elizabeth's life as the cen
love and happy endings."

"Appealing . . . a refreshir

✦ *Between Two Queens* ✦

→ The Pleasure Palace ←

"Emerson creates a riveting historical novel of the perils of the Tudor court, vividly fictionalizing historical characters and breathing new life into their personalities and predicaments."

—*Booklist*

"Jane Popyncourt is not the idealistically virginal heroine but a skillful player in the intrigues of the Tudor court, who manages to get what she wants without selling too much of herself in the bargain. It is this heroine that separates the book from the pack."

—*Publishers Weekly*

"This beautifully researched novel [is] the first in a fascinating new historical series. History, love, lust, power ambitions—*The Pleasure Palace* is a pleasure indeed."

—Karen Harper, author of *The Irish Princess*

"Rich and lushly detailed, teeming with passion and intrigue, this is a novel in which you can happily immerse yourself in another time and place."

—*RT Reviews*

All the gripping historical novels in the
***Secrets of the Tudor Court* series are also available as eBooks**

Also by Kate Emerson

The Pleasure Palace

Between Two Queens

By Royal Decree

⊹ At the ⊹

KING'S

Pleasure

KATE
EMERSON

GALLERY BOOKS
New York London Toronto Sydney New Delhi

G

Gallery Books
A Division of Simon & Schuster, Inc.
1230 Avenue of the Americas
New York, NY 10020

First Gallery Books trade paperback edition January 2012

GALLERY BOOKS and colophon are registered trademarks of Simon & Schuster, Inc.

For information about special discounts for bulk purchases, please contact Simon & Schuster Special Sales at 1-866-506-1949 or business@simonandschuster.com.

The Simon & Schuster Speakers Bureau can bring authors to your live event. For more information or to book an event contact the Simon & Schuster Speakers Bureau at 1-866-248-3049 or visit our website at www.simonspeakers.com.

Manufactured in the United States of America

1   3   5   7   9   10   8   6   4   2

Library of Congress Cataloging-in-Publication Data
Emerson, Kate.
At the king's pleasure / Kate Emerson.—1st Gallery Books trade pbk. ed.
p.   cm.
1. Ladies-in-waiting—Great Britain—Fiction. 2. Mistresses—Great Britain—Fiction. 3. Nobility—England—Fiction. 4. Buckingham, Edward Stafford, Duke of, 1478–1521—Fiction. 5. Henry VIII, King of England, 1491–1547—Fiction. 6. Great Britain—Court and courtiers—Fiction. 7. Great Britain—Kings and rulers—Paramours—Fiction. 8. Great Britain—History—Henry VIII, 1509–1547—Fiction. I. Title. II. Title: At the king's pleasure.
PS3555.M414S424 2011
813'.54—dc22
2011010993
ISBN 978-1-4391-7782-2
ISBN 978-1-4391-7784-6 (ebook)

Another one for Sandy

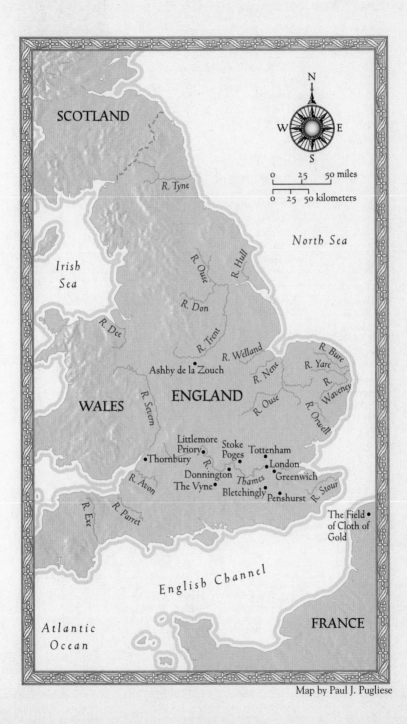

SCOTLAND

R. Tyne

North Sea

Irish
Sea

R. Ouse
R. Hull

R. Don

R. Dee

R. Trent

R. Welland

R. Nene

R. Bure

R. Yare

Ashby de la Zouch

ENGLAND

R. Ouse

R. Waveney

WALES

R. Severn

R. Orwell

Littlemore
Priory

Stoke
Poges

Tottenham

Thornbury

R.

London

Donnington

Thames

Greenwich

The Vyne

Bletchingly

Penshurst

R. Stour

R. Avon

R. Exe

R. Parret

The Field
of Cloth of
Gold

English Channel

Atlantic
Ocean

FRANCE

Map by Paul J. Pugliese

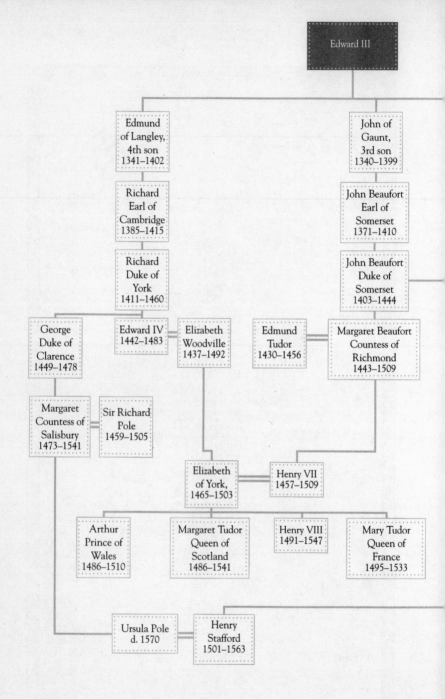

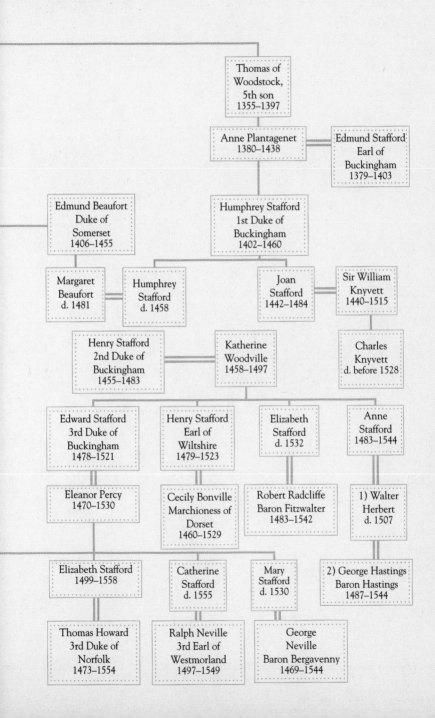

Thomas of Woodstock, 5th son 1355–1397

Anne Plantagenet 1380–1438

Edmund Stafford Earl of Buckingham 1379–1403

Edmund Beaufort Duke of Somerset 1406–1455

Humphrey Stafford 1st Duke of Buckingham 1402–1460

Margaret Beaufort d. 1481

Humphrey Stafford d. 1458

Joan Stafford 1442–1484

Sir William Knyvett 1440–1515

Henry Stafford 2nd Duke of Buckingham 1455–1483

Katherine Woodville 1458–1497

Charles Knyvett d. before 1528

Edward Stafford 3rd Duke of Buckingham 1478–1521

Henry Stafford Earl of Wiltshire 1479–1523

Elizabeth Stafford d. 1532

Anne Stafford 1483–1544

Eleanor Percy 1470–1530

Cecily Bonville Marchioness of Dorset 1460–1529

Robert Radcliffe Baron Fitzwalter 1483–1542

1) Walter Herbert d. 1507

Elizabeth Stafford 1499–1558

Catherine Stafford d. 1555

Mary Stafford d. 1530

2) George Hastings Baron Hastings 1487–1544

Thomas Howard 3rd Duke of Norfolk 1473–1554

Ralph Neville 3rd Earl of Westmorland 1497–1549

George Neville Baron Bergavenny 1469–1544

SECRETS OF THE TUDOR COURT
✣ *At the King's Pleasure* ✣

1

Manor of the Rose, London, June 18, 1509

*T*his latest news from the court pleases me," said Edward Stafford, third Duke of Buckingham, "but my brother's continued confinement in the Tower of London is worrisome."

"A mistake, surely, my lord," Charles Knyvett murmured.

Squarely built and florid-faced, with thinning hair and small, pale eyes, Knyvett had been in Buckingham's service from childhood and was one of the few men he trusted, perhaps because they were also linked by blood. Knyvett's mother had been a daughter of the first duke. His father, Sir William, now nearing his seventieth year, still held the honorary post of chamberlain in the ducal household.

"All will be sorted out in good time," agreed Buckingham's chaplain, Robert Gilbert, a tall, thin, hawk-nosed fellow with a deeply pocked face and intense black eyes.

The duke made a little humming noise, neither agreement nor disagreement, and studied the small group of women surrounding his wife at the far end of the garden gallery of his London house. His sisters, Elizabeth and Anne, were among them. They might prove useful to him, he thought. At least no one, not even the new king's overcautious councilors, would be likely to order the arrest of either of them on suspicion of treason.

"Lord Henry's confinement is doubtless the result of malicious lies," Gilbert said. "No formal charges have been made against him."

"And the only other members of the late king's household who are under arrest are inferior persons: lawyers and accountants," Knyvett chimed in.

"And a surveyor of the king's prerogative," Gilbert reminded him with a little smirk.

Knyvett glared at him, offended by the jab but reluctant to quarrel outright over it in the duke's presence. Officially, Charles Knyvett was Buckingham's surveyor. That it was a relatively minor post in a household large enough to need a chancellor, an almoner, a receiver general, and a clerk of the signet had been a source of frustration for him for some time.

Buckingham ignored the sparring between his two retainers. He was accustomed to it. In truth, he preferred antagonism to complacency. He also expected his men to spy on each other and keep him informed of everything they discovered. He deemed it wise to keep his allies at odds with one another. In an England that had for decades been torn apart by wars over the succession, it paid to know what your enemies were thinking. It made even more sense to keep a close watch on your friends.

As for his younger brother Hal's situation—that worried the duke more than he let on. They had been on uneasy terms for some time before his arrest. Hal had taken offense when his brother, as head of the family, had attempted to reallocate the funds he'd earlier promised would be Hal's for marrying the dowager Marchioness of Dorset, a match Buckingham himself had arranged. Hal had stubbornly refused to cooperate, with the result that Buckingham had found himself, at the start of a new reign, more than six thousand pounds in debt to the Crown.

Even before news of the death of King Henry the Seventh had been announced, Hal had been imprisoned in the Tower of London on suspicion of treason. Some people, Buckingham thought sourly, no doubt imagined that *he* himself was responsible for Hal's troubles. But for all his younger brother's failings, Hal was still a Stafford. Buckingham had known nothing about his arrest until several days after the fact.

Who, then, had caused Hal to be seized and held? And why? The idea that Hal had been planning rebellion was laughable. Hal's only interest in the royal court lay in the competitions to be found there—he lived for jousting. To Buckingham's mind, that meant that the charges against Hal had been intended as a warning to him as Hal's brother.

Had it been the old king's outgoing Privy Council who'd ordered the arrest? They'd been anxious to keep King Henry the Seventh's death secret until his son's succession was secure. That they should fear Buckingham as a rival claimant to the throne amused the duke. It was true he had more royal blood in his veins than the new king did, but there were others who had even more. Regardless, he'd never thought to seize the throne for himself. He was a loyal subject, sworn to support the Tudor dynasty.

It was tiresome to have to prove his loyalty to a new king, but Buckingham did not suppose that he had any choice in the matter. The Staffords must make themselves indispensable to young Henry the Eighth.

He looked again at the women clustered around his wife, Eleanor, a plain, even-tempered woman, and the sister of the Earl of Northumberland. She and her brother had been raised, as had Buckingham and Hal, in the household of Henry the Seventh's mother, the Countess of Richmond. Fatherless, they had all become wards of the Crown. Just after his twelfth birthday, Margaret Beaufort, Countess of Richmond, had arranged a marriage between her charges.

It was a good match, the duke thought now. He and Eleanor had always been fond of each other. She was soft-spoken and made him an excellent wife. In the years since they'd wed, she had provided him with a son, his heir, and three daughters to use to forge alliances with other noblemen. Unfortunately, none of his four children was old enough yet to be of use at court. Elizabeth was twelve; Catherine, ten; Henry, eight; and Mary only six.

Buckingham's gaze slid over assorted waiting gentlewomen, including plump, pretty Madge Geddings and Knyvett's half sister, Bess, to come to rest on his own siblings. His sister Elizabeth was a year his senior. He had contracted a match for her with Robert Radcliffe, Lord Fitzwalter. They'd been together for nearly four years now and Elizabeth had done her duty, giving her husband two sons. The elder was three years old and the younger an infant.

Then there was Anne. She was twenty-six years old. Buckingham had thought he'd had her settled in a marriage to Sir Walter Herbert, the old Earl of Pembroke's younger son. But Herbert had died in a fall from a horse afterward and, for nearly two years now, Anne had been back in her brother's house. Widowed, she'd returned to Thornbury, the Stafford family seat in Gloucestershire, bringing with her over a dozen servants but no heir for Sir Walter's estate. She had failed in the primary duty of a wife by not producing a single child of either sex to inherit.

Anne had moved away from the group and now sat alone on a window seat, her head bent over her embroidery frame. Buckingham's eyes narrowed as he assessed her attributes. She was more attractive than his other sister, although no great beauty. Her chin was too sharp—an outward sign of an unfortunate stubborn streak—and her complexion lacked the pink and white prettiness that was so popular at court. Still, she'd do.

"Go about your business," he told his men. "I must speak in private with my sister."

2

ady Anne looked up from her embroidery to find her brother Edward staring at her from the far side of the garden gallery. As was his wont, he wore extravagant clothing, even in the privacy of his own home. His gown was damask, heavily embroidered and studded with garnets and seed pearls. Neither rich fabrics nor costly decoration, however, could disguise the predatory nature of his smile.

"I wonder what dear Edward is plotting now," Anne murmured.

If there was more than a hint of wariness in her voice, she felt it was warranted. While it was true that she had voluntarily returned to her brother's household after the death of her husband, she had never intended to place herself quite so thoroughly under his thumb. Yet, somehow, within a month, she'd ended up granting Edward full control over her dower lands. Now she was beholden to him for everything she had, from the roof over her head and the food that she ate to the garments she wore and the jewelry that adorned them.

Only Madge Geddings, a young gentlewoman with a pink and white complexion and a small, turned-up nose, sat near enough to Anne to overhear the soft-spoken words. Madge glanced toward the duke, then quickly away, cheeks flaming.

Poor Madge, Anne thought. These days, anything to do with

Edward left her flustered and blushing. For some time now, the duke had been trying to persuade Madge, his wife's waiting gentlewoman, to share his bed. If Madge gave in, she would not be his first mistress. He'd had at least two, and had the illegitimate sons to prove it. Anne was only surprised that it had taken her brother so long to notice that the young woman had blossomed into a beauty. Madge had been part of his household for nearly ten years. True, she had been a girl of twelve when she'd first entered the duchess's service, and she had been assigned to the nursery until recently, but the duke made it a practice to keep track of everyone in his service.

The other women in the garden gallery, as yet unaware of the duke's presence, continued to converse together, heads bent over a large embroidery frame that held an altar cloth. Anne sat a little apart from those working on the project. She preferred to spend her time on emblem embroidery, creating small motifs, usually in tent stitch, which were then cut out and applied to large velvet panels for use as hangings, bed curtains, coverlets, or cushions. It was a negligible show of independence, especially when the emblem at hand was the golden Stafford knot, but it salved her pride to have tangible proof that Edward did not control *every* facet of her life.

Anne's sister, Elizabeth, looked up from her stitches at the sound of approaching footfalls. At once, a calculating look came into her eyes. Anne hid a smile. She could read her sister's expression as easily as she could interpret the sampler she'd made as a child and, just as she no longer needed to refer to the sampler as she embroidered, neither was it necessary to rely upon anything but past experience to know that her older sister wanted something from their brother. Elizabeth's face, although it had the same heart shape Anne saw in her own looking glass, was dominated by lips held too tightly compressed, so that they habitually formed a thin, hard line. Her smiles always looked forced, and they never reached her eyes.

Edward, Anne decided, seemed a trifle agitated. That was nothing unusual. Having his attention fix on her, however, *was* out of the ordinary.

"I would speak with you in private, sister," he announced in a peremptory tone of voice.

Elizabeth looked miffed, for there was no mistaking which sister he meant.

"As you wish, Edward." Anne set aside her small embroidery frame and rose from the cushioned window seat.

The gallery in the Manor of the Rose ran north to south, as did the garden it overlooked. All the windows had a view of Laurence Pountney Hill and the steeples of St. Laurence Pountney and St. Martin Orgar and, at a little distance, St. Margaret Bridge Street and St. Leonard Milkchurch. Anne's brother walked her to the southern end of the gallery, near to where it adjoined a four-story tower. From that vantage point, they could almost see the Thames and did have a clear view of the turrets of Coldharbour, the London house of the late king's mother. Margaret Beaufort, Countess of Richmond, was in residence there with her youngest grandchild, the new king's sister Mary, who went by the title Princess of Castile by virtue of her long-standing betrothal to a Spanish prince. The princess, who could not be more than fourteen years old, would have taken her father's death hard. Anne's heart went out to her.

Occupied by such thoughts, Anne waited with apparent patience, hands demurely tucked into her sleeves, for the great and powerful Duke of Buckingham to make known his reason for wishing to speak to her alone. She was not afraid of him, but she had learned that a show of respect made dealing with her brother far easier. At Thornbury Castle, Penshurst Place, or Bletchingly Manor, his country houses, she was able to avoid him for days on end. Here in the smaller London house, that was impossible.

"You will recall," he began in a patronizing tone, "that the late king, His Gracious Majesty, Henry the Seventh, required you to sign a recognizance for one hundred and sixty pounds."

"I do. Although no one ever troubled to explain to me just why I was obliged to provide that surety."

"You would not comprehend the legal details, sister. Suffice it to say that Hal and I signed similar documents. Our new king, His Most Gracious Majesty, Henry the Eighth, has seen fit to cancel them."

"That is excellent news," Anne said. "Has he also freed Hal from the Tower?" Why her other brother had been a prisoner there for nearly two months was something else no one had bothered to tell her.

Edward scowled. "No, he has not, and we will not speak further of the matter."

"As you wish," Anne murmured, lowering her gaze so that he would not guess how angry and frustrated such dictates made her feel. "Shall I return to the other women now?"

"My business with you is not yet complete. It is time you remarried, sister. I am considering young Lord Hastings."

"*Young* Lord Hastings?" Anne echoed, caught off guard by his announcement. "*How* young? I do not wish to be yoked to a child."

"You will suit well enough."

"How old is he, Edward?" She met his eyes now, letting him see her determination to have an answer. She was loath to challenge him on most matters but she did have one legal right as a widow. She could refuse to marry a man who displeased her.

"George Hastings is twenty-two."

She breathed a sigh of relief. A four-year difference in their ages was not so bad, not when the bride Edward had found for Hal had been nineteen years his senior. "Will the new king approve?" she asked. As their liege lord, King Henry also had the right to put a stop to a betrothal, should he dislike the match.

"That young fool married for love," Buckingham snapped. "What do you think?"

"I think that the king's devotion to Catherine of Aragon is admirable," she replied, although she knew full well that Edward had not expected her to answer him.

"His Grace is as impulsive as a young puppy. By the Mass, I cannot fathom why he would wed his brother's widow. And before his coronation, too. They're to be crowned together six days from now." He shook his head, his bewilderment almost tangible. "Young Henry will never be the king his father was if he does not learn how to govern a too-tender heart."

"Have a care, Edward," Anne warned, daring to bait him. "He *is* the king."

"I will speak my mind in my own house!" His eyes flashed with irritation.

"You always do," she said, and sent him a smile of surpassing sweetness.

His hard stare told her that he was uncertain how to take that last remark, or her attitude. After a moment, he apparently decided that she would never laugh at him, or be so bold as to criticize him to his face. "If all goes well in the negotiations over your dowry and jointure," he said, "you will be wed by the end of the year."

Anne accepted this dictate with equanimity, certain that if George Hastings proved distasteful to her, she could refuse to marry him. She did not know much about the Hastings family, other than that their seat was in Leicestershire. She would have liked to ask for more details, but Edward already had hold of her arm and was towing her back to the other women.

"Is there any news from court?" Elizabeth demanded as soon as Anne had been returned to the window seat. "I have been waiting to hear about a place in the new queen's household."

"You have already been given the honor of escorting the Princess of Castile in King Henry's funeral procession," Buckingham chided her. "You must not be greedy."

He laughed when her face fell.

"Have no fear, my dear. There can be no doubt but that you will be included among Queen Catherine's ladies. Both my sisters will have places of honor with Her Grace. How could it be otherwise when the Staffords are the foremost family in the realm?"

3

wo of the king's grooms of the chamber, summoned by His Grace, hurried toward the privy bedchamber. It was after midnight, but Will Compton was not at all surprised that Henry Tudor was not yet abed. Oh, he'd have been disrobed and put into his long white silk nightshirt. He'd have washed his face and cleaned his teeth. An attendant would have combed his hair and put on his embroidered scarlet velvet night bonnet. But Will had seen the heated looks that had passed between the king and his bride earlier in the evening. It had only been a little more than a month since their wedding. They'd not yet tired of bed sport.

Will and his fellow groom, Ned Neville, passed through the presence chamber, where the yeomen of the guard were on duty, and along a short passage into the privy chamber. The two yeomen of the chamber, who would spend the rest of the night on pallets outside the bedchamber door, were already yawning at their posts. They could sleep if they wished. The king would not be calling for them again.

Beyond the privy chamber were the quarters that were truly private. The royal bedchamber came first, dominated by a massive bed and hung with exquisite tapestries. The two grooms of the chamber passed through it to a second bedchamber, the one in which His Grace actually slept. The light given off by several quarriers—square blocks of expensive beeswax—showed Will windows hung with purple, white, and black striped satin curtains stuffed with buckram. The floors were oak painted to look like marble, and a very fine tapestry showing a hunting scene decorated an inner wall. Small, exquisitely made carpets covered not only the tabletops but also the floor beside the royal bed.

The king had only one attendant. This gentleman of the bedchamber would sleep on a pallet at the foot of the royal bed, but for now he stepped back, yielding his royal charge to Will and Ned, and busied himself rounding up the royal pets—a beagle, a greyhound, and a ferret—to prevent them from trying to follow their master.

Henry the Eighth, Will thought, looked every inch a king, even when he was wearing nothing but a nightshirt. Barely eighteen years old, His Grace had been blessed with a strong, long-limbed, muscular body honed to perfection by long hours of practice in the tiltyard. His face, too, was pleasing to look at, even when, as now, it wore a frown.

"What took you so long?" His pale eyes narrowed as he glared at them. The king had an unpredictable temper, but Will doubted he'd stay angry once he was on his way to his bride.

"Your pardon, Your Grace." Ned scooped up the royal night robe—a mantle of crimson velvet furred with ermine—and assisted the king into it.

Will collected a torch to help light the way to the door of the bedchamber where the queen awaited her husband. They did not have far to go. The king's apartments at Greenwich were connected to the queen's by a privy gallery. An ordinary man might have yielded to his impatience to see his bride and made the trek alone, but protocol demanded that a ruling monarch go nowhere unescorted, not even to his wife's bed.

His Grace set a brisk pace, paying no attention to the shadowed contents of the gallery or the view outside the many windows that graced both sides of it. There was no moon, but the palace courtyards were lit by lanterns.

They were met at the bedchamber door by a small, dark-haired woman, one of the queen's Spanish servants. She dropped into a deep curtsey as soon as she recognized the king, then backed away as he entered the room. She'd exit quickly by the door on the far side, then settle down to wait, just as Will and Ned must now do. The rule that a king could not be left unattended at any time obliged them to remain nearby until His Grace was ready to be escorted back to his own bed.

"We could be here all night," Ned complained.

Will gave a grunt of agreement. His Grace was a lusty young man married to an attractive woman. It was their royal duty to couple, but it was plain they both took pleasure in that obligation. It might be hours before King Henry left his queen's bed.

"What a pity that toothsome young wench who opened the door must remain on the queen's side of the chamber," Ned mused. "She fancies me, I think. Did you see the look she gave me?"

"One of abject terror, I thought. I presume your ugly face frightened her."

"Ugly, am I?" Ned laughed. "Have a care, Compton. Insult me and you come close to insulting the king."

"I am not one of those who think you bear a strong resemblance to His Grace."

Ned Neville and King Henry were both very tall—a head taller than any other men at court. Both had auburn hair and muscular builds. They'd traded places in a disguising once, to the astonishment and chagrin of all those who had been fooled into thinking Neville was the king. Close up, the differences were obvious, especially to Will. He had known both Ned and the king since they were all young boys.

Will Compton had become a ward of the Crown at eleven, when his father died. He'd been sent to young Prince Henry's household as a page. Ned Neville had arrived soon after. The third son of Lord Bergavenny, Ned had been one of the boys chosen to be children of honor—companions for the young prince. They'd grown up together—Will Compton, Ned Neville, and Henry Tudor. Later others, both older and younger, had joined their circle and become close friends, in particular Charles Brandon, Harry Guildford, and Nick Carew.

Retreating to a wide, cushioned bench set into one of the gallery's window recesses, Will decided it was a great pity that it was not long enough to serve as a couch. He placed the torch he'd been carrying into a wall bracket, sat down, and produced a pair of dice from the pouch suspended from his belt.

"Shall we pass the time at hazard?" he asked.

Ned joined him on the bench. "What are the stakes?"

"I am obliged to play for pennies," Will admitted. Paying his tailor's bill had taken all the ready money he had.

They rolled one die to see who would go first and Will's six beat Ned's four. "The main is five," he said, and sent both dice spinning across the window seat. He kept rolling until the five came up, then rolled again and lost with a three.

Ned claimed the dice and took his turn. "I'd not mind a taste of Spain," he said as he rolled a six, collected the dice, and tried again. "That Salinas wench is a pretty young thing."

Only a handful of Spanish-born servants remained in Catherine of Aragon's household. Four were women, but only two of them were from noble families, Maria de Salinas and Inez de Venegas.

"So she is," Will said, "but Lord Willoughby d'Eresby has his eye on her. And I hear Lord Mountjoy plans to make Mistress de Venegas his second wife."

"It must be nice not to be obliged to wed a fortune." Ned rolled a five, then another to win. If he rolled a five on the next toss, he'd lose. When a six came up instead, he continued to play.

"Some of the queen's English ladies have both beauty and wealth," Will remarked.

"Most of them also have husbands."

"I was thinking of widows. One in particular. Have you taken note of Buckingham's sister? Sir Walter Herbert's widow?" She was a bright spot in an otherwise dull assortment of ladies-in-waiting.

"She is too old to suit me," Ned said with a laugh. He was all of twenty-two, several years Will's junior. He rolled a twelve and lost.

"Would that age were the only difficulty! You know the duke's opinion of those of us who were raised with the king." Will rolled a three, then a four.

"Aye. Upstarts. Fortune hunters. He stops just short of calling us baseborn curs. He'll never approve of you, Will. Besides, didn't I hear that he's cast a line toward George Hastings?"

"I'm surprised the noble duke thinks a mere baron good enough for his sister." He tossed the uncooperative dice back to his friend.

Will's thoughts remained with Lady Anne while Ned took his turn. He did not know why the duke's sister piqued his interest. She was no great beauty and, as Ned had rightly pointed out, she was no longer young. She might even be barren, since she'd borne her first husband no children. But there was something about her that appealed to him and had from the first moment he'd noticed her among the queen's ladies. She had a freshness about her that made her stand out.

Perhaps, he thought, it was because she seemed to take a genuine interest in her surroundings. Lady Anne never affected boredom, as so many courtiers did, but was always looking around her, as if she eagerly anticipated each new experience. She responded to the ongoing pageantry of court life with unfeigned delight. And she had a wonderful laugh.

But she was not for him.

Ned handed over the dice and Will promptly lost again. "God's bones! I'll have to pawn my new doublet if this keeps up!"

His friend laughed and took another turn. "I'll give you a chance to win it all back the next time we're in the tiltyard. Or we could wager on another kind of jousting." He nodded his head toward the still-closed door.

"On the king's prowess?" Will grinned. "Have a care, Ned. That comes perilous close to treason."

"Only if you underestimate His Grace," Ned shot back. "But that is not what I meant. I had in mind a competition to see which one of us can entice a certain laundress into bed first. You know the one I mean."

Will did. The wench had a bold stare that made a man certain she'd be willing. But where was the challenge in that? He'd never had any difficulty convincing women to couple with him. Nor had Ned. Still, he shook his head, rejecting the wager. "The game's not worth the candle."

"You're slowing down, old man," Ned taunted him.

"Not slowing. Just changing course," Will corrected him. "The beginning of this new reign means more than an escape from the old king's tightfisted ways. We may lack titles and land, Ned, but we have the king's ear. We have his trust. At his pleasure, he can grant his friends anything and everything."

"You want a title?"

"I'd rather have land. And annuities. And lucrative wardships. I inherited a dilapidated old manor house in Warwickshire from my father. One day I'd like to rebuild it into a great mansion."

Ned gave this due consideration, then said, "I'd rather be a baron like my brother. Or better yet, an earl." He laughed. "If such things are to rest entirely upon the king's pleasure, then is it not possible that one of us might even be elevated to the level of a duke? That would give old Buckingham a turn!"

Will reclaimed the dice and continued to play, hoping his luck would change. Commoner all the way to duke? He smiled at the thought. Not likely!

4

*E*dward had been right, Lady Anne thought as she watched King Henry dance a pavane with his Spanish-born queen. Although the measures were slow and formal, all gliding movements designed to show off the dancers' skill, His Grace had a bounce to his step that put one in mind of a large, enthusiastic puppy.

The king had not quite lost the plump features of boyhood. He had the size of a man, towering over everyone else in the great hall, but his face was round and rosy, the skin so fair as to be the envy of any woman. Instead of a beard's shadow, only the finest, fairest golden down showed on his flat, clean-shaven cheeks. Some of his features were delicately cast and his blue-gray eyes, small mouth, and cleanly made lips gave him an almost cherubic look. He was only saved from a too-feminine appearance by a strong, square chin with a deep cleft in it and a high-bridged nose.

His Grace laughed as he danced to the sound of rebec and lute, shawm and sackbut, delighted with himself and with his bride. And why not? They were young and beautiful and had everything they desired. The diamonds sewn onto their clothing sparkled in the light of hundreds of wax tapers. The king's mass of red-gold hair glinted, too.

Catherine of Aragon was much shorter than her husband and nearly six years older than he was. A plump, dainty little woman, she had large, dark eyes and neat, regular features in an oval face. Her complexion was as fair as the king's and she wore her long, thick, reddish-gold hair loose under a Venetian cap, a luxury only permitted to virgins and queens. That hair was a deeper shade of auburn than King Henry's. When the queen wore it down, as she often did, she looked more like a child of ten than a woman of twenty-three.

The king and queen danced together in the great hall at Greenwich, surrounded by courtiers who were almost as vividly appareled as they were. Anne's brother, as always, wore particularly fine clothing. The Duke of Buckingham's crimson gown was heavily studded with pearls. He had taken care, however, not to outshine the king. Both Henry and Catherine were attired in cloth of gold.

From her quiet corner, Anne enjoyed both the spectacle and the opportunity to match faces to names. She was still very new to the royal court and, after spending so many years in Wales, where Walter's lands had been located, remained a bit uncertain as to who was who.

As her brother had predicted, she and her sister, Elizabeth, had been appointed to positions at court as two of the new queen's eight ladies-in-waiting, a select group chosen from the highest ranks of the nobility of England. The other six were all the wives of earls—the countesses of Derby, Shrewsbury, Essex, Oxford, Suffolk, and Surrey. Their duties were light and largely ceremonial, consisting of such things as offering a bowl of washing water to Her Grace before meals, but Anne was required to live at court, at least part of the time. The ladies-in-waiting served in rotation, except on state occasions. Then all eight of them were required to attend the queen.

When she was not on duty, Anne was free to spend her time elsewhere. For the most part, she chose to remain in proximity to the queen. Although Queen Catherine spent an inordinate number of hours on her knees in prayer, her household was also the center of all the most amusing entertainments at court. King Henry enjoyed the company of his bride and her women and brought with him to her apartments all the witty and athletic gentlemen, some nobly born and some not, who were his boon companions.

At other times, Queen Catherine and her ladies provided an admiring audience when the king played tennis or bowls. They also attended tournaments and disguisings. The latter entertainments were always splendidly mounted by the king's master of revels. But above all else, Anne loved the dancing. Her foot tapped in time to the music, stopping only when, out of the corner of her eye, she saw a man approaching.

She did not acknowledge him, although she knew full well who he was. Strange as it seemed to her, he had his own distinctive smell, just slightly different from other men who wore the same musky scent and dressed in the same fabrics. She never failed to recognize it.

"None of the other dancers are so graceful at executing the steps as you are, Lady Anne," Will Compton murmured in his low, compelling voice. "Will you do me the honor of being my partner for the next set?"

As it was considered bad manners to take your partner's hand while wearing gloves, Compton slipped his off with the grace and speed of a trained courtier. Then, with his left hand, he doffed his hat, a fine, plumed bonnet with a garnet pinned to the band. He bowed to her as he extended his right hand in her direction.

"You are bold to ask, sir." She continued to avoid looking directly at him, but as it was also bad manners to refuse an invitation to dance, she did not plan to hold out very long.

"Ah, my lady, you wound me to my very soul. I am but a humble supplicant, hoping for a crumb from your table, a touch of your gentle hand, a kiss from—"

"Master Compton, you forget yourself." Anne did turn then, fighting a smile.

Like most of the men with whom King Henry surrounded himself, Will Compton was pleasing to look at, a strapping specimen of manhood with a broad chest and good legs. His eyes were hazel, his hair golden brown. He was close to her own age, but far more experienced in the ways of the court.

He was also one of the men her brother disdained—the schoolfel-lows of His Grace's childhood, his opponents when he'd learned to joust, and now his closest companions, whether it be for a day of hunt-ing or a night of revelry.

"Come, my lady," Compton persisted. "Let us show the others how a passamezzo should be performed." The pavane at an end, the musicians were about to play a faster version of that stately dance.

"You cannot mean to suggest that we should outshine the king," she quipped, permitting the barest hint of a smile to show on her face, "for surely His Grace is the most skillful of us all . . . at everything he does."

"It would be politic to say so, to be sure," Compton agreed, his eyes alight with good humor. "And yet, to show off your skills to the world, my lady, I would gladly risk offending my liege lord."

"What? Would you endanger your career at court?" she teased him. "Mayhap even your life?"

"For you, my lady, I would slay dragons."

She had to laugh at that. "Then perhaps I do not wish to risk *my* life."

Suddenly serious, he stepped closer to whisper in her ear. "Is it true that you are to wed Lord Hastings?"

"You are impertinent, sirrah!" Anne tried to step away from him but he caught hold of her hand.

"You feel it, too. You must. There is a strong attraction between us."

"I do not know what you mean."

As soon as she spoke, she realized it was a lie. Being this close to Will Compton put her in mind of soft feather beds and long nights with the hangings closed tight.

"He's not good enough for you," he said.

"Nor are you," she shot back. Compton was gently born, but he had not even been knighted yet, while she was the daughter of one duke and the sister of another.

"I can make your life far more interesting than he ever will."

The heated feel of her face told Anne that she was blushing, but she managed to make her voice as cold as an icy morning in January. "I am to marry Lord Hastings, as you have heard. Therefore be gone, Master Compton. There is nothing for you here."

"Are you certain?" he whispered.

Before she could reply, he surprised her by obeying her command. He slipped away as quickly and quietly as he'd appeared, leaving her to stare after him in dismay.

Furious with herself, she tamped down the maelstrom of feelings his nearness had aroused. Wicked man! He knew that harmless flirtations—Compton would no doubt call it "courtly love"—were acceptable behavior. But this encounter had borne little resemblance to the chivalric ideal in which a knight worshipped his lady from afar. Compton wanted to bed her. She had no doubt of it.

Perhaps, she thought, if the difference in their rank had not been so great, he might have offered to marry her. But that was clearly impossible. He was too inferior in station and too poor to compete for her hand, even if she wanted him to. And she did not, she assured herself. She was content with the plans her brother had made for her. Within a few months, she would marry George Hastings.

Lord Hastings would make her an excellent husband. True, she had spoken with him only a handful of times, but he was pleasing to look at and courteous. And she did not intend to remain dependent upon her brother forever. Nor did she wish to be exiled to the drafty old castle in Wales where she'd lived with her first spouse. Or rather, she amended, where she had lived with a handful of servants while Walter had spent the bulk of his time hunting, and swiving his mistress.

Anne was well pleased to be done with that dull and stodgy existence. She had a place in the lively, intoxicating whirlwind that was the royal court and she meant to keep it.

One of the queen's lesser ladies, a fair-haired, blue-eyed woman with a sweet face, approached Anne when the music stopped and the dancers broke apart. "It might be wise to remain in company," Lady Boleyn murmured, "lest you provoke evil rumors. He watches you, even now."

"Who?" Anne asked. "Compton?"

Bess Boleyn laughed softly. "Your brother the duke. He was born, I think, with a suspicious nature."

"Say rather that it was bred into him."

In common with many others at court, including the woman standing beside her, the Stafford siblings were descended from noblemen who had been condemned for treason for choosing the losing side at some point during the seemingly endless conflict between the houses of Lancaster and York. Anne did not remember her father. She'd been an infant when he was executed.

Bess Boleyn's grandfather had been Duke of Norfolk at the time of her birth. Her father had been Earl of Surrey. But before she'd been full grown, Norfolk had died in battle and her father, only three months after inheriting that title, had been attainted for treason and imprisoned in the Tower. The unmarried daughters of attainted noblemen had little to offer a husband. Anne had wed a younger son of an earl. Bess had married Tom Boleyn, a gentleman whose grandfather had been a London merchant.

Although Bess was a few years older than Anne, and had three small children at home, she was young in spirit, with an infectious laugh and a cheerful outlook on life. She had also been a great help to Anne in sorting out who was who at court. That Bess's father was no longer a prisoner and had been restored to his lesser title of Earl of Surrey gave Anne hope that her brother Hal might soon be granted his freedom.

"Do you suppose we will remain here at Woking long?" Anne wondered aloud as they circled the great hall, watching the dancers. They were careful to skirt the place where Will Compton stood with two other untitled gentlemen who were high in the new king's favor, Ned Neville and Harry Guildford.

"We will stay as long as the hunting is good," Bess predicted. A few days earlier, the court had taken up residence at Woking, one of the king's lesser houses. Rebuilding the Great Hall had been one of the last architectural projects of the last king's reign.

They encountered two of Bess's younger brothers on their next circuit of the room, Lord Edward Howard and Lord Edmund Howard.

"Why are you not dancing, Lady Anne?" Lord Edmund asked. "I vow you have a most excellent light step."

It was flattery, but it was also true. When Anne realized that the next pavane was to be danced in threes, with one man partnering two women, she gave in to temptation. "I have only been waiting for you to offer to lead us out, Lord Edmund," she said.

"My pleasure." He extended his right hand to Anne and the left to his sister.

The dance began with curtseys and bows to the king and queen. King Henry, flushed of face and smiling hugely, bestowed a nod of recognition on Anne as she took her place at Lord Edmund's side. His Grace looked genuinely pleased to see her join in, although he'd spoken barely a word to her in all the weeks she'd been at court.

As Anne executed the steps, taking special care with the long train of her gown when she danced backward, she was intensely aware of being watched. Although she would have been happier without her brother's scrutiny, she could not help but be pleased by the admiring glances from the others. The king approved of her. He looked often in her direction, even though he was once again dancing with the queen. Anne also had the full attention of two of the most toothsome unmarried gentlemen in the Great Hall—Will Compton and George, Lord Hastings—and that made her feel like the most fascinating woman alive. As she executed the intricate steps of the dance, she laughed aloud in delight.

Oh, yes—she did love life at court!

5

*L*ady Anne sang like an angel. Seated on a stone bench in the garden and surrounded by other courtiers, she accompanied herself on the lute. George Hastings waited until she trilled the final note of the ballad before he went to sit beside her.

"Never have I heard that song performed better," he said, relishing the smile she lavished on him, "not even by the king's choristers."

"You are kind to say so," Lady Anne replied, "but others are far more talented than I am and there are those who can play more instruments, as well."

"Better to excel at one than butcher many," Will Compton quipped.

Compton sat on the ground near Lady Anne's feet, as did Ned Neville and Charles Brandon. The second bench in the little bower was occupied by Lady Boleyn and Lady Fitzwalter. The latter, George knew, was Lady Anne's older sister, Elizabeth. George did not think they liked each other much. As if to prove it, Elizabeth Fitzwalter sent her sister a sly look and sighed deeply.

"You must confess, Anne. Tell them what other instrument *you* play."

"I am not ashamed of my skill," Lady Anne shot back. "Not everyone can master the rebec."

"Why would anyone want to?" Lady Fitzwalter idly strummed her own lute. "Its high pitch and shrill quality are most annoying."

George had never thought much about the rebec. It was a pear-shaped instrument with three strings and was played with a bow. He'd heard it was far more difficult to coax music from than a lute. That was not surprising. Everyone at court could pick out a few of the most popular songs on lute strings.

"Some compare the sound of a rebec to a woman's voice," he blurted out.

"Is that meant as praise or condemnation?" Lady Anne had a teasing light in her eyes.

"Some women," Neville interjected before George could reply, "cackle like hens."

Bess Boleyn threw a ball of yarn at him. She always seemed to have needlework at hand. Neville caught the missile one-handed and tossed it back, laughing.

"The rebec is a useful instrument in courtship," George said, directing his words solely to Lady Anne. "It is ideally suited to playing duets."

"With the lute?" Her full lips curved into a pleased smile at the thought.

"With the lute," he agreed, "or with the harp, the gittern, other rebecs, double pipes, double shawms, panpipes, or the voice."

"Stick to the lute," Brandon advised in a lazy drawl.

Charles Brandon was accustomed to doling out advice. Although not much older than Compton, he had more experience of the world than the rest of them put together. He'd been master of horse to the Earl of Essex by the time he was George's age, and he'd gone on from there to serve King Henry the Seventh as an esquire of the body. No one could equal him in the tiltyard, and he was undeniably appealing to females. If the rumors George had heard were true, he'd already been married three times, twice to the same woman.

"Will you sing if I play, Lord Hastings?" Lady Anne's question caused him to lose interest in anyone else.

"I do not have a strong voice," he warned her.

"No matter. I am certain we will do very well together."

She strummed a few notes and, caught, George complied with her wishes. He faltered, then gained strength and, as it was a song everyone knew, his nervousness quickly vanished. Performing a duet with Lady Anne proved most congenial . . . until the other gentlemen joined in. All of them, especially Compton, had better voices than George did.

The moment the song ended, Compton seized the lute. He accompanied himself while he warbled a mournful love song. Lady Anne appeared to be impressed by the performance.

George felt an unaccustomed surge of annoyance as he watched her flirt with the other man. He remembered another occasion, more than a year earlier, when he and Compton and some of the other young men at old King Henry's court had spent an evening in a tavern near Greenwich Palace. There had been a pretty serving wench on the premises. She'd been responding to George's advances . . . until Will Compton enticed her away with his charming smile and ready wit.

This situation was far different, George assured himself. The Duke of Buckingham had already promised his sister to George and Compton knew it. George touched one tentative hand to Lady Anne's sleeve, recapturing her attention.

"Will you walk with me, Lady Anne? There is more to enjoy in these gardens than a single bower."

That she rose at once and went with him pleased George beyond measure. The strains of the lute and the sounds of the others singing together now became no more than a pleasant background accompaniment to their stroll. He never remembered afterward exactly what they said to each other. He only knew he was in heaven.

6

City of Westminster, September 19, 1509

*A*s far as George Hastings was concerned, the matter of his marriage had been settled well before he answered the summons to visit his grandmother at her third husband's house in the city of Westminster. Several weeks had passed since his walk in the garden with Lady Anne. He'd seen her almost every day since. True, they had generally been part of a large company, but she'd singled him out for attention and had danced with him more than she had with any of the other men. He'd come to adore this lively, appealing creature with the sparkling eyes. She was graceful in movement, pleasant in speech, and shapely in form. He could hardly wait to be bound to her at bed and at board till death did them part.

It was a shock, therefore, to be confronted by his mother, his sister, and his grandmother and told that all three of them were opposed to this marriage.

"I do not understand what you have against Lady Anne."

George's words dropped into a deep pool of silence. He had to fight not to shift his weight from foot to foot or run a finger under the collar that suddenly felt too tight around his throat. Women, he thought, were the very devil to deal with.

"Lady Anne is unobjectionable enough," his grandmother conceded, "but that brother of hers is trouble."

George's grandmother was a very small woman, but she had a big presence. Her solar was not the overtly feminine chamber found in most houses. Instead it contained shelves full of books and manuscripts. Ledgers were stacked on the worktable that dominated the room. The only embroidery in sight belonged to George's sister Nan, and she'd abandoned it on a window seat. The three women stood ranged against him like combatants at the barriers in a tournament.

"I know Hal Stafford is in the Tower," George began, "but he's not been charged with any crime. He—"

"We do not speak of Lord Henry," his mother interrupted. "Buckingham is the problem. The man's unstable, just as his father was. Ambitious. Proud. Hot-tempered. No good can come of an alliance with the Stafford family."

Like her own mother, George's dam was slight of build and large of character. She stood a bit taller than the older woman, and was as yet unbent by age. She kept her hands tucked into her long sleeves, but there was otherwise nothing demure about her.

"The king himself approves of the match," George said in his own defense.

His mother and grandmother exchanged a speaking glance that George could not interpret, although he had the feeling that it did not flatter King Henry. Nan looked only slightly more sympathetic to his cause.

At twenty-five, George's sister was the youngest of the queen's high-ranking ladies-in-waiting. As Countess of Derby, she served with Lady Anne at court and therefore knew her far better than either of the others. George thought of appealing to Nan for support, but if their objection was not to Lady Anne herself, what good would it do?

He tried another argument. "It is no bad thing that the premier nobleman in the realm wants me as a brother-in-law. But beyond that, I find Lady Anne most pleasing to be with. I consider myself a lucky man on that count."

"You must not let physical attraction sway you, George," his mother said.

Christ aid! That was rich, coming from her. His mother had married where she'd pleased the moment old King Henry was dead, hoping in the confusion of a new reign to avoid the penalty for wedding without royal consent. True, she had been a widow for three long years and was old enough to know her own mind, but some sons might have seen her new husband, Richard Sacheverell, as a fortune hunter.

George's mother, Mary, as the only heir to the Hungerford barony, was extremely wealthy in her own right. She was still addressed as Lady Hungerford, rather than as Lady Hastings or Mistress Sacheverell, because Hungerford was the greater title.

George refrained from criticizing her remarriage, but only just. He admired his mother. She had seen to it that he'd had an excellent education, something not all noblemen valued. After his father's death, when he'd become a ward of the Crown and gone to live at court, she had moved into his London house in Thames Street so that she would be close by. At the time, he'd resented her hovering, but even then he'd known that she'd been motivated by her love for him.

He was not so certain about his grandmother. She frankly terrified him. Nearly seventy years old, but spry for her age, she knew how to turn her walking stick into a vicious weapon. Grandmother's first of three marriages had been to Lord Hungerford, George's grandfather, and she still used that title. Her second husband had been a mere knight. Her third, Hugh Vaughan, had not even been knighted yet when they wed. That marriage had taken place several years before George's birth, but he'd heard the story so often that he knew it by heart. His grandmother, the widow of a baron and the daughter of an earl, had married a commoner because she'd admired his prowess in the lists. In his day, Hugh Vaughan had been a champion jouster.

At present, Vaughan was responsible for royal prisoners in the Tower of London. He must have been, George realized, the one who oversaw Lord Henry Stafford's arrest and imprisonment. George narrowed his eyes at his grandmother and sent her hard look for hard look. "What do you know to the detriment of the Staffords? *Has* Buckingham been plotting against the Crown?"

There were always rumors. Most could easily be discounted. But Grandmother was the daughter of the third Earl of Northumberland. The Duke of Buckingham's wife, Eleanor, and Eleanor's brother, the current earl, were her niece and nephew. Between Grandmother's current husband and members of her own family, she was privy to as many state secrets as any of the king's ministers. She'd know if there was any truth to the stories about Buckingham's desire to be king and Hal's alleged part in an aborted plot to put his brother on the throne instead of King Henry the Eighth.

"Well?" he prompted her when she seemed hesitant to speak.

"I have heard only that some of my nephew's servants think Buckingham should have been named Lord Protector, since our new king is so young. And that Northumberland himself should have been given control of all the lands north of the Trent."

"King Henry is fully capable of governing this realm. Age has naught to do with it."

Even though His Grace had not yet attained his majority at the time of his father's death, he'd convinced the Privy Council to abandon any thought of appointing a regent. It would never have been Buckingham, in any case. The councilors had proposed that the king's grandmother, Lady Margaret Beaufort, Countess of Richmond, take up that role. As matters had fallen out, it had been just as well that the king took the reins of government at once. Lady Margaret had died of old age only a few days after her grandson's coronation.

"It does appear that His Grace is mature for his age," Grandmother reluctantly conceded, "but he is still young enough to be in need of guidance, just as you are, my boy."

George took a deep breath. He did not wish to distress his mother and grandmother, but the choice of a wife was his to make. "I am of age to make my own decisions."

"It is never wise to rush into marriage," his mother said bluntly. "Have you spent any time with Lady Anne? Do you know her likes and dislikes? Have you interests in common? These are things more important to a couple than the urge to scratch a mutual itch." She paused long enough for a gleam to come into her eyes. "Although I must admit that to be compatible in bed is a great deal more pleasant than the alternative."

George felt the heat rise in his face and was glad his skin had been darkened by the sun. It was bad enough to be henpecked without giving his womenfolk proof that they could embarrass him by speaking so frankly. Having a mother still young enough at forty-one to enjoy coupling with a man her own age was something he preferred not to think about.

Nan spoke up for the first time. "Marriage is for life," she reminded him.

"Say rather, until death."

Lady Anne's first husband had died, and so had Nan's. George's sister had been married very young to old Baron Fitzwalter, the father of the Lord Fitzwalter who was currently wed to Lady Anne's sister. Two years ago, Nan had remarried, taking the Earl of Derby as her second husband. She had already provided him with a son and heir. George wondered if they were happy together, but he did not ask. Instead, he squared his shoulders and faced down all three of his kinswomen.

"Do you know anything to Lady Anne's detriment?"

"Only that she bore her first husband no children," his mother said.

That gave him pause. He needed a son, as did every titled nobleman.

"The fault may have been with Sir Walter," Nan suggested. "He had a longtime mistress and never got any children on her, either."

George understood enough of animal husbandry to realize that Nan was probably right. There was no reason to think that another man could not sire sons on Lady Anne, even if Sir Walter had not. As for Grandmother's tittle-tattle, that did not seem to amount to much. He gave no credence to the idea that Buckingham wanted the throne for himself. The duke had never seemed to take much of an interest in government when Henry the Seventh was king.

"I am going to marry Lady Anne Stafford." Just saying the words filled him with a sense of joyous anticipation. He held up a hand to stop further argument. "Accept that the decision has been made. It only remains for the three of you, for my sake, if not for hers, to show my wife both love and respect when you welcome her into our family."

7

Greenwich Palace, December 2, 1509

*L*ady Anne went to her wedding attired in her finest clothing. Her gown was made of cloth of silver with train so long that she needed an attendant to carry it. Even though she had been married before and was no virgin, she wore her hair hanging loose down her back. A gold circlet crowned her head.

The king had insisted that they marry in the chapel at Greenwich Palace. Edward had been pleased by this sign of favor. He took it as proof of His Grace's goodwill toward the Staffords, much needed so long as Hal remained a prisoner in the Tower.

With the moment at hand when she would pledge to honor and obey George Hastings for the rest of his life, Anne strode purposefully toward the place where he waited beside one of the king's own chaplains, Thomas Wolsey, a heavyset priest in his late thirties who wore a somber expression on his face but had a twinkle in his eyes. Anne had no qualms about making her vows. She and George suited each other well and he looked magnificent in a white damask gown trimmed with gold and lined with sarcenet. Beneath the formal outer garment he wore a jacket with sleeves of crimson satin bordered with black velvet. His hose were scarlet and his costly cambric shirt was embroidered with gold thread. For jewels he'd chosen rubies.

Anne had spent enough time with George since coming to court to know that beneath the finery was a pleasant young man, considerate and eager to please and possessed of no vices that she could detect. He was, perhaps, a trifle dull, but there were worse qualities in a husband. And it would be no hardship to couple with him. She'd seen him in less concealing clothing, playing tennis with the king and in the tilt-yard, training with His Grace at the quintain and the rings. George Hastings had strong, well-shaped legs, muscular arms, and a masculine grace that gave promise he would be as skillful in bed as he was in the lists.

The priest began the ceremony with an address in Latin on the dignity of Holy Matrimony. It went on twice as long as Anne would have liked, especially when she could not understand a word of it, but finally it was time for George to take her by the hand and repeat the matrimonial formula *per verba de praesenti*. She did know what that bit of Latin meant. When she took her own vows, she and George would be sealing the covenant of betrothal as well as the covenant of marriage.

"I, Anne," she said in a clear, steady voice, "hereby do accept thee, George, to be my husband and spouse, and consent to receive thee as my husband during my natural life. I will have, hold, and repute thee as my husband and spouse, and hereby I plight thee my troth."

George placed a thick gold band on the fourth finger of her right hand, counting from the thumb—the one said to have a vein that led directly to the heart. The ring was inscribed with a motto on the flat inner side: *God Above Increase Our Love*. George kissed her lightly on the lips as the circle slid home.

Moments later, the marriage schedule had been signed and the priest began to sing the Nuptial Mass. More Latin. Anne let her mind drift, thinking of the changes she would make in the lodgings she and George were now to share. She paid attention again only when the king's chaplain divided the consecrated wafer between them. Accepting her half, playing her role by rote, she made a halfhearted effort to fix her mind on spiritual matters. Instead her thoughts strayed to her first wedding. She'd been nervous and excited then, and not quite certain what the night would bring.

It had been a disappointment.

Walter Herbert had done his duty quickly and efficiently and then he'd rolled over and gone to sleep. He'd snored. She'd wept.

This wedding night would be different. She was no longer an innocent. She knew what to expect from the earthy side of marriage. Sir Walter's swiving had never produced either grand passion or simple affection. Still, although infrequent, it had been thorough enough that she'd eventually developed a healthy appreciation of her own capacity for physical pleasure.

At last the ceremony was over. Holding hands, Anne and George turned and made their obeisance to the king and queen. Then it was on to dinner and a banquet. Musicians played during and after both, and then there was dancing. The celebrations went on for hours. But when the bells rang for eight of the clock, Anne's sister and Lady Derby, her new sister-in-law, hustled her away to the sumptuous bedchamber where a bridal bed had already been blessed and sprinkled with holy water. Others of the queen's ladies followed to help strip her of the cloth of silver gown and a kirtle of dark blue velvet. Even her chemise was whisked away, leaving her in naught but her stockings and garters. When a satin night robe settled around her shoulders, she tugged it tight. In spite of a charcoal brazier and the fire in the hearth, the room felt drafty.

The queen appeared briefly to offer a prayer and her wish for much happiness and many children, but then she excused herself because she was breeding and tired easily. Anne was not sorry to see her go, accompanied by Maria de Salinas and Maud Parr, two of her favorite ladies. Anne did not dislike Queen Catherine, but Her Grace's lingering Spanish accent—which the king seemed to find charming—was difficult for Anne to understand, and the extreme piety Catherine expected of her ladies made Anne uncomfortable.

Catherine of Aragon spent many long hours in her oratory, kneeling on a bare floor before a Spanish crucifix and statues of St. Margaret and St. Catherine. Her Grace studied the Office of the Blessed Virgin daily, rose every midnight to say Matins, and heard Mass each day at dawn. The queen confessed her sins once a week, whether she had committed any or not, and received the Eucharist every Sunday. She fasted, too, not only during Lent, but every Friday and Saturday and on the vigils of saints' days. Her Grace could not compel her ladies to do likewise, but she did insist upon reading aloud to them from pious works after dinner. Her wedding gift to Anne and George had been a beautifully illustrated book of hours.

There were times when Anne wondered what the king saw in his wife. Perhaps she was not so pious in bed. Smiling to herself at the thought, Anne bent down to loosen her garters, so that they could more easily be removed.

Anne's tiring maid, Meriall ap Harry, lifted the circlet from her head and began to comb the tangles from her hair. Small and dark, like so many of the native Welsh, Meriall had not stood out among Sir Walter Herbert's servants when Anne first became his bride. Only during the years that followed had she gradually become both friend and confidante. She had left all that was familiar to her behind to accompany Anne back to Thornbury after Sir Walter's death. In the duke's household, she had often been the only one Anne could be certain would put her wishes first and those of the Duke of Buckingham second.

Now Meriall smiled warmly at her mistress in the reflective steel of the standing glass and bent close to whisper a blessing in her ear. Behind them, Anne could see the two Ladies Hungerford adding more decorations to the nuptial bed. December was the wrong month for fresh blooms, but there were plenty of dried flowers to strew and colorful ribbons had been attached to every available surface. The whole room smelled of violets and essence of jasmine.

A commotion outside the door heralded the arrival of Anne's new husband. Courtiers poured into the room, pushing George ahead of them. He had been stripped of his wedding finery, just as she had. His friends had allowed him to keep only his shirt. It fell almost to his knees, but the linen was so fine that it was nearly transparent.

His color high, George hurried toward the bed. His companions blocked his way, swarming around the newly married couple. Ribald comments and suggestions vied with demands for Anne's garters.

Prepared to follow tradition, Anne stepped forward and carefully extended her right leg. Her care to untie the garter beforehand made it hang low, but Will Compton's hands still managed to stray halfway up her thigh. A whoop of triumph and more laughter filled the room as Ned Neville claimed the second loosened garter and fastened it to his bonnet.

Anne quickly stripped off her stockings, handing them over to another of the unmarried gentlemen. George's friends had already given the hose he'd worn to two of the single women in the room.

"Into bed with you!" Bess Boleyn cried, and pulled back the covers.

At the same moment Anne slipped between them, George's sister relieved her of her night robe. George's shirt was ripped from his body by Lord Edmund Howard and Sir Charles Brandon. In a trice, the newly-weds found themselves in bed together, naked as the day they were born.

Anne shifted to a more comfortable position, careful to keep the coverlet pulled up over her breasts. She had nothing to be ashamed of in her appearance. She knew herself to be slender and well shaped and healthy. But she was four years older than George and feared her flesh might show signs of it. The tradition of putting newlyweds to bed, she decided, was far more enjoyable when someone else was the center of attention.

All the hangings had been pulled back as far as they would go, to give the wedding guests a clear view. That meant Anne could see them, as well. Her brother and sister looked vaguely disapproving of the rev-elry and stood a little apart, but the king was at the center of the group of young men who'd accompanied George into the chamber. Rosy-cheeked and delighted to have been a part of their wedding, His Grace strode to the side of the bed, leaned in, and kissed Anne full on the lips. He was an enthusiastic but sloppy kisser. She had to fight the urge to wipe her mouth when he released her.

"You are a fortunate man, George," the king declared. "She is a prize indeed."

"So I believe, Your Grace," George said.

"So you will soon know," Neville called out.

"Now we must discover who will be next." Bess Boleyn herded several of the queen's unmarried gentlewomen toward the foot of the bed. They took turns throwing George's stockings over their shoulders, to the accompaniment of wagers and raucous laughter. It was widely believed that the maid who managed to hit the bridegroom in the head would soon be married herself.

The unmarried men took their turn next. Anne thought it a silly superstition that the same fate awaited the first man to hit her with one of her own stockings, but she kept a smile fixed on her face and endured. This time the rolled-up fabric flew backward with considerably more force behind it. Seeing Will Compton take aim, Anne gave a little squeak of alarm and slid down beneath the covers, but the stocking still struck her square on the nose.

"Your turn to marry next, Compton!" Neville hooted with laughter.

"Only if I can find myself a bride as beautiful as Lady Anne." Compton went down on one knee beside the bed. "I beg a boon, my lady."

"What would you ask, good sir?" Anne narrowed her eyes, instantly suspicious that he meant to demand a kiss, as the king had. That prospect caused a strange little flutter in her belly.

"I would have your stocking back, my lady," he whispered in far too intimate a tone, "to carry as a token that even in the darkest night, true love burns as brightly as the sun."

Before she could respond to this nonsense, George reached across her body to take possession of the prize. "You have the garter, Compton," he said. "Be content with that."

Catcalls and ribald suggestions drowned out Compton's reply. Anne thought that was just as well. Clearly, Master Compton had been imbibing freely of the wine. There was no telling what ill-advised comment he might make.

When Compton was pulled away by his friends, Anne's sister took his place. Elizabeth had brought the nuptial posset, a drink made with milk, wine, yolks of eggs, sugar, cinnamon, nutmeg, and other ingredients. This strengthening caudle was specially prepared to relax the bride and embolden her new husband. The wine was sack, which was supposed to make men lusty. The sugar in the mixture had been added to also make him kind.

Anne swallowed her portion quickly and George followed suit. She could feel how tense he was and wondered suddenly if he was as experienced as she'd assumed.

"It is time for our guests to leave," he announced when the goblet was empty.

No one paid him any mind.

"Be off with you, my lords and ladies," George said in a louder, more forceful voice, although it was difficult to appear as a figure of authority when one was naked and in bed.

The ladies giggled, even George's elderly grandmother, who had been making her own inroads into the supply of wine. George's mother sent the elder Lady Hungerford an exasperated look and approached the bed, leaning down to whisper a suggestion in her son's ear. George looked startled at first, but then he grinned at her.

As soon as Lady Hungerford stepped back, George grasped the bedclothes, as if he meant to shove them aside and leap out of bed. "If you will not go," he bellowed, affecting rage, "then I must throw you out!"

Several of the women shrieked and scurried toward the door, pretending to be frightened by the threat of seeing a naked man. The other ladies followed them, but George's friends remained, more ribald in their comments than before. It was not until King Henry stepped in that they gave up the game. At a signal from His Grace, they obediently trooped out of the room. The king lingered until the others had gone, then he, too, went away, closing the door behind him.

Silence descended on the bridal chamber, sudden and complete. Most of the illumination had vanished, too, as the courtiers had carried off all but two of the candles. Anne extended one bare arm and pinched out the tall wax taper on the table at her side of the bed. A moment later, George's candle went out, too, leaving them to lay side by side in complete darkness.

Nothing happened.

"George?"

He sighed.

"We are supposed to consummate our marriage now. The union will not be fully legal until we do so."

"I know."

She felt a moment of panic. Did he not desire her? Had she just made a terrible mistake by marrying him?

"There is no reason to delay our coupling," she said, her voice coming out more sharply than she'd intended. "I am hardly a blushing virgin."

She felt him roll toward her. His words were a low growl of sound. "Are you certain we are alone? I have no wish to be interrupted by drums and fiddles or drunken laughter."

"Everyone has gone. I am sure of it." She had heard not a sound from the outer chamber for several minutes.

"They could return."

"If they do, then you will run them off again." She smiled in the darkness. "Brandish your sword at them."

After a moment of startled silence, he laughed aloud. Then he slid his arm around her shoulders and eased close enough to kiss her.

Their first coupling was a trifle awkward but George was not, as Anne had briefly feared, inexperienced. Neither was he a practiced seducer, and that pleased her. She had heard lurid tales about some of the king's boon companions, especially Neville and Compton and that dark-haired devil, Brandon.

In the end, George proved both lusty and kind, and Anne did not believe that was only because he'd drunk deeply of the nuptial posset. The physical side of marriage was even more satisfying than she'd remembered. Edward had chosen well for her, she decided as she drifted toward well-sated sleep. George Hastings was an excellent choice for a husband.

8

estminster Palace was situated between the river Thames and Westminster Abbey. It was a sprawling place surrounded by the shops and tenements built up on land leased from the monks. When the entire court moved there three days after their wedding, Anne and George were allocated a single small, cramped chamber. They might have lived in their own house in London instead, but as it was December and a cold journey, whether by boat or on horseback, Anne much preferred to remain in one place and George was inclined to humor her. He spent his days in attendance on the king while she enjoyed the convivial ambiance of the queen's apartments.

The outer rooms were open to everyone. Even when she was not on duty, Anne customarily joined the other ladies in the presence chamber. Some of them held appointments like her own. Others were the wives and daughters of members of King Henry's household.

On their first full day at Westminster, Anne sought out her friend Bess Boleyn. She found her hard at work on a complex design of bright blue forget-me-nots on a pair of black velvet sleeves that were to be Bess's New Year's gift to the queen.

Bess's stitches slowed, then stopped altogether when Anne joined her on a long, backless bench drawn up close to one of the charcoal braziers that provided extra heat to the cavernous room. "Does married life suit you as well as you'd hoped?" Bess asked.

"What a question!" Anne took out her own needlework, a shirt she was decorating with geometric designs. "I am well content to be Lady Hastings."

"And yet you have rarely been seen with your husband since your wedding day, not at Greenwich and not here."

"We each have our separate duties," Anne protested.

"But I had hoped for better for you," Bess said with a sigh. "George is in love with you. Anyone can see that."

"And so I must therefore fall madly in love with him?" Astonished, Anne stared at her friend. "Love is scarcely a necessity in marriage. We have liking between us. That is more important."

"Is there at least attraction?"

Anne felt her cheeks warm. "We are both well pleased with each other in bed. And well pleasured, too."

"He loves you," Bess said again.

Anne did not know how to reply. She had never considered her marriage in terms of the kind of love the poets wrote of. It was a business arrangement, arrived at for the benefit of both parties and their families. Her brother had overseen the marriage settlement she'd signed, looking after her interests and making certain that she would have her dower rights should she again be left a widow. She was fond of George. She would gladly bear his children. But love?

"I am not sure I know what love is," she murmured after a moment.

"You will know what it is when you have children," Bess predicted. "A mother cannot help but love her babies."

Anne chuckled. "I do not believe that is quite the same thing as love for a man."

"Perhaps not," Bess agreed. "And motherhood has its own frustrations, especially when the children must be left behind with nurses and tutors in order for one to dance attendance upon royalty."

Bess had left a son and two daughters, all under the age of ten, at Blickling in Norfolk, Anne recalled. She might have chosen to stay with them, but instead she'd come to court, where her husband was already in Henry Tudor's service.

"Do you love Tom?" Anne asked.

"In truth, I do, and did so even before we married. He can be difficult at times, but he has a way about him . . ." Her voice trailed off as her lips curved into a secretive little smile that made Anne suspect that Tom Boleyn's excellence as a jouster in the tiltyard extended into the bedchamber.

The same could be said of George Hastings. Each night of their marriage so far, he had come to their bed with gratifying enthusiasm. They coupled, sometimes more than once, before they fell asleep. But they rarely talked. And he had never *said* that he was in love with her.

Unnecessary, she thought again. Marriages were made for the purpose of providing heirs. Had the priest not charged them to be fruitful and multiply? He had not said anything about romantic love.

That night, however, after Anne and George had coupled, she lay awake listening to his soft snores and wondering if what they had between them would be enough to satisfy her as they grew old together. Would they drift apart as time passed, as so many husbands and wives seemed to? Would they have nothing in common but their children?

Anne knew it was possible to have more than that between husband and wife. She had sensed the genuine bond of affection between Bess with her Tom even before Bess confided in her. And she had observed George's mother with her second husband, Richard Sacheverell—the second husband she'd chosen for herself after she was widowed. Lady Hungerford enjoyed a true partnership with him. They were friends as well as lovers.

She turned her head to look at George, deep in untroubled sleep beside her. She did not love him, but she thought that one day she might. In the meantime, she was determined to enjoy what they did have. With a wicked smile curving her lips, she slid one hand down his chest and lower, waking him in a way that pleased them both enormously.

9

Richmond Palace, Christmas 1509

The court traveled to Wanstead on the sixteenth of December and then moved on to Richmond for Christmas, where Lord and Lady Hastings once again had double lodgings. The queen often retired early, but the king and his companions kept late hours. Anne and George joined wholeheartedly in the revelry, which almost always concluded with dancing. Anne never lacked for partners.

King Henry singled her out for the more energetic dances, knowing that her skill equaled his own. Anne was flattered.

She was also anxious, but only at first. She soon forgot to be nervous of the king and threw herself into the performance.

His Grace dominated every room he entered, drawing every eye. And he set every female heart to beating just a little faster whenever he passed by. Even though Anne was a full seven years older than King Henry, and married besides, she was not immune to his boyish good looks or his enthusiasm. By the end of each dance with him, her smile matched the expression of delight on her liege lord's face.

She told herself the warmth that suffused her entire body was only due to exertion. The rapid steps had her gasping for breath and wishing fashion did not require such tight lacing.

"Your hood is askew, Lady Anne," His Grace said, and reached out to straighten it himself.

Even through the layers of velvet lined with silk that made up the gable headdress, Anne thought she could feel his touch. When he went on to adjust the bands that hung down at the front of both sides of the hood, his fingers trailed over the fabric of her bodice and she shivered.

"Tell me, Lady Anne," the king said, chucking her under the chin and lifting her face so that she was forced to meet his eyes, "is Lord Hastings to your liking?"

For an instant, she thought she saw something calculating in his gaze. Then she told herself she was being foolish. The king was merely flirting with her, and she must reply in kind, keeping the banter between them light and friendly. Those who amused King Henry stayed in his favor.

"I find him adequate, Your Grace," she quipped, "though any man must pale before his king."

She meant the words in jest, and for the king's ears only, but Charles Brandon was close enough to overhear. He bleated a laugh and within moments had repeated her quip to Neville, Guildford, Compton, and the rest. To Anne's horror, George was also told what she'd said of him.

From across the room, she saw his face darken with embarrassment. The tips of his ears turned bright red. Anne wished she could take back her hasty words, but to say more now would only make matters worse. She sent a silent look of apology in her husband's direction, but he did not see it. Then the king stepped between them, blocking their view of each other, and whisked her away into another dance.

His Grace was oblivious to George's distress. Anne forced herself to smile and act as she always did, continuing the easy banter that was expected of all courtiers, but, all the while, she worried. She'd never meant to embarrass her husband. She resolved to make amends the moment they were alone in their chamber.

But when Anne at last retired to their lodgings, George was not there. He did not come to her bed that night. In the morning, one of his men delivered a note to Meriall, Anne's tiring maid. It was curt and to the point. He had business to attend to on one of his estates. He would not return for several days.

Anne told herself not to worry. When George came back, she would shower him with affection to make up for her careless words. She had not meant to disparage his abilities as a husband. Surely he would understand that. Besides, he knew what Brandon and the rest were like. He should never have taken their taunts so seriously.

She did not sleep well at night while George was gone but the celebration of Yuletide kept her too busy during the day to dwell on her rift with her husband. Anne was just breaking her fast in her chamber on the morning of St. Stephen's day when her sister appeared in the doorway.

"Have you quarreled with George?" Elizabeth demanded.

"Certainly not." Anne gestured toward the food and drink on her small table, silently inviting her unexpected guest to join her.

Elizabeth seated herself on the other stool. "Did the king send him away?"

"Why should he?" But the manchet loaf suddenly tasted as coarse as horse bread. What had Elizabeth heard?

"I am not blind." Elizabeth helped herself to a cup of barley water and took a long swallow.

"Then I must be, for I fail to see any connection between your two questions." Anne abandoned her meal and clasped her hands in her lap. She had a bad feeling about this early morning visit from her sister.

"King Henry fancies you."

Anne was surprised into a laugh. "His Grace is devoted to the queen. He is as pleased with her over her pregnancy as a child with a new toy."

Incredulous, Elizabeth made a snorting noise. "Have you not seen the way he looks at you? Other men show an interest, too. They think you are ripe for the plucking, now that your husband—the husband you yourself deemed only adequate—has gone away."

"That is arrant nonsense! And George will return in a day or two." Anne hoped she spoke the truth. She'd heard not a word from him since his departure. She did not even know where he was. He owned land in several counties.

"You are always at the center of a group of laughing gentlemen."

Anne heard envy as well as suspicion in her older sister's voice and tried to rein in her irritation. No one flirted with Elizabeth. She had a haughty air about her that discouraged the court gallants. "It is best to keep the king sweet. Do not forget that our brother the duke hoped that you and I would be able to exert some small measure of influence here at court."

Elizabeth gave a disdainful sniff and stood, taking the last of the bread with her. "We are here to please the queen, not the king."

Anne was glad to see her sister go, but she spent the remainder of the day in a thoughtful frame of mind. That night, as Meriall combed and braided her hair in preparation for bed, she was still brooding over what Elizabeth had said.

"Meriall," she asked, "do I flirt too much? Have I encouraged men other than my husband to think I might welcome them into my bed?"

The tiring maid's fingers stilled for a moment in Anne's hair, then resumed their skillful braiding. "You are pleasant to everyone, my lady."

In the looking glass, Anne saw her own lips twist into a wry smile. "That is not quite what I asked. I beg you to be honest with me, Meriall. You have been with me long enough to know that I will not fly into a rage if I do not like your answer."

"Unlike your brother the duke." Meriall continued braiding and did not speak again until her task was complete. "There is something about you, my lady, that draws men to you. You are not a great beauty, but you have the ability to charm all those you meet."

"But it is only a game," Anne protested. "Knights and ladies and chivalry, like the pageantry at a tournament or the stories in the *Roman de la Rose*. All the poetry and songs and disguisings are pretty conceits, nothing more."

"The queen is with child," Meriall said.

"I do not take your meaning." Anne turned to look at her maidservant in confusion.

"When wives are great with child, husbands stray. Sometimes the alliances outlast the pregnancy."

Anne frowned. Wives did not always remain faithful, either, but *she* had no intention of putting a cuckold's horns on George's head. She could not imagine what she had done since coming to court that might make anyone—except for her sister, who had always been surpassing critical of her—think that she would.

"Flirtations are expected at court," she said in a firm voice. "There is no harm in indulging in them."

Meriall applied herself to putting away the wooden box that held Anne's combs and brushes. "If you say so, my lady."

10

*I*t was late when Lady Anne returned to her lodgings. The queen had received her New Year's gifts early that morning. The rest of the day had been spent in revelry, culminating in a disguising and the inevitable dancing. As was her wont, Anne had smiled and flirted with and partnered the king and several of his gentlemen but, as always, she had returned to her bedchamber alone.

Elizabeth had made no further accusations, but she was always watching, as if she hoped to catch her sister in some wrongdoing. For the most part, Anne ignored her. Let her think what she would, Anne was not about to offend King Henry by rebuffing his attentions in public. She was on amiable terms with His Grace and wished to remain so. Tonight the effort had been rewarded.

She was smiling as she entered the outer room. The expression vanished and she was beset by an intense wariness when she realized that it was not Meriall who awaited her within. A man stood in front of the hearth, backlit by the fire, his face in shadow. All she could see of him at first was his silhouette.

Then he took a step toward her, closer to the candle she held. "George," she exclaimed in delight. "You're back."

Anne reached out to him, but he evaded her. She could read

nothing in his expression. Very carefully, she set the candlestick down on the small table.

"I have missed you," she said.

"And I, you," he replied, "but I cannot imagine that you have been unhappy in my absence. You were smiling when you came in."

"I have just received a most excellent New Year's gift. His Grace has ordered Hal's release from the Tower. My brother is to resume his place as one of the king's companions. It will be as if he was never arrested at all."

"I am glad to hear it." George sounded sincere, but Anne could detect no relaxation in his stiff posture.

"Have you had a long journey? Shall I heat a cup of spiced wine for you?"

"Such wifely devotion," he muttered. "A pity you do not always think first of my comfort."

This time Anne did not allow him to avoid her touch. She caught his hands in hers and waited until he met her eyes. "Do you mean to let a careless word come between us? I did not intend to impugn your manhood."

"And yet you did. You made me a laughingstock, Anne. That is hard for a man to bear."

"I know. And I am sorry for it. Truly, I am. But your friends were the ones who made much of it, not I. And you made matters worse by going off alone to lick your wounds. The matter would have been forgotten by now had you remained here with me."

"I could not stay." He pulled free and turned his back on her to stare into the fire.

Anne watched him, wary now. "Why did you think you could not stay?"

He hesitated, then blurted out the truth. "I was afraid I would be incapable of giving you pleasure."

"What nonsense!"

"Is it? Such things happen."

A horrible suspicion crept into Anne's mind and her temper ignited. "Did you find some other woman to demonstrate your prowess?"

"What?" He turned to look at her, his face a mask of astonishment. "No. Never."

"My last husband would have." She heard the bitterness in her voice and despised it. "Walter preferred his mistress's bed to mine in any case."

For a long moment, George just stared at her. Then he abruptly closed the distance between them. "It's your heat I need to warm me, Anne, only yours."

Her heart sang as he swept her up into his arms and carried her into the bedchamber. And when he proceeded to prove that her careless quip to the king had not unmanned him, her body sang, too.

11

Richmond Palace, January 12, 1510

*L*ady Anne shivered in spite of the warmth of her fur-lined cloak and the speed of her steps. It was a bright, sunny day, but so desperately cold that it almost hurt to breathe. "Bess, wait," she called. "I am no longer certain I wish to spend the afternoon out of doors."

Bess Boleyn's laughter floated back to her. "Think of this weather as invigorating. Besides, you cannot cheer for your husband if you are not present when he enters the lists."

Thinking she'd be just as happy to hear about the jousting after the event, when she and George were snug and warm in their lodgings inside the palace, Anne nevertheless picked up her skirts and hurried after her friend. What had sounded like a great adventure with charcoal braziers and fires in all the hearths fighting off wintry drafts, now seemed the height of folly.

So was this "secret" tournament some of the king's courtiers had devised.

Nothing stayed secret long at court. By now everyone must know that several of King Henry's more energetic gentlemen, made restless by the long cold spell, had decided to amuse themselves by participating in a mock tournament. Earlier that morning, George himself had told Anne what was planned, and that he intended to participate.

She found herself smiling slightly as she hurried after Bess toward the tiltyard at Richmond. Since the night of his return to court, George had made no further mention of the unfortunate incident that had prompted his departure. To others who asked, he maintained that there was nothing unusual about his sudden decision to visit his estates. Anne had been happy to go along with this fiction and happier still that, when she'd shown an interest in his travels, he'd regaled her with amusing tales of his tenants at Ashby de la Zouch in Leicestershire, the Hastings family seat, and nearby Kirby Muxloe Castle, which he also owned.

He had also been gratifyingly attentive, bringing her little gifts of flowers and candied fruit and finely made lace. For her part, Anne had showered her husband with affectionate gestures, both in private and in public, to let everyone see how highly she regarded him. That morning, before he'd left their lodgings for the tiltyard, George had begged a ribbon from her to tie to his lance.

When Anne reached her, Bess was already at the entrance to the tiltyard, stamping her booted feet to keep them warm. No brightly colored pavilions had been set up, as there would have been for a proper tournament, but a goodly number of spectators filled the wooden benches that surrounded the field. Only the covered grandstand, where the king and queen usually sat, stood completely empty. No pennants flew. There were no rich blue hangings embellished with gold, or cloth of gold cushions, or canopies of estate.

Anne took a moment to study the crowd. She and Bess were almost the only women present, and they were the only members of the queen's household. At random, they chose one of the benches and sat.

Shading her eyes against the glare of sun on snow, Anne tried to pick George out from among the combatants. Although they were all dressed much alike, it took her only a moment to locate him. Her husband was a little shorter than most of his fellows, and more stocky in build, and he wore his dark brown hair a little longer than was fashionable. She marveled that she had not known him at once that night in their lodgings.

Both of Anne's brothers, Edward and Hal, were also among the participants. So were the king's good friends, Charles Brandon and Ned Neville. Neville always stood out, being so much taller than anyone but the king.

Anne frowned as she realized that there was another man present who towered over the rest. It had to be King Henry, but could His Grace really mean to compete? While it was true that he exercised almost daily, practicing with the others in the tiltyard, for a ruler to risk his life by taking part in a tournament was unheard-of. Jousting was a dangerous game.

Bess tugged on her sleeve. "Do you see that man with his visor down? I believe that is the king." She looked as worried as Anne felt.

"This is not a real tournament," Anne murmured, trying to reassure herself as well as Bess. "There will be no fighting on foot at the barriers, nor a tourney fought by small teams on horseback. There will only be jousting."

"Men had been blinded, disabled, even killed, in the lists ere now," Bess said, "and that with officials on the scene to assure their safety."

Anne shaded her eyes, blinking in the bright sunlight. In a joust two men, mounted and armed with lances, charged at each other. A high wall erected between riders prevented collisions. But for this secret event, the combatants were running *volant*. The lists, with their wooden barriers, had not been set up. Worse, the ground, although it had been cleared of snow to reveal a layer of gravel sealed with plaster, was slick with ice.

As the first two competitors took their places, the spectators let out a roar of approval.

"They are all well trained." Anne knew she sounded doubtful, but Bess followed her lead.

"Indeed, they are. And they would think us very foolish to worry. So, shall we wager on the outcome? I say my Tom will break more lances than your husband."

"What stakes?" Anne told herself her fears were groundless. King Henry's gentlemen would not let anything happen to His Grace. And if the competition was safe enough for the king, then it was also safe for all the others, George included.

"Will you wager that new kirtle your brother's wife gave you as a New Year's gift?" Bess had been admiring the finely woven garment for days.

"Only if it is against your silver pomander ball."

"Done."

Having agreed on the wager, they turned their attention to the field. Scoring was based on the number of hits and where each landed on one's opponent's armor. A strike to the helmet scored highest, followed by the breastplate. If the lance broke—and they were hollow with blunted points, designed to shatter on impact—that was worth more than a glancing blow.

Each match was hard fought, just as in a real tournament. When two jousters collided with a mighty crash, long wooden splinters flew in every direction, adding to the excitement. Dozens of lances were broken and although there were a few falls, no one was seriously injured. An hour into the contest, George Hastings and Tom Boleyn had identical scores, but the competitor who'd won joust after joust was the king. Even though he never removed his helmet, word of his identity had spread through the spectators.

Another competitor had also done well, and now prepared to ride against Ned Neville. "Is that Will Compton?" Anne asked. Like the king, he had kept his visor down throughout the jousting, but everyone else in the king's circle of close friends was accounted for.

"It must be," Bess agreed. "Likely he is the one who told His Grace about the tournament. Perhaps he even persuaded King Henry to participate."

Anne smiled a little at that notion. "No one would have had to talk the king into anything." This day's adventure was exactly the sort of reckless activity an impulsive young man would plunge into without a thought for his own safety.

The two great warhorses pawed at the ground, then charged toward each other, hooves thundering on the frozen ground. There was a resounding crash as both lances shattered. Neville's blow caught Compton square in the middle of the chest, unseating him.

Earlier bouts had ended the same way, but in those the fallen man had always clambered awkwardly to his feet and walked away. This time was different. Will Compton lay ominously still. A hush fell over the crowd.

Anne stared in shock at the motionless form. She felt exactly as she had when she'd been told that her mother was dead: beset by a paralyzing sense of loss and despair. Her gloved fingers instinctively sought her rosary and she murmured a fervent prayer. Beside her, Bess began to weep.

The other competitors milled around their fallen comrade. A physician was summoned. Anne saw the king, mounted and still wearing his concealing visor, speak briefly with Neville, then turn as if to leave. But if His Grace thought to slip away before his disguise was penetrated, he had left it till too late. A spectator, seeing him about to depart, set up a shout.

"God save the king!" he called out, and instantly a hundred voices took up the cry.

King Henry turned back, removed his helmet, and acknowledged the cheering crowd. If he was concerned for his friend, it did not show. He never even glanced Will Compton's way before he rode off in the direction of the palace, attended by Tom and George and several other gentlemen.

"We need to leave," Bess whispered, tugging on Anne's arm with one hand while she dashed moisture from her cheeks with the other.

"He has not stirred." Anne could not stop staring at the motionless figure. Was he dead? Of all the king's men, Will Compton had always seemed the most alive, the most vibrant. It would be a sin against nature if he had so carelessly lost his life.

"There is nothing we can do. And, look—there is Dr. Chambre, one of the king's own physicians. He'll have Compton on the mend in no time."

As they walked swiftly away from the tiltyard, Anne tried in vain to still her trembling hands and quell the sick feeling in the pit of her stomach. Why should she care so much? Will Compton was nothing to her—just another of the king's boon companions. But she hoped with all her heart that he would not die. She had danced with him, flirted with him, and had grown, she now realized, quite fond of him. Fingering her rosary as she scurried into the palace, Anne went not to her lodgings but to one of the chapels, where she prayed harder than she had in years that Compton would survive. Then, as Bess had, she wept.

"Is there any way I can assist you, my child?"

Anne looked up into the concerned face of one of the king's chaplains. She recognized him as Thomas Wolsey, the priest who had performed her wedding ceremony. "It is Master Compton, Sir Thomas," she blurted out. "He has been sore wounded while jousting and I fear he will die."

"His destiny is in God's hands," Wolsey reminded her. "Trust in the Lord to do what is right."

He offered to pray with her and afterward Anne felt comforted, but hours later, when George returned to their lodgings, she was still deeply upset by what she had witnessed in the tiltyard. She made no pretense of unconcern. "Is he yet living?" she asked the moment her husband walked through the door.

"He'll mend."

"He'll *mend*? Is that all you can tell me? Have you no idea how terrible it was to see him lying so still?"

"His head was cracked open and he was unconscious for hours. At one point, the king's physicians feared for his life. But then he came back to himself. Demanded a cup of ale to quench his thirst."

"Has he other injuries?" Anne asked.

"Nothing of note. He broke a number of bones, and his nose. He'll have to stay behind when the rest of the court moves to Westminster on the morrow."

Anne frowned at him. Was it her imagination, or had George seemed *pleased* by that? "I do not understand what possessed the king to compete. How terrible it would have been if His Grace had been the one who was injured."

"We all knew who he was." George poured himself a goblet of sack and drank deeply.

"I did not suppose that Neville *meant* to injure Compton," Anne said with a trace of asperity. "Why do men take such risks?"

"To ready themselves for war. And to impress women." George gave a self-deprecating laugh.

Belatedly, Anne recalled how well he'd acquitted himself, and that he'd been wearing her favor. "I very nearly won Bess's silver pomander ball wagering on you," she admitted.

That seemed to please him.

Anne set herself to charming her husband out of his ill humor. By the time they retired to their bed, they were in harmony again.

12

*L*ady Anne yawned as she approached the royal bedchamber. Had it not been her turn to wait upon the queen, charged with handing her the royal washing water and supervising the chamberers and other lesser ladies who helped Her Grace dress, she'd have stayed in bed for at least another hour herself. It was no consolation at all that George had been obliged to rise even earlier than she to attend King Henry. She was not certain why. George was no groom of the chamber to be at the king's beck and call. Something special was afoot, she supposed. An early morning hunt or some other male foolishness. Perhaps another snowball fight, since that pastime had become so popular of late.

Her Grace the Queen would have been up at midnight to pray in her oratory, the small closet that adjoined her bedchamber. Now, at third cockcrow, she insisted upon being roused from slumber yet again, this time to hear Mass. Anne would have to accompany her to the chapel, as would all the other ladies on duty this morning. There the priest would drone on, keeping them on their knees far longer than necessary.

That the queen would give birth to a child in a few months and was exhausted with carrying it made no difference to either Catherine of Aragon or her Spanish chaplain. Her Grace insisted upon regular and frequent devotions. Anne thought the queen spent an excessive amount of time in prayer, and in fasting, too. Those who knew more of such things than she did had tried suggesting that the baby would be the better for a more rested and well-fed mother, but the queen would not listen. Her own mother, as Her Grace continually reminded them, had given birth to children on the battlefield during the holy war she had waged against the infidel.

Anne doubted that Isabella of Castile had been fasting at the time. Pausing at the final doorway before she reached Queen Catherine's presence, she carefully schooled her features to reveal nothing of her disrespectful thoughts.

The queen's bedchamber was dimly lit. The curtains were still drawn around Her Grace's bed. With quiet movements, a Spanish chamberer, Isabel de Vargas, heated washing water over a charcoal brazier while Bess Boleyn inspected the garments that had been sent up by the queen's wardrobe mistress. The sleeves, skirt, and bodice, together with the elaborate gown that went over the rest, had already been brushed by another of the queen's chamberers.

Anne nodded to Bess, then glanced toward the bed. Her sister, Elizabeth, was about to part the hangings and gently awaken Her Grace. Elizabeth gave a start when a small door on the far side of the chamber abruptly popped open. A dozen large men, each one dressed in a short cloak and hood of Kendall green and armed with both swords and bows, spilled into the room.

Eyes wide, Anne stared at them. She'd managed to stifle a gasp, but some of the other women shrieked in alarm before they realized who these intruders must be. The door gave onto a passageway that led to the king's secret lodgings. No one could enter that way except with His Grace's permission . . . and with His Grace.

The mask covering the king's face did nothing to hide Henry Tudor's identity. Ned Neville might be as tall and have similarly broad shoulders, but only one man at court had that shock of bright red-gold hair.

Anne had only seconds to decide how to react. To curtsey would acknowledge that she recognized the king when he plainly thought himself well disguised as the legendary outlaw, Robin Hood. Acting on instinct, she flung her arms wide instead, as if to prevent him from reaching the queen's bed.

It was the right choice. The king's hearty laugh boomed out. Then he moved Anne out of his way by the simple expedient of putting both hands on her waist and lifting her aside. He winked at her as he did so. The cloth visor did nothing to conceal the wicked merriment in his pale blue-gray eyes.

Anne retreated, searching among the "Merry Men" until she found her husband. This, then, was why George had been obliged to wait upon the king so early in the morning. There were a dozen invaders in all—the king as Robin Hood, ten of his companions as the Merry Men, and a Maid Marian dressed in a green gown and yellow wig and wearing a mask that covered all her features, not just her eyes.

"The Maid Marian is a woman," Anne whispered, too surprised to keep the observation to herself. The role was traditionally played by a man in female clothing.

"It was to have been Compton," George whispered back, "but he's still recovering from his injuries."

The king, meanwhile, had swept back the hangings that enclosed his wife's bed and discovered her still groggy with sleep. Her Grace gave a startled cry, but a few quiet murmurs calmed her fears.

"Rise and dance with us, madam," the king ordered in a voice loud enough for everyone to hear, "for I vow we will not depart until you agree to our demand."

"You give me no choice, sirrah," Catherine replied in her deep, throaty voice with its distinctive hint of a Castilian lisp. "I yield."

The king lifted his wife out of her bed and set her on the small carpet beside the bed. Her fair skin flushed with embarrassment, right down to her bare feet, and she immediately turned in to him, using his much bigger body to shield her from prying eyes. Wearing only her nightgown and with her hair down, the queen appeared even tinier than she usually did, especially standing next to her massive husband.

His Grace plainly took delight in teasing and embarrassing his wife, but he was not unkind. He called for her velvet night robe and demanded fur-lined slippers for her feet. Only after she'd been bundled into these warm accessories did he signal for one of his Merry Men to strum the lute he carried.

With great care, the king danced with his wife. George partnered Anne, and others of the Merry Men persuaded the remaining giggling ladies to join in. Anne could tell by the look on Bess Boleyn's face that she was dancing with her Tom, but was less certain of the identities of the other gentlemen.

"Who is that?" she whispered to George, angling her head toward the Merry Man dancing with the Maid Marian.

"Harry Guildford."

"And the woman?"

He laughed and shook his head. "No one but Harry knows that. He's the one who arranged the disguising."

Solicitous of the queen's health, the king insisted that she rest after only one dance. Her Grace sank gratefully into a padded chair, one hand resting protectively over her womb, but she watched with apparent pleasure as her husband and his band of Merry Men disported themselves with her ladies.

Anne took her cue from the queen and gave herself over to enjoying the unexpected respite from morning Mass. She danced with her brother Hal and then with a man she thought was Harry Guildford's older half brother, Sir Edward, although she could not be sure. He barely spoke two words to her. It hardly mattered. Flirtation with "strangers" was the order of the morning.

When His Grace selected Anne to be his next partner, having already danced with Bess and Elizabeth and Isabel de Vargas, too, she accepted the honor with exaggerated delight. "Ooh, you're a big one, Master Robin Hood," she cooed, and fluttered her eyelashes at him.

Amused, the king responded in kind, playing his role of outlaw to the hilt. "The better to hold you for ransom, mistress," he declared. "Now you must give me a kiss to pay for your freedom, or it's off to the greenwood with me and my men."

Before she could think of some witty response, His Grace had cupped his big hands beneath her elbows and lifted her off the ground. When her lips were level with his, he met them with a kiss that made up with enthusiasm what it lacked in finesse. Anne felt the heat rush into her cheeks as he set her down again, but she managed not to stumble as he led her into the first movements of a lively country dance.

Less than two weeks later, the queen went into labor prematurely. The child, a daughter, was stillborn. Anne wondered ever after if the king's early morning raid on his wife's bedchamber had somehow precipitated the loss.

His Grace's response to the tragedy was to assure the queen that they were young yet and would have more children.

13

*A*fter more than ten years in the Duke of Buckingham's household, Madge Geddings was accustomed to the duke's rages. It did not take much to set him off. Last month, he'd been upset about a romp instigated by the king—an early morning raid on the queen's bedchamber. Madge had been unable to decide if the duke had been so chagrined because King Henry's companions were all "upstarts," as he called them, or because he'd been left out of the fun.

The women of the duke's household had heard another version of the tale from the duke's sister, Lady Anne. According to her, the revelers had also included an earl, the duke's own younger brother, Lord Hal Stafford, and two of the duke's brothers-in-law, Lord Hastings and Lord Fitzwalter.

This time, the duke's temper had apparently been ignited by the fact that the king had granted Lord Hal a title. Buckingham had left court immediately following the investiture of his brother as Earl of Wiltshire, a ceremony that had taken place with great pomp at Westminster.

"I should have thought that such an honor coming into his family would please His Grace," Madge whispered to Bess Knyvett.

"Hah!" Bess said, but softly. "Nothing ever satisfies him."

Bess should know, Madge thought. She had already been one of the duchess's ladies when Madge arrived to take up her duties in the ducal nursery. Bess's father, Sir William Knyvett, was the duke's chamberlain, although he was wealthy in his own right. Her brother, Charles, was also part of Buckingham's household. Bess herself always had fine clothing and money to gamble with.

Madge continued to watch the duke. To her eyes, he lacked nothing. Not only was he noble and wealthy, but he was an attractive man. Barely past his thirtieth year, he was in excellent physical condition, able to compete in the lists with much younger men. Madge had seen him practicing once and had been mightily impressed.

Her heart beat a little faster as he stalked toward the small circle of women who sat sewing by the windows of his newly erected gallery. He had embarked upon an extensive building campaign at Bletchingly since the new king's coronation, for the manor lay within easy traveling distance of court. Nowadays, they were more apt to stay here than at Thornbury Castle in distant Gloucestershire.

Madge quickly turned her attention to the sampler that young Lady Mary was stitching. The youngest of the three girls, she was a child of six and making her first efforts to create a guide to the stitches and patterns she'd use for the rest of her life. She'd laboriously made rows of the most common stitches—tent stitch, cross stitch, back stitch, stem stitch, split stitch, and chain stitch. Now she was attempting to copy her favorite patterns and motifs in green and black silk.

"What will you do for the border?" Madge asked her when she'd admired the little girl's work.

"A running scroll," Lady Mary replied at once.

"You should decorate it with columbines," said her sister, Lady Catherine, who was four years Lady Mary's senior.

"A lozenge design of lined hexagons is prettier," Lady Elizabeth chimed in, using the know-it-all voice that so aggravated her younger siblings. She was fast approaching womanhood and lorded it over the other two that, as the eldest, she'd have her pick of husbands from among the nobility of England. She'd been unable to hide her chagrin when her little sister pointed out to her that, since their father was England's only duke, they would perforce have to settle for a nobleman of lesser rank.

Into this homey little scene stepped the duke himself. He took a moment to bend down and examine the work of all three girls, and bestowed upon them a few curt words of praise, but it was clear his mind was elsewhere. He turned next to his wife.

"Madam, a word?"

She sent a quelling look his way. "Have you forgotten the date, my lord? Yesterday was Ash Wednesday."

A chilling quiet descended on the chamber. The duchess was not excessively religious. She had no desire to declare herself a vowess devoted to chastity and prayer for the rest of her life. But she did believe that a devout woman should give up something of value during Lent. She chose, year after year, to forgo the pleasures of the marriage bed.

"The date?" he echoed. "It is the fourteenth day of February. St. Valentine's Day. At court they celebrate with the giving and receiving of gifts."

"I am certain that her most gracious majesty the queen will maintain a sense of decorum," the duchess said.

"Unlikely," her husband replied. "Not with all the young wildheads that surround the king."

"How do they celebrate, Father?" Lady Catherine piped up.

For a moment, Madge thought he might ignore her question, but then he relented. "They choose their valentines by lot," he explained. "Then each man has to give a gift to the lady who selected him."

"Even if she is not his wife," the duchess said with a disdainful sniff. She stood and began to gather up her sewing, a signal for all her ladies to do likewise.

"Especially if she is not his wife," Buckingham shot back.

Head down, Madge scurried after the others, nearly running over Lady Mary when the little girl stopped short in the doorway. "I left my sampler behind," Lady Mary said, and started to return.

Madge glanced over her shoulder at the duke. He looked so alone, standing there amid the scattered cushions and stools. As she watched, he sank into the only chair, the one his wife had just vacated. He stared out the window at the bleak and snow-covered garden, shoulders slumped. He was making the little humming sound that meant he was mulling something over in his mind.

"I will fetch it," Madge told the child. "You go along after your mother. She'll be expecting you."

Cautiously, she approached the Duke of Buckingham, but her wariness lessened as she drew close. He was just a man, and a sad and rather lonely one, at that. Instead of reaching for the sampler, abandoned among the cushions on the floor, she touched his velvet-clad arm.

He looked up, his gaze so intense that for a moment Madge forgot how to breathe. In one swift movement, he freed himself from her grasp and seized her about the waist, tugging her onto his lap. His mouth clamped down hard over hers.

The kiss went on and on, frightening at first and then, abruptly, turning into something wonderful. Madge responded, kissing him back. He laughed softly as he tumbled them both to the floor among the cushions. Before Madge could gather her wits, he shoved her skirts aside and himself into her body.

She gave one squeak of protest when her maidenhead was breached, but the pain faded quickly, replaced by myriad pleasurable sensations. Afterward, her only regret was that it was over too soon.

The duke straightened his own clothing first, then restored hers to order and helped her to her feet. Then he gave her a playful swat on the bottom on his way out of the gallery, telling her to hurry back to her duties, lest she be missed.

Madge stared after him in disappointment. He might have lingered for just a little while. Or bestowed some word of praise upon her. She sighed deeply. What had she expected?

It troubled her that she'd just lain with her mistress's husband, but not overmuch, not when the duchess had given up conjugal relations for Lent. Men were carnal creatures. Everyone knew that. They needed women, especially if they had serious matters weighing upon them. The duke would soon realize that he needed *her,* Madge told herself as she gathered up Lady Mary's sampler. Given time, surely she'd win his affection, too.

14

Greenwich Palace, May 1, 1510

*L*ady Anne rolled over in bed to blink sleepily at her husband. His manservant had dressed him all in white satin. In one hand he carried a gilded bow. He'd slung a quiver of white-and-gold-fletched arrows over his shoulder.

"Do you mean to shoot the flowers?" she asked.

George chuckled. "I would not put it past His Grace to try. He does enjoy showing off his marksmanship."

"It is May Day. You mean to go into the woods to gather green boughs and May blossoms. I see no need for weapons."

Anne yawned as George checked his accoutrements one last time to make sure he had everything. Then he returned to the bed to kiss her in farewell.

"Will you be waiting in the gardens to watch for our return?" he asked.

"Everyone will be," she assured him.

She tugged the coverlet up over her head as soon as he was gone. Lethargy crept over her. There was no reason for her to rise at dawn just because George had. She was not one of the queen's attendants today.

Catherine of Aragon was no doubt already at Mass. Although it had only been a few months since she'd lost her first child, she was already breeding again. Anne fervently hoped that, this time, His Grace would have sense enough to leave his wife out of his more energetic revels. Anne took it as a good sign that the king had not insisted that the ladies join this morning's expedition into the woods. Hoping that no one would be struck by a stray arrow, Anne ignored a slight queasiness brought on by that thought and, trusting Meriall to wake her in good time to dress, drifted back into sleep.

Three hours later, she sat on a bench in the garden where the maypole had been raised, listening to music provided by the king's blind harp player. King Henry and his entourage had not yet returned. Anne's sister sat next to her. Their brother the duke stood beside them. Their other sibling, Hal, was with the king.

Anne smiled to herself. Above and beyond forgiving Hal for whatever imagined sins he had committed, His Grace had granted him the title of Earl of Wiltshire. Edward, although he was pleased to see their brother advance at court, had not been entirely happy with that development. He'd rather have seen another gift of property come his way instead, or perhaps a profitable wardship.

"What news from Bletchingly?" Anne asked. Edward's wife, Eleanor, along with most of the ducal household, were currently at the manor house in Surrey, close enough to London for Edward to visit them regularly.

"The rebuilding progresses apace," the duke said.

Anne was not surprised that he should think first of the improvements he was making to the house. He had already added a long gallery for winter exercise. From the start, he'd taken a personal interest in the construction. Anne was slightly taken aback, however, when he produced a drawing from inside his doublet and unrolled it so that both his sisters could admire the design for a double courtyard.

"I mean to commence rebuilding at Thornbury Castle early next year," he said. "On the front of the new gatehouse I will put an inscription to tell all who see it who it was that built such an opulent palace."

"Never tell me that you mean to list all the masons and carpenters!" Anne exclaimed. Thornbury Castle in Gloucestershire was the family seat. She'd lived there both before her first marriage and after she'd been widowed.

Edward ignored her.

"What will it say?" Elizabeth asked, always more than ready to encourage their brother to boast of his accomplishments.

"This gatehouse was begun in the year of Our Lord God 1511, the second year of the reign of King Henry the Eighth, by me Edward, Duke of Buckingham, Earl of Hereford, Stafford, and Northampton."

Edward rambled on, describing the spacious outer courtyard he had planned, with towers and a wooden gallery that would provide the inhabitants with a covered walkway from the family lodgings to the parish church. There would also be a fine, new enclosed park with good glades for coursing.

Anne frowned. "The land thereabout is fertile and arable farmland, Edward. Is it not wasteful to convert it to parkland, especially when there is already a park only a mile away from the castle?"

"I mean to enlarge the latter, too, increasing its size to six miles in circumference."

That would cause a good deal of grumbling among his tenants, Anne thought, but in his own little corner of Gloucestershire, Edward was king. He could do as he wished.

A trumpet fanfare interrupted Edward's detailed description of how he hoped to make a channel from the small tidal creek that flowed into his land from the Severn, in order to lead the water up to the castle. The sound heralded the return of the king and his courtiers, their arms full of green boughs. They were carrying so many flowers that Anne wondered whether any remained unpicked, and more greenery decorated their caps.

Queen Catherine and her ladies waited beneath the maypole. Gaily colored ribbons streamed down from its top, ready to be seized by dancers who would follow the tradition of cavorting around the pole. Later there would be horse races and jousting and cakes and cream to eat. Anne made haste to abandon her brother and sister and join her husband, who greeted her with the gift of a nosegay and a kiss.

15

With envy in his heart, Will Compton watched Lady Anne accept a posy from her husband. She was a paragon among women, he thought. What a pity it was that he'd lacked the where-withal to court her before she married George Hastings. George was a decent sort, but a bit of a dull stick. The lady deserved better.

The king noticed the direction of his gaze and, grinning, slung an arm around his shoulders. Will maintained his balance only by dint of long practice. Sometimes His Grace did not know his own strength, and Will was still not fully recovered from his injuries in the tourna-ment. That he'd nearly died, he supposed, accounted for his uncharac-teristic tendency to dwell on what might have been. Ordinarily, he did not take time for regrets.

"Lady Anne is a saucy wench," King Henry declared. "Full of energy. Always cheerful. Those are good qualities in a woman."

"Indeed, Your Grace. Your Grace is fortunate in that the queen is both energetic and cheerful, as well." Will balked at calling Queen Catherine saucy.

The king's smile dimmed. "Her Grace worries too much," he muttered.

Will waited. If the king wished to confide in him, he had no choice but to listen.

"She took the loss of the child hard and now that she's to have another, she spends even more hours every day in prayer. I vow, she will wear out the floor with all that kneeling."

"Her Grace is young and healthy. I am certain all will be well this time." Will was sure of no such thing, but it would not be politic to say so. He sent a silent prayer winging heavenward that the queen would not only survive childbirth but also produce the son and heir every monarch needed to secure the throne.

The king lowered his voice to the point where Will had to strain to catch his words. "Her Grace should be spared amorous attentions during this delicate time."

"Is that what the physicians suggest, Your Grace?" With an effort, Will hid his alarm. Had he heard correctly? Did the king intend to avoid his wife's bed for the rest of her pregnancy?

"They are not of one mind on this matter, but Dr. Vittorio thinks to do so would ensure the queen's good health and the health of the child she carries."

The Spanish physician had charge of Her Grace's care. No wonder King Henry was inclined to listen to his advice. Will said only, "Celibacy is a difficult course, Your Grace."

King Henry's booming laugh drew the attention of every courtier in the garden. His hand landed on Will's shoulder with a hearty smack. "Who said that I meant to remain celibate?"

The king left Will's side and headed straight toward Lady Anne. She appeared to be delighted by the attention and George smiled, too. Only Lady Anne's sister, Lady Elizabeth, watching from the shade of a rose arbor, seemed to read anything ominous into the king's sudden show of interest.

16

ith a sigh of pleasure, Lady Anne relaxed under her tiring maid's ministrations. They were in the inner chamber of her lodgings at court, finished at last with a long day in the queen's service. Anne had bathed and washed her hair. She'd dried it over a brazier and now Meriall was brushing the long, dark brown strands. Anne felt deliciously lazy. Her cheeks were still slightly warm from having been so close to the glowing coals. She let her velvet nightgown fall open to cool her flushed skin.

The creak of the outer door opening in the other room startled both mistress and maid. Anne glanced at the little clock on the table. George had left some hours earlier for the nearby village of Greenwich. His stepfather, Richard Sacheverell, was there, staying in an inn for a day or two. Anne did not expect her husband to return for many hours yet. He'd planned to spend the evening gambling with Sacheverell and other gentlemen of his acquaintance.

"See who has come in," she instructed Meriall, and retied the sash of her robe with a secure knot.

The little maid clutched the hairbrush in one hand, as if she thought to use it as a weapon, and crept to the door that stood open between the inner and outer rooms of Anne's lodgings. There she stopped and stood stock still and staring for a long moment before she spoke. The look she slanted at her mistress contained both worry and confusion. "It is Master Compton, my lady."

Anne frowned. What was Will Compton doing here at this hour? The logical answer was that he'd been sent to find George. The king must want her husband for some reason. She was about to rise and go out to talk to him when the man himself brushed past Meriall and entered the inner chamber uninvited.

Compton had come back to court hale and hearty once he'd recovered from that fall in the tournament. He'd laughed off his injuries, claiming that the worst of it was the broken nose. He now had a slight bump in an appendage that had previously been perfectly shaped.

"Forgive the intrusion, my lady." He doffed his bonnet and bowed to her.

In the candlelight, he cut a fine figure. Anne felt a little flutter of excitement low in her belly and quickly adjusted the collar of her night robe. She decided not to stand up. Doing so might reveal an unseemly length of leg, for she was naked beneath the soft dark blue velvet.

"It is late, Master Compton. Why are you here?" She was pleased to hear that her voice was steady, even though she was all aquiver inside.

"I require a word with you in private." He sent a pointed glance in Meriall's direction.

Anne frowned, but she knew that Will Compton would not have come to her chamber at this late hour if the matter were not important. "Has something happened to George?" she asked.

Even as she voiced the question, she knew that was not the reason. If Compton had come to deliver bad news, he'd have wanted Meriall to stay.

"George has naught to do with this," he said when they were alone. "The king sent me."

"Why?"

"You truly have no notion, do you?" Looking exasperated, he came closer, and she saw that he'd twisted his bonnet into a knot. "Dearest Anne, His Grace desires you. So do I, but I have not the power to command your love."

"Is this some tasteless jest?" Even as she asked, the pained look in Compton's eyes told her it was not.

"I wish it were," he muttered.

"The king . . . *wants* me?"

He nodded.

"But . . . but he loves the queen. You know he does."

"His Grace believes he is being noble," Compton said. "He would spare the queen his attentions while she carries his child. And during that time . . ." His voice trailed off. Clearly, he did not care for the king's plan any more than she did.

"Let him find someone else!"

"His Grace seems set upon having you. If you mean to refuse him—"

"If? There is no question of *if*. And does he think my husband will sit idly by and let me go to another man's bed, even the king's? Does he think my *brother* will?"

Compton's expression turned grim. "I do not believe His Grace has thought past the pleasure of coupling with you."

His words sent a spike of fear through her. She willed herself to be calm, to think clearly. "I will never be his mistress. You must tell His Grace that."

"It would be best if you told him yourself."

Now it was her turn to show exasperation. "Are you afraid of the king, Will Compton?" she taunted him.

"At times, His Grace terrifies me. I doubt that you have seen it, my lady, but King Henry has a temper when he is thwarted and has since he was a boy."

There was such honesty in the simple statement that Anne felt a moment's sympathy for him. Compton served at the king's pleasure and had no powerful kin to protect him from his master's wrath should he refuse to obey a command.

"There may be a way out," she said slowly. "For both of us. You did say that the king is loath to do anything that might harm a woman who is with child?"

Compton nodded.

"Then he will not wish to meddle with me any more than he does with the queen."

His gaze darted to her belly.

"It is early days yet, but I am all but certain that I am with child." Her breasts were tender. For the last week, she had felt a little ill in the morning. She had not yet told anyone, not even George. She had wanted to wait until she was sure. "Will my condition dissuade the king from his pursuit?"

"I have no doubt of it." Compton started to smile.

Relief washed over her. The king would not take offense at her refusal to become his mistress. Not in these circumstances. And as soon as George returned from his visit to Richard Sacheverell, she would inform him that in six or seven months he would be a father.

"Will you be bold enough to inform the king?" she asked, rising carefully to her feet, her robe snugly wrapped and covering all but her bare feet. "Or must I slay my own dragon?"

His smile turned into a grin. "Never fear, my lady. In this instance, I am prepared to fulfill the duties of a chivalrous knight."

She couldn't help but smile back at him. "I thought for a moment there that you expected me to don armor and enter the lists."

"Now there is a sight I would like to see!"

They were laughing together when the door to the outer room slammed open with a resounding crash. Anne's brother stormed into her bedchamber, closely followed by their sister.

The Duke of Buckingham stopped short when he caught sight of Anne standing so close to Will Compton. "I did not believe it!" he roared. "I told Elizabeth she must be mistaken. But now I see that she was not. Whore! You bring shame on the good name of Stafford."

Elizabeth's smug expression removed any need for words from her.

Compton rounded on the duke. "My lord, you have no cause to revile Lady Anne."

Anne placed one hand on his sleeve to stop him from saying more. "What is it, my lord brother, that you *think* you see?" She had her own full share of Stafford pride. She drew herself up straighter and met Edward glare for glare. She might be wearing nothing but a velvet night robe, but she would not oblige her officious older brother by showing any sign of shame. She had done nothing to warrant his anger.

Edward clearly thought otherwise. "What is he doing here in the middle of the night? Have you no pride, Anne? He is a commoner. A nobody."

Will made matters worse by laughing aloud. "Ah, I see," he said. "It would be acceptable, then, for your sister to become a nobleman's mistress? Or perhaps the king's?"

Edward's face turned an ugly shade of red.

"I told you the king was sniffing around her!" Elizabeth said, her voice triumphant. "I tried to warn you, Edward."

"There is nothing untoward in my connection to His Grace," Anne protested.

"Then why is *he* here?" Elizabeth demanded, pointing an accusing finger at Compton. "If not for himself, then there is only one other for whom he'd solicit your favors."

Anne sent her sister a withering glance but, before she could answer, Compton did.

"I came to read the lady a poem I wrote to her left eyebrow. It is a poor piece, but mine own. Shall I recite it for you?"

"Can you never be serious?" Anne scolded him. "He is jesting, Edward." Her brother looked as if he were about to explode.

Compton opened his mouth to say more, but Anne silenced him with a look. He was incorrigible. Under other circumstances, she might have found his quick wit amusing, but not when her brother's anger was rapidly building into rage.

"Staffords are no game for Comptons," Edward said with a supercilious sneer, "nor for Tudors, neither."

"Am I a hind to be hunted?" Anne felt her own temper spike.

Neither man answered her. They were too intent on scowling at each other. Edward's hand rested, ominously, on the pommel of his sword.

"Upstart!" he flung the word at Compton like a curse.

"Fool!" Compton lobbed back.

Before they could draw weapons or come to blows, both treasonable offenses at court, Anne launched herself between them and gave her brother a hard shove. Taken off guard by the sudden movement, he staggered back a few steps, giving her enough room to round on Compton.

"Leave my lodgings at once, sirrah. You are not welcome here."

He started to protest, but when he got a good look at her face, he sketched a bow instead. "As my lady wishes. But perhaps we might speak tomorrow, properly chaperoned, that I may assure you of the outcome of certain matters we discussed tonight?"

"She'll not be speaking to you ever again, Compton!" Edward bellowed. "At first light tomorrow she'll be on her way to a nunnery!"

"Edward!"

"Silence! You have played the wanton and you must suffer for it. It is my duty as your brother to protect you and, failing that, to correct you."

"The king shall hear of this," Compton vowed, and on that promise he turned on his heel and left the chamber.

Anne took several deep breaths in an attempt to regain control of her emotions. Only when she was calmer did she turn to her brother and speak to him through gritted teeth. "You are being unreasonable. And you have no right to send me anywhere, least of all a nunnery."

"We will see about that. I've sent a man to fetch your husband."

"I have done nothing to warrant your condemnation, or his."

"Liar! Women are weak vessels. Those who succumb to the lure of the flesh must be chastised. Consider yourself fortunate that I do not insist that your adultery be punished by public penance."

"I have not committed adultery, Edward." Anne enunciated each word carefully, but he was not listening to her.

"How could you be so disloyal to Queen Catherine?" Elizabeth chimed in. "Her Grace will be most distressed when she hears of this."

"And you will no doubt delight in telling her!" Disgusted, Anne turned her back on them both.

Edward and Elizabeth continued to revile her for another quarter of an hour, but when she refused to acknowledge them they finally gave up. Unfortunately, they did not go far. Announcing that he would wait in the outer chamber until George returned, Edward slammed out of the inner room.

Anne heard the key turn in the lock and had to fight an overwhelming urge to attack the thick wooden panels with her fists. She stood very still instead, arms wrapped around herself to contain the shaking. George would set things right. He would never believe Elizabeth's slurs or pay heed to Edward's ranting. She would tell him the truth and all would be well—or as well as it could be when George learned that his king had tried to cuckold him.

A very long time passed before she heard any sound from the other side of the door. Then there were voices, speaking too low for her to understand the words. The conversation seemed to go on forever before the key was once again turned in her lock. Anne held her breath, letting it out with a whoosh when George entered the chamber alone.

She had taken only a few steps toward him before she caught sight of the expression on his face and froze. She had never seen him so angry. He was furious . . . at her.

"Was Compton in this chamber?" he asked.

She took a step back. "Yes, but—"

"Alone with you?"

"Yes, but—"

"Enough! You have shamed me, Anne." He turned to shout at Meriall, who hovered in the doorway. "Pack all your mistress's belongings. We leave at first light."

"Leave? I cannot leave the court without the queen's permission."

"Her Grace will be glad to be rid of you."

Anne did not trust herself to speak. She'd rail like a fishwife if she gave voice to everything she felt at this moment. And then it was too late to say anything. George had stormed out of the room, once again locking the door.

He would come to his senses by morning, she told herself. Or the king would intervene. While Meriall quietly began to pack, Anne climbed into bed and closed the hangings around her. She kept back a scream of frustration only by holding her clenched fist to her mouth. Then the tears came.

Wisely, George did not try to join her in their bed that night, but she could hear his voice in the outer room from time to time, and Edward's, too. She did not think she would sleep, but eventually exhaustion claimed her.

George woke her with a rough shake. He stood over her, glowering, a candle held in one hand. For a moment, Anne could not think why he was so wroth with her. Then everything that had happened the previous evening rushed back. She gathered herself, determined to set the record straight, but he gave her no opportunity to explain. Every time she opened her mouth to speak, he cut her off.

"Dress yourself for travel or I will order my men to stuff you into your clothing," he snapped when she caught at his arm. He shook her off and once more retreated to the outer room.

"Oh, Lady Anne, whatever are we to do?" Meriall wailed. "There are men waiting to escort you to a litter. Your brother's men."

A quick glance around the chamber showed Anne that her belongings had been removed. Any money and valuables were out of her reach, at least for the present, and the guards Edward had set would prevent her from asking for help from any of her friends at court.

She had depended upon George to defend her. His defection left her with no recourse, for a wife had few legal rights and fewer resources.

She had been betrayed by the one person who should have stood by her. George had given in to Edward's demands with nary a whisper of protest. Her husband had taken his brother-in-law's word over his wife's.

Bitterly disappointed, frustrated, hurt, and angry, Anne began to dress. An hour later, in the pale light of dawn, she and her maid were escorted out of Greenwich Palace and tucked inside a litter. The curtains had been pinned together on all sides so that no one would see who was within. Anne sank down onto the cushions and into despair.

17

Greenwich Palace, May 7, 1510

*L*ady Anne was taken away by her husband at dawn, Your Grace," Will Compton said. "No one knows her destination."

King Henry's expression was a combination of disbelief and irritation. He did not like to have his plans thwarted. He'd been disappointed but not angry the previous night, when Will had returned to the royal bedchamber alone. The duke's arrival at his sister's lodgings had been sufficient excuse for Will's failure to bring Lady Anne back with him. He'd been able to avoid telling His Grace that she had declined the honor of becoming a royal mistress. He'd also neglected to mention that she was breeding.

The king had declared himself content to wait a bit before he tried his luck with her again, but now Lady Anne was gone. Will could scarcely believe it himself, or how strongly he'd reacted to hearing the news. Over and above desiring her, he *liked* Lady Anne. And for all his banter, some of it admittedly ribald, he knew full well that she had never done more than laugh and talk with any man but her husband. Everyone carried on harmless flirtations at court. It was expected.

"I never thought the Duke of Buckingham would carry out his threat," he said, half to himself. Too late, Will remembered that he'd not given the king any particulars of the duke's visit to Lady Anne's chamber.

His Grace's eyes narrowed to slits. "What does Buckingham have to do with his sister's departure?"

There was no help for it. Will supplied the details he'd left out of his earlier account, including the duke's arrogant claim that a Stafford was too good to be a Tudor's mistress. A part of him was glad to do so. He'd spent an uneasy night, wondering if the duke had dared lay a hand on Lady Anne, or had provoked George Hastings into doing so. A man had the right to beat his wife for far less than the possibility that she'd committed adultery, but the thought of bruises on Lady Anne's delicate skin had turned his stomach.

"Bring the Duke of Buckingham to me," the king commanded, barking the order at one of his gentlemen ushers. When he turned back to Will his face was a mottled red, a sure sign of rising temper. "How dare he remove one of the queen's ladies-in-waiting from court without Her Grace's permission?"

Will started to speak, then stopped himself. The king in this mood was not to be trifled with. But King Henry had known him too long and too well.

"Say what is on your mind, Will. You'll not be flogged for it."

"I was wondering if perhaps he had it. The queen's permission, that is. After all, it was Lord Fitzwalter's wife, sister to both Buckingham and Lady Anne, who shared her suspicions with her brother. Lady Elizabeth is one of Queen Catherine's favorite ladies. Perhaps she also whispered in Her Grace's ear. Your Highness's lady wife might welcome the opportunity to rid the court of a rival."

"Catherine is queen. Her position is secure."

"Who knows how women think, especially when they are breeding?"

At this none-too-subtle reminder of the reason why the king meant to avoid his wife's bed and seek the favors of another woman, King Henry looked thoughtful. His Grace, at eighteen, had not had many dealings with females, thanks to his father's overprotectiveness. He seemed uncertain how to react to the possibility that his wife was jealous, especially since he had no intention of admitting that he'd done anything wrong.

"I believe, Your Grace," Will said by way of distraction, "that Lord Fitzwalter's wife is to blame for everything that transpired last night. Had she not alerted her brother, Lady Anne would still be at Greenwich."

"Then she will be banished," the king decided, "and her husband with her."

The Duke of Buckingham's arrival at that moment solidified His Grace's resolution. Buckingham radiated arrogance. He barely sketched a bow to the king, as if he considered them to be equals.

King Henry rounded on his highest-ranking subject with a roar. "How dare you interfere with my pleasures?"

"Any man has the right to look out for his family!" Buckingham shouted back. "A duke more than most!"

"I decide who stays at court and who goes, not you. Or have you forgotten who is king here?"

It was a dangerous moment. If the look in Buckingham's eyes was anything to go by, the king's cousin would have liked to lay hands on his sovereign and thrash him to within an inch of his life. At the very least, Will expected him to burst out with a statement so treasonous that it would land him in the Tower.

Buckingham barely managed to contain his temper. "Am I not the head of my family, Your Grace? Is it not my responsibility—nay, my duty—to discipline those in my care, even as Your Grace exacts punishment from wrongdoers in this realm of England?"

"Your sister left your care for that of her husband. I was witness to their marriage myself."

A wise man, Will thought, would be wary of that look in the king's eyes and even more cautious when His Grace used that soothing tone of voice. Buckingham was not a wise man. He was unwilling to admit that he might have overstepped his authority.

"George Hastings relies upon me for advice," he said. If he'd been taller, he'd have been looking down his long, patrician nose at the king.

"He agreed with me that his wife would benefit from a period of contemplation away from court."

"Send for Lady Anne," the king commanded. "I prefer to have her here at court."

Buckingham was unable to hide his smirk. "May I suggest you ask the queen if she will accept my sister back before I go to the trouble of fetching her, Your Grace?"

"Her Grace will have need of Lady Anne's services," the king replied, "since she will be losing those of Lady Elizabeth."

Buckingham's color rose. "Your Grace, I must protest. My *elder* sister did nothing to merit dismissal."

"Did she not? She meddled where she had no business meddling. She must go. I will not have her here."

"Have you spoken to the queen of this?" Buckingham demanded.

Will winced and almost felt sorry for the duke. That had been the wrong thing to say.

"The queen will do as I command!" King Henry bellowed. "As will you, my lord Buckingham, if you wish to remain at court."

Temper combined with an overweening pride pushed the duke into hasty speech. "I have no wish to stay where my wisdom and experience are not valued!"

"Go, then. And do not return until I recall you."

Buckingham backed out of the privy chamber, as protocol required, and the yeomen of the guard gently closed the door behind him as soon as he'd passed through.

King Henry looked surprisingly cheerful as he reached for a goblet of wine. "It will be no hardship to do without my lord Buckingham's presence for a time."

But the king was not smiling later that day, after his interview with the queen. When Her Grace heard she was to lose Lady Fitzwalter, she objected in the strongest terms anyone had ever heard from that gentle lady. Finding the king adamant, she burst into tears. That did her no good, either. The king disliked such displays and left her apartments in a rage.

"Come with me to the tennis play," he barked at Will, who'd been waiting for him in the queen's presence chamber.

It took an hour for the king to work off his pique, but he was calm again by the time he'd trounced Will soundly in every match. They were both drenched in sweat.

"Will you recall Lady Anne?" Will dared ask.

The king considered for a moment, then shook his head. "Better to make a clean sweep of Staffords in the queen's household. I will promote Tom Boleyn's wife, Bess, to fill one of the vacancies. She's a duke's granddaughter. And I will be generous and allow the queen to choose the other replacement."

Will longed to protest, but knew better than to do so. Once the king made a decision, he did not change his mind.

18

They stopped briefly in London, at Hastings House in Thames Street. Lady Anne knew the sounds and smells of the city even before she was freed from the litter, escorted indoors, and fed. Afterward, they traveled until dusk, but she had no way of knowing in what direction. The manor house at which they stopped for the night was not one Anne had ever visited before and the few servants she glimpsed did not look familiar to her. While Meriall went off with one of George's men to fetch food and drink, he escorted his wife to a bedchamber and locked her in.

Wearily, she sank into the room's single chair. The bitter thoughts that had plagued her throughout the long, uncomfortable journey left her feeling restless and agitated. She had nursed her resentment for hours. The two men who should have defended her honor—her husband and her brother—had turned against her when she had done nothing to deserve their mistrust.

It had been her brother's certainty that she'd sinned, with Will Compton if not with the king, that had convinced George to believe it, too. Hypocrite! How dare the duke condemn her for taking a lover—especially when she had not!—when he himself had kept more than one mistress over the years?

Had he succeeded in seducing Madge Geddings yet? No doubt he had, for Madge had already been half in love with him before Anne left the ducal household to marry George. Anne could not fathom why her arrogant, much older brother would appeal to a pretty young woman. She could only suppose it had something to do with the power he wielded.

Dismissing Madge from her thoughts, Anne surveyed the room in which she was imprisoned. In the last light of the day she made out a bed with a lumpy mattress, a small table, a wardrobe chest, and a wooden screen. With an effort, she rose and lit the candle on the table, then went behind the screen to make use of the close stool she found there. No one had thought to provide washing water. She was not surprised. She doubted their arrival had been expected.

The room had a single window that looked out over a courtyard. She could see no sign of the church spires of London in the distance, nor any other landmarks that might tell her in which direction they had traveled. She did not know where she was or where they were bound.

Edward had threatened to send her to a nunnery. She found it difficult to believe that he might have meant what he said, and yet everything about this debacle defied belief. Edward and George should have accepted her protestations of innocence without question. She did not lie. Nor had she ever lain with any man who was not her husband.

At the sound of the door opening behind her, Anne whirled to face her accuser. Of their own volition, her hands curled into tight fists.

One of George's henchmen came in first, bearing a tray. He set it on the table and left. Then George entered, closing the door behind him. He pulled the chair up to the table and gestured for her to sit.

She remained where she was. "Why do you refuse to believe me?" she demanded. "I have told you nothing but the truth."

"Sit and eat. I do not intend to starve a confession out of you." His voice was harsh and he refused to meet her eyes.

She wondered why she bothered trying to talk to him. It was obvious that he had set his mind against her. "If you imagine I would ever confess to something I did not do, you are more of a fool than my brother is!"

As she stalked past him to the table, she caught a brief glimpse of his face. For just that moment, she thought she saw a flicker of distress in his expression. Hope flared in her that he might weaken and listen to her at last, but when he spoke again his words were as cold and unyielding as ever.

"What we do is for your own good, Anne, and for the good of your soul."

"According to my brother?" She had no appetite, but she picked up a chicken leg and took a bite. She had a feeling she would need her strength in the coming days.

"Yes, according to your brother, who bore witness to your sin."

"He saw nothing untoward."

"That is not what he says."

"And is he the king, now, that he must be listened to? Or God?"

"You will not aid your cause by blaspheming."

"I will fill the air with my curses if I must listen to such hypocritical pap for much longer!" She flung the drumstick at him. It struck his doublet, leaving a greasy smear.

"I will send your maid to you," he said stiffly. "You will want to get a good night's rest. We leave again at dawn."

"Oh, yes," she muttered as he slammed out of the room. "I must be well rested to ride all day in a closed litter." She was tempted to throw the entire tray at the door. Instead she forced herself to eat every bit of the food.

She had just consumed the last morsel when Meriall arrived with washing water and toiletries. The maidservant's brow was knit with worry and she looked as if she had been weeping.

"Well?" Anne demanded. "What have you discovered?"

"Oh, madam, they are taking you to a nunnery, just as the duke threatened."

"What nunnery?"

"I do not know. All I was able to overhear was that it will be a journey of some sixty miles in all."

There were hundreds of nunneries in England, both large and small. The distance from Greenwich ruled out some of the best known. George was not taking her to Syon or to Barking, the wealthiest and most prestigious of the lot. "Trust Edward to find some remote hole to stuff me into," Anne muttered.

"Oh, madam, what are we to do?"

"A journey of sixty miles will take four or five days," Anne mused. "If we give the guards no trouble, they will be lulled into thinking I have accepted my fate. Then we will act."

"Escape?" Meriall's eyes went wide, but whether from admiration or fear, Anne could not tell.

"If we can. You must discover what road we are on. Then perhaps I can think of a place to go and a way to get there."

The wicked thought that she might be able to reach Compton Wynyates, Will Compton's family seat in Warwickshire, slipped unbidden into her mind. She thought better of that idea at once. She had no intention of giving George another reason to believe that she was Compton's mistress.

"What a tangle!" she lamented as Meriall helped her prepare for bed. And it was all her wretched brother's fault. It would be a long time, she vowed, before she forgave the Duke of Buckingham. And if she ever had the opportunity to pay him back in kind and soil his reputation as he'd soiled hers, she would seize upon it without hesitation.

19

*A*s they set out on the third day of travel, George Hastings cast a worried look at his wife. She was still not speaking to him. He had a feeling that if he'd not had several large and sturdy henchmen with him, she would also have refused to climb into her litter.

It was plain for its kind, with undecorated canvas side curtains and few amenities within. The horses, one before and one behind, supported the weight of the whole. Traveling this way, they made slow progress, barely fifteen miles a day, plodding along roads that were still muddy with the spring rains.

In the cool of the early morning, they left Uxbridge and set out for Beaconsfield, seven miles distant. They'd stop there briefly to dine, then continue on to Tetsworth. If the weather held, they might be able to travel as far as East Wycombe before stopping for the night. George hoped they could manage that much. If they did, they'd reach their destination on the morrow. He'd be quit of this distasteful burden.

Unfortunately, he'd also be short a wife.

The Duke of Buckingham's parting words echoed in his head: *Do not weaken. Where women are concerned, you must have a firm hand and a steady resolve. She will emerge from the contemplative life the better for it and become the obedient wife you deserve.*

George had liked Anne the way she was, but it was obvious to him now that he had allowed her too much freedom. If she'd dallied with Will Compton . . .

He did not like thinking about it. It made his chest hurt to picture them together. He'd spent enough time with Compton at court to know that women always preferred his charm and hyperbole to George's quieter, more sincere flattery. He'd hoped Anne would be different, that she'd be faithful to him, but he'd have been a fool indeed not to have seen the signs. He'd forgiven her too easily for her careless words about him to the king. And he'd chosen to ignore the depth of her concern for Compton when he'd been hurt while jousting.

She'd always had a ready smile for Will Compton. From there it must have been but a short step to desire, and thus had she gone willingly to another man's bed. The image of his passionate, laughing Anne in someone else's arms—Compton's arms—had him seething and hardened his resolve. She must be taught that she could not play the wanton. He was her husband. He would not allow it.

He found himself staring at the litter as he rode along beside it. What was she thinking, hidden away in there? Did she regret her actions? Or was anger at him still her paramount emotion? She was not sorry for what she had done, only sorry that she'd been caught. She had been furious to find herself a prisoner. She'd thrown things at him—it had been a chamber pot the previous night.

George had not slept well since he'd learned the terrible truth about his wife. Every night on this journey, he'd left her under guard and gone off to a lonely bed in another chamber. He wondered now if he should have forced himself on her, but he found the idea repugnant. She must be willing, even if she was not pure. And she must be removed from temptation until she saw the error of her ways. Buckingham had been right about that.

It had been Buckingham who had made all the arrangements. He'd sent Charles Knyvett on ahead, so that they would be expected at their destination. If all went well on the road, they would reach there on the morrow. That meant, George realized, that tonight might be his last chance to speak in private with his errant wife.

They stopped at dusk at an inn in East Wycombe. Knyvett arrived in time to sup with them in the inn's best chamber, the one George had given over to Anne's use.

"My Lord Hastings. Lady Anne." Knyvett's greeting to George's wife, who was his kinswoman, was distinctly cold. "All is in readiness at the priory to receive you."

Anne glared at him. "Good dog, Cousin Charles. Your master will give you a bone."

Knyvett's already florid coloring deepened. His small, pale eyes narrowed. Then he gave a nasty laugh. "You will not be so quick to mock, Lady Anne, when your hair has been shorn and you are wearing coarse wool instead of brocade."

"What are you prattling on about?" Anne affected disinterest and helped herself to a serving of beef stuffed with forcemeat and vegetables, but George heard the wariness in her voice.

"Did you think your brother was joking when he vowed to send you to a nunnery?" Now it was Knyvett's turn to taunt and he seemed to relish the opportunity.

George intervened before Anne could hurl her wine goblet at him. "There will be no shaving of heads. She is not taking vows, Knyvett. Only living as a guest of the nuns for a time."

"A guest is permitted great freedom and may even leave if she so chooses. It is the duke's wish that his sister do penance for her sins. She must live as a cloistered nun, subject to the rule."

"Where, exactly, am I to do this penance?" Anne interrupted. "Where on God's green earth *are* we?"

"This is East Wycombe, on the Oxford road," George answered.

She frowned. "Then you are taking me to Godstow?" She named a large Benedictine nunnery situated just beyond the city of Oxford.

"No."

"Then where? I have a right to know." She tore a section of bread from the loaf with so much force that crumbs flew the length of the table.

"You have forfeited your rights," Knyvett said.

Anne ignored him to turn pleading eyes to her husband. "I have done nothing wrong, George. That you so willfully choose to believe otherwise makes me wonder why you agreed to marry me in the first place."

He looked away from her. He could scarcely tell her the truth, that he'd thought for a time that they might be among the fortunate couples who could find love in marriage. She would laugh at that, surely—laugh at *him*. "Your destination is Littlemore Priory," he said in a voice tight with emotion. "We should arrive there tomorrow evening."

"I have never heard of it."

Neither had George, but Buckingham had assured him that it was the perfect place to send a disobedient wife. The duke had been told by one of his many informants that the prioress there was exceedingly strict when it came to disciplining her nuns.

The rest of the meal passed without conversation. Anne sulked, although that did not impair her appetite. Knyvett gloated. George retreated to his own chamber as soon as he could, but he was too restless to sleep. Instead he passed the time reading by the light of a candle. He customarily carried a book with him on long journeys and he kept a small collection of favorites wherever he lodged. Several times during the last few months, he'd read aloud to Anne in the quiet of an evening. She was particularly fond of tales of chivalry.

Deliberately pushing thoughts of his wife out of his mind, George forced himself to concentrate on rereading one of Master Chaucer's tales. Silence fell over the inn and continued for some time, until it was broken by an odd scraping sound.

George glanced at the wall that separated his bedchamber from Anne's and frowned. When the sound was repeated, he rose and went to the window. The upper floor overlooked the stable yard. There was no balcony, only a straight drop to the cobbles below, but when he peered out he saw a flash of white to one side—the direction of Anne's room. A makeshift rope made of sheets tied together slithered down the wall. A foot and a shapely ankle followed it over the sill.

Torn between laughter and curses, George could not help but admire his wife's ingenuity. Collecting the guard he'd posted in front of her door, he descended the stairs and went out into the stable yard. Moving silently, he arrived beneath Anne's window just as she reached the ground. All her attention was directed upward, toward her descending maidservant. She had no notion he was there until he seized her roughly by the arm.

At Anne's cry of alarm, the maid above them lost her grip on the makeshift rope. She fell the last two feet to land on her bottom with a grunt.

"Meriall! Are you hurt?" Anne tried to run to her servant, but George's firm grip prevented her.

"Her skirts provided adequate padding to prevent any injury." He could not see Anne's face clearly in the dimly lit stable yard, but he was certain she was scowling. "Running off to join your lover?" he asked.

"Wouldn't you, in my place?" she shot back.

The question both startled and annoyed him. It was as good as a confession. George hauled her back to her chamber and went in with her, shutting the door on the guards. Still without speaking, he crossed the room to free the end of the makeshift rope she'd tied around a bedpost. The scraping sound he'd heard earlier had been Anne and her maidservant shoving that heavy piece of furniture closer to the window. He let the sheets drop into the stable yard below, far out of reach should she decide to make another attempt at escape.

"You are my wife, Anne," he said when he turned to face her. "I have no desire to harm you. If you had not first sinned against me, I—"

"Why will you not believe me when I say that I never betrayed you?"

He took a step closer, watching her face. "Because I know Will Compton. And I saw how upset you were when you thought he might die. You may have come to my bed all those nights, but he is the one you really desired. Do not trouble to deny it."

"Will Compton is a toothsome fellow. That much is obvious. And just now, given your fawning obedience to my thickheaded brother, I must indeed admit that he seems much more appealing to me than you do!"

What more proof did he need? She condemned herself with her own words. "And the king? Would you have gone to his bed, too?"

"I refused him, George."

"If His Grace wanted you, he could have had you. By taking you away from court, I have prevented you from further dishonor."

"How little you think of me! Why would I wish to become the king's mistress?"

"Ambition?" he suggested. "Curiosity? Fear of reprisal?"

"Perhaps those things motivate *you*, but had Edward not interfered, I would have dealt with the king myself. I had the means at my disposal to persuade King Henry to accept my refusal with good grace. I—"

He would not let her finish. "Your brother's quick action prevented a scandal."

"No, it did not, but I have no doubt but that it created one."

George frowned, momentarily disconcerted. He did not know what had happened at court since their departure. He'd had no word from the duke.

"I have always been faithful to you, George. I would have continued to be so."

"And yet you've just admitted that you are attracted to Compton."

"Do you sleep with every woman you find attractive?"

"That is not the same."

"It should be."

He wanted to believe her, but his doubts were too strong. They were like a great weight crushing his chest. Fearing he was about to lose the ability to breathe altogether, he pushed Anne aside and fumbled with the latch. He had to get away from her, out into the fresh air.

"Guard her well," he growled at his men as he stumbled toward the stairs.

Behind him, George heard Anne call his name. She was begging him to come back and listen to her, insisting that she had something important to tell him, but he was unable to halt his headlong flight. He burst out into the stable yard, head pounding as he gulped in great gouts of air.

Slowly, he calmed enough to breathe normally again. As he mopped sweat from his brow, his gaze fell upon the pile of discarded sheets. He knew then that he had no choice. He must deliver his wife to Little-more Priory and leave her there. Then he must take himself as far away from her as possible. They might be bound together until death parted them, but it would be a very long time before he could bring himself to forgive her and let her back into his life. And never, he vowed, would he allow her back into his heart.

20

fter four days of confinement inside the litter, unable to see more than a sliver of the passing countryside, jounced about until she had bruises all over her body, Anne was grateful to reach their destination, even if it was a nunnery. At first glance, its sturdy stone walls turned brilliant white by the late afternoon sun, Littlemore Priory did not seem too dismal a place. It sat in a green and pleasant landscape where wildflowers bloomed in profusion.

Charles Knyvett led the way into the outer court, his boots crunching on gravel. It boasted the usual outbuildings that were part of any small manor. There appeared to be lodgings for a gatekeeper, a priest, and a steward, as well as to accommodate guests. Anne recognized a brewhouse and a bakehouse, stables, a dovecote, and a pigsty among the other structures. And there was a minuscule church.

"The sisters will receive Lady Anne, but the rest of the party will stay in the guesthouse," Knyvett said. He had been at Littlemore only two days earlier and, considering himself an expert on the place, assumed a lecturing tone. "No men are allowed among the cloistered nuns."

"What of my maid?" Anne demanded.

The glance George and Charles exchanged told her that they'd not previously given a moment's thought to what would happen to Meriall.

"It is not meet that she remain with you," Anne pointed out.

Knyvett's sneer was worthy of his master the duke, but George, after a moment's hesitation, gave a careless wave of one hand. "Keep her with you, then."

"That will not be permitted."

George ignored Knyvett's protest. His jaw was set in a hard line. Knyvett annoyed him, and that gave Anne a tiny flicker of hope that, if properly appealed to, George might be inclined to soften the conditions of her imprisonment, if only to spite her brother's man. Then, too, there was one argument she had not yet tried, one that might make him change his mind about leaving her here.

A priest and a nun entered the courtyard from the cloister.

"That is the priory's chaplain, Sir Richard Hewes," Knyvett said, "and the prioress, Dame Katherine Wells."

Anne studied both individuals with interest. Sir Richard was remarkably attractive for a priest, blessed with a tall, straight, long-limbed body and a strong-featured face. Dame Katherine appeared to be very young for a prioress. She was plainly dressed in the black habit of her order and wore no adornment on her person save a single gold cross around her neck, but her eyes were large and wide-spaced and her face was a perfect oval with pale, flawless skin.

George stepped in front of Knyvett, preventing the other man from taking charge. "There are two alterations to the orders you previously received," he informed the prioress. "Lady Anne will be keeping her maidservant with her. And not one hair on her head is to be touched."

Dame Katherine looked taken aback by George's forcefulness, but she inclined her head in agreement. "It is not the custom," she said in a mild voice, "for locks to be shorn until the final vows are taken."

"The Duke of Buckingham promised us a generous contribution," the priest cut in. "Will he change his mind if we follow your orders and not his?"

George managed a withering stare. "I am the one who will pay for my wife's keeping. Step aside with me and we will discuss the financial arrangements."

Left with Dame Katherine, Anne tried to assess the woman who would have charge of her for the foreseeable future. The other woman's bland expression gave nothing away, nor did she speak.

A few minutes later, the three men rejoined them. George and the chaplain, Sir Richard, looked satisfied. Knyvett did not. "You are to go with Dame Katherine, Anne," George said. "She will take you to the nuns' dormitory."

"I have something to say to you first, my lord. In private."

Eager to please, Sir Richard offered to show them to the guesthouse.

"Wait here," George ordered his men. "You, too, Knyvett," he added when Anne's cousin started to follow them.

Sir Richard escorted them to the chamber George would occupy that night. The floors and walls appeared to have been freshly scrubbed, but there was a lingering odor of decay about the place. Anne did not think much of the narrow bed and sparse furnishings, either. She wondered if these accommodations would seem luxurious after she saw where she and Meriall were to sleep.

When Sir Richard left them alone together, Anne tried and failed to find the words to tell her husband that she was with child. Something in her rebelled at using her unborn child to win her freedom. George *ought* to want to take her away from here for her own sake. She cleared her throat. "You may want to reconsider your decision to leave me here. I—"

"A reprieve is out of the question!"

Irritated, she answered in kind. "What if I were to 'plead my belly,' as the lawyers say? Would that win me a stay of execution?" Bitterness laced her words.

"You had best pray you are not breeding, madam. And if you are, then pray you lose the brat, for given the circumstances that brought you here, I could never be certain who the father was."

Anne's pride would not allow him to see how much his harsh words hurt her. She wanted to wail, to abandon every vestige of self-control and fly at him in a rage, raking his face with her fingernails and calling down curses on his head. Instead she made her voice as cold and emotionless as his had been. She would not humble herself further by begging him to accept that she was innocent.

"How long am I to stay here?" she asked. "Or am I to be incarcerated for life?"

"Until I decide to forgive you."

"I do not *want* your forgiveness! I want you to *believe* me! If you leave me here, you need not bother to come back, for I will never forgive *you* for doubting my honesty."

A flicker of doubt crossed his face, as if he realized, for the first time, just how deeply he had wounded her. "Anne, I—"

"Have you changed your mind? Will you take me with you? Take me back to court where I belong?"

"For the nonce, you must stay here."

"Then I never want to see you again."

He gave her a long, hard look, then turned his back on her. "So be it," he muttered as he stalked out, leaving her alone in the guesthouse. She heard him calling for the horses, shouting that they would travel on to Oxford and stay the night at an inn rather than spend one more moment in such proximity to his wayward wife.

Anne almost went after him. She saw her hand stretch out in the direction he had gone, her fingers reaching blindly for her husband, for the father of her unborn child. She snatched it back when she heard the clatter of hooves and knew that George was riding away from Littlemore Priory with his men. Those same fingers curled into a fist.

"I do not deserve to be treated so," she whispered. "I have done nothing wrong."

A faint rustle of fabric from the doorway had her straightening, chin thrust out in defiance. The prioress stood just inside the chamber with Meriall behind her. Anne's tiring maid looked as bereft and miserable as a lost puppy, but when she saw that her mistress was looking in her direction, she managed the ghost of a smile.

"Come," Dame Katherine said. "It is time to retire to your cell."

With no choice but to obey, she followed the prioress across the courtyard, where both wardrobe trunk and traveling litter had been abandoned, and into a walled space to the east of the church. A dozen steps brought them into a private garden. On the far side was the main building of the convent.

The nuns' dormitory was located on an upper floor in the most inaccessible part of the priory, to protect the innocence of the inhabitants. The space was divided into two rows of tiny rooms. Dame Katherine led her into one of them, furnished with a narrow bed and a candlestand and nothing more.

"Where is my maid to sleep?" Anne demanded.

"She will have to make do with a pallet on the floor."

"And my wardrobe trunk? Where am I to put that?"

"You will have no need for fancy garments. Your husband may have countermanded the duke's order that your head be shaved, but he said nothing about your clothing. You will wear a novice's habit while you are here and be treated as a lay sister. You will do your share of the work. If you transgress, you will be punished without regard to the nobility of your birth or the wealth of your family."

So saying, the prioress left Anne and her maid alone in the tiny room. Its single window, Anne noted, was too small to climb through.

"Find out where they will store my trunk, Meriall," Anne ordered. "Did you manage to pack anything of value?"

"The supply of coins you kept on hand to wager with at court was confiscated by the duke," Meriall reported, "along with all your necklaces and brooches and rings. But he left your book of hours, my lady, the one the queen gave you as a wedding gift. And you still have your wedding ring and the jewels that are sewn onto your clothing."

Pearls, Anne recalled, and semiprecious stones. Perhaps they could be detached and sold. Or used for bribes. As for the book of hours, it was a guide to prayer designed for use by a layman, but it might find favor with the prioress. Anne did not believe that Dame Katherine Wells was quite so pious as she wished to seem. As she'd left Anne's cell, Anne had heard the distinctive swish of a silk underskirt.

"For the present, we will do nothing," she said. "I need time to think. To plan."

She would give George a few days to change his mind about leaving her at Littlemore. Then, if he did not return, she would find her own way out. She would have to learn the lay of the land. She must not do anything in haste. She knew none of the local landowners and therefore could not ask any of them to shelter her. Oxfordshire was foreign territory to her. No doubt that was why Edward had chosen it.

Anne sank down on the rock-hard mattress with a sigh. If only she had access to the properties she'd brought with her into her marriage. With that income, she'd be able to equal, perhaps even surpass, whatever contribution Edward had promised the priest, and top George's gift to the priory, too. But as matters stood now, she was penniless.

One of the nuns, bright-eyed with curiosity, arrived with the novice's habit. Anne dutifully donned a plain garment made of undyed wool, although she retained her own soft cambric shift. The tunic was grayish white and scratched her skin. It was worn with a leather belt. Over it went a loose scapular. A veil and wimple completed the costume. Anne also kept her own shoes and stockings rather than slide bare feet into poorly made leather-soled sandals.

"You are better dressed than I am now," she remarked to her maid.

"You will find a way out of here, madam," Meriall said loyally.

"So I will, with your help, my friend. Is there paper and ink in my trunk?"

Meriall brightened. "Indeed there is. No one told me not to pack your writing supplies."

"Then we must think who best to send letters to."

The ringing of the bell for Compline prevented any further discussion. Anne's stomach growled as she left her cell. It was after sunset and she had yet to be offered any supper. Perhaps that was to be part of her punishment, she thought—frequent fasting. The queen would approve. A grim expression on her face, she fell into line behind three black-clad Benedictine sisters and followed them down a flight of steep stairs and into the priory's tiny church.

21

Littlemore Priory, May 11, 1510

n her first morning at Littlemore Priory, Lady Anne was put to work scrubbing floors. No one spoke to her. She was not surprised. She'd always heard that, in a convent, unnecessary conversation was not only discouraged, but forbidden.

During that first day, she heard the nuns speak only in whispers, save for when they performed the psalms and chants required by the liturgy. Choir service was, it seemed, the principal work of these Benedictine sisters. They spent several hours each day in the rather ramshackle church, singing and praying. The rest of their time appeared to be occupied with tending the small enclosed garden and keeping the priory and its furnishings clean. There were also periods for meditation and study.

The routine of the priory was simple, tedious, and repetitious. When in church, Anne was not permitted to sit in the choir with the nuns. She occupied a balcony that had been erected for residents of the guesthouse. There were none at present, or if there were, they did not attend services. In solitude, she cast a wary eye heavenward. The church gave evidence of having been repaired in a haphazard manner over the course of several centuries. To her normal prayers, she added one to prevent the roof from falling in on them during services.

There were only five nuns in Dame Katherine's charge. They did not acknowledge Anne as they filed into the church and took their places, but each time they assembled, Anne noticed that one or two of them sent curious sidelong glances her way.

They broke their fast with bread and ale after Prime. At nine the office of Terce was sung, followed by Sext at twelve. They dined before None at three. Vespers was at six. They supped at sunset, just before Compline, after which everyone retired for the night. And so the cycle began all over again.

Anne's back ached and her knees were sore. The previous night, when she'd been ordered to bed right after Compline, she'd thought she heard voices from one of the other cells but had decided she was imagining things. It had taken her a long time to fall asleep, and then she had been jerked awake by the bell for Matins at midnight. Lauds had followed at three in the morning and Prime at sunrise.

On her second night at Littlemore Priory, she fell instantly asleep and did not stir between bells. But on the third night, as Anne again lay awake, too tired to sleep, she once again thought she heard voices. She listened harder.

"Is that a lute?" she whispered into the darkness.

"I hear it, my lady," her maidservant answered. The cell was so small that her pallet was only inches away. "Shall I go and investigate?"

"We will both go."

Anne slid out of bed, careful not to step on Meriall, and fumbled for the tinderbox to light the single candle she'd been allowed. She slid her arms into the blue velvet sleeves of her night robe—rescued from her trunk along with writing materials, the book of hours, and a gown heavily decorated with expensive baubles—and tied the sash. She did not bother with shoes.

There was no sign of life behind the closed doors nearest her cell, but light spilled out beneath the one at the far end of the row. As Anne approached, she heard muffled laughter. She exchanged a puzzled glance with Meriall, then boldly reached for the latch.

The door swung open to reveal three young women who did not look the least bit like nuns. They were in their night robes and sat together on the bed, sharing a jug of wine. One of them had a lute in her lap.

The same nun who had brought Anne her novice's habit sprang to her feet at the intrusion. Her hair was a pretty gold color and streamed down her back as if it had been freshly washed and combed. She relaxed as soon as she recognized Anne and Meriall.

"I was afraid that you were Dame Katherine," she said. "If you wish to join us, come in and close the door behind you."

"The prioress, I assume, would not approve?"

Another nun giggled. She was a fresh-faced girl with long, reddish-brown hair who looked too young to have taken final vows. She might have been a beauty, had it not been for a strawberry birthmark on the left side of her face.

"Dame Katherine approves of very little . . . for us," the first nun said, "but her lodgings are in the west range, near the guesthouse and the priest's chamber. She cannot hear what goes on here. I am Juliana Wynter. These are my sisters, Eliza Wynter and Joan Wynter."

"Your sisters are . . . sisters?"

Dame Juliana nodded and offered wine to Anne and Meriall. Anne accepted the jug and took a swallow. The taste was surprisingly pleasant. She passed the container to her maid.

"There were seven girls in the family," Eliza explained, "and only money enough for four marriage portions." Like her siblings, she had been a nun long enough for her hair to have grown long again. It reached nearly to her waist in red-gold waves.

"Who are you, Lady Anne?" Juliana asked, resettling herself on her narrow bed alongside her sisters. "No one has said, you know. Nor told us why you are here." For lack of other seating, Anne and Meriall sank to the floor to sit tailor-fashion on the bare stone.

"The prioress knows," Anne said.

Juliana made a noise suspiciously like a snort. "As if she would tell us anything!"

"And Sir Richard does also."

"Thick as thieves, those two are. And not inclined to share with anyone else." All three nuns laughed at that, and Juliana sent Anne what could only be interpreted as a lewd wink.

Anne took another swallow of wine, giving herself time to think. Plainly there was more going on at Littlemore Priory than she had suspected. "I will gladly tell you who I am and why I am here," she said after a moment, "if you will help me send word to those who can help me leave."

"Nuns cannot exchange letters or gifts with anyone, not even relatives, nor journey out of the convent without the prioress's permission," Joan said primly. She was the one with the birthmark. Then she giggled again.

Juliana grinned. "We are not permitted to talk to outsiders alone, either. Is it not fortunate that the three of us were sent here together?"

"Dame Katherine thinks we spend too much time in each other's company," Eliza complained.

"And you do not want to cross her," Joan warned. "She enjoys meting out punishment."

"She has told me that I am to be treated like a lay sister while I am here," Anne said. Then she gave them an abridged version of her story.

They listened in fascination, as if she were recounting a tale of romance and chivalry. Anne supposed it must sound like one to them, but she had lost her own illusions. If some brave knight meant to come to her rescue, he had left it till rather late.

As the wine jug gradually emptied, Anne learned that the other two nuns at Littlemore were older. Anna Willye occupied the cell across from Juliana's, but she was conveniently deaf. A second Juliana, Juliana Beauchamp, who called herself Dame Julian, was the subprioress. She was also the sacristan, in charge of chalices, books, vestments, reliquaries, and candles and charged with ringing the bells to call the nuns to worship. The Wynter sisters were not worried about being heard by her because on this night Dame Julian was keeping a private vigil in the church.

"She is also the cantrix," Juliana added, looking aggrieved, "so she is the one who sings all the solos. She complains that the rest of us pause in all the wrong places, both in singing and in saying the other hours. And she says we sing too fast. Well, who would not? It is excessively dull to perform divine services the same way every day of every week, with only the occasional feast day to enliven the ritual."

"Surely you must find other ways to alleviate the boredom," Anne said. The ember of an idea had caught at the back of her mind and now burned fitfully.

"Here and there," Juliana admitted, but she would say no more on that subject.

When the wine was gone, Eliza played a decidedly secular song on her lute to end the evening. By the time Anne made her way back to her own room, she was barely able to keep her eyes open long enough to pound her pillow into a more comfortable shape and tug the single quilt up to her chin. And yet she still could not sleep. Too many thoughts coursed through her brain, tumbling around like leaves in the wind.

The Wynter sisters had been careful not to give too much away. Anne understood that she was, after all, a stranger to them. She might report them to the prioress. But she had begun to suspect that they were not entirely cut off from the outside world. After all, they had procured that jug of wine from somewhere. If she could win their confidence, they might be able to help her escape from Littlemore . . . once she had solved the problem of her lack of funds.

Anger and disappointment still weighed heavily upon her, as they had since she'd been forced to leave Greenwich Palace. She had been betrayed by all those who claimed to care for her and her brother was the worst of the lot. She pictured the mighty Duke of Buckingham imprisoned in a small, bare cell, his hair shorn and his expensive garments replaced by a black monk's habit with a hair shirt beneath.

Without warning, her thoughts turned to Will Compton. He'd disappointed her, too. She'd been flattered by his desire for her in her early days at court and had grown fond of his company after her marriage. She had been upset when he'd been hurt and relieved when he recovered. She'd thought of him as a friend when they devised a way to dissuade the king from pursuing her, but it was clear to her now that he lacked any true affection for her, else he'd never have tried to persuade her into the king's bed.

She did not think much of King Henry, either, and George had abandoned her. Anne rolled over and thumped the pillow again. If she had the sense God gave a goose, she'd never trust any man again!

22

*D*ame Katherine's private parlor looked much like any well-born lady's chamber. It was furnished with a table, a chair, two stools, and several cushions with embroidered covers. A tapestry showing a scene from the Bible graced one wall and the windows had brocade curtains. The floor was covered with rushes that had been recently changed and smelled of rosemary.

Anne had written two letters, sealing them with wax and her signet ring. The first solicited the support of Bess Boleyn, asking her to work toward Anne's return to court. The second was a humble plea for assistance to George's mother. Anne had met Lady Hungerford on only a few occasions, but she had sensed in her a strength of purpose and a ready wit that she could not help but admire. She knew that Lady Hungerford had not approved of George's decision to marry a Stafford, but if there was to be an heir to both the Hastings and the Hungerford titles, Anne and George must, despite the current enmity between them, be reconciled.

She had not mentioned the possibility, which grew more certain with each passing day, that she might already be with child. If she was, it would be December before the baby was born. Conception would have occurred some time in March. That was early enough that no suspicion of bastardy would be attached to the child, despite the uproar Edward's accusations must have caused at court.

Anne's hands were hidden by the sleeves of her novice's clothing. Surreptitiously, she touched her still-flat belly. Dame Katherine could not see the movement, but she regarded Anne with suspicion. "What do you want, Lady Anne? You shirk your duties to come here without an invitation."

"I would ask your permission to send two letters to friends, Mother. I left court in such haste that no one knows where I am. There are people who will be concerned for me."

"You are here as punishment for your sins, my lady. You are not permitted luxuries."

"It is no luxury to ease the fears of others," Anne objected.

"Letters from you are unnecessary. Your noble brother and your husband will inform your friends of anything they wish them to know. Return to your assigned tasks at once."

Juliana had warned her that the prioress would not grant her any favors, but Anne wished to test the waters for herself. "I am not a novice," she said. "Nor am I a slave."

"But you are a prisoner in my charge," Dame Katherine said coldly. "If you wish to eat, you will work."

"Perhaps I prefer to starve myself to death," Anne shot back. "That would not please my *noble* brother." At least, she hoped it would not. She was no longer certain how Edward felt about her. Perhaps he would be relieved if she died here, alone and forgotten.

"I have other means of enforcing my will," the prioress said smoothly. Anne did not trust the ghost of a smile that appeared on her pale, perfect face. "Come and see."

The window to which Dame Katherine led her looked out over the cloister. Anne frowned. A large wooden structure occupied a secluded corner she had not noticed before. Set atop a sturdy post was a heavy piece of wood with three holes cut into it, one for the head and two for the hands.

"Stocks? You have *stocks* in your cloister?"

"Those who defy me are punished." Dame Katherine's smile broadened. "Just as every village has a pillory to exhibit those who break the law, so we have this for sisters who break the Rule of St. Benedict. Go back to your duties, Lady Anne. Scrubbing floors is good for the soul, and much less trying than a day spent out there in the sun without food or water."

Dismissed, Anne fled. She told herself she was not afraid of Dame Katherine, but neither was she prepared to openly defy the prioress's authority.

That night, after Compline, she confided the prioress's threat to Meriall.

"The stocks are indeed used to discipline the nuns," her maid confirmed. "The cook told me that Dame Joan had to stand in them for an entire day because she laughed aloud during church service."

"This is most strange," Anne murmured. Such punishment was usually reserved for the baker who sold bread that was underweight or the vintner who added colored water to the wine. Or, sometimes, for a woman charged with being a scold. With head and hands locked in place, the malefactor was obliged to stand in the center of the village, an easy target for rotten vegetables as well as taunts. But to Anne's knowledge, the stocks were never used to punish a gentlewoman, let alone a member of the nobility.

"The prioress is very strict, my lady," Meriall said, "in *some* ways."

In the darkness of her cell, Anne heard an odd note in her tiring maid's voice. "What do you mean?"

"Only that I heard a baby crying when I was in the kitchen this morning. There is something strange about that."

"Perhaps the nuns run a school for local children," Anne suggested. The long day and the restless nights that had come before had caught up with her. She yawned and closed her eyes, only half listening to what Meriall was saying.

"Oh, they do. Several young boys come daily for their lessons. But it was not a child from the village that I heard. It was too early in the morning and it was an infant, not a boy of an age to learn letters."

"Perhaps someone is staying in the guesthouse," Anne murmured, beginning to doze off.

"Perhaps." Meriall did not sound convinced, but she failed to offer any other explanation before her mistress gave in to exhaustion and slept.

23

The nine days of Ascensiontide leading up to Whitsunday, the nineteenth day of May, had commenced on the very day that Lady Anne arrived at Littlemore Priory. On Whitsunday itself—fifty days after Easter—the residents of the nearby village and all the priory's servants, as well as those who lived in seclusion within Littlemore's walls, went to church to receive communion. Flowers had been strewn in the choir. Sir Richard Hewes wore the priest's traditional red vestments. And there was a baptism. A little girl, dressed all in white, was brought in by no less a personage than the prioress herself. Perhaps the child had been abandoned at Littlemore, Anne thought, and had been taken in by the nuns.

After the choir sang the hymn that began "Veni, Sancte Spiritus, / Et emitte caelitus / Lucis tuae radium," which even those who did not understand Latin knew meant "Come, Holy Spirit / and from thy celestial home / Shed a ray of light divine," a dove was released through the "Holy Ghost hole" near the east end of the church. The sound of a rushing wind was achieved by the nuns shuffling their feet. Next came a shower of rose petals, to imitate the "tongues of fire" also described in the Acts of the Apostles. Anne was glad they did not use pieces of burning straw, as some churches did. In this rickety old building, that would surely have led to a conflagration.

In common with many other villages, Littlemore held a Whitsun ale, a celebration that featured Morris dancers, jugglers, and other simple amusements. The cloistered nuns were not permitted to attend these festivities, but even from inside the convent walls they could hear the music.

The celebrations continued well into the evening. Right after Vespers, Dame Juliana Wynter tapped on Anne's door. In her arms she carried two of Anne's gowns, liberated from her traveling trunk. Without a word, she removed her wimple and veil and put one of the gowns on over her habit.

Anne exchanged a glance with Meriall. Was this the chance they'd been waiting for? The opportunity to escape? She removed her own headdress and took the second gown, grateful that she'd not been forced to cut off all her hair. Meriall, who had been allowed to keep her own clothing, did not have to alter her appearance at all before the three of them crept out of the dormitory and through the church.

A kiss from Dame Juliana paid the gatekeeper's fee. Once out of the convent, a path led straight to the village. Juliana took the lead, covering the short distance at a rapid pace. Anne understood why as soon as the young nun joined the dancers on the green. She went straight up to one particular gentleman, a man who did not have the look of a humble villager. Anne smiled to herself at this proof that Juliana had connections to the outside world. It only remained to find a way to convince her new friend to help a penniless noblewoman.

While she considered the situation, Anne accepted a meat pie from one of the villagers. She had just bitten into it when, on the other side of the bonfire, through a haze of smoke, she caught sight of a familiar face.

Her heart stuttered in her chest and her breath caught. Then she started to choke on a succulent morsel of meat. By the time she stopped coughing, Will Compton had reached her side. She touched trembling fingers to his chest.

"Are you real?"

He grinned. "Here in the flesh. Dance with me?"

He swept her into a country measure that left her breathless and laughing. Afterward, he collected two tankards of ale and drew her apart with him, into the shelter of a stand of trees. They leaned against the trunk of an ancient oak, their shoulders just touching, and sipped the slightly sour brew.

"Have you come to rescue me?" Anne asked.

"Alas, my love, that is the one thing I cannot do."

That was not the answer she'd been expecting. Disappointment pierced her, sharp as a splinter from a broken lance. "Then why are you here?"

He stared at the bonfire, reluctant to meet her eyes. "To make certain you are unharmed."

"Did you think George would beat me?"

"I would not have been surprised if your brother had."

"And yet you let them spirit me away without a murmur of protest."

He did look at her then, his expression somber. "I objected, loud and long, and to the king himself. Rest assured that your brother did not escape unscathed. He had the poor sense to argue with the king and was banished from court, and your sister and her husband with him."

Anne frowned. A part of her was glad to know that both Edward and Elizabeth had been punished, but she had been born and raised a Stafford. This wholesale dismissal of her family did not bode well. "And Hal?"

"Oh, he's still there." A little silence ensued before Compton spoke again. "You do not ask about your husband."

"Perhaps I do not care what fate befell him."

Compton continued as if she had not spoken. "Lord Hastings sent word to the king that he wished to retire to Stoke Poges, Lady Hungerford's house in Buckinghamshire. The king graciously granted permission. Of you, Lady Anne, nothing at all has been said. Not since the day you left court. His Grace quarreled with the queen over the matter of dismissing your sister, but he has since found it more convenient to believe that I solicited your favors for myself. The king likes to think himself a virtuous husband."

"And next, I've no doubt, he will contrive to forget that he exchanged harsh words with my brother." Anne grimaced at the thought.

"There are certain advantages to having my lord of Buckingham at court," Compton agreed.

"To keep an eye on him?"

Compton nodded.

A little silence fell between them while they watched the dancers. The villagers did not seem real to Anne. She wondered suddenly if she was dreaming, but she could smell Compton's musky scent and feel the heat of his body, so close to her own.

"Am I to be conveniently *forgotten,* too? Is that why you mean to leave me here?"

"It is never wise to cause the king embarrassment. I risked His Grace's displeasure simply by sending men in search of you, but I wanted to be certain you were not being ill-treated." He glanced toward the walls of the convent. "Littlemore is a humble place, but you might have been sent to worse."

"You know nothing of conditions within the priory."

"But I do know how matters stand at court. I have spent almost my entire life in His Grace's service. All that I have belongs to me only at the will and pleasure of the king. I am no great and powerful nobleman like your brother. I am dependent upon King Henry's goodwill."

"In other words, you'd have done nothing to help me, no matter how pitiful the situation you found me in."

"But you are *not* in any danger, Anne, and you will not have to stay here forever. George Hastings is not such a fool as to—"

"George Hastings, thanks to you and the king and my brother, believes me to be wanton. You have destroyed my marriage. The least you can do in return is provide for my comfort. You have a house in Warwickshire, do you not? Take me there."

"To do such a thing would only make matters worse. And the king would—"

"Oh, yes," she said bitterly. "The king. We must not offend His Grace, no matter how much he offends me!"

"Have a care, Anne," he warned.

"Why should I? Let the whole world hear my complaint! I am the one who was wronged, not George Hastings or Edward Stafford. And most certainly not Will Compton!"

He backed away from her, hands in front of him as if to ward off a blow. "It was a mistake to come here. I can see that now. I will not trouble you again."

She wished she were a man so that she could pummel Will Compton as he deserved. Instead she had to watch in fulminating silence as he abruptly turned his back on her and almost ran to the horse and a man he'd left waiting for him at the edge of the clearing. Moments later, he'd mounted and ridden out of her life.

Juliana and Meriall found her still standing there, staring after him, when it was time to return to the priory. They would be missed if they did not appear for Compline.

Later that night, Juliana again came to Anne's cell. "I thought perhaps you might wish to talk to someone," she said.

"I did not think nuns heard confessions."

Juliana laughed softly. "I'd have something to confess myself if I warranted a visitor as toothsome as that one!" Without waiting for an invitation, she settled herself on the end of Anne's bed. "Did you see the young gentleman I danced with? He is a clerk in Oxford now, but I knew him when I was a girl." She drew her knees up to her chest and hugged them tightly, almost as if she imagined herself embracing her clerk.

"Do you plan to run away with that young man?" Anne asked, forcing thoughts of Will Compton from her mind. She could count on no help from him. She must make her own plan of escape.

Juliana sighed deeply. "The church would only find me and bring me back here. I took my final vows. I am not permitted to change my mind any more than a wife is allowed to take a second husband. But so long as I do not run away, I can still see him now and again."

"At Whitsun ales?"

"And other times."

Anne kept her head down and toyed with the frayed edge of her coverlet, hoping to hide her eagerness from Juliana. "Do you leave the priory often?"

"I visited him in Oxford once. It was not so very difficult to get away. There are horses in the stable and the distance is under three miles."

"Would it be possible for you to smuggle letters out for me?"

Juliana was not fooled by a careless manner. She leaned closer. "It may be . . . so long as you have the wherewithal to pay for their delivery."

"I have no money."

Juliana waited.

"The seed pearls that once decorated my clothing have some value. They could be sold."

"Or used to barter with. Give me your letters and the pearls and I will see what I can do."

When the nun had gone, Anne gave herself a stern lecture. She must endeavor to be patient. She would have to wait a reasonable length of time for what she'd written to yield results. If nothing came of those efforts, then she would have to persuade Dame Juliana to show her the way to Oxford.

It was at that point that her confidence faltered. She knew no one in that city or at the great university there. If she identified herself as Lady Hastings, the authorities would notify her husband and he would likely send her straight back to Littlemore. Or to some worse place.

If only she could make her way to Wales, she thought. She had inherited a castle and two manors there from her first husband. Then she remembered—they had all become George's property when Anne married him. She had nothing of her own, not land nor chattel nor ready money. Even if she sold her book of hours and all the gemstones decorating her clothing, she would lack the means to live for more than a few weeks.

24

George Hastings stood with one hand braced against the side of the casement as he stared out at the South Buckinghamshire countryside. Stoke Poges, a castellated manor house, was nearer to London than the family seat at Ashby de la Zouch, and more comfortable, too. He'd been in residence since he left his wife at Littlemore Priory nearly four weeks earlier.

In brooding silence, he quaffed more ale, then leaned his head against his forearm. The duke was pleased with him. The king was not. And George did not know what he thought of himself. He was plagued by indecision and an uneasy conscience. Could he truly have been so blind to Anne's faults, so completely deceived, so enamored of his own wife that he'd overlooked every hint of her true character? Or was Anne innocent, as she claimed? If she had been faithful to him, then he had done her a great disservice.

But Will Compton *had* been in her chamber, he reminded himself. And Anne had been wearing nothing but her night robe. What else was he to think but that they were lovers? A virtuous woman avoided even the appearance of misconduct.

Compton! The hand on the windowsill clenched into a fist. Women always flocked to Compton. They loved his flamboyance, his confidence, his easy way with them. They never even noticed pudgy little George Hastings when tall, toothsome Will Compton was in the same room. While it was true that George was no longer the shy, awkward boy he'd once been, he doubted he'd ever hold a candle to the king's boon companion. How could Anne *not* be fascinated by Will Compton?

Anger and jealousy flowed through him, swamping all gentler emotions. He struck the stone wall at the side of the window with his fist. The pain brought him back to himself, and to a sudden awareness that he was no longer alone in the small room he used for prayer and contemplation.

"Feeling sorry for yourself?" his mother asked.

"Do I not have the right?"

"For myself, I am inclined to pity your wife. She has written to me."

Slowly, George turned to face her. Lady Hungerford had made herself comfortable in his Glastonbury chair and was idly flipping through the correspondence on his writing table. "Did you reply?"

"I did not," his mother said. "According to her letter, she is forbidden correspondence, or any other communication with the outside world. I imagine she had to have the missive smuggled out. You could do worse than be married to such a resourceful woman."

"Resourceful enough to betray me."

"Did she? Or did her brother lose that infamous temper of his and leap to conclusions? Did you trouble to investigate or did you simply accept Buckingham's word?"

She read the answer in his face and shook her head, her expression full of remorse.

"You were eighteen when you inherited your father's title and went to court, George. I'd have thought you old enough to know the grain from the chaff."

"I have seen firsthand how appealing Will Compton is to women. All women. As for the king—he has been called a young god and the comparison is apt." King Henry had male beauty, wealth, and power. How could any woman resist him?

"Did you *ask* either of them if they'd seduced your wife?"

"No, but—" He broke off, at a loss for words. Compton would have told him the truth and he would have believed the other man, even though he doubted the word of his own wife.

If Compton *had* been her lover, George would have found it unbearable to remain at court.

"Let me summarize," his mother said. "Lady Fitzwalter and Buckingham thought His Grace was sniffing around Anne and that the king sent Compton to test the waters. Is that likely? She is years older than His Grace."

"Anne is a most attractive woman, and spirited, and the queen is breeding again." It was all too easy for George to imagine other men lusting after his wife.

Mary Hungerford made a tsking sound. "You miss her." It was not a question and he did not answer it. "Tell me this, George—do you plan to poison her? Or apply to the pope for a divorce?"

He felt as if he'd been kicked in the stomach. "I would never harm her." And he could not imagine himself with any other wife.

His mother heaved a deep sigh. "Search your heart," she advised, "and while you are taking your time about it, as it seems likely you will, use your head, as well. Without a wife, there will be no heir. If you do not want your title, and mine, to fall into abeyance when you die, then you must bring yourself to get a child on Lady Anne."

"A part of me wants to take Anne back, to forgive her, even if she did sin against me, but how am I to be certain of her honesty in the future?"

"What if she did not lie to you? What if she is guiltless in this matter?"

"Then I have wronged her sorely." He bowed his head. "I do not know what to do."

"Are you asking my advice?"

He crossed the room to her chair and flung himself at her feet. She stroked his hair as she had when he was a child. Her touch still had the power to soothe him.

"Go back to Littlemore," she advised. "Talk to your wife. *Listen* to her, this time. Do not, under any circumstances, use the word 'forgive' unless it is to ask her to forgive you."

"But—"

She silenced him by touching her fingers to his lips. "First mend your fences, George. Then bargain with your wife for what you want. Marriage is a business contract like any other. It is possible to negotiate a successful partnership even with someone you dislike and mistrust."

"That is not the sort of marriage I hoped for."

"It is better than nothing. You made your bed, George. Now you must lie in it. How comfortable it is will depend on how well or ill you treat your wife."

25

*B*e patient, my lady," Meriall advised.

"I have used my last reserves of patience. If no one is going to rescue me, then I will have to find my own way to escape."

"But where can you go?" Meriall asked.

"Oxford. Oxford is not that far. I can *walk* there. I will sell the rest of the jewels we removed from my clothing and my book of hours, too."

"And then?"

Anne glared at her. "Must you *always* be the voice of reason?"

She knew her plan was flawed, but she grew daily more frustrated with her situation at Littlemore. Did George mean to leave her here forever? There were times when it seemed to her that he did. She'd written again to George's mother, but she'd still had no reply. She told herself that she should not expect to receive one in writing. The prioress would have confiscated any letter that came for her. But she'd expected a messenger to come. She'd *hoped* George would, in spite of the fact that she'd told him she never wanted to see him again.

She paced the tiny cell, trying to convince herself to be grateful that Dame Katherine had accepted the changes George had insisted upon. Otherwise, Meriall would have been sent away. She forced herself to smile for her maidservant. Her tiring maid was a prisoner here, too.

Meriall cleared her throat. "There is one possibility, my lady, although I hesitate to mention it."

"I will listen to any plan, no matter how fanciful."

"Not fanciful, my lady. But I fear that it is something the duke would do, were he ever in your position."

"An unlikely circumstance." Anne felt her face relax into a genuine smile. "Tell me."

"This priory is not what your brother believed it to be. The duke thought, because he had been told that the prioress was strict in disciplining her nuns, that she must also be a paragon of virtue."

Anne frowned. "What have you learned?"

"That the priory chaplain, Sir Richard Hewes, spends every night in Dame Katherine's bed. The baby girl who was christened on Whitsunday is their child. If you threaten to betray her secret—"

"How would that profit me? If Littlemore is deemed unfit for my prison, I might be sent somewhere worse. In a proper nunnery I would have even less freedom than I do here, and no chance at all to escape."

"You would not need to carry out the threat, my lady, only let Dame Katherine *think* that you mean to. If you can convince her that you have smuggled a letter out, a letter detailing her sins, a letter that is to be opened and acted upon only if you do not appear in person to reclaim it within a certain period of time, then surely she will let you leave, and give you the wherewithal to live upon, too."

Anne turned the idea over in her mind. It was a clever plan, but it had one drawback. "To make Dame Katherine believe me, I would have to prove that it is possible to send a letter from Littlemore. That would mean betraying Dame Juliana. Would you have me leave her behind to face her prioress's wrath?"

"Your kind heart does you justice, madam," Meriall said.

"But you think I would be a great fool to listen to it." Anne sighed. "Perhaps so, but I think I will take a less devious route to freedom."

It took three days to make the arrangements. On the twenty-second of June, when the moon was high and full in the night sky, Anne and her faithful maidservant left the cramped cell behind and sallied forth to meet Juliana.

It was just possible, once her eyes had adjusted to the dimness, to find her way through the priory and out into the night without lighting a candle. Meriall crept quietly along behind her, carrying a bundle containing the few possessions they had left. Anne's remaining wealth had been sadly depleted by the necessity of paying bribes. Even her soft cambric shifts had gone to compensate Dame Juliana for the risk she was taking.

The young nun walked several paces ahead of them, keeping an eye out for their friendly gatekeeper. Once away from the priory there would be more obstacles to face, but for the moment all Anne cared about was gaining her freedom. They would ride first to Oxford, where temporary shelter had been arranged. Then they were bound for Wales. Meriall still had kin there who would keep them both safe while Anne decided what to do next. She was inclined to think that a petition sent directly to the king might work best. Surely His Grace would not ignore a direct plea for help. All she had to do was find a way to send it to him without either Edward or George getting wind of it.

Juliana signaled for them to wait while she crossed the cobbled courtyard. She would not be coming with them. Indeed, outwardly, in her black habit with her head bowed and her hands tucked demurely into her sleeves, she appeared to be the most circumspect of nuns.

It was eerily quiet where Anne and Meriall waited, pressed against the smooth stone wall of the convent. The only sounds Anne could make out were the soft slap of Juliana's leather-soled sandals and the distant whuffle of a horse.

The challenge came out of nowhere. "Halt! Who goes there?"

Suddenly the courtyard was blindingly bright, lit by torches carried by burly priory servants. The gatekeeper advanced directly toward the spot where they were hiding, flushing them out like birds for a band of hunters. His face was impassive, revealing no hint of his earlier willingness to aid in their escape. Close behind him came the prioress.

"So, this is how you repay my hospitality," Dame Katherine said.

Anne managed a haughty, defiant look, but inside she was weeping in disappointment and despair. With the failure of this attempt, all hope of escape was gone.

The prioress ordered all of Anne's belongings confiscated. The bundle Meriall carried was seized and taken away. "Who helped you?" Dame Katherine demanded.

"No one, my lady."

Anne saw no purpose in implicating Juliana or the gatekeeper, especially since the young nun had vanished. Anne hoped she'd managed to flee back into the dormitory in all the confusion. Juliana had taken a great risk. Even if everything had gone as they'd planned, she might well have been blamed when Anne's disappearance was discovered on the morrow.

Dame Katherine slapped Anne across the face. "Who helped you?" she repeated.

Anne gasped, more from shock at such effrontery than from pain.

"Who helped you?" The prioress's hand lifted, ready to deliver another blow.

Anne fought not to cringe. Her cheek stung and she knew she'd have a bruise. "How dare you strike me? I am a duke's daughter."

"You are nothing here." She barked an order to her henchmen. "Put her in the stocks."

Seized by rough hands, Anne was half carried, half dragged to the corner of the garden. Her hands and head were forced into the slots allotted for them and the heavy upper piece lowered to hold her there. The lock snapped into place with a loud click.

"Release me at once!" Anne shouted, but no one paid her any mind. Moments later, she was left all alone, and they had taken the torches with them.

The moonlight, which earlier had seemed so friendly, now picked out eerie shadows. Anne found herself remembering every story she had ever heard about creatures that roamed in the night. Sudden panic overwhelmed her. She struggled to pull her hands free but only succeeded in making her wrists bleed. One incautious movement sent pain lancing through the back of her head as it struck solid wood.

The blow knocked sense into her. She settled. There was no point in fighting against her restraints. She could not escape.

Dawn would come, she told herself. Eventually. And Dame Katherine would not keep her here forever. She might have been given leave by the Duke of Buckingham to ill-treat his sister, but she would not risk doing permanent harm to a noblewoman.

Slowly, Anne gathered her shattered self-control and steeled herself to endure. The position was horribly uncomfortable. Her toes barely reached the ground and her neck was forced to bend at an awkward angle. Splinters abraded her wrists.

Her thoughts turned, unbidden, to the budding life inside her. Would her child be harmed by this treatment? Anne's stomach clenched. Her chest tightened to a point that was nearly painful. No. She would not let that happen. In the morning, she would reveal her secret to the prioress. Surely Dame Katherine, a mother herself, would show mercy to a woman who was with child. Considering how best to broach the subject distracted Anne for fully half an hour.

It did not occur to her until much later that Juliana might have betrayed her. Someone had, she realized. If it had not been Juliana, then it must have been the gatekeeper, or one of Juliana's sisters. She clenched her fists and fought tears. She had trusted too easily again.

Anne spent the rest of the night and all of the next day in the stocks. No one came near her, not even when she called out. She received neither food nor water. As the hot sun beat down on her head, she wondered if she would be freed if she gave Juliana's name to the prioress, but she could not make herself do it. Juliana's punishment would be to take Anne's place and even if the young nun *had* betrayed her, no one deserved to be treated with such cruelty.

By the time Anne was finally released from the stocks, she was so weak that two of the nuns had to help her walk up the stairs to her cell. They locked her in and left her there for another full day without sustenance.

On the third day, the prioress freed her from strict confinement but informed her that her maid had been put to work in the kitchen. Meri-all, like Anne, was to be locked in at night, and from now on would live separate from her mistress.

"You do not need the services of a tiring maid," Dame Katherine decreed.

That was all too true. The only possessions Anne had left were her nun's garments. Even her book of hours had been taken away. Without it, Anne prayed more fervently than she ever had before, begging God for deliverance . . . or for the strength to endure until she could find a way to free herself. She was grimly determined to escape from Little-more and equally resolved not to be returned to the stocks.

26

*E*very time the court stayed at Windsor Castle, Will Compton imagined himself in St. George's Chapel receiving the Order of the Garter from the king's own hands. This visit in mid-July was no different. The Garter was an honor generally reserved for noblemen and foreign princes, but more humbly born men than himself had begun from nothing and gone that far ere now.

His goal was the same as it had always been—to make himself invaluable to King Henry and reap the rewards. A knighthood would come first, then a title. He'd earn both by listening to His Grace's petty complaints, fetching and carrying, and escorting willing young women to the royal bed.

Will wondered if His Grace ever thought of Lady Anne. He doubted it. She'd been a passing fancy, easily abandoned when having her proved too much bother. That was Henry Tudor's way—convince himself he had no share of the blame, then go on as if nothing had happened. As Lady Anne herself had predicted, His Grace had even managed to forget that the Duke of Buckingham had lost his temper in the royal presence and left the court in a rage. Barely two months after the incident, Buckingham was back. Moreover, the king had granted him the young Earl of Westmorland's wardship. That included the right to arrange Westmorland's marriage. Doubtless the duke would wed the earl to one of his own daughters. Even if he did not, he'd have control of Westmorland's lands and fortune until that young man reached the age of twenty-one.

It was a convenient ability, Will thought, to be able to ignore what one could not change. Queen Catherine possessed the same skill. In the end, she'd accepted the loss of Lady Fitzwalter's services and been reconciled with her husband.

King Henry was eagerly anticipating the birth of their child, due at Yuletide. In the meantime, His Grace had been practicing his own form of discretion by bedding only women the queen was not likely to notice. The first one Will had brought to the secret lodgings had been the laundress whose favors Ned Neville had already sampled. The second had been a visiting country gentlewoman with a complaisant husband.

"A pity we cannot go direct to Woking," Neville commented as he came up beside Will on the castle battlements, "instead of meandering between gentlemen's houses and monasteries for so many weeks first. It has been far too long since we've had a proper tournament."

The court was about to embark on a royal progress through Hampshire and Dorset. It would be late September before this annual ritual, a chance for the king to be seen by his people and to deal in person with various small matters of government, would come to an end with a stay at Woking. The royal manor house there was in need of rebuilding and was much smaller than the palaces at Greenwich, Richmond, Westminster, and Windsor, but it did boast a fine tiltyard.

"Aye, it has been." Will bore Ned no ill will for the injuries he'd suffered at Richmond. Being hurt now and again was part of the sport.

It would have been good to have the distraction of testing his skill with a lance. Will had spent far too much time of late brooding about Lady Anne. When he'd ridden away from Littlemore Priory, he'd told himself that she was safe and in good health, even if she was unhappy. He'd meant to forget about her, but she refused to become a distant memory. Instead she remained in the forefront of his mind, nagging at him like a sore tooth.

He'd done the honorable thing, he assured himself, and the only sensible thing. Had he abducted the wife of a baron and carried her off to Compton Wynyates, he'd have lost everything, including any hope of rebuilding the dilapidated house he'd inherited from his father. No woman was worth that, not even Lady Anne.

Neville clapped him on the back. "Care to take me on in the tennis play? I'm willing to wager a crown that I'll beat you in every match."

Always in need of ready money, Compton agreed, although he knew gambling was as likely to deplete his purse as fill it. There would be endless opportunities to lose money in the coming weeks as the progress moved from Easthampstead to Reading and on to Rumsey, Bewley, Chichester, Canford, and Corfe Castle. They'd visit Shaftesbury and Salisbury, too. And they'd pass nowhere near Littlemore.

Will cursed himself for a fool as he followed Neville toward the tennis play. It was no good pining for what he could not have. Lady Anne had married George Hastings and George was hale and hearty. It seemed unlikely she'd be widowed a second time. A rueful smile made his lips quirk upward. Even if she was, she'd never marry him now, not after he'd so cruelly abandoned her. Women did not easily forgive such treatment.

He sighed. Forget Lady Anne. He must set himself the task of finding a wealthy widow who *would* wed him!

27

Littlemore Priory, July 26, 1510

A little more than a month after her thwarted attempt at escape, Lady Anne begged an audience with the prioress and asked Dame Katherine to inform Lord Hastings of the impending birth of his child.

"I suppose you think that news will persuade him to take you away from here," the prioress said, looking displeased.

"The heir to a barony should be born at the family seat. That is only right."

"Your husband, Lady Anne, may not believe he is this child's father. He has shown no faith in your honesty so far."

Anne glared at her. "Still, under the law, the child is his, no matter who fathered it, simply because I am his legal wife."

He *would* come for her, she told herself. She had to believe that. Her only other recourse would be to fall back on the plan Meriall had once suggested, using threats to win her freedom. She would not mind striking back at the haughty, heartless prioress, but she was still loath to sacrifice Juliana to do so.

She breathed a sigh of relief when, exactly a week later, George rode up to the gates of Littlemore Priory. She had wondered, after her meeting with the prioress, if her message would even be sent.

Dame Katherine escorted Anne to the guesthouse, the expression of someone who has just bitten down on a sour persimmon marring the perfection of her face. She was reluctant to leave them alone together, but George ordered her away, assuring her that they did not need a chaperone.

A long silence ensued after the prioress departed. George stared at his wife as if he'd never seen her before. Anne supposed she did look far different from the noble court lady he'd left behind. Her novice's habit was very plain and, being light colored, was sadly in need of laundering. Just as she felt she would scream in frustration if she had to endure his penetrating stare a moment longer, he spoke.

"I wish to be reconciled," he said.

"I never had any desire to quarrel with you."

"My mother suggests that we retire to Ashby de la Zouch Castle, the Hastings family seat."

"What do *you* want, George?"

He ignored her question. "There are conditions. You must agree to remain there until you have borne me a healthy son and heir. After that, you may do as you wish, even return to court."

Anne took offense at his tone. She'd heard him put more enthusiasm into negotiations to buy a broodmare. She wanted to ask if he was willing to acknowledge that he had misjudged her, but she did not quite dare voice the question.

"Well," she said instead, "that should not take long. The baby is due at Yuletide."

The look of shock on his face was almost comical. He backed away from her, his gaze now fixed on her midsection.

Anne frowned. Her rough wool habit was loose and concealing, but her condition should not have come as a surprise to him. She'd all but told him she was breeding before he left her here, and Dame Katherine had written to him . . . hadn't she?

"I thought you'd received a letter from the prioress. I thought that was why you came."

"The prioress?" He shook his head, still staring.

With a sinking heart, Anne realized that he had not known. Worse, he still believed she'd coupled with Will Compton. Or with the king. Or with both. "This is *your* child, George," she said in as calm a voice as she could manage. "I swear it by all the saints and by the Virgin, too."

He swallowed hard, then held out his hand. "I have already offered you my terms. Do you accept them? Will you come to Leicestershire with me?"

She grasped his fingers and held his gaze. "I will go with you and remain there until you have a healthy son and heir. I am your *wife*, George. We pledged ourselves to each other for life."

Surely, she thought, if they spent time together at Ashby de la Zouch, they could learn to trust each other again. It was even possible that renewed affection might grow between them. Anne vowed she would strive to forgive him for doubting her. How else could they build a new life for themselves and their children, starting with the life that grew within her?

George signaled his agreement with a curt nod. "We will leave at daybreak. Have your maid pack your belongings."

Then he sent her back to her cell for one more night.

28

The chamber high in the Great Tower of Ashby de la Zouch Castle, where Lady Anne lay in a richly appointed canopied bed to await the birth of her child, was airless, overheated, and crowded with females of every persuasion. It was customary for a woman's "gossips" to gather at such a time, to offer advice and lend support and to bear witness to the outcome of her pregnancy.

Lady Anne could have done without so much company. She was glad to have Meriall near at hand, and the midwife, and she did not mind the presence of George's mother, Lady Hungerford, but the others were all but strangers to her.

Then Cecily, Dowager Marchioness of Dorset, swept into the room as if she owned it, coming straight up to the bed and leaning in to brush Anne's cheek with her dry, scratchy lips. "My dear girl, you look splendid," she declared.

"I feel," Anne told her, "as if I am about to burst."

Cecily patted her hand. "The first is always the hardest. I should know. I birthed fourteen babies in my day."

Now in her fiftieth year, Cecily looked remarkably unscathed by the experience. Perhaps, Anne thought with a wry twist of her lips, it had something to do with being married to a man nearly twenty years her junior, for Cecily's second husband was Anne's brother Hal. Two of Cecily's surviving sons, Thomas Grey, the current Marquess of Dorset, and Lord Leonard Grey, were older than Hal was.

Lady Hungerford appeared on the other side of the bed. "How good of you to make the journey from Bradgate, Lady Dorset," she said, "when the brief hours of daylight at this time of year needs must make your visit here so short."

Anne stared at her mother-in-law, appalled at this breach of hospitality. Lady Hungerford should have been offering Cecily a bed for the night instead of rudely hurrying her on her way.

"You must stay the night, dear *sister*," Anne said quickly. As wife of the current baron, *Anne* was mistress of Ashby de la Zouch and had the final say in such matters.

Cecily's eyes flashed with wicked amusement. "I perceive that no one has told you about the feud," she said. "Members of the Grey and Hastings families have been at odds for generations."

Although she declined Anne's invitation to remain overnight, Cecily did not permit herself to be hurried on her way. She stayed long enough to inquire into the details of the nursery and offer advice.

"All is in readiness," Anne assured her. "I have selected a lady mistress to supervise the staff, chosen a wet nurse and a dry nurse, and appointed two young girls as rockers."

"Is the wet nurse qualified?"

Anne shifted in the bed, trying to get comfortable. "She has recently given birth. She has a good supply of milk."

Cecily made a dismissive gesture with one plump hand. "That is the least of it. A wet nurse must be of good character, else the child will drink in her bad habits and ill nature when he suckles. I am not surprised that Lady Hungerford did not know this, having had only two children."

George's mother, overhearing, was quick to take offense. "I assure you, Lady Dorset, that the young woman in question is without vice. She has all the qualities the most notable physicians believe are desirable in a wet nurse. She is in her twenty-fifth year, with broad breasts, rosy cheeks, pale skin, and an amorous disposition."

"She must abstain from carnal coupling while she gives suck," Cecily warned.

"She understands that, and that she will be responsible for any ill health her young charge suffers. If he has colic, she will be purged. If her supply of milk proves inadequate, she will be required to eat stewed goat's udders and powdered earthworms to increase the flow."

Nodding her approval, Cecily next inquired as to Anne's physical condition, demanding details of her pregnancy and even poking at her belly. After predicting that the child would arrive within a week, she finally left. By then, Anne was heartily glad to see the last of her.

Two hours later, Anne's labor began. It continued through the night. Near dawn, exhausted, she felt the child slip from her body. Then she knew no more until, as if from a great distance, she heard voices.

"The child was a boy," the midwife said, "but he never drew breath."

"We must accept this as God's will," George murmured.

Through her pain and grief, Anne heard the note of profound relief in her husband's voice.

After a moment, George spoke again. "How does my wife fare? Will she be able to bear more children?"

"She is healthy," the midwife said, "but you must give her time to recover before you get her with child again."

"For your good service." Coins clinked as George paid the old woman.

The midwife shuffled out of the bedchamber, but George remained behind. Anne could feel him staring at her.

She kept her eyes tightly closed as hot tears pricked the backs of her eyelids. George was *glad* their baby was dead. That could mean only one thing. He had not accepted her word that he was the child's father. He still believed that she had taken a lover at court.

This betrayal was all the more hurtful because she had come to enjoy his company during the months they'd spent together in Leicestershire. Affection, even love, had begun to grow. Now she felt it wither and die, leaving behind a cold and empty place in her heart.

Fabric rustled as he approached the bed. She turned her face away.

"Let her be, George," Lady Hungerford said from the far side of the chamber. "She needs to rest."

"I only wished to bid her farewell. The king has summoned me back to court for the New Year's revels."

"You will no doubt return before she's noticed that you were gone," Lady Hungerford predicted. "After all, it is customary for a woman who has just given birth to remain in the birthing chamber for a further three days, keeping the room dark and quiet. And the period of purgation is twenty days." Her voice grew fainter as she led George away, ascending the stairs to the Great Chamber on the floor above. "When a month has passed, I will arrange a quiet churching. After that you may return and set yourself to beget an heir."

Alone save for the faithful Meriall, Anne finally allowed herself the release of tears. An audible sob escaped her.

"Wail and scream, too, if you've a mind to, my lady," Meriall said. "You have every right."

Instead Anne gave a choked laugh and opened her eyes. The bedchamber was dimly lit. A fire smoked fitfully in the hearth, adding to the gloom. The windows were closed tight because cold air was supposed to be bad for a new mother. But she was not a mother, Anne thought. Her son had been born dead.

"Why?" she whispered. "Why am I being punished? I did nothing wrong."

Meriall offered her a draught of poppy juice, but Anne waved it away.

"Why?" she repeated. "Why did my baby die?"

"It is God's will and His reasons are not ours to question. You know full well not all babies thrive. Even the queen lost her first child. Most mothers count themselves fortunate if half the children they bear live past their first year."

Meriall's words gave Anne no comfort, but they brought to mind another mother and another child. Memories flooded back—all those hours in the stocks, her exhaustion, the denial of food and drink. Fresh tears flowed.

"I failed to protect my unborn child. I should have told the prioress at once that I was breeding."

"Hush, my lady," Meriall soothed her. "It would have made no difference. She's a cruel and wicked woman, that prioress. She'd likely have left you there even longer if she'd known."

"She's the one who should be punished," Anne muttered. She had no way to prove that Dame Katherine's actions had harmed the child she'd carried, but Anne knew in her heart that Meriall was right. The prioress was an evil woman.

"All in good time, my lady," Meriall said, and once again offered the poppy syrup. This time, Anne drank it down without protest and welcomed the drugged sleep that followed. By the time she awoke, George had already departed for court.

29

wo days after Lady Anne was churched—blessed by the priest and deemed pure enough to attend services again in a ceremony that was also intended to mark her fitness to return to her husband's bed—Lady Hungerford informed her that she had her own house to attend to. She meant to return to Stoke Poges on the morrow.

The weeks since the stillbirth had passed in a blur. Anne remembered little of Yuletide. Lady Hungerford had presided over the festivities held for the tenants and household staff while Anne stayed in her chamber, lying listless in her bed.

She awoke on the day after Lady Hungerford's departure to the sound of horses and wagons arriving in the courtyard. A spark of curiosity stirred within her. "Who has come, Meriall?" she whispered.

But Meriall was not in the room with her. She had already gone down to investigate. Impatient, and more alert than she had been since the loss of her baby, Anne rose from the bed. If she wanted an answer anytime soon, she would have to find it for herself. She made her way to the window on unsteady legs and flung back the curtains, setting up a great clatter as the gilded rings that held them rattled along the fixed rod.

The panes of glass were coated with frost, but when she scrubbed at them with the side of her hand she could make out a portion of the inner court below. She frowned when she saw the Stafford knots prominently displayed on the hangings of a litter and several men in the Duke of Buckingham's red and black livery milling about. She had not seen her brother since that disastrous day at court and could not imagine what he would be doing here. Nor did it seem likely that his duchess would visit Ashby de la Zouch in January.

The explanation came a moment later, when the door to Anne's chamber was flung open and Madge Geddings rushed in. "Lady Anne!" she exclaimed. "You will catch your death of cold standing about in nothing but your nightgown."

Clucking in the manner of a mother hen, even though she was several years Anne's junior, Madge spied Anne's warm night robe and insisted that she don it. That accomplished, she stirred the embers in the hearth until they produced a satisfactory flame, then called for bread and ale so that Anne might break her fast. No doubt she would have found some other service to perform had Anne not caught hold of her arm.

"What are you doing here, Madge? Did Edward send you to spy on me?"

Once she was no longer busying herself with domestic tasks, Madge's unease suddenly became obvious. She could not meet Anne's eyes.

Meriall's arrival, just ahead of servants bringing food and drink, prevented Anne from insisting on an explanation. Instead she seated herself at a small table and invited Madge to join her. Madge waited until they were alone again, then slowly removed her cloak.

Anne stared. Madge was expecting a child, and before much longer, too. "What madness is this, to send you out on winter roads? Or did my brother hope some accident would befall you and the child?"

"Lady Anne! What a thing to say! I came to visit you and brighten your spirits. And to spare the duchess the awkwardness of having me give birth to her husband's child under her own roof at Thornbury."

"My brother has much to answer for," Anne muttered, helping herself to a generous portion of beef and bread. There was both ale and mulled cider and she chose the former. Meriall had been nagging her to eat to rebuild her strength.

"What do you mean?" Madge looked wary and did not touch the food.

"Edward condemned me unfairly. He judged me wanton and sent me into imprisonment in a terrible place. The prioress at Littlemore truly is a wanton, and cruel with it. I blame her treatment of me for the loss of my child." The story of her ordeal in the stocks poured out of her in a rush and afterward she felt better for telling someone what had happened.

Madge's initial shock was quickly replaced by denial. "I am certain your brother knew nothing of this. I admit he has a temper, and he was wroth with you for what he saw as behavior that reflected badly on the Stafford name, but he is at heart a compassionate man, and to poor religious houses in particular, he is wont to be generous. This Littlemore—is it a small place?"

"Small, backward, and neglected," Anne conceded.

Madge nodded, as if this confirmed her opinion. "Your brother has a weakness for such priories. He tries to do good. Why, at Hinton, near Bath, he pays the fees for one of the prior's servants and he has recently taken an interest in a lad recommended by one of the monks. He talks of sending the boy to Oxford."

"Where he, too, can be corrupted by the nuns at nearby Littlemore," Anne muttered.

"I will tell the duke what the prioress did to you."

"No!"

"But why not? He will see to it that she is punished."

Would he? Anne had her doubts, but she said only, "I wish to take revenge on her myself."

"How?"

"By writing to her bishop to complain of her. Except that I am not sure he will pay any attention to my letter if he has heard why I was sent there." Anne shoved her trencher aside. Her appetite had fled.

"You need an intermediary," Madge said. "You might send your chaplain."

Anne made a face. George's chaplain, Sir John Canne, was no friend to her. She much disliked having him as her confessor. But Madge's suggestion gave her an idea. She did know another priest, one who might even have some clout.

Thomas Wolsey, the royal chaplain who had performed her wedding ceremony, had been kind to her when he'd come upon her weeping in the chapel at Richmond. Since that time, he had acquired several ecclesiastical honors and been appointed to the king's Privy Council, too.

"Your brother is very good to me," Madge said, distracting Anne from her plotting.

Anne gave her a hard look. "Madge, you are of gentle birth. You should be married to some country squire, bearing him sons to inherit his land. Edward is a selfish pig."

"But I love him!"

Anne opened her mouth, then closed it again. She had seen that starry-eyed look on other women's faces. If Madge fancied herself in love with Edward, it was useless to try to convince her that no good could come of continuing her liaison with him. Nor did Anne speak to Madge of her desire to see Edward suffer as she had suffered. Time had dulled her sharpest cravings for revenge, but she would still be glad of an opportunity to inflict damage on her brother's reputation.

When she was alone again, she took out parchment, pen, and ink and composed a long letter to Thomas Wolsey, king's chaplain, almoner, and confessor, member of the Privy Council, and dean of both Lincoln and Hereford. She complained in detail of Prioress Katherine Wells and then, to cause her brother what little embarrassment and trouble she could, suggested that his charity to the priory at Hinton might be just as ill-advised as the favor he'd shown to Littlemore.

30

The schedule for each year's royal progress was published at court in June, listing all the proposed stops and the dates the court would be at each. Visits could last anywhere from one night to three weeks, and the distance the whole entourage traveled in a day ranged from five to nearly twenty miles. Since leaving Windsor Castle in mid-July, the king and his court had visited Northampton and Harrowden, stayed at Pipewell Abbey and Lidlington, and spent two nights in the abbey at Leicester, some fifteen miles from Ashby de la Zouch. Now they were settled in at Nottingham Castle, where they would remain until the end of the month.

They were too close for George's comfort—only about eighteen miles from Ashby de la Zouch.

Nottingham was a large town, well built, with perhaps the finest marketplace in all of England. The town's main street was extremely wide and evenly paved. George's route took him across an arched stone bridge and into the town from the south, then westward, to where an imposing stone castle dominated a rocky hill above the River Leen.

George could understand why Nottingham Castle had been selected to house the king. It was sturdily built, both outside and in. He rode across a bridge over the ditch that separated the outer from the inner wards. It was said to be protected not only by the portcullis, but also by the carvings of beasts and giants on the pillars. He did not set much store by such superstitious nonsense, especially when he noted that the buildings on the western side of the inner ward were in terrible disrepair.

On the north side a new stone tower rose to three stories and was topped by an upper floor of timber. It boasted large, semicircular bay windows that were both imposing and beautiful to look at. Peering down at him from one of them was a familiar face. Lady Boleyn lifted a hand in greeting, then promptly disappeared. George was not surprised to see her reappear in the courtyard a few minutes later.

"What news of your wife, Lord Hastings?"

"Lady Anne is well." George would have gone on into the tower in search of the king had she not taken a firm grip on his arm.

"It has been some time since I heard from her," Lady Boleyn said.

"I was not aware that she had written to you at all."

Bess Boleyn's eyes narrowed and went cold, although her smile remained in place. "She is a dear friend, Lord Hastings. I care deeply about her."

He stopped trying to free himself to stare at her in astonishment. Did she think he *beat* Anne? Quite the opposite was true. He pampered his wife. He had forgiven her for her transgression. Why, just during the last few weeks, he'd arranged all manner of entertainments for her, even hiring a troupe of players to stay for a week and perform their entire repertoire. He thought Anne was softening toward him, too. He knew with certainty that she was looking forward to the birth of their child. If she worried that, like the last, it would not survive, she never let her fears show.

"I assure you, madam," George told Lady Boleyn, "that my lady wife is in good health and fine spirits."

"Then why is she not with you?"

"She is expecting a child in November, Lady Boleyn. A long and tiresome journey would not be good for the babe."

"Nonsense. It is healthy to take some exercise when one is increasing."

"The roads between Ashby de la Zouch and Nottingham are not the best. Even in a litter, she would be most uncomfortable."

Lady Boleyn was obliged to take his word for it, but she continued to look skeptical.

Fearing that she might be contemplating a visit to Ashby de la Zouch, the very thing he had come to Nottingham hoping to discourage, George hastily added, "She wishes to live quietly, without visitors, for these last months before she is delivered, having lost the previous child."

"I thought you said she was in good health."

"She wishes to *remain* so."

He felt a twinge of guilt, as he always did when he thought of the boy who had died. He had his doubts about the child's paternity, and had been relieved that he would not have to spend the rest of his life bearing the burden of doubt about his heir's legitimacy. Still, the loss of a life, any life, troubled him deeply. He had left Anne afterward—nearly eight months ago now—and gone back to court. When he'd returned to Ashby de la Zouch, richer by a loan from the king of one thousand pounds, he had been determined to reclaim her affection. The loan, he'd suspected, had been a bribe to encourage him to leave court. He'd had no problem accepting. He'd found court life exceedingly dull without Anne there with him.

He was anxious to return to her now. It had taken him months to get her to soften toward him. She'd never denied him his rights, but until recently there had always been an aloofness about her, even in bed. He did not want to risk losing the gains he had made, and he did not want her distracted by old "friends" from court.

"I must make myself known to the king," he said, gently disengaging Lady Boleyn's grip on his arm. "Is His Grace within, or out hunting?"

"He rode into Sherwood Forest at the break of day."

George was not surprised.

"He took *all* his favorites with him," Lady Boleyn continued.

"Charles Brandon. My brother, Lord Edward Howard. Tom Knyvett. Ned Neville. *Will Compton.*"

George kept his expression bland. Lady Boleyn rambled on, filling him in on the latest news of court and courtiers. Compton and Brandon were at odds, vying for first place in the king's affections. Thomas Wolsey, the priest who had married George and Anne, was now the king's confessor. Compton's sister had made an excellent marriage. George hadn't known that Compton had a sister and did not much care.

At length, the hunting party returned and George duly made himself known to King Henry. He was greeted with indifference, which suited him well. Compton also pretended a lack of interest, although George strongly suspected that the other man longed to ask after Anne.

"The Hastings title will have an heir come November," George announced, and was pleased to see a sour look on his rival's face.

The king made the expected responses, and accepted without comment George's statement that Lady Anne was well but disinclined to entertain visitors. That should settle the matter, George thought. No one from court would intrude upon their privacy.

He was in a cheerful frame of mind as he prepared to return home. Seeing Compton enter the stable yard, he called out a friendly greeting. "You should take a wife yourself, Will," he added. "Marriage has much to recommend it."

"I have been considering it," Compton said.

George rode back to Ashby de la Zouch in excellent spirits . . . until he reconsidered Compton's words and realized that the wife the other man intended to take might be his own.

31

*M*adge Geddings glanced up from her embroidery frame in alarm when the Duke of Buckingham stalked into the private room situated between his dining chamber and his bedchamber. Madge wondered what had gone wrong at the meeting with the monk at Hinton Priory.

Buckingham's lips, compressed into a hard, thin line, relaxed a little when he caught sight of her. The vein in his forehead stopped throbbing. Slowly, she rose, dipping into a curtsey. The duke liked such displays of servitude, even from the woman who warmed his bed at night. Perhaps especially from her.

He raised her up, then jerked her into his arms for a heated kiss.

"My lord!" she exclaimed with a teasing laugh. "It is the middle of the day!"

Since they both had fond memories of other afternoons, and mornings, too, he only grinned at her.

Madge reached up to touch his smooth cheek with her fingertips. "What troubles you, Edward. Is there aught I can do to help?"

He hesitated, then seemed unable to stop himself from blurting out a question. "Do you believe there are those who can see into the future?"

The question startled her, but she answered as honestly as she could.

"There were prophets in ancient times, were there not? And if such things were possible in days of old, then it follows that a man might exist today who can do the same." Now it was her turn to hesitate, but she had heard the rumors. "Is Nicholas Hopkins a prophet?"

Instantly suspicious, he released her and stepped back. "What do you know of the monk?"

"Everyone hereabout has heard of him." Hinton Priory was no more than fifteen miles distant. The duke had sent his chaplain, John Delacourt, thither at dawn. Delacourt had returned less than an hour ago.

"What do they say?"

"That he is a holy man, a monk of the Carthusian order, and that he utters cryptic predictions. The Carthusians live in their charterhouses like hermits, do they not? Spending their days alone in prayer and contemplation? Such a man might well be blessed with the gift of prophecy. People venerate him, and hope that he will one day see good fortune in their futures."

"Ordinary people do?" the duke asked, looking thoughtful.

Madge heard the odd note in his voice and her interest quickened. "It is not like you, my lord, to care what the country folk think."

"I have been advised to win the love of commoners," he muttered.

"By the monk?"

As if he suddenly became aware of his surroundings, the duke grabbed her hand and towed her after him down the privy stairs that led to a private garden about a third of an acre in size. Just as the duke's lodgings at Thornbury had been the first to be rebuilt, so had he taken the trouble early on to fill this space with trees, flower beds, and shrubbery.

Madge was fond of Edward's little garden. There were gooseberry and lilac bushes in addition to roses and peonies. Several willow trees offered shade while a pear tree still had a few pieces of fruit left among its branches. A variety of herbs kept the space fragrant even in winter.

Edward led the way to a stone bench in the farthest corner of the garden. The thick stone wall behind it would prevent anyone from creeping up on them to listen to their conversation.

Madge's gown was lined with fur and the kirtle beneath was made of the finest wool, but she felt a chill run through her. It was unusual that Edward practiced such discretion in his own house. When something annoyed him, he was wont to let everyone in earshot know of it. He had never troubled to be cautious of his words, not even when he criticized King Henry.

"You must swear never to reveal what I am about to tell you," he said when they were seated.

Madge agreed without a qualm. She prided herself on her loyalty. Besides, they shared a child. Little Margaret bore the Stafford surname and slept in the ducal nursery. Edward had promised that she would receive the same upbringing and education he'd provided for his legitimate children and that he would find a noble husband for the girl.

"Hopkins," Buckingham said, "predicts that I will have all."

"All what?"

"All of England. I will one day be king."

Madge felt her eyes widen. "Surely it is treason to speak of such things," she whispered.

"It could be seen as such," Buckingham admitted. "That is why Delacourt has taken an oath never to reveal what the monk told him. Except to me."

"Oh, Edward!" Her concern increased tenfold. It was dangerous to covet the Crown and he, of all men, should know that. His own father had died for trying to replace one king with another.

Buckingham must have heard the anguish in her voice because he clasped her close again, resting his chin atop the simple coif she wore over her hair. "The message he sent today was that I should endeavor to win the love of the community. Royal blood is not enough to claim the Crown. Come to that, there are others nearer the throne than I am. The new-made Countess of Salisbury for one. Margaret Pole is the daughter of George, Duke of Clarence, younger brother to both Edward the Fourth and Richard the Third."

Madge knew who the countess was—a widow with five children who had just recently been granted the earldom of Salisbury in her own right, a most unusual circumstance. There had been talk of that among the duchess's ladies when it happened, and even more speculation a few weeks later, when it was rumored that the king's boon companion, Will Compton, was angling to marry the newly made countess. The king, however, had not approved the match, and now it was said that Compton intended to wed the wealthy widow of Sir Francis Cheyney instead.

"His Grace is young yet," Madge said carefully. "Surely he will father more children." The death of his son and heir, only a few weeks after the prince's birth, had been a hard blow, not just to King Henry, but to the entire realm.

"But will they be the queen's?" Buckingham asked. "She is six years older than he is."

Age was not an issue, Madge thought. Not yet. Both of Edward's sisters were as old as the queen and they'd both produced healthy children.

Madge spared a thought for Lady Anne, of whom she was most fond. They had exchanged letters regularly ever since little Margaret's birth. Lady Anne was one of the child's godmothers.

While it was true that Anne had lost her first child, she had given birth to a daughter since. Madge had no doubt she'd soon be with child again. She might already be.

"I must return to court soon," Edward said. "There is talk of war with France, a joint effort with the King of Aragon, Queen Catherine's father."

Panic seared her. "Would you have to fight?"

"No more than the king will, but His Grace will have need of my advice if he intends to send troops abroad. When I know which way the wind blows," he mused, speaking more to himself than to Madge, "it may be worth my while to consult again with the monk. To know the future is to have a powerful advantage."

32

*G*eorge Hastings returned from months of death and disease in an army encampment on the border between Spain and France to find that death had also struck much closer to home. When he'd gone away at the end of May, Anne had been breeding again, healthy and happy. The child, a boy, had been born in early October. He had lived less than a week.

He found his wife in the nursery with their daughter, Mary. Anne was seated on the floor on a large cushion, holding the child upright while they touched noses. The little girl was nearly a year old, at the age when children began to explore their limited worlds. She was providing a distraction for her mother, George thought. That was good.

But when his wife looked up and their eyes met, he saw his own deep sorrow reflected tenfold. No other child could make up for the one she had just lost, not for either of them. Without a word, he went to her side and sank down onto his knees in the rushes. Heedless of the giggling maidservants, he took both wife and daughter into his arms and hugged them hard.

Mary squealed and laughed. Anne just clung.

It was much later, when they had left the nursery for Anne's solar, before they spoke of their lost child. "We named him Henry," Anne said.

George nodded. For the king. It was expected. He listened as she told him of the child's burial, still in the chrisom, but he did not really hear. His own thoughts, he kept to himself. He did not think she would find the comfort he did in reminding himself that they were young yet and could have more children.

He tamped down, too, on the desire for her he felt. She was in no condition to welcome him to her bed, and tradition, in any case, forbade the resumption of marital relations until a month after childbirth. But he was loath to leave her. He had missed the simple closeness of living together under one roof.

"I am glad you came home unscathed," Anne said after another long silence. "We heard terrible rumors."

"Not rumor. Truth." George could not hide his bitterness.

They had been deceived. The queen's father, Ferdinand of Aragon, had promised to join with King Henry for an invasion of France. Ten thousand Englishmen had sailed from Southampton in late May and landed at San Sebastián on the coast of Spain in early June. They had advanced twelve miles, to Feunterrabia, and there they had remained for the next three months, waiting for Spanish troops that never came.

"You had doubts," Anne said, reaching up to touch his face with gentle fingers. "Even at the beginning."

He caught her hand and brought the palm to his lips, placing a kiss squarely in the middle. He felt her shiver. "Do you truly want to know?" he asked. "It is not a pretty tale."

"I have spent months wondering and worrying. I would like to hear a little, at least."

"I will spare you the details. I have no desire to remember them myself, but aside from the king's foolish decision to trust his father-in-law, His Grace made a second mistake in choosing the Marquess of Dorset to lead the expedition."

"That is not just old enmity speaking," Anne remarked, watching his face in the candlelight.

"No. My dislike of all the Greys, the marquess in particular, is well founded, but even I would have thought he'd manage better than he did."

"He had no military experience," Anne pointed out. Her body might still be weak from childbirth, but her mind was as sharp as ever.

"Few did. The king chose Dorset because he is an excellent jouster." After a thoughtful pause, he added, "No matter who had command of the troops, many would have died. We had no cavalry or transport, no proper provisions—not even beer to drink. It was hot there, much more so than England ever is, and all we had was Spanish wine to quell our thirst. Some said that was the cause of the disease. I cannot say, but three thousand men fell ill and some eighteen hundred died of the flux. I blame Dorset for keeping us there so long. It was soon clear that our allies were not coming, but it was not until the troops all but rebelled that Dorset gave the order to return home."

Anne had her head against his shoulder, her arm around his waist. There were tears in her eyes. "So much waste."

He bent to kiss her forehead. "All for the glory of England."

She gave a small laugh at his tone and wiped the moisture from her eyes. "You are home. It is over. We will begin anew."

"How?"

"We will go out into the park. We will . . . we will go hawking. It has been months since I've been on a horse. And you have been cooped up on board a ship during the journey home from Spain. It will be good for both of us."

"You are certain you are well enough?" It was a sport they both loved, and George employed his own falconer.

"Quite certain," she said in a brisk voice that brooked no argument.

And so, early the next morning, they set out on stout, steady-going horses accompanied by four spaniels to quest and retrieve. George carried his favorite hunting bird, a goshawk he'd named Athena. She was not hooded. Unlike long-winged hawks, she did not need to be, but she did have bells tied to her legs, to aid in tracking her when she flew.

Anne, like most ladies, hunted with a sparrowhawk. Colorful tassels hung down from the lower point of her gauntlet, swaying in a light breeze. They matched those on the drawstring of the silk pouch attached to her belt, storage for leashes, jesses, and hoods. Anne had decorated it herself. George recalled seeing her work on it at court in the days before their marriage. She had embroidered upon it all four of the Stafford badges—the golden knot, the silver swan, the blue-ermined mantle, and the spotted antelope.

Ahead of them, a partridge rose into the air. George cast Athena from his fist. Like most of her breed, she had been difficult to train and was ill-tempered, but she could take any ground game or low-flying bird with ease, even bustard and pheasant, and had once brought down a hare. True, she had not killed it, but her grip had held it until a dog arrived to help. Now she flew at her quarry with a determination and skill that had him grinning ear to ear.

"There's supper tonight!" he called to his wife.

Face flushed, eyes alight, Anne reveled in the moment. "Wait till you see what prey my Rosebud takes down."

The most common quarry for a sparrowhawk was a blackbird or a thrush, but George had known a good hunting bird to take down partridge, woodcock, and even a young pheasant. Rosebud, he remembered, was as savage as she was small, but she had been well trained to carry her dead prey back to the hand of her bearer.

And so the hunt continued. They rode through the parkland, flying their hawks at random, taking down partridge, quail, lark, and pheasant until the game bags were overflowing. "We shall sup," Anne declared, "on Sparviter's Pie—three plump partridges, six quails, a dozen larks, and diced bacon strewn over all in a pastry case made of pure wheaten flour and eggs."

George's mouth watered and his heart sang. Not tonight, he reminded himself, but soon, supper would be followed by renewed coupling, and in another year, perhaps less, there would be a son to share the nursery with little Mary.

33

Thornbury Castle, Gloucestershire, April 26, 1513

The Duke of Buckingham stood by a window hung with scarlet curtains. Madge could tell he was lost in thought. He was making that peculiar little humming sound again. And she knew why he was so preoccupied. That morning he had once more dispatched his chaplain, John Delacourt, to deliver a letter to Nicholas Hopkins, the resident prophet at the Carthusian priory of Hinton. The duke desired to know the outcome of King Henry's war with France.

Abandoning her embroidery, not even noticing when her needle fell to the floor, Madge left her cushioned bench to go to her lover's side. Greatly daring, she slipped an arm around his waist. While the duchess was at Bletchingly, she had Edward all to herself at Thornbury. True, Lord Henry and Lady Mary were also in residence, but they had known her since they were babies and did not seem to mind that she was their father's mistress, or that Madge's daughter, little Margaret, shared the nursery with Lady Mary.

"At last!" Edward exclaimed as he caught sight of an approaching rider.

Madge faded into the wainscoting again and, once she'd found her needle, resumed her stitching. A moment later, the sound of boot heels striking tile preceded Delacourt's entry into the duke's privy chamber.

The chaplain had a long face that narrowed toward the chin, hollow cheeks, and murky green eyes that seemed stuck in a perpetual squint. His looks, Madge had always felt, went well with his manner. With clerkish precision, he extracted a sealed letter from the pouch at his waist and presented it to the duke.

"Leave us," Edward ordered.

Delacourt bowed deeply and obeyed with alacrity, wary of the duke's notoriously short temper.

As soon as the door closed behind him, Edward ripped open the monk's reply. His brow furrowed as he read, then smoothed out as a satisfied smile overspread his features. Only after he had burned the letter in the candle flame did he seem to remember that Madge had remained behind when the chaplain left. He shot a narrow-eyed look her way. She continued to embroider roses. If Edward wished to share his secrets, he would do so. If not, she would not be offended. Pleasure warmed her when he came and sat beside her on the bench.

"Good news," he said. "The monk predicts that England will emerge victorious from this conflict. Well, there was never any doubt that we would defeat those poisonous frog eaters."

"I am pleased to hear it," Madge said. Edward had always disliked the French. She was not sure why.

"He was more specific than usual this time. He predicts that King James of Scotland will invade England as soon as English forces cross the Narrow Seas to France. That is not unexpected, either." He leaned back, at his ease, regarding her with heavy-lidded eyes. Madge had no doubt but that his thoughts would soon turn amorous.

"Even when the king's sister is married to the Scots king?" She enjoyed learning about the ways of the great and powerful, and relished Edward's company as much out of bed as in it.

"It is said that King James's mistress has more influence on him than his wife."

"Why, my lord—how can that be?"

He responded to her teasing with a laugh. "In any case," he continued, "James will see England's invasion of France as an opportunity to lay claim to English land in the north. I will advise the king to leave behind some part of his army, to defend our northern borders. His Grace will no doubt send the Earl of Surrey with troops. Surrey has more battle experience than any other, even if he is in his dotage."

He spoke disparagingly of the earl, but his main complaint against Surrey was that he had not yet died and been succeeded by his son, who had recently married Lady Elizabeth, the duke's eldest daughter.

"Perhaps you should stay instead, Edward," Madge suggested. Even though the prophecy was for victory, she feared for his safety in far-off France.

"There is no need to worry about me, Madge. My destiny is foretold." He took both her hands in his, chafing them when he found them icy. "The prophet saw something else, too—that the king will have no male issue of his body."

King Henry, as yet, had no issue at all, although not for lack of trying on the queen's part. Madge knew that Her Grace had lost one child before he was two months old and had endured at least one stillbirth and one miscarriage. News came slowly to Thornbury, but it reached Gloucestershire eventually. Lady Elizabeth sent letters full of news of court to her younger sister.

Madge often heard from Lady Anne, too. In her last letter, the duke's sister had written that her husband, Lord Hastings, had been ordered to be ready to embark for France by the ninth day of May. That was when Edward was to leave for war, too.

"Did you hear what I said?" the duke demanded, tightening his grip on her hands.

"That the king will have no son to succeed him." Madge frowned. "What if he has a daughter?"

He scoffed at that. "No woman will ever rule England. Such a thing could only lead to disaster. It is a king we must have and I am the one best suited to wear the Crown. In time, King Henry will see that and name me as his successor. I have only to be patient."

Patience was not Edward's strength, as he proved only moments later. Instead of carrying her off to the soft featherbed in the adjoining chamber, he tumbled them both to the floor for a quick coupling. The oak boards were covered with plaster of Paris painted to look like marble. Rush matting padded some of the hard surface but not all, and not well enough to prevent bruising.

AFTER EDWARD LEFT for the war, Madge tried from time to time to imagine him as king. He was already accustomed to ruling over extensive holdings in several counties and he had a privy council, just as kings did. She had known him to be arbitrary on occasion, and he had most assuredly been wrong to treat Lady Anne the way he had, but for the most part he was a benevolent overlord. He had given her a number of generous gifts and her widowed mother had both an annuity and the use for life of a comfortable cottage on the estate at Penshurst.

If Edward were to become England's ruler, Madge wondered, would he take her to court with him? Surely a king could keep his mistress close if he wished to. While she waited anxiously for news from France, she allowed herself to dream.

The first word to reach Thornbury was of the expected invasion from Scotland. The queen, acting as regent in her husband's absence, had mustered troops under the command of the Earl of Surrey and repelled the Scots. They had suffered a terrible defeat at a place called Flodden Field. Even their king had been slain, making King Henry's sister Margaret regent of Scotland for her infant son.

Shortly thereafter the entire country heard that English forces had sent the French running for their lives. The encounter, near Thérouanne on the sixteenth day of August, quickly acquired the name "the Battle of the Spurs" because, it was said, the English troops saw naught but the backs of the Frenchmen's spurs as they fled the battlefield.

In early September, Madge received a letter from Lady Anne. Lord Hastings had taken part in the Battle of the Spurs, serving under the Earl of Shrewsbury, who was his uncle by marriage. After the battle, King Henry had knighted many gentlemen who distinguished themselves, including Richard Sacheverell, who was Lord Hastings's stepfather, and William Compton. Lady Anne did not need to identify him.

Madge wondered why she mentioned Compton at all, especially when the next bit of news she shared was that she was once again with child. The baby was due early in the new year.

Madge was happy for her friend. If the child turned out to be a boy, Lady Anne could return to court. That had been the bargain she had made with her husband.

IN OCTOBER, THE king and most of his noblemen returned to England, but several more months passed, until the spring of 1514 was well advanced and Lady Anne had indeed given birth to a son, before Madge saw her lover again. The Duke of Buckingham arrived at Thornbury in a foul mood, cursing everything from the muck and mire of the roads to the clumsiness of the servant lad who dropped a painted wooden box and sent the contents—expensive imported oranges— tumbling to the floor of the duke's bedchamber.

Madge sent the boy on his way and knelt to retrieve the individually wrapped pieces of fruit herself. When she'd collected all the oranges and returned them to their container, she plunked herself down on the chest at the foot of the bed. Feeling she might need a makeshift shield, she snatched up a plump cushion with tassels and held it clasped to her bosom.

She had been permitted to speak freely to her lover in the past. She told herself she was foolish to feel nervous about doing so now. If Edward did not like what she had to say, then he could sleep alone this first night home.

"The roads are always bad," she began, "and servants are often clumsy, especially when someone is shouting at them. What is the real reason for your anger, my love? And what can I do to soothe you?"

The duke's glare would have intimidated anyone who did not love him. After a moment it softened, but his temper did not cool by a single degree. "By the Mass, Madge, I vow I am done with court. King Henry is an impulsive, ill-advised young fool."

Thus began a litany of complaints, the least of which was the king's reluctance to confirm him in the office of Lord High Constable of

England, to which the Staffords had an hereditary claim. A worse crime had been the king's advancement of Sir Charles Brandon, one of the "upstarts" Edward had so often railed against. First the king had granted Brandon the title of Viscount Lisle, in the right of the young woman to whom Brandon, a widower, was betrothed. Then, for no apparent reason other than blatant favoritism, His Grace had elevated Brandon in the peerage, creating him Duke of Suffolk.

"And almost as unwarranted," Edward complained, throwing himself into his chair, "His Grace named his former chaplain, Thomas Wolsey, Archbishop of York. Another nobody!"

"Well, at least the war is over." Madge toyed with the tassels on the cushion, hoping she'd said the right thing. England had, after all, defeated the French.

"Oh, yes. We have peace." The duke's sour expression was a good match for his bitter tone. "And what does the king plan to do next? Why, to marry his younger sister, Mary, who until lately was betrothed to Charles of Castile, to old King Louis of France. That is to be part of the treaty with the enemy we so lately vanquished."

Madge stared at the heraldic beasts embroidered on the bed hangings, trying to think of a way to shift the duke's mind to some less controversial topic. The cloth was high-quality wool, more expensive than even silk velvet. The duke was very wealthy, even after providing dowries for two of his daughters.

"I hear that Lady Elizabeth is now a countess," she blurted out.

Elizabeth's husband had been named Earl of Surrey and Surrey's father, who had previously held that title, had been restored to his old honor as Duke of Norfolk. Too late, Madge realized that they must have been elevated in the peerage at the same time Brandon was made Duke of Suffolk.

Edward sprang up from his chair, his face an unhealthy purplish red. "By the Mass!" he swore again, both fists clenching. "That was yet one more slap at me, for now it will be the Duke of Norfolk who will head the delegation that escorts the king's sister across the Narrow Seas to her wedding. That honor should have gone to me. I am still the highest-ranking nobleman in the land."

Madge abandoned her seat and went to his side. "But my love, surely the last thing you want is to spend more time in that benighted country."

"That is not the point."

She reached up to smooth her fingers over the stubborn line of his jaw. "There may be two new dukes in England, but if anything but good should happen to the king, you are the only duke in the line of succession to the Crown."

The reminder seemed to please him. He allowed himself to be drawn toward the bed. "That is just what I told Westmorland at the time of their elevation."

Madge froze. "Oh, Edward!"

"There was no harm in it, my dear. The Earl of Westmorland is my son-in-law, after all."

That young man was married to the duke's middle daughter, Lady Catherine, but Madge wondered if that was enough to ensure his loyalty. "It is one thing to speak of the monk's prophecy to me," she scolded him, "but to boast of it to others is not only unwise, it could be dangerous."

Edward stared at her as if she'd grown another head. Then he laughed. "It is good to know that I can always count on your loyalty, Madge. But you must not worry your pretty little head with such matters. Come, let me show you what I have brought from London."

He led her to the stack of parcels piled near his wardrobe chest. The top one was cone-shaped and had a fitted silk cover. He whisked it off to reveal a cage containing a gaily colored bird of a species Madge had never seen before.

"These are all the rage at court," the duke said, "where gilded birdcages hang at every window in the queen's apartments. This is, therefore, a gift fit for a queen, and I bought it just for you."

34

Ashby de la Zouch Castle, Leicestershire, February 20, 1515

*H*ave all the arrangements been made for the christening and for my churching?" Lady Anne asked. She would not be permitted to resume normal activities until she had been churched.

"They have." George stood on the far side of the bedchamber, in front of a wall hanging that depicted the goddess Venus presenting a gift of armor to the warrior Aeneas.

"Then you may begin to plan for our departure for court."

"Anne—"

"Your presence is needed in the House of Lords, is it not?"

"The king has given me license to absent myself from Parliament."

"Well, then, His Grace will be pleasantly surprised that you are so mindful of your duties that you return of your own free will."

She glared at him, her temper primed and ready to ignite, across the expanse of the high, ornately carved and painted bed. She sat propped up against the headboard, a plump bolster covered in soft, tufted velvet at her back and a coverlet of cream-colored silk tucked in around her hips. When George remained silent, Anne's hands curled into fists and her chin came up.

"Do you intend to forbid me the court, George? You did promise that I could return when I had borne you a son. I have given you two!"

The birth of Francis, a healthy boy, had fulfilled her part of the bargain with George. She'd expected to return to court in time to celebrate the proxy wedding of the king's sister, Mary, to King Louis of France, but fate had had other ideas. The reason for the change in plans was soon to be christened Thomas. He slept peacefully in a cradle near the hearth, unaware that his conception had confined his mother to Leicestershire for nearly a year longer than she'd planned to stay.

"Have you been so unhappy here, Anne?" George asked. "I have been generous with you, providing servants to wait on you, delicacies for you to eat, and rich fabrics in which to clothe yourself."

"So you have," she muttered, unappeased by the reminder. George had showered her with affection, too. She had no doubt but that he was fond of her. But he still did not trust her. "We had a bargain, George. I mean to hold you to it."

"Is that all we've had?" He sounded so forlorn that for a moment she weakened.

Anne extended a hand toward him. "You know it is not, but I have been immured here in the country for five long years."

"You have the children."

"And I love them dearly. There is a part of me that does not want to leave them, but if I do not return to court I will lose something of myself." She had missed the excitement, the contact with other people of her own station in life, the constant whirl of entertainments. She had not danced in years. "It is only a visit, George."

A *long* visit, she added to herself. In truth, she wanted both court and country to be part of her life from now on. There was no good reason why they could not spend part of the year in each place, or even bring the children closer to court on a permanent basis. Lady Hungerford had been talking for some time about moving to Leicester. Once she vacated Stoke Poges, they could take up residence there.

George at last approached the bedstead. He leaned close, bracketing her shoulders with his strong, long-fingered hands. His shoulders were broad enough to block out the candlelit room behind him. "You have just given birth, Anne. It is not meet that you travel so soon."

She reached up to toy with the laces holding his collar closed. What was it about her husband, she wondered, that gave him the power to stir her senses, even when she was wroth with him? His betrayal of her nearly five years ago and his stubbornness now should have been enough to make her despise him. Instead she felt a strong desire to pull him closer, down into the bed with her, and indulge in an activity that was even more unmeet this soon after childbirth.

A flick of her fingers knocked his bonnet clear off his head.

The glitter of arousal came into his eyes as the expensive head covering landed among the rushes on the floor and Anne's hand came up to cup the back of his neck.

"Take me to London," she whispered. "We will both enjoy the journey."

"If I go there," he whispered, nuzzling her neck, "it will only be to attend Parliament. You will be as bored at Hastings House as you are here. More so, since you will not have the children to distract you."

"I will go to court," she informed him.

He lifted his head and fixed her with a steely stare. "Without me, you have no place there."

"And whose fault is that?" Her playful mood evaporated like dew on a sunny morning.

George jerked away from her. "Christ aid! I do not have patience for this wrangling. Most women would be content with their lives. We have a daughter and two fine sons. It is your duty to care for them, and for this household when I am away."

"I have done that!" She threw a cushion at him. It glanced off the side of his head and landed on a storage chest. "I have been everything you could want in a wife. How, then, can you continue to think that I wish to return to court only so that I may dally with other men?"

Anne despaired of ever recapturing the promise of the early days of their marriage. Her brother had blighted that prospect with his meddling. After all this time, George was still quick to believe the worst of her.

"The court is rife with licentious behavior," he said, further discouraging her.

"Have *you* taken a mistress?"

"How can you suggest such a thing? I cleave only to you." He looked so affronted by the suggestion that Anne almost laughed aloud.

"Then why do you think it so impossible for me to live at court and enjoy its entertainments without taking a lover? Am I so weak-willed that I cannot withstand the least temptation?"

His sheepish expression answered her even before he spoke. "You are the most willful woman I know." He came close again and touched his fingers to her face. "Perhaps that is what I am afraid of."

"You miss me when you are away and I am here. I know you do."

"Yes, I do," he admitted.

For a moment, she thought he would join her in the big bed. Instead he gave her a speculative look, then strode to a nearby pedestal table. The rushes underfoot whispered as he passed, giving off a hint of marjoram.

Covered with an exquisite piece of Persian carpet, the table held a pitcher of Xeres sack and another of barley water. George filled one goblet with each before returning to Anne's bedside. He handed her the barley water, then used that hand to catch hold of the Spanish chair. He pulled it up close to the bed and straddled it. All the while his intense gaze bored into her, as if she were a puzzle he needed to solve.

Anne met his eyes with a boldness she was far from feeling. She thought that he loved her, although there had been a long period of time when he had tried not to. Why else would he be so jealous of other men?

That was better, she told herself, than if he did not care for her at all. A man could tup a woman without feeling anything toward her, especially if he was desirous of begetting sons. The very intensity of their attraction to one another seemed to belie the idea that she was only a convenience to him, but it also meant that they would never have a peaceful marriage.

Resigned to that, Anne searched for some way to convince her husband that she would be a good and faithful wife to him, whatever he believed about her past behavior.

When George spoke again his voice was silk over steel. "Perhaps some time apart would be good for us. I will go to London, but alone."

"It is cruel of you to keep me a prisoner here." She let her lower lip slip forward into a pout.

He kissed away the sullen expression, then removed the empty goblet from her hand. "I do not trust you, Anne, when you pretend to be my sweet and obedient wife."

"Then let me be truly honest with you. If you leave me here alone, you will force my hand. I will not take a lover, although I could, for I desire no other man but you. But if you do not make a prisoner of me in truth, I will leave here and take the children with me."

She jabbed a finger into the center of his chest. Startled, he spilled some of his wine.

"I will lead you a merry chase all over England," she continued, inventing punishments as she went along, "and create such a scandal that you will never stop being a laughingstock at court. Is *that* what you want, George?" She poked him again. "Or will you keep your part of our bargain so that we may continue to live in harmony?"

"Christ aid," he muttered, but a rueful smile followed the curse. He knew she was not serious, but her words had given him pause. His left hand slid up along her shoulder. The fingers toyed with a lock of her hair. "We will set out for London right after Easter. Will that suit you?"

Easter Sunday fell on the eighth day of April, a date well past the time when George would expect to do far more than just kiss his wife. Anne told herself that even if he did get another child on her, they'd be well away from Ashby de la Zouch before she knew for certain that she was breeding again. Another pregnancy would not trap her in the country.

"That suits me very well," she said.

35

*I*t felt strange to be back at court after nearly five long years away. Anne and George had left Leicestershire right after Easter, stayed for a week at Stoke Poges, and then journeyed on to Greenwich, arriving just in time to be swept into the pageantry and pomp of the annual celebration of May Day. It was very early that morning when Lady Anne found herself mounted on a gentle bay mare and riding beside Bess Boleyn.

They followed the queen's party into the countryside. Queen Catherine was surrounded by twenty-five damsels on white palfreys, all wearing gowns slashed with gold lamé. Most were young and pretty, in startling contrast to their mistress.

"Her Grace does not look well," Anne whispered to Bess.

"That gown does not flatter her." It was in the Spanish style and might have enhanced the beauty of a tall woman, but the queen was tiny. Four pregnancies had left her far heavier than she once had been and the result was an appearance both squat and unattractive.

Anne pitied the queen. None of Her Grace's children had lived. King Henry still lacked an heir.

"You seem to be thriving in my old post," Anne told her friend.

"I've envied you more than once these last few years," Bess confided.

"I hardly know my daughters. My son, George, is here at court now, as a page to His Grace, but Tom sent our daughter Nan to serve Archduchess Margaret of Austria and little Mary went with the king's sister to France and is to stay there, in the household of the new queen, Claude, where Nan is now to join her." Mary Tudor's elderly husband, King Louis, had not long survived his wedding to a vivacious younger woman. The French king now was Francis the First, a man the same age as King Henry.

"Your girls are very young for such service, surely? I do not recall that any of Catherine of Aragon's maids of honor were less than fourteen years old and most were considerably older."

"Tom got the idea from Charles Brandon—or should I say m'lord Suffolk, who sent one of his young daughters by his first wife to be educated at the archduchess's court."

"Ah, yes—Brandon." They exchanged a speaking glance.

Even far away in Leicestershire, Anne had heard of it when Brandon was elevated in the peerage. For a commoner to be made a duke was unprecedented. Anne had wondered at the time if Will Compton would be awarded a similar title, but as yet he had obtained no higher honor than his knighthood.

"Why was Brandon singled out?" she asked Bess as they rode toward the greenwood.

"He has always been the best jouster, and of all His Grace's companions, he is the king's closest friend." Bess bent forward to stroke her horse's neck and added, in a whisper, "And now he is even closer to His Grace."

"Friend. Duke. What is left?"

"He has married the king's sister. The newlyweds are even now in Calais, awaiting permission to return to England."

"Charles Brandon, a mere knight when I left the court, has grown so in power that he dares marry royalty," Anne marveled. Not only was Mary Tudor the king's sister, she had been crowned herself as Queen of France.

"My father was ready to call for Brandon's execution when he heard," Bess said. "No doubt your brother felt the same way. As the only other dukes in England, they both resent Brandon's meteoric rise."

Anne felt herself stiffen. "I would not know. Edward does not confide in me." He rarely even spoke to her and the five years that had passed since he'd wrenched her away from court had done little to lessen the resentment she felt toward him.

They rode on in silence until they had traveled nearly two miles from the palace and could see the king and his men waiting in the distance. King Henry was dressed all in green and surrounded by a great company on horseback. George was somewhere among them, but there were nearly a hundred men in all, many wearing identical short green velvet gowns gored with yellow satin. She could not pick him out from the crowd.

Just inside the wooded area, the queen's cavalcade came to a halt. In addition to the mounted men, a multitude of archers, all in hooded green coats, awaited them. One was clearly meant to be Robin Hood and another Friar Tuck . . . in a green habit. Beside them stood a figure in a red kirtle and a green gown—the man playing the Maid Marian. Anne was forcibly reminded of another morning and another band of Merry Men. She never had learned the identity of the woman who had, quite outrageously, taken on the role of Robin Hood's lady love.

If there were a hundred noblemen and gentlemen on horseback, there were twice that many archers. Anne's gaze slid over them to fix upon the king. His Grace was a truly magnificent sight. Mounted on a beautiful bay, jewels sparkling in the sun, he drew every eye, but it was not just his splendid appearance that held the crowd's attention. At a soft-voiced command he set his horse in motion, first to execute a double turn in place, then a half turn and a full turn.

Bess leaned close once more. "His Grace has been taking instruction in the Italian art of the manage. His mount, Governatore, was a gift from the ruler of Mantua."

Anne did not expect to see anything truly spectacular. Everyone would applaud enthusiastically no matter how poorly the king performed. But she had underestimated His Grace's skill. He used a wand to touch his horse on the shoulder and Governatore reared up on his hind legs.

"Holla, holla, ho boy, there boy," King Henry murmured. Then he pressed his calves into the horse's flanks and clicked his tongue.

Governatore raised both forelegs at the same time and kicked out with his hind legs, so that all four were in the air at the same time. Anne could not hold back a gasp of surprise and pleasure. She'd never seen a horse do anything like that before, and certainly not at a rider's command. To the sound of applause and whistles, the king patted Governatore's neck and spoke softly to him again, murmuring words of praise.

King Henry, Anne decided, was no longer an enthusiastic, oversized puppy. He'd matured and learned control.

An archery contest followed the king's demonstration of horsemanship. Both noblemen and archers competed but no one was surprised when it was the king who won. Afterward, Robin Hood invited the queen and her damsels to follow him deeper into the greenwood.

"Do you dare venture into a thicket with so many outlaws?" King Henry teased his wife.

"Where you go, so am I content to follow," Queen Catherine replied.

Laughing, the king took Her Grace's hand and led her onward. Trumpets blared, almost drowning out the sound of dozens of singing birds imprisoned within the interwoven boughs of a series of bowers. Flowers and sweet-smelling herbs had been twined around the branches. Inside, tables heavy laden with platters of venison and casks full of wine awaited the royal party.

The king's musicians played throughout the breakfast that followed. There were lutes and flutes and drums, and even an organ. For further entertainment, two pageant wagons were drawn into the woods by gaily caparisoned horses. One displayed the giants Gog and Magog in pasteboard. The other was occupied by a pretty young girl representing Lady May. She was attended by four damsels and all five were dressed in white and green sarcenet and had flowers in their hair.

When the meal was over, the entire company, pageant wagons and all, formed a triumphal procession for the journey back to Greenwich. It seemed to Anne as if every person in the realm had come out to see the display.

How she had missed this, not only the pageantry, but the camaraderie! There was nothing to equal the rush of excitement and pleasure that came from simply being among other nobly born ladies—to talk, to share, to enjoy.

With so many people in the cavalcade—thousands, it seemed—she had to wait her turn to dismount. Another rider came between Anne and Bess, spooking Anne's horse. She murmured soothing words and brought the mare under control again without difficulty, but when she looked up, she found she had become separated from the other ladies. Instead, a gentleman rode beside her. Will Compton looked down at her from his seat on a big black gelding.

"Lady Anne." He doffed his bonnet—green, as was every piece of clothing he wore, even his shoes.

"Sir William." She regarded him with what she hoped appeared to be cool detachment, for inside she felt decidedly unsettled at seeing him again after so long. He looked exactly the same as she remembered him—tall, toothsome, and smiling that engaging smile.

With a mild sense of surprise, she realized that she was no longer angry with him. Five years was far too long to bear a grudge against someone who had done nothing worse than tell her the truth. He did serve at the will and pleasure of the king. No matter what his feelings for her had been, he'd had no choice but to leave her at Littlemore.

"It is good to have you back at court," Compton said.

She could not help but smile. "It is good to be back."

"The king sends you greetings. His Grace noticed you riding alongside Lady Boleyn."

Her smile dimmed. She was uncertain she wanted to attract the king's attention. Having it had not done her much good five years ago.

As if he'd read her thoughts, Compton laughed. Then he leaned across his horse's neck and spoke softly, for her ears alone. "Never fear, my lady. These days our Bessie keeps the king busy."

"Bessie?" she echoed, thinking for a moment that he meant Bess Boleyn.

"Mistress Elizabeth Blount," Compton explained. "She has been the king's mistress for some time now and he shows no sign of tiring of her."

"I am delighted to hear it." Anne urged her horse forward, forcing Compton's mount to sidle out of her way.

He fell in beside her again. "I, however, have never forgotten my sweet Lady Anne."

She rolled her eyes at this nonsense. "You, Sir William, have a wife now, and I left three young children behind when I returned to court."

"I have a daughter." His voice was warm with pride. "She's called Catherine, after the queen."

"I congratulate you. Is your wife here at Greenwich?"

The warmth abruptly vanished. "She is not." Dismounting, he helped her down from her horse. He kept his hands on her waist longer than he needed to.

Anne slipped deftly out of his grasp, wagging an admonishing finger at him. She was glad she had when she caught sight of George on the far side of the stable yard. He was watching them with a scowl on his face.

"The past is best forgotten, Sir William," Anne said firmly. "This is a new beginning."

He regarded her with clear hazel eyes for a long moment before he nodded. "Indeed it is," he said and, with a courtly bow, he took himself off to rejoin the king.

36

he official English wedding of the king's sister to his dearest
friend, Charles Brandon, Duke of Suffolk—actually the third
time they'd exchanged their vows—took place in the presence of all the
nobles then at court. Others arrived in time to share in the festivities,
even though many found little cause for celebration. What was Charles
Brandon, after all, except a jumped-up country gentleman who'd won
his title through his prowess in the tiltyard?

George Hastings studied his brother-in-law, the Duke of Buckingham, with wary eyes. The duke was a prideful man who much disliked
the king's tendency to give preferment to commoners. Buckingham was
also a force to be reckoned with within his family and, unless George
was much mistaken, he was even now making his way to Anne's side.
An encounter between brother and sister was unlikely to be harmonious.

They had seen one another only rarely during the years Anne had
spent away from court. After one such occasion, George had named his
brother-in-law steward of all of George's Welsh properties, essentially
giving Buckingham control of their revenues, just to stop him from paying another visit to Ashby de la Zouch.

He was too late to intercept the duke, but arrived in good time
to see the militant gleam come into his wife's eyes at the sight of her

brother. She sank at once into a curtsey, but her jaw was set and her teeth clenched tight to hold back hasty words. George prayed she would be able to contain her ire. An open feud would benefit no one.

Buckingham was either oblivious to his sister's feelings or discounted them as unimportant. He had always treated her like a child and did not seem likely to change this condescending attitude. Nor would it occur to him to refrain from meddling in her life.

"Are you pleased to be back at court, sister?" he asked.

"Indeed, I am, Edward."

"Then, in gratitude, perhaps you will do something for me in return."

Taken aback that he would so blatantly take credit for arranging her return, she gaped at him. George covered the last few feet between them in a rush, coming up beside his wife and placing a restraining hand on her arm.

He arrived a second too late. Anne found her voice. "Do you mean to claim," she asked with deceptive calmness, "that it is only with your permission that I remain?"

"You *were* sent away in disgrace," the duke reminded her.

"I was taken away against my will, and not by the king's wish."

He made a dismissive gesture with one heavily beringed hand. "That scarce matters now. Water over the dam, as they say. And I have a task for you, dear sister."

"You have another sister. Use Elizabeth!"

"Elizabeth is not at court at present. You are."

"Honestly, Edward, for sheer gall you—"

He talked right over her words. "In your absence, there have been changes at court, and few of them have been for the better."

George could see his wife's anger and resentment simmering just beneath the surface, although Buckingham remained unaware of his danger. Somehow, Anne managed to hold her tongue. She made a curt gesture to indicate that her brother should continue.

He glanced warily over his shoulder to make sure no one was nearby, then leaned closer. "I have enemies here at court."

Neither Anne nor George made any reply. The truth of the duke's statement was too obvious.

"They would keep me from my rightful place," Buckingham continued. "It is therefore necessary that I learn of their plans in advance, so that I may protect myself *and my family*." He put particular emphasis on those last three words, reminding Anne that, as his sister, she would share in both his triumphs and his defeats.

George could feel Anne's muscles tense beneath his fingers. She wanted to refuse to do anything her brother asked, but she had as strong a streak of duty to family as he did. And she had children to protect. Anne loved their daughter and two little sons. George had seen that clearly when it had been time to leave Ashby de la Zouch. As much as she'd longed to return to court, it had broken her heart to leave them behind.

"You have spies aplenty already," Anne told her brother. "You forget how well I know you, Edward. I have often seen you set one servant against the other. Charles Knyvett is so eager to win your favor that he'd let you know of it if one of your chaplains sneezed out of turn."

Buckingham did not seem to notice her sarcasm. "How else am I to learn if my men are loyal? I do not need your advice on how to run my household."

"But you do need my assistance here. Is that not what you just said, Edward?" She was openly taunting him now. A wise man would have retreated.

Buckingham seized the opening to make more demands. "You are friends of old with Lady Boleyn. She knows how to show proper obedience to the head of her family. The Duke of Norfolk makes use of all of his children here at court. I would know his mind."

"Ask him yourself. Your daughter is married to his eldest son. Better yet, let *her* spy for you."

Buckingham's daughter, named Elizabeth like their sister, *was* at court, and on good terms with Queen Catherine, too. But clearly the duke did not care for this suggestion. His frown deepened.

"You have age and experience and can manage matters more subtly." In an obvious attempt to ingratiate himself to her, he affected a smile.

It did not reach his eyes. "My daughter," he added in a confiding tone of voice, "is cursed with a volatile temperament."

"I wonder where that came from?" Anne muttered under her breath.

"Besides, you are the best one to gain access to another individual whose movements I would have watched. You can keep me informed of Sir William Compton's plans."

George's grip tightened on his wife's arm, but it was toward Buckingham that he aimed his incredulous words. "You must be joking."

Anne spoke at the same time. "That is out of the question."

The duke buffed his nails on the front of his doublet. "I will have your obedience in this, Anne."

"You do not control my movements," she shot back.

He lifted a supercilious eyebrow.

"Enough!" George's interruption startled them both. "You may be a duke, my lord, but I will not permit you to threaten my wife."

Anne stared at her husband in amazement. Then she began to laugh. "Too little, too late, my dear. Where was this bold and chivalrous knight five years ago?"

George felt his color rise, along with his temper. How could she compare his defense of her now to what had happened then? The hurt and disappointment of that night flooded back as if only days had passed instead of years. He had to forcibly remind himself that he had forgiven her long ago for her misbehavior with Will Compton.

Even so, he knew he could not tolerate seeing the two of them together. Who knew what would come of it if she did as her brother demanded? As much as he might wish to avoid conflict with his powerful brother-in-law, George was determined to take a stand.

"My wife will not spy for you, Your Grace. Nor will she whore for you."

He heard Anne gasp, but he kept his attention on the duke. Buckingham's eyes went cold and hard.

"Defiant puppy!" Contempt underscored every word the duke spoke. "Correct me if I am wrong, George, but as I recall, you hold no state or court office. You are not a member of the king's Privy Council. You have no diplomatic duties. You have, in fact, no excuse to be at court at all."

They stood only inches apart, poised like two stags ready to lock antlers and fight to the death. Then Anne stepped between them.

"If you wish to avoid attracting the king's attention, and that of his guards, you will go your separate ways at once and speak no more of this."

"My wife is a wise woman," George said through gritted teeth. Fighting at court was forbidden, and harshly punished. "Far wiser than her brother."

"Impudent churl!" But Buckingham backed off. With a swirl of his costly cape, he stalked off.

George turned back to his wife and bowed stiffly to her. Then he, too, strode away. He'd had enough of Staffords for one day.

37

*A*fter he had heard Mass and broken his fast on midsummer day, the king mounted his horse and rode into the parkland surrounding the palace. It was the beginning of hart hunting season and he was eager for a kill. King Henry hunted every day he could manage it, sometimes coursing with greyhounds and at others shooting at deer from a standing. He laughed aloud with delight as three loud blats on a hunting horn signaled the release of the first relay of the running-hounds. The sound of their baying filled the clear morning air.

Accompanying the king was a small company of favored courtiers and some of their wives. The sisters married to Harry Guildford and Nick Carew giggled together as they set out. Lady Anne, who was some years their senior, disdained the company of these silly girls and chose to ride instead at her husband's side.

In and out of the bedchamber, George was, for the most part, congenial company. Anne supposed that in their time together at Ashby de la Zouch she had learned to love him, after a fashion, in spite of the fact that he continued to doubt her ability to remain faithful to him. If jealousy was proof of love, she thought, then George must be most horribly in love with her! Ever since their encounter with her brother the previous month, he had been particularly attentive, bringing her little gifts and being even more generous in his lovemaking than he ordinarily was.

The hart they were chasing had been selected the previous evening after several of the king's huntsmen, using lymers—hounds with extraordinary scenting abilities that had been trained to work on a leash and to trail only harts—had reported their findings to the king's master of game and compared descriptions of potential quarry. The hart was the noblest prey, an animal that combined guile with innocence and, it was said, could not die of fright because it had a certain special bone in its heart. This bone, when retrieved from the carcass, was highly valued as a talisman. Anne herself had an amulet made from one. George had given it to her during her second pregnancy.

The progress of the hunt was tracked by various combinations of short and long notes on the horns. These told the riders how great the distance was between hart and hounds and signaled the release of each relay of hunting dogs. The hounds pursued their quarry in full cry, but the success of the hunt was never a sure thing. The scents left by other deer in the forested park sometimes confused them, and the hart itself, clever beast that it was, had been known to interrupt its own line of scent by crossing through streams or doubling back.

For the most part, there was constant noise from the baying of the hounds and the shouts of encouragement from the riders. But from time to time there were lulls when nothing could be heard but distant birdsong and the rustle of leaves overhead. It was during one of these that the king rode back to join Anne and George. His face was flushed and his eyes were bright.

"Go speak to the huntsman, Hastings," His Grace ordered, and reined in at Anne's side, taking her husband's place.

Flustered, Anne kept her gaze averted from her king. She was not sure she wanted his undivided attention.

"You absented yourself from Court for a long time, Lady Anne," His Grace remarked.

"I assure you, Your Grace, had I had the wherewithal to return on my own, I should have done so. But, as Your Grace knows, and as is only right and proper, all a woman's possessions become the property of her husband upon their marriage."

The king looked momentarily startled, although whether by the notion that women were so powerless or by Anne's forthright speech, she could not tell. He seemed to be mulling over what she'd said while he patted his mount's neck and murmured soothing words to the restless beast.

"You may request a loan from my privy purse should you ever have need of it in the future," he offered.

"I do not wish to be in your debt, Your Grace."

His lips quirked with an amusement Anne did not share. "Would you also refuse an outright gift?"

Anne did not want to appear ungracious, but she resented the idea that she could be bought. "Perhaps Your Grace might be willing to grant me some unspecified boon at a later date? At present, I have all I could desire—a good husband, thriving children, and the company of the most noble monarch in Christendom."

"Done," he said.

Anne was still stammering her astonished thanks when the horns sounded the *requeste*. The hounds had found the scent again. King Henry spurred his mount forward. Almost at once, another rider took the king's place at her side.

Even before Anne got a good look at him, she recognized Sir William Compton by his distinctive smell, that combination of musky perfume and leather and man that was uniquely his own. It still had the power to set her nerves on edge. Already annoyed, she glared at him when he seized her pommel to prevent her from responding to the call of the horn and the distant baying of the hounds.

Oblivious to her irritation, he grinned at her. "A lovely day for a ride in the wood, is it not, Lady Anne?"

"I *was* enjoying it."

"We will all be doing a great deal more riding soon. I understand that the king's summer progress will take us westward this year, and the first part of the journey will be a landscape familiar to you. We will pass quite close to Lady Hungerford's house at Stoke Poges."

Although the last thing she wanted was to engage in conversation, Anne forced herself to be polite. Compton was, after all, one of the king's most influential courtiers, his closest personal servant. Offending him was not a good idea.

"I am certain there will be many stops, at courtiers' houses and royal manors alike. After all, the purpose of a royal progress is to allow the king and queen to show themselves to their subjects. And to seize upon every opportunity to hunt along the way. Do we travel as far as your home in Warwickshire, Sir William?"

"Compton Wynyates is not yet fit to receive the king." The rest of the hunt had left them behind and still he gripped her pommel.

"What a pity." Anne jerked on her reins, making her palfrey sidestep.

Compton let go, but deftly used his horse to block her way.

"I thought I'd heard that you married enough wealth to fund a complete remodeling."

"The work is ongoing."

Recognizing annoyance in his clipped speech, Anne thrust the needle deeper. "I should have welcomed the opportunity to meet your wife," she drawled. "Why is it that you never bring her to court, Sir William? I am certain you must miss her terribly."

"I scarce think of her at all."

Anne frowned. He'd wed for money and to get an heir. She'd known that already. Most of England's nobility and gentry did the same. And yet, for some reason, it suddenly struck her as terribly sad that a man as vital as Will Compton should have had to settle for a loveless marriage. "I am sorry that you are unhappy in your choice."

"Mine is not a unique situation, as you well know, Lady Anne." Their eyes met and held.

"Only a fortunate few enjoy true contentment in their marriages," she agreed. "I have been luckier than most."

"You did not always think so."

"I have grown quite fond of George." And she'd admired his courage when he'd stood up for her with Edward, even if she did still wish he'd been that valiant five years sooner.

" 'Content,' " Will murmured in a thoughtful voice. " 'Fond.' Those are not words that denote undying passion."

"Passion is overrated, Sir William." She made a little clicking sound to set her horse in motion. They had tarried longer than she'd intended.

"You might find more than contentment outside of the nuptial bed."

"You are blunt, Sir William."

"Shall I woo you instead with poetry and baubles?" They rode side by side out of the forest and into a clearing.

"I should prefer that you not try to tempt me at all. The cost is too dear." And yet, in spite of the nervous fluttering of her stomach when she was around him, she realized that she was enjoying their flirtation. She had missed this—the lighthearted banter, the playing at courtship.

"There are ways to elude your watchdog," Will said, "should you wish to use them."

"He is not—"

Compton gave a derisive snort. "Lord Hastings does not trust you, my lady. He watches you like the hawk watches its prey, only waiting for the least mistake to pounce." With a jerk of his head, he directed her gaze to the far side of the clearing and there was George, glaring at them.

Anne sighed. In spite of repeated and often heated denials, George continued to believe that she had betrayed him with Will Compton, and perhaps with the king, too. Even after all this time, he still accepted her brother's word over hers.

The huntsmen who were with the pack blew the signal that the hounds had the hart at bay. George momentarily forgotten, both Will and Anne urged their horses forward and rode hard toward the sound, arriving in a second clearing just in time for the kill.

The hart, with its sharp antlers and flying hooves, had already maimed one of the dogs. Although King Henry was to deliver the final blow, a royal huntsman approached the animal first, to ensure His Grace's safety. While the hart was distracted by the hounds, he struck from behind, severing the main tendon in its hind leg.

Laughing, the king stepped in to slit the hart's throat and help the huntsmen turn it on its back, so that its antlers pressed into the earth. With quick, decisive movements, one of the huntsmen slit the skin along the length of the neck, slashed downward at each end to form two flaps, and then cut through the flesh, down to the bone. Only after he stood back did the other huntsmen blow the "death" notes for the hart.

The hounds bayed, straining to get to the carcass. They were warded off with short staffs until the horns had done sounding. Then they were set loose and permitted to tear at the flesh of the neck, but only long enough to reinforce their hunting instincts before they were dragged away again and harnessed. When the lymers had been similarly rewarded, the king and his courtiers began their long ride back to the palace, leaving the huntsmen behind to slaughter the hart.

George once again took his place at Anne's side. She expected him to make some comment about Sir William, but he said not a word. And when he came to their bed that night, he presented her with a rose, all the thorns thoughtfully removed. Then he made love to her with as tender a thoroughness as she'd ever known.

A strong physical attraction had always existed between them, even when they were at odds about everything else. But this night, for the first time in years, Anne felt as free to indulge her appetites as she had during the early days of their marriage. She threw herself fully into the enjoyment of their coupling, daring to touch everywhere with mouth and hands and encouraging George to do the same. When they were finally sated, she felt such a sense of intimacy surrounding them that she was filled with a new confidence. She was certain George no longer doubted her and that she had finally convinced him that she would cleave only to him.

38

While King Henry sat on the royal close stool, Sir William Compton waited patiently nearby, pretending not to notice the smell that lingered in the small antechamber. The stool was a pretty, costly thing, covered in velvet and padded so that the royal bum did not have to touch the wood beneath, but it was a common jakes all the same. Beneath the hole was a chamber pot that Will would have to empty, after he'd shown its contents to one of the royal physicians.

As groom of the stool, Will was the king's most intimate body servant, and his most trusted. Gifts of property and generous annuities had accumulated at a steady pace over the last few years. In addition, Will controlled the king's privy purse. It was an honor, he reminded himself, to serve the king, even in such a menial capacity. Besides, when His Grace was constipated, as he was this morning, he was inclined to share his thoughts. That gave Will additional opportunities to exert an influence over the king's decisions.

"Shall I send for sweet butter, Your Grace?" Will asked.

King Henry made a face. Rancid butter, especially when mixed with buckthorn seeds, was a sovereign remedy for what ailed him, but the effects of the cure were usually more unpleasant than the original condition. "We will wait awhile," he decreed. "In the meantime, I need distraction."

"Shall I send for my lute?" Will asked. "Or order your musicians to play in the adjoining chamber?"

"Talk will provide sufficient diversion."

Will did not care for the way His Grace was looking at him. Those small blue-gray eyes had narrowed to slits and a slight smile curved the royal lips.

"Tell me about your latest conquests," the king commanded.

Henry Tudor had long taken a prurient interest in the amorous adventures of his friends. Although, at present, the King of England was among the most intelligent men in the known world, skilled in languages and music and renowned for his athletic prowess, and these days had no shortage of women willing to couple with him—and would not have had such a shortage, even if he had not been the king—the many years during which his father had kept him close, never letting him experience life for himself, had left their mark. In his youth, he had been forbidden to experience the joys of the flesh firsthand. He'd taken vicarious pleasure in listening to tales of the erotic exploits of those who served him. Demanding explicit details from his friends had since become his habit.

"I do not wish to bore you, Your Grace," Will said.

"No willing wench in your bed these days, eh? No luck with the beauteous Lady Anne?"

One did not refuse to answer his sovereign's question, no matter how personal. "She flirts with me, as ever she did, but the only man she allows to touch her is her husband."

Five years earlier, Will had admired Lady Anne. Since her return to court, he'd been even more powerfully drawn to her. This time around, his interest had not been at all casual. Not on his part. To his own chagrin, Will had discovered that he had deep feelings for her.

"She reminds me that both of us are married," he added.

"Marriage should not stop a man from taking a mistress, but perhaps you would do better to find yourself one who is young and malleable."

The king smiled, clearly thinking of the plump, pretty blonde who warmed his bed. Bessie Blount adored her royal lover.

"I should like nothing better, sire, but I fear I have fallen in love with Lady Anne. I care more for her happiness than for my own satisfaction."

King Henry laughed out loud. "Love is naught but a passing fancy. Make her your mistress and that will soon disabuse you of the notion that her wishes are more important than your own."

"No doubt you are right, Your Grace, but at present the lady is decidedly unwilling."

"Are you so certain of that?" The king's grin widened. "Have you not seen the way she looks at you? She will be more than willing, Will, if you catch her alone at the right time and in the right place."

The king might have said more, but at that moment there was a tap at the door. At King Henry's gesture, Will slipped out of the stool room and into the connecting bedchamber. Ned Neville waited impatiently on the other side of the door.

"This is not a good time to disturb His Grace," Will warned, but even as he spoke his sharp hearing picked up a grunt of relief. "Perhaps in a moment," he amended. Then he took note of his friend's expression. "What news, Ned?"

"Nothing unexpected, and yet I wonder what it portends. Word has just come from Rome. Thomas Wolsey, our own beloved Archbishop of York, has been elected to the Sacred College. He is now a cardinal of the Church of Rome."

"Wolsey." On Will's lips, the name became a curse.

From a minor appointment as one of the royal chaplains at the start of the reign, Thomas Wolsey had risen to become one of the most powerful men in the land. The king trusted him. Indeed, he relied upon Wolsey to handle all the dull, day-to-day matters involved in running the kingdom.

Wolsey might be a churchman, but he was no saint. He had a mistress and two children. And he amassed wealth as greedily as any secular gentleman. In the spring, he had started constructing a redbrick, double courtyard house at Hampton, fifteen miles from Westminster. Archbishops were entitled to palaces, it was true, but this building appeared likely to rival Greenwich or Richmond when it was complete. And it was not as if the man did not already have a fine house in Westminster. York Place had been suitable for an archbishop before Wolsey took up residence there. Since then he had built a new chapel and a massive great hall and made other improvements, as well.

"One more reason for him to lord it over the rest of us," Will grumbled.

Soon—very soon—he would have to make a decision. He could wholeheartedly support Wolsey, or he could openly ally himself with the man but covertly oppose him. There would be considerable irony involved if he took the latter course. Should he choose it, he would be climbing into bed with a Stafford, but it would not be the luscious Lady Anne. Will would have to form an alliance with her brother, the Duke of Buckingham.

39

ourtiers crowded the docks at Deptford, a little upstream from Greenwich Palace, eager to follow the king and queen aboard the ship Queen Catherine had just christened *The Virgin Mary*. Lady Anne hung back, feeling slightly queasy even though she still stood on solid ground.

She was thinking of finding her horse and returning to Greenwich, rather than join the rest of the court on board for a feast and an inaugural sail, when a familiar figure appeared beside her. Robert Gilbert, once her brother's chaplain and now his chancellor, was the most trusted man in the Duke of Buckingham's service. Anne had heard that he was in London, buying up great quantities of cloth of gold, cloth of silver, and silk. Given Edward's love of fine clothing, that news had not surprised her. Edward owned one purple satin doublet that was decorated with gilt spangles, little golden bells, and appliquéd antelopes and swans made of fine gold bullion.

She looked around for her brother but did not see him. That did surprise her, since it seemed to her that every other nobleman in the kingdom was present. Her gaze rested briefly on the Duke of Suffolk and his wife. The king's sister was glowing, obviously well content with her second marriage. She had the best of all possible worlds, Anne thought.

She had wed a man of her own choosing, one with whom she was in love, *and* she'd kept the title Queen of France from her first, arranged marriage.

"A word, my lady?" Gilbert's black eyes bored into her, demanding her cooperation.

"I've time for little more than that," she warned him.

"His Grace the duke wishes you to send word to him at Thornbury," he said quickly, "should you hear any news of Archbishop Warham."

"What sort of news?" In addition to being Archbishop of Canterbury, William Warham was Lord Chancellor. He was also a dull old stick.

"There are rumors afoot that he may resign his post. He is said to be weary of public life. If the chancellorship goes to Cardinal Wolsey, Wolsey will have unprecedented power for a man without a drop of royal blood in his veins. By adding Lord Chancellor to his other offices, he will be able to run roughshod over the royal household, the Privy Council, and Parliament, too."

Anne grew tired of hearing about the upstart cardinal. He was supposed to have begun life as the son of a butcher. Whether that was fact or fiction she had no way of knowing, but she did not hold it against him if it was true. Many poor boys made something of themselves through advancement in the church.

"Leave me out of the duke's schemes, I pray you," she said wearily. "Go back to your cloth buying." Had she not told Edward that she would not spy for him? As usual, her brother had not listened to a single word she'd said.

Gilbert's pockmarked face took on a look of deep consternation. "What do you know of my mission in London, my lady?"

"I know nothing, nor do I wish to."

But Gilbert's reaction made her wonder if there was more to his shopping spree than the duke's desire to dress himself in the finest and most costly fabrics. Expensive cloth could also be used as a gift, or rather for a bribe, but who did Edward wish to keep sweet? And why?

"Where is my brother?" she asked as Gilbert started to turn away.

"Why, at Thornbury, Lady Anne. Where else should His Grace be?" Gilbert seemed genuinely surprised by her question.

Relieved that no new encounter with Edward was imminent, Anne dismissed her brother's man and returned her attention to the ship. She could see the king on the deck, dressed in a sailor's coat and breeches of cloth of gold. He intended to pilot *The Virgin Mary* himself, taking her down the Thames to the sea. If appearances were anything to go by, King Henry thought the only skill required for this task, aside from dressing the part, was the ability to blow the large gold whistle he wore around his neck. This he did, loudly and repeatedly, to call the members of his party aboard. Anne hoped that more experienced sailors were standing by, to keep His Grace from running the ship aground on her maiden voyage.

Anne hurried up the ramp just as a crew from the dockyard came out to remove it. She was resigned to enduring the voyage. At least it would be blessedly short.

The Virgin Mary was enormous, requiring 120 oars to power her when she was not under sail. She had been designed to carry a thousand men and two hundred big guns. Anne had assumed, given the size of the vessel, that the ride downriver would be smooth. She soon discovered that she was mistaken.

A dizzying combination of smells rose up to taunt her from tables spread with the rich food prepared for the king's feast. The aromas did not mix well with the sway of the ship. Queen Catherine was the first to retire to a cabin, followed soon after by the Queen of France. On unsteady legs, Anne made her way to the nearest rail. She did not feel an enclosed space would suit her just now. She stared at the passing shoreline, hoping that by watching a fixed point she could persuade her roiling stomach to settle.

Will Compton found her there a few minutes later. "Lady Anne?" He sounded concerned. "Are you ill?"

"The chop of the waves is . . . unfortunate."

"I know a sovereign remedy for seasickness."

"I fear you cannot cure what ails me, Sir William. In common with Queen Catherine and the Duchess of Suffolk, I am breeding."

She glanced up in time to surprise a peculiar expression on his face.

"What are you thinking?" she asked. She did not know why, but she suddenly felt it was crucial that he answer her.

"I was wishing the child were mine," he said bluntly.

She should have been offended. Strangely, she was not, but she was puzzled. She knew well enough that Will Compton would have liked to bed her. There was nothing new in that. In truth, he had told her that he desired her so many times that she'd become inured to his claims of undying devotion, just as she'd grown accustomed to the harmless flirtation they'd resumed upon her return to court. She enjoyed his company and knew he enjoyed hers.

But there was something different about this declaration, something that suggested his feelings for her might go far deeper than she'd imagined. Anne's gloved hands gripped harder on the painted rail in front of her. She did not know what to say. How could she engage in lighthearted banter with him if he truly meant what he'd so often said to her—that he was in love with her?

"Will you return to Leicestershire?" he asked after a long, strained silence.

"No." In that matter, she had taken a firm stand with George. "I will travel no farther than Stoke Poges, and only retire there at the last."

"Good," Will said. "I would rather have you here and out of my reach than not have any sight of you at all. Now, come and try a bit of marmalade. It is marvelous good for settling a queasy stomach."

40

*L*ady Anne gave birth to a girl at Stoke Poges just three days after Queen Catherine's daughter, christened Mary after her father's sister, was born at Greenwich Palace. Lord Hastings chose to name his newest child Catherine.

Anne was anxious to return to court and planned to remain where she was only until her churching. For that month, she chose to remain indoors, not only because George insisted upon it, but also because the winter was uncommonly cold. Even inside the snug manor house, it was difficult to keep warm. Anne spent much of her time in the well-heated nursery and it was there that her mother-in-law, Lady Hungerford, located her on a blustery mid-afternoon in early March.

"Sir William Compton is here with a message from the king," she announced.

"Have you sent someone to find George?" Anne asked. Her husband had gone out on horseback early that morning, as he often did, to visit tenants and tend to estate business.

"Sir William asked for you." Lady Hungerford sent a disapproving look Anne's way. Until she'd been churched, a woman was not supposed to entertain anyone, let alone a gentleman. Only the fact that he'd come from court, apparently on official business, had persuaded George's mother to fetch Anne to him.

Puzzled, Anne followed the older woman into her private parlor, an upper chamber warmed by both hearth and brazier. It was filled with all manner of treasures, everything from reliquaries and crosses and jeweled caskets to elaborate, intricately made chamber clocks. George's mother had also indulged in the great extravagance of a carpet for the floor. In most houses, carpets were used only to cover tables.

Most of the rest of the females in the household were already there. They surrounded Will Compton, one of them helping him out of his snow-covered traveling cloak and all of them peppering him with questions. Everyone wanted to hear the latest news from court.

Will turned, smiling, as Anne entered the chamber. His bold gaze ran over her, as if to assess how much damage childbirth had done to her figure. What he saw appeared to please him and a mischievous glint came into his eyes. It was impossible not to respond to such obvious admiration, even with George's mother watching her every reaction.

"Lady Anne," Will said, bowing low and sweeping off his bonnet. "You are well, I trust?"

"Very well indeed, Sir William." She sent a servant for food and drink and stared at the waiting gentlewomen until they returned to the large embroidery frame where they had gathered to work on an altar cloth.

"I have a matter of some importance to discuss with Lady Anne on the king's behalf," Will announced. He glanced toward Lady Hungerford, still hovering nearby. "It is, for the moment, a matter that requires secrecy."

Lady Hungerford looked annoyed but, given no other choice, dutifully left the chamber, taking her women with her. Giggles and speculative backward glances accompanied their retreat. When Meriall brought wine and seed cakes, Anne seated herself at the small table where the tray had been placed and fixed her guest with a steely-eyed gaze. "My maidservant stays, for propriety." She'd learned that lesson a long time ago.

"As you wish." Will agreed so readily that she grew suspicious.

"I thought your mission demanded secrecy."

"I lied to rid us of Lady Hungerford's looming presence. Do you want me to call her back?"

Anne had to smile. Again. "No."

"Good." He sat opposite her, picked up his wine goblet, and took a sip of what Anne knew to be an excellent Burgundy. "You may have heard that the king's older sister, Queen Margaret of Scotland, fled her adopted homeland several months ago."

"She was regent of that country until she married a Scottish earl," Anne murmured, recalling what little she knew of the matter. "That turned the other noblemen against her. She must have feared for her life, poor woman. The Scots are a vicious people." Anne had never met Margaret Tudor, but since Will had been in her brother's service from an early age, he must have grown up with Her Grace.

"Queen Margaret," he said, "left England to marry the King of Scotland more than a dozen years ago. She did not have an easy time of it. Although her royal husband did his duty and she duly gave birth to an heir to the Scottish throne, King James was not faithful to her, or even kind. Nor did he care much for the treaty with England their marriage was intended to seal. When we went to war with France three years ago, and King Henry and his army were occupied across the Narrow Seas, James followed a long-standing tradition and invaded England from the north. He was slain in battle at a place called Flodden Field. The new king is not old enough to rule and will not be for some years to come."

Anne listened to this recitation with growing impatience. She knew all this. "I do not need a history lesson, Sir William."

"Queen Margaret was breeding when she left Scotland. She tarried in the north of England to give birth to a daughter and now intends to travel south with that child, Lady Margaret Douglas. She wishes to visit her brother at court. King Henry has agreed. The queen's party will arrive at the beginning of May, but certain preparations must be made first. That is where the king needs your help."

"I, too, serve at the will and pleasure of the king." Mirroring Will's movements, Anne sipped her wine.

"Queen Margaret will occupy Baynard's Castle during her sojourn in the south of England. It is His Grace's wish that you prepare it to receive the queen. You are to take whatever is needed from the royal wardrobe of beds, and order provisions, as well."

Anne frowned. "The king has household officers to attend to such matters. Why does His Grace choose to entrust the details to me?" The officers of the wardrobe and their assistants were accustomed to traveling ahead of King Henry when he went on progress, specifically to prepare houses along the way for royal occupation.

"Perhaps the king thinks this occasion requires a woman's touch."

"Even so, why mine? Surely the queen has someone among her ladies who might better undertake the task."

"Your London house is in Thames Street, hard by Baynard's Castle. Do not quibble, Anne. To be sought out for such a duty is a great honor."

She selected a seed cake and nibbled. After the enforced boredom of her lying in, she could not help but respond to the challenge, and it would be delightful to furnish an entire palace at the king's expense. "I would need assistants," she said aloud.

Compton set aside his goblet and leaned closer. "There will be someone living in Baynard's Castle to help with furnishing and provisioning the place. One of the king's most trusted gentlemen has been assigned to serve you in any way that you require."

And suddenly it all made sense. "You?"

He grinned at her. "Your humble servant, my lady."

"George will not be pleased."

"I believe His Grace said something about requiring Lord Hastings's presence at court."

"I am certain that even if he is living at Greenwich or Richmond, my husband will manage frequent visits to London." Anne spoke in her most repressive voice.

"I thought you objected to being kept prisoner."

Anne felt her face grow warm and hastily took another swallow of wine.

"You are a miracle, Lady Anne," Will said in a low, husky voice. "You have a bloom in your cheeks and a bounce in your step. Dare I hope my presence accounts for a small portion of your response?"

Disconcerted by the intimacy of the moment and her own reaction to it—an intense and unsettling desire to move closer to Will Compton—Anne abruptly stood.

Will also rose, but was considerate enough to keep his distance. "It is the king's wish that you prepare Baynard's Castle, but you may refuse."

"As I tried to refuse him once before?"

The irritation in her voice surprised a quick grin out of him. "Even so."

Anne drew in a strengthening breath. One did not say no to the king without good reason, but she was under no obligation to act upon the physical pull she felt toward Will Compton, no matter how compelling it seemed at this moment. When she had performed this task for His Grace, she would return to court, with George, and reap the rewards of royal gratitude.

"Tell His Grace that I will take up residence at Hastings House on the last day of March," she said. "That will give me a full month to prepare Baynard's Castle for Queen Margaret's arrival."

41

Baynard's Castle, London, April 1, 1516

ill Compton welcomed Lady Anne into Baynard's Castle wearing a wide grin. "Do you really need two chaperones?" he teased her.

"I do not need even one. I am perfectly capable of resisting your crude blandishments on my own."

"Alas, how well I know it. But why, then, did you move into Hastings House with both Lady Hungerford and her mother in tow?"

"For the pleasure of their company," Anne assured him in lofty tones. They had entered the great hall and her words echoed in the huge, open space. Empty, the place had a bleak and disused appearance.

"Well," Will said, "since it appears you are gifted with their presence, you may as well take advantage of their expertise. Lord Hastings's grandmother should have knowledge of Queen Margaret's likes and dislikes. As I recall, she knew the queen well before Her Grace's marriage."

"She did," Anne agreed, "and relishes telling stories of her days in the household of Queen Elizabeth of York, Queen Margaret's mother. At first, from the way she spoke, I assumed that she was still the unmarried daughter of the Earl of Northumberland at the time. But when I gave the matter closer thought, I realized that she had, in fact, been twice widowed by the time she became part of the court of King Henry the Seventh."

Will chuckled. "She scandalized the entire court by taking Hugh Vaughan as her third husband. True, he was a champion jouster, but he had no title. As yet, he had not even been knighted."

"That does not mean she *approves* of scandal," Anne admonished him, and produced a list of the many things that needed to be done to make Baynard's Castle ready for Queen Margaret's arrival.

During the days that followed, Anne and Will established a surprisingly good working relationship. She could not help but enjoy his company, especially since, aside from the occasional suggestive remark, he was a model of propriety. By the second week she had stopped being nervous around him and was able to give herself over to her enjoyment of the task of decorating one of the king's houses.

Baynard's Castle had been renovated by King Henry the Seventh to remove fortifications and make it more comfortable as a dwelling. It boasted two octagonal towers, one of which contained the privy lodgings. It also had its own watergate, a cobbled courtyard, and a large walled garden. Just to the north, and most convenient from which to transport furnishings, was the royal wardrobe of beds, where all manner of household furnishings were stored.

Anne paused on one bright morning to look out over the city toward the redbrick walls rising at Bridewell, the palace the king intended to replace the burned-out shell of Westminster Palace. Ever since a fire had destroyed most of that ancient edifice, the court had been obliged to use the Archbishop of Canterbury's palace at Lambeth as a London residence. The many offices that had once been located in Westminster had been moved to temporary quarters constructed on the green in the Tower of London.

"Building at Bridewell does not seem to progress very rapidly," she remarked to Will when he came up beside her to see what had caught her attention.

"Cardinal Wolsey is in charge of the construction. Since he is using some of the same men and materials to renovate his own house of York Place, which is building apace, Bridewell feels the neglect."

Anne heard the derision in his voice. Her brother spoke in the same way of the cardinal. "Is Wolsey grown so very powerful that he can neglect the king's interests in favor of his own?"

"Some think so. They may be right."

"Is he . . . a friend of yours?"

Will's expression hardened. "We understand one another."

Anne started to ask another question, then stopped herself. She had no wish to become involved in a discussion of politics. Neither did she wish to seem to favor any faction at court. When she returned there, it would be to enjoy its pleasures and pastimes and the company of her husband, not to indulge in intrigue.

As for Cardinal Wolsey, she winced to recall that she had once bared her soul to him. In a letter written from Ashby de la Zouch when she was at her most vulnerable, she had detailed her mistreatment at Littlemore Priory and revealed the prioress's lack of chastity, too. The only result of this outpouring had been a curt reply, dictated to a secretary, telling her Wolsey would take the matter under advisement. Nothing, so far as Anne could tell, had ever been done to investigate the priory, nor had there been any repercussions for the mighty Duke of Buckingham.

Over time, Anne's desire for revenge had faded, but she could not help but resent Thomas Wolsey's attitude in taking her complaints so lightly. She had no desire to have any further dealings with the priest who was now a cardinal.

42

Lordship House, Tottenham, May 3, 1516

When all was in readiness to receive Queen Margaret, Lady Anne received her reward. First she would join the king to greet his sister just outside London. She would ride into the city with them to escort Her Grace to Baynard's Castle. Once that task was complete, she would be reinstated at court as a member of Queen Catherine's household. She and George had already been assigned one of the double lodgings at Greenwich.

Anne had missed her husband, especially during the long, lonely nights at Hastings House. During the days, Will Compton had distracted her. Once or twice, to her chagrin, she had caught herself wondering what it would be like to have him warm her bed. She had firmly resisted the temptation to find out, but she was very aware of his eyes upon her as she entered the great hall of his house in Tottenham.

"Sir William," she exclaimed, her gaze going unerringly to the shadowy corner where he stood, "I had no idea this was such a magnificent establishment." The moated manor house, situated a half day's ride from London, appeared to have been newly renovated.

Will came toward them, on the surface paying equal attention to each of the noble ladies in Anne's party and greeting their husbands with equal animation. But before long he attempted to draw her away from the others for a private word. He was not successful. George kept pace with them, one hand possessively gripping Anne's elbow as they walked.

"I acquired this property two years ago," Will said, "along with two other manors in Tottenham—rewards for my service to King Henry. I had the newest sections rebuilt in brick, the same building material I am using in the construction at Compton Wynyates. Is the place worthy to receive a queen, do you think?"

"Entirely suitable for royalty," Anne assured him.

"Since Queen Margaret will not be staying here," George Hastings said, "the condition of the house matters little."

"George," Anne chided him. "How can you say that? Her Grace travels with her six-month-old daughter. Accommodations at any place she stops to rest, whether for an hour or a month, are most important." She gave a light, nervous laugh. "Why else should I have spent so much time of late making certain all is in readiness for her at Baynard's Castle?"

"Why indeed," George asked, and glowered darkly at Will.

"Cry peace, Hastings," Will said in a low voice. "The king does not desire enmity between us."

"Then His Grace should not have tried to separate me from my wife."

"Stop it. Both of you." Irritated, Anne stepped between them. "No matter what the king's intention, I did naught during the last few weeks but furnish rooms for his sister."

Will sighed. "She is telling you the truth, Hastings. Much to my regret, I admit. You are married to a paragon of virtue. A pity you cannot appreciate that."

"You dare—!"

"George!" This time, Anne got a good grip on *his* arm. She hauled him away into a window embrasure. "You claim to trust me," she hissed at him.

"I do. It is Compton I cannot put my faith in, especially when he has no less a personage than the king playing matchmaker for him."

"With all these people about, I believe I am safe from any acts of impropriety."

Looking a bit sheepish, George conceded her point.

"Then permit me to speak with him for a few moments alone. You may glare at us from the opposite side of the chamber if you like, but keep your distance. This is neither the time nor the place for a brawl."

"George Hastings does not deserve you," Will said when she reached him. "I would trade all I have for such a wife."

"Stop your nonsense!" Anne snapped at him. "We've no time for it, not with Queen Margaret due to arrive at any moment." Her Grace had been staying the last few nights at Sir Thomas Lovell's house in Enfield and that was but a short ride from Tottenham.

Will did not touch her, did not even stand close to her—there were too many people watching them—but his voice dropped to a lower pitch that compelled her attention. "If I do not say this now, I may never have the chance again, and I want you to know how I feel about you, Anne. Even when you were great with another man's child, I could not stop myself from thinking about you, longing for you. No other woman will ever mean as much to me as you do."

Anne squeezed her eyes shut and shook her head from side to side in denial. Perversely, this seemed to encourage him.

"You do not strike me, or scream, or—worse—mock me. I believe that is because you feel what I feel. Perhaps you already love me, although surely not as much as I love you."

Anne's eyes popped open. "Stop, I beg you. I love George."

"Perhaps you do, but you have always had feelings for me, too."

She swallowed convulsively and clasped her hands in front of her to still their trembling. "For pity's sake, Will, speak no more of this. Do you want me to be sent back to Littlemore Priory?"

Startled by the suggestion that she might be imprisoned again, he took a step back. Anne inhaled deeply, struggling to rein in her emotions. She had barely regained her composure when the fanfare sounded to announce the arrival of the Queen of Scots. Her opportunity to speak privately with Will was at an end. George reappeared at her elbow and they went outside.

Queen Margaret was dressed in fine clothing—supplied by her brother—and accompanied by a number of ladies and gentlewomen. The nursery staff followed. Anne heard the wails of an unhappy baby inside an ornate litter.

"It is a delight to see you again, Your Grace," Will greeted the woman who dismounted in his courtyard. He wore a fixed smile on his face and Anne was grateful that their years at court had taught them both how to school their features.

In the years she had been in Scotland, Margaret Tudor had grown old and stout. The beauty of her youth had fled, and with it had gone the carefree girl Will remembered. This Margaret was frightened, Anne realized, and trying not to show it. She had no idea what kind of reception to expect from her brother the king.

"Master Compton, is it not?" she asked. Her voice was sweet and low and much like that of her younger sister, Mary.

"Sir William Compton these days, Your Grace, but still at your service."

His courtliness seemed to bolster the queen's confidence. Anne knew all too well the effect it had on most women. Then it was time to come forward and be presented. She firmly pushed all personal thoughts of Will Compton to the back of her mind.

When the queen's party had refreshed themselves, they set out again. This time Queen Margaret was mounted on a snow-white palfrey sent to her by Queen Catherine. A series of signals had been arranged to assure that King Henry and the lords and ladies he'd brought with him would reach the market cross in Tottenham at the same time that his sister, approaching from the opposite direction, arrived there. Their carefully staged public reunion went off without a hitch. Then, riding together, they set out for London, some eight miles distant.

The noblemen accompanying the king vied with one another for attention, both in dress and in the number of attendants they brought with them. Liveried retinues were the order of the day, from the king's own servants in Tudor green and white to Anne's brother's men in their red and black livery with the silver Stafford knot as a badge. The retainers of the Marquess of Dorset and of each earl and baron had their own distinctive colors. Riding all together, they made a splendid sight.

Crowds gathered all along the way, appreciative of the display and cheering for the king and his sister. Margaret insisted upon stopping every time a child appeared carrying flowers to present to her. As a result, it was late afternoon before they made their triumphal entry into the city, and nearly six in the evening before they arrived at Baynard's Castle, where a late supper awaited them. That meal marked the end of Anne's responsibilities, but the entire month of May was to be spent in feasting, jousting, and pageantry at court. Anne intended to enjoy every moment of it.

43

Manor of the Rose, London, May 16, 1516

George Hastings, disinclined to enjoy the afternoon's entertainment, nevertheless pasted a smile on his face and applauded when the eight players and a boy took their bows. They had acted in something called *The Four Elements*, which had included music and dance, but George had been too preoccupied with his own thoughts to pay much attention to the story.

He told himself that he should be glad of the respite of a day spent in London, as he found it well nigh intolerable living at court. True, he had his wife in his bed every night, but during the day she laughed and flirted with other men, just as she always had, and Will Compton was always among them, lapping up her smiles. Realizing that he'd clenched both his fists and his teeth, he forced himself to relax, but the tension that rode him, day and night, did not lessen one whit.

He heartily wished the Duke of Buckingham would come to the point. George's brother-in-law had not extended this invitation to dine for no reason. Buckingham never did anything without having two or three purposes in mind. The fact that he'd included George's stepfather, Sir Richard Sacheverell, in the invitation only heightened the likelihood that the duke was up to something.

George's best guess was that it had to do with the Earl of

Northumberland. The earl had recently spent twelve days in the Fleet Prison before being released and fined ten thousand pounds—an impossible amount!—for illegally keeping more retainers in livery than were permitted by law. Two days ago, Northumberland had met with the king in His Grace's privy chamber. George did not know what had been said there, but the earl had emerged looking relieved and had immediately set off for his properties in the north.

After the entertainment was over, the other gentlemen in the dinner party began to drift away to their own houses, but Buckingham indicated that he wished George and Sir Richard to linger. "Let us go out into the garden," the duke suggested.

It was more private there than indoors, shielded as it was on the one side by the hill leading up to the church of St. Laurence Pountney. Buckingham, with uncharacteristic familiarity, took each man by an arm and led them deeper into the concealing shrubbery.

"I sent for you two to let you know a part of my mind. My last day at court, my lord cardinal and I chanced to sit together without any others nearby. He broached the idea that I should send for my son, Lord Stafford, to come to court and become acquainted with the king and the queen."

George lifted an eyebrow at this. "Your Grace has but one son."

"So I told Cardinal Wolsey. And I reminded him that the boy is not yet wed nor a father. With the contagion lately spreading through the land, I would not risk him for the world."

Sacheverell started to speak, perhaps to remind the duke that the contagion Buckingham spoke of appeared to have been—God be praised!—confined to Nottinghamshire and a bit of Derbyshire. But Buckingham was already speaking again and neither George nor Sacheverell cared to interrupt.

"Wolsey seized on that, taking my words to mean that once young Henry had a wife and child I would no longer object to his coming to court." The duke plucked a rose and with a savage flick of one finger, beheaded it.

"Had he suggestions in mind?" George asked.

"Oh, yes. The first was the daughter of the Countess of Salisbury. That was a test, I think. Why should Wolsey wish to see two strains of royal blood combine?" Once again, he did not give either man time to comment. "A moment later, as if struck all of a sudden by the thought, Wolsey proposed that my son wed the Earl of Shrewsbury's daughter, Mary Talbot."

"Another trap?" George asked. "Shrewsbury and Northumberland have all but completed plans for a betrothal between Lady Mary and Northumberland's heir, Lord Henry Percy."

"And if it was Wolsey who contrived Northumberland's arrest, he may wish to thwart any alliance between the two greatest magnates in the north."

George sent a quick glance in Sacheverell's direction. They had both served under Shrewsbury at the Battle of the Spurs and neither would willingly cause the earl any trouble.

"Wolsey asked me if I knew what Shrewsbury's plans were for the marriage of his son and heir," Buckingham continued. "I replied that I did not, but that I was certain the earl would never marry off his son without the advice of the king's grace. 'Why, my lord,' Wolsey said then, 'this I dare promise you, that if my lord Shrewsbury were here, the king's grace would speak to him with all his heart on your behalf. And if he does not come soon to court, His Grace will write to him and bid him come thither without delay. It is the king's wish to see you two knit together. And this shall I say, that if you vary in anything the king shall give the stroke betwixt you himself.' And with that, my lord the cardinal left me alone to ponder all he'd said."

So that was why they had been invited to dine, George thought. Buckingham wished to use their connection to Shrewsbury to propose a marriage alliance between the Staffords and the Talbots. George wanted no part of it, most especially if Wolsey was behind it. But it puzzled him that Buckingham did not appear to be more suspicious of the cardinal's motives.

"Here is what I propose," the duke said, drawing Sacheverell down onto a bench under a secluded arbor. "There should be cross marriages between my son and the earl's daughter and the earl's son and my daughter. I ask that you, Sir Richard, since you are one of Shrewsbury's regular correspondents, should write to his lordship on my behalf, to sound out his feelings on the matter. You may tell him that I will ask a thousand marks less as a dowry from him than I would from anyone else. I will tarry in London and not depart for Thornbury until I have his reply. Or better yet, let him come here in person to discuss the matter."

Wolsey wanted Shrewsbury in London, George thought—perhaps so he could be arrested and charged, as Northumberland had been, with illegal retaining. Or else so he could be forced to agree to the marriage alliance Wolsey wanted. Either way, the journey would not end well for the earl.

Buckingham sent a sly glance George's way. "It would be useful, Hastings, if Sir Richard could convey your endorsement of the plan to the earl in his letter."

Sacheverell dutifully promised to write to his lordship as soon as he returned to his lodgings, but George managed to avoid committing himself. A short time later, the two men left the Manor of the Rose to walk to George's house in Thames Street, located just across from Paul's Wharf.

The Queen of Scotland had left Baynard's Castle for Greenwich, where tournaments in her honor would begin in two days' time. The neighborhood had an empty feel to it that suited George's sour mood.

"I suppose I must write to the earl," Sacheverell muttered once they'd made themselves comfortable in one of the smaller chambers where the fire, ready laid, did not take long to catch. Although it was mid-May, the cold of winter still clung to houses near the riverfront.

George gave the embers a last stir and, satisfied it would soon warm them, returned the poker to its rack, put the fire screen in place, and crossed to a cushioned chair near the writing table where Sacheverell sat toying with quill and inkpot. "It must be Shrewsbury's desire to ally himself with Northumberland that prompted the cardinal's suggestion. Rumor says that Wolsey is the one who contrived to have the earl arrested. Perhaps, had Shrewsbury not fallen ill of the contagion, he'd have ended up in the Fleet, as well."

"But why? The charge of retaining made against Northumberland had no true merit. Everyone has men in livery." He laughed. "Even I do, for my servants wear your mother's badge."

One of George's retainers arrived at that moment, bearing wine and an assortment of nuts and cheeses. He delayed his reply until he and Sacheverell were alone again, sipping from goblets filled with Rhenish wine. The fire crackled merrily in the background.

"Money," he said succinctly. "Even if the fine levied against Northumberland is reduced, it will still bring a huge sum into the royal treasury, and Wolsey is the one who has charge of finances. The king is too busy with pageants and tournaments to oversee such petty details."

Sacheverell looked thoughtful. "I wonder if there is more to it than that? Northumberland has not been particularly effective in controlling disturbances on the border with Scotland. And it is clear that neither the king nor the cardinal trusts him. Why else question him about plans for his son's marriage?"

"Was he asked about that during his examination before the Star Chamber?"

Sacheverell took another swallow of wine and watched George over the rim. "He was questioned privately, too, by Sir William Compton on behalf of the king."

"Compton and Wolsey," George muttered. "Strange bedfellows, and yet they are reputed to be great friends these days. Plotting together, no doubt."

"No stranger that Wolsey and Buckingham, and they, too, seem to be working in concert."

George's sympathy lay with Northumberland, who was, after all, his cousin. That the earl was also one of Buckingham's brothers-in-law had not seemed to sway the duke. That was hardly surprising. For all his claims to act in the best interests of his entire family, Buckingham looked out for his own interests first.

"What do you hear from Worksop?" he asked Sacheverell.

"Shrewsbury has taken the precaution of sending all his horse keepers away and turning his horses to grass, but no one has fallen ill there for five or six weeks now, and there have been no new deaths."

"It might be best not to tell the king that. You know what a great fear His Grace has of any sickness. If he believes there remains any possibility of contagion, he will not want Shrewsbury anywhere near the court."

"But what of the duke's proposal? I have promised to suggest this double marriage alliance to the earl."

"Find a way to phrase it that will incline Shrewsbury to a cautious reply," George advised.

As Sacheverell began to pen a letter to the earl, George left his chair to stand beside the hearth. He felt uncommon chilled.

That both Sir William Compton and the Duke of Buckingham were in such favor with the cardinal disturbed him deeply. There was no love lost between the two of them and he knew just enough about the cardinal's machinations to be as wary of Wolsey as he was of the duke. There was no question in his mind but that the Earl of Shrewsbury should stay away from court. George heartily wished he could do likewise.

44

*T*he first day of the tournament in Margaret Tudor's honor, a Monday, dawned hot and dry. The display of pageantry was one of the finest Lady Anne had seen. The king himself led the challengers, along with the Duke of Suffolk, the Earl of Essex, and Sir Nicholas Carew. They and their horses were all in black velvet, decorated with branches of honeysuckle appliquéd in fine flat gold. The embroidery had been done in such a way that the leaves and branches appeared to move and shimmer in the sunlight.

Anne's eye was drawn first to the king and then to the dozen or more knights on horseback who were waiting in attendance. The knights were all dressed alike in blue velvet fringed with gold and wore identical blue velvet bonnets, but three figures stood out among them—George, George's old enemy, the Marquess of Dorset, and Sir William Compton. At the king's pleasure, they were compelled to work together as a team. Anne felt a sense of unease creep over her as she studied the three men. She could almost feel the tension bubbling just beneath the surface.

Fourteen trumpeters in blue sarcenet coats and blue hose and bonnets sounded the call to begin the tournament. Although Anne continued to keep a watchful eye on her husband and the other two men, nothing untoward occurred. When George returned to their lodgings that night, he had been gifted with the blue velvet bonnet and was in a cheerful frame of mind. The challengers had triumphed over the answerers in every event.

The second day of the tournament began in a fashion similar to the first, only this time the king, Suffolk, Essex, and Carew wore purple velvet embroidered with golden roses and rose leaves. Their mottos had been picked out in pure gold on the borders. The lords and knights were in yellow velvet, gored and guarded with cloth of gold, while the king's gentlemen wore yellow satin. The trumpeters were attired in yellow damask, with yellow bonnets and hose. The opposing team sported garments of white and gold.

Every eye fixed on the king as he unhorsed Sir William Kingston. But despite the cheering of the crowd and the exuberant spirits of the other ladies seated near her, Anne could not quite shake the uncomfortable feeling that all was not well. Again she sought her husband's familiar form among the king's men, and this time she saw that her instincts had been sound. He was turned in his saddle, watching a scuffle that had broken out near the colorful pavilions erected beside the tiltyard. Even at a distance, Anne recognized the livery of the men involved. Some wore George's colors and others had the badge of the Marquess of Dorset sewn onto their sleeves.

The skirmish did not last long, thanks to quick action by members of the royal household, but the damage had been done. Anne spent the rest of the tournament worrying that George would be held responsible for the exchange of blows. To fight at court in anything but a sporting competition was expressly forbidden. A man could lose a hand for striking another in the king's house.

Although there was a banquet in the queen's apartments after the tournament, Anne retired to her own lodgings instead and sat disconsolately before the cold hearth. When Will Compton appeared at her door, her first thought was that he'd come with word of George's arrest.

"I will stay only a moment," he promised, "while your husband is engaged in deep conversation with your brother."

"I have told you before that I will not lie with you." His persistence was wearying.

"Ah, yes. Because you have a husband and he is right here at court. And yet I live in hope."

She rolled her eyes heavenward. "Oh, do go away, Will. You can scarce expect me to take you into my bed when George is likely to walk in at any moment!"

"That is why I've brought you a substitute." He stepped back outside her door and returned a moment later with a basket. "One of my spaniels recently whelped."

The small, intriguing sounds coming from inside the container lured Anne closer. Big brown eyes in a furry white face looked up at her. A pink tongue darted out to lick the hand she'd not even been aware of extending. She blinked and stepped back. Following her movement, the puppy came up on its hind legs, dancing to keep its balance, and braced a pair of floppy front paws on the edge of the basket. When the little dog gave an excited yip, Anne's heart melted. She plucked the brown and white body out of the basket and held it against her chest. Warm and wiggly, determined to lick her face, it made her laugh out loud.

"Think of me when you hold her," Compton whispered, and left before she had gathered sufficient wit to thank him for the gift.

45

*D*espite Lady Anne's fears, the incident at the tournament had attracted little attention. Court gossip focused instead on the king's displeasure because the quality of the competition he'd faced on the second day had been so poor. His Grace had shattered five fewer lances than the Duke of Suffolk, a dismal performance, and afterward he'd vowed never to joust again unless it was against an opponent as good as himself.

At the end of May, giving every appearance of remaining high in the king's favor, the Duke of Buckingham left court. The Duke of Suffolk also retired to his country estates, taking his royal wife with him. Queen Margaret, in the meantime, moved from Baynard's Castle to Scotland Yard, the traditional lodging for Scots kings who visited England.

"What a waste of time it was to prepare Baynard's Castle for Her Grace's occupancy," Lady Anne complained to her maid.

"There were other benefits," Meriall reminded her as she continued to brush one of Anne's gowns.

"There were . . . distractions." Anne sighed. That was a good word for Will Compton, she decided. At times he was a welcome distraction, at others an annoying one. She turned to watch the little dog he had given her frisk across the floor of her lodgings at court. She'd named the spaniel Dancer and had found her to be a most engaging companion.

Anne had just scooped Dancer into her arms and was fending off a tongue eager to lick her face when Sir John Canne, the Hastings family chaplain, requested an audience. The look of agitation on his face alarmed her. He was ordinarily the most unemotional—and unsympathetic—of men.

"What is it, Sir John?" Anne asked, motioning for him to enter her inner chamber.

"Lord Hastings sent me to warn you, my lady. Perhaps it is nothing, but, well . . ."

"Spit it out, man."

Impatient, she handed Dancer to Meriall and crossed the room to confront the chaplain. He was a little man with deep bags under his eyes and an air of defeat in the best of times. Now he looked as if he'd just lost his last friend. Eye to eye with him, Anne fixed him with a withering look and waited for an answer.

He stammered as he told her that both George and Sir Richard Sacheverell had been summoned before the Privy Council in the Star Chamber. "The name derives from the fact that the ceiling in the chamber in which it first met, back in the reign of Henry the Seventh, had stars painted on the ceiling," he added, as if Anne might care.

"This is most alarming," Anne conceded, "but not disastrous. The Privy Council investigates matters on behalf of the king, but it is not a court of law."

"Perhaps not," Canne said, "but it was the Star Chamber that examined the Earl of Northumberland, after which he was imprisoned in the Fleet."

"Of what is my husband accused?"

"I do not know, my lady. But he was told to bring with him a list of every servant in livery who was with him at the time of the Scottish queen's arrival."

"Illegal retaining, then," Anne said. "Just like Northumberland."

It was an easy charge to make against anyone who maintained a household of any size and it was usually unfounded. No nobleman she knew of wished to raise a private army for any reason, let alone to use against the Crown. Armies were too expensive to maintain.

"Why George?" she murmured, more to herself than to the priest. "And why now?" A charge of illegal retaining usually resulted in a ruinous fine, but George was not particularly wealthy. He had been the one to borrow money from the king a few years back, not the other way around.

"There is something else that is most peculiar," Canne ventured.

"What is that?"

"The Marquess of Dorset, the Earl of Surrey, and Lord Bergavenny were put out of the council chamber just after the Star Chamber began its session."

Peculiar indeed, Anne thought. Why those three? Dorset would have been glad to see any member of the Hastings family in trouble, but Surrey was married to Anne's niece and might be inclined to support a kinsman. She frowned over Bergavenny's name. He was Ned Neville's older brother, and Ned was close friends with Will Compton. What did that signify? Perhaps nothing. She hoped it was nothing. She did not like the thought that Will might somehow be behind George's troubles.

She waited with growing anxiety for her husband's return and knew the moment he walked into their lodgings that her worries had been justified. George's face wore a haggard look that tugged at her heart. She hastily poured a cup of wine and brought it to him.

George accepted the offering and drank deeply, draining the goblet before he handed it back to her. "Sir John told you where I was?"

"He did. What happened, George? Why were you summoned?"

"Both Sir Richard and I are charged with illegal retaining. The case will be heard before the King's Bench. A court of law," he added, in case she was not familiar with the name.

"But you have done nothing wrong!"

His short bark of laughter told her how little that mattered.

"And if they find you guilty? What then?"

"'If'? Say rather 'when.' A fine, no doubt, similar to the one levied against the Earl of Northumberland."

"But we do not have ten thousand pounds!"

"Neither did Northumberland." George ran the fingers of one hand through his dark brown hair, leaving tufts standing on end. "I fear I may have made matters worse for myself. When I first arrived, Dorset could not resist making a snide remark. I lost my temper with him. I came within a hair's breadth of attacking him bodily. If Sacheverell had not held me back—"

"Oh, George! How could you?"

"I lost my head. I admit it." Showing a renewed spark of anger, this time directed at her, he stalked to the table where the wine was kept and refilled his goblet.

"But . . . but I thought Dorset was put out of the Privy Council."

"He was. *After* we nearly came to blows."

"And Surrey? Bergavenny?"

George just shook his head. "I wish I knew, just as I wish I knew what was behind this. The charges of retaining cannot have been made because my men and Dorset's had an altercation at the tournament. Nothing was said about that. And I am not powerful enough to be a threat to the king."

"The king," Anne said carefully, "allows those he trusts to make some decisions for him."

George frowned. "Wolsey?"

She nodded, but she was thinking that Will Compton was such another. Her gaze slid to the little spaniel sleeping on a cushion in the corner of the room. Either man might be complicit in George's troubles.

"Christ aid!" George exclaimed. "That has to be it!"

Startled by his vehemence, Anne stared at him. "What does? What have you remembered?"

He told her then, for the first time, of an after-dinner conversation with her brother that had taken place a fortnight earlier. "Sacheverell duly wrote to the Earl of Shrewsbury, proposing the cross weddings, but he worded his letter so as to warn the earl not to come to court unless he was prepared to fall in with all of the cardinal's plans. As Shrewsbury is set upon a marriage between his daughter and Northumberland's son, he has wisely stayed put, insisting that he is still too ill to travel."

"How could Wolsey know that you and Sir Richard acted to thwart his plans?"

"The man has spies everywhere, and so does your brother, who is hand in glove with him in this matter."

Anne opened her mouth to protest, then closed it again. Edward was, most conveniently, on his way to Thornbury, safe from accusation and from any taint attached to having yet another brother-in-law accused of illegal retaining.

George's theory seemed to satisfy him and it spared Anne the necessity of offering an alternative. She kept the possibility that Will Compton might be involved to herself, hoping she was wrong.

Another two weeks passed with excruciating slowness. Watching George wait and worry wrenched at Anne's heart. The only bright spot during that time was that the Marquess of Dorset was also charged with illegal retaining, along with Lord Bergavenny and Sir Edward Guildford.

"The Star Chamber must be trying to show how unbiased they are in meting out justice," George sneered.

They were still awaiting word of George's sentence, expecting a fine but fearing that a cell in the Fleet or in the Tower might also be in his future, when Anne was summoned to the queen's apartments.

Queen Catherine had done her best to ignore Anne's presence at court and her attendance on ceremonial occasions, but now she looked at her directly, leaning a little forward in her chair of estate, as if she wished to commit every detail of Anne's appearance to memory. Anne rose from a deep curtsey with her heart in her throat. For once, she did not manage to show a calm exterior. She felt beads of sweat pop out on her forehead and knew, by the flicker of pleasure that crossed the queen's face, that Her Grace had noticed.

"Lady Anne," the queen said in her deep, husky voice. "You are to have a permanent place in the privy chamber."

Caught off guard by this unexpected announcement, Anne had to swallow several times before she found her voice. "I am most pleased to hear it, Your Grace."

The oath was administered then and there, after which she was dismissed. Her head was spinning. This change in her status made no sense to her. Anne had resumed her post as one of the honorary ladies of the household after her return to court, but she'd not been called upon to be in daily attendance on Her Grace. Now she would serve in a more intimate capacity and be in frequent contact with both queen and king. A lady of the privy chamber had less prestige than a great lady of the household, but the position offered more opportunities to solicit royal favor.

Anne returned to her own lodgings to find servants carrying out traveling trunks. "Stop!" she cried. "I cannot leave court without the queen's permission. She has appointed me to her privy chamber."

George turned at the sound of her voice, a look of such revulsion on his face that she shrank back. His voice was cold, the words falling like chunks of ice and shattering as they landed on the tiled floor. "While I, dear wife, have just been banished from court. Why do you think that is, hmmm?"

"For . . . for illegal retaining?"

"For attempting to retain my own wife, more likely. Did you think I would not guess? That I could not see the fine hand of the king's *good friend* behind this?"

"Wolsey. It must have been Wolsey. You said so yourself." She heard the note of desperation in her voice but could do nothing to control it.

"It was Compton." He all but spat the name. "And you knew all along."

"I did not." She'd suspected, but that was not the same thing.

Anne wanted to scream at her husband, to pound his chest with her fists and proclaim her innocence to the world at large, but she was too proud to beg. Let him go, she told herself. Let him live all alone in the country. None of this is my fault.

But she knew now where the fault *did* lie and as soon as George departed for Stoke Poges, she sought out Will Compton. She found him in his lodgings, hard by those of the king. It was the last place she should have gone, but she was too angry and upset to care.

He was not alone. Ned Neville was with him, and Nick Carew, and Harry Guildford. They were gambling, laying down bets on the outcome of a game of cards. She sneered at them. "Have you no care for your friends?" she demanded. "For your brothers?" This last was directed at both Neville and Guildford. Lord Bergavenny and Sir Edward Guildford had also been banished from court.

"Half brother," Harry Guildford muttered, but he had the grace to look ashamed of himself. Ned Neville just shrugged and studied his cards.

"Is there something we can do for you, Lady Anne?" Compton's tone reproved her for her audacity in coming to his chamber, but his eyes betrayed a different reaction.

"I would speak with you, Sir William. Alone."

He blinked, less sure of himself now, but he wisely refrained from making any rude remarks. For a salacious comment, she would have struck him. Had he been flippant, she'd have railed at him. Her temper was balanced on a fine edge and the other gentlemen seemed, belatedly, to realize that. They hastily scrambled to their feet and departed.

Will rose more slowly, adjusting his doublet and hose and avoiding her eyes. "This is not how I imagined your first visit to my rooms."

She ignored the little flare of heat in her belly. "I must ask you a question," she said, "and I would have honesty from you, no matter the cost."

"Cost to me or to you?" He appeared intrigued by the notion and when he looked at her at last, she could read nothing except curiosity in the clear hazel depths of his eyes.

"Were you behind the charges of retaining made against my husband?"

"No."

"No?"

"No. Now the only question left is this—do you believe me?" He leaned back, lounging with one shoulder propped against the window casement, but he was far from relaxed.

Anne knew what it was like to not be believed. She understood full well how painful a lack of trust could be. And she found, with a sense of surprise, that she could accept Will Compton's single-word answer. He had not questioned the number of George's retainers. He had not been responsible for her husband's banishment from court—a better outcome, now that she thought about it, than a ruinous fine or imprisonment or both. And he had not contrived to keep her at court in the queen's service when she should have been obliged to leave because George did.

She gave him a one-word answer of her own—"Yes"—and turned on her heel to leave his lodgings. She returning to her own as swiftly as possible.

"Meriall?" she called as she entered. "Dancer?"

Her maidservant materialized from the bedchamber, holding the little dog in her arms. Her face was streaked with tears—one of George's manservants had been courting her—but she managed a watery smile for her mistress.

"The queen has sent for you, my lady," she said. "She wants you in the privy chamber as soon as may be."

Anne had no choice but to go, since she now served at the *queen's* pleasure. But she took the time first to wash the streaks of tears from her face and to cuddle the puppy close. Contrary to what George might believe, Dancer was the only one who would be sharing her bed in his absence.

46

*L*ady Anne rode along the low-lying land toward a cluster of buildings, her mind occupied with the queen's comfort and the many duties Her Grace expected Anne to perform. She had not given much thought to where she herself would lodge during the royal visit to Farnham Castle, and only gradually did it dawn on her that they had come rather a long way on this hot and airless day. Her throat was parched, and even her soft chemise felt uncomfortable against her skin.

"Where are we?" she asked, using the reins to bring her palfrey to a halt.

Sir William Compton, who rode beside her, gestured toward two clusters of houses no more than a few hundred yards apart and a small nearby manor house surrounded by a curtain wall. "The hamlet is called Vyne Green. The village is Sherborne St. John. And the house is The Vyne. I understand that this entire area is often flooded," he added, showing a landowner's interest in the site.

"No chance of that this year." It had been hot and dry all summer, to the point of drought. The fields they'd passed on the royal progress had shown all the signs of a poor harvest to come.

"The king stayed at The Vyne last year," Will continued, "but this time the house will only be used for overflow."

"Overflow?" Anne echoed, startled. "Since when is a lady of the privy chamber considered overflow?"

Compton grinned at her. "Since I was given charge of deciding who would sleep where."

Alarmed, she turned in her saddle and was not surprised to discover that she was the only one of the queen's ladies to be billeted so far from the rest of the court. She sent Will a fulminating glare. He just kept smiling as he dismounted to oversee the disposition of men and horses.

A short time later, they were ensconced in a parlor decorated with green silk curtains and a tapestry showing a hunting scene. Anne sat in a chair with an antelope carved on the back and Will was seated in one that boasted a hart for décor. In spite of the thick stone walls of the manor house, the room felt close and uncomfortable. While Anne sipped a cool drink, she studied Will with wary eyes.

Nearly two months had passed since George had been sent away from court. Every day of that time, Will Compton had insinuated himself more deeply into her life. He did not thrust himself forward or make demands on her. He was simply *there. Always* there. Waiting for her to notice him. Tempting her.

She did not know what had become of the servants, either their own or those belonging to the house. But it was Will who went away for a few minutes and returned with a light supper of sliced meats and cheeses, nuts and fruit. He placed a small table between their chairs and somehow, as the meal commenced, Anne found herself taking bits of food from his fingers instead of her own.

His scent surrounded her, further weakening her resolve. Had she been drinking Xeres sack, she'd have blamed her light-headedness on the drink, but she'd had nothing more potent than barley water. It was her own weakness that lured her closer to him. It seemed only natural that she end up in his arms after the meal was finished. And once their lips met, the rest of the world vanished. Anne could think of nothing but Will. The power of his kisses sent tremors of excitement and longing singing through her veins.

Will literally swept her off her feet, carrying her up a winding stair set into the thickness of a wall to the great chamber above the parlor. He spun around with her still in his arms, laughing, and pointed to the tapestries decorating the walls. They showed the story of Cupid, the ancient god of love. Then he set Anne down atop an enormous bed. She bounced lightly on the feather mattress and stared in bemusement at the red damask canopy overhead. Before she could fully gather her wits, Will landed beside her and an instant later he was kissing her again with long, drugging kisses that she didn't want to end.

They struggled with points and laces, equally desperate to touch and be touched. And then, freed of the most restrictive of their clothing, her corset and his codpiece, they came together in an explosion of mutual need. Never before had she climbed so rapidly to the pinnacle. She felt as if she'd touched fire.

The instant passed far too quickly, leaving her only momentarily sated. She reached for him as he rolled away from her, although he clearly intended to do no more than remove the rest of his clothing.

Sanity returned in a rush.

He was beautiful, this naked man she'd just taken into her body. And she could not fail to know that it was love as well as desire that she saw in his eyes. But the enormity of what they had done together struck her with the force of a fist. They had committed the sin of adultery.

"Anne?" His voice was filled with concern for her. He braced one knee on the bed and leaned toward her, not with carnal intent but to take her face gently between his hands and study her expression. "Did I hurt you? I have waited so long. I—"

"You brought me pleasure," she assured him. "But we must not . . . we cannot—"

Had his smile been self-satisfied or smug, she'd have found the strength to leave him, but the look in his eyes told her he understood her sense of guilt, even if he did not share it. "I will go if you wish," he whispered, running one hand over her tangled hair. She did not know what had become of her headdress. "But surely, now, it is no greater sin to go on with what we have begun. I crave your smiles, Anne. Your touch. I can live without more, but must I? Will you deny us both, my love?"

"I . . . I do not know. I cannot think."

"Thinking is unnecessary. Just feel."

And with that, he drew her into his arms again, divested her of skirt and bodice and chemise, leaving her in only her stockings and garters. His lovemaking was slower this time, but they climbed again to the same wondrous heights. Anne realized, with a sense of despair, that she loved Will Compton.

That knowledge haunted her as the progress continued. It drove her to meet her lover in secret again and again. Each time, she gave in to the desire that consumed her. And each time, afterward, she was tormented by remorse.

She loved Will Compton.

But she also loved her husband.

How could that be? How could she love two men at the same time? And how could she expect George, who had found it so hard to trust her when she'd done nothing wrong, to forgive her now that she'd sinned in truth?

She missed her husband terribly. She had been furious with him when he'd first left court, hurt that he'd believe the worst of her. In her more rational moments, she supposed that was part of the reason she had encouraged Will's advances, relished his interest, and, ultimately, given in to her own desire.

But Anne knew full well how foolish it was to continue as Will Compton's mistress. There were those on progress with them who suspected they were lovers. Some of them would not hesitate to spread the tale.

She knew it was madness to allow Will to seduce her time and time again. But when they were alone, the temptation was too strong to resist. She gave in and then, when her lover had gone and she was alone, she despaired of her marriage . . . and feared for her soul.

47

"We will join the progress at Donnington Castle on the edge of Windsor Forest," Cardinal Wolsey announced, "where the Duke of Suffolk is to entertain the king, the queen, and Queen Margaret. Suffolk's own wife, the Queen of France, will not be there. She is staying at one of their country houses, Letherington Hall, with their young son. You can make your case to end your banishment while I spend a few days going over state business with the king."

George Hastings wondered if he was a fool to trust the wily cardinal, but he told himself that the simplest explanation was usually the one that was true. Wolsey had made his point, proving to George that he could punish those who dared oppose his plans. Now, secure in his belief that George would never do so again, he saw the advantage to having another ally at court. George was no use to him left to rusticate in the country. For that reason, when the invitation had come to accompany Wolsey to Donnington, George had leapt at the chance. Soon he would see Anne again. He had missed her horribly.

They had traveled on the cardinal's luxuriously appointed barge most of the way from London, only resorting to roads for the last stage of the journey. Thus Wolsey arrived at the castle wearing a pristine robe of figured scarlet velvet trimmed with black velvet and the fur of sables and a red cardinal's hat with tassels. He looked every inch the powerful, prosperous prince of the church that he was.

He rode on a mule, a tradition intended to convey humility, but Wolsey's mount had rich trappings of crimson velvet purled and fringed with gold. The harness was velvet, too, and the stirrups were gilt. A second mule, caparisoned in gold and red, was led before him and he was attended by four liveried lackeys.

Neither George's clothing nor the trappings of his big bay came close to competing with such splendor. As they drew near their destination, second thoughts plagued him. How would the king receive him, with favor or with fury? And, more important, what reception would he have from his lady wife?

He was all too aware that he'd treated Anne abominably. He'd lashed out at her because she'd been handy, when the true object of his anger had been the very man who was now taking him back to her. George watched the cardinal pass through the gatehouse into Donnington Castle from well back in his entourage. When it was his turn to enter, he quietly made his way to the stables and, after making certain his horse would be seen to, went in search of his wife.

"She's gone hawking with the king," Anne's tiring maid told him. "They left at dawn, right after Mass. At least a hundred people went, and dogs with them. The king has a new falcon," she added.

George was not surprised. He'd expected either hunting or hawking. The king was nothing if not predictable. On such an expedition, beaters would flush ducks from the river marshes by banging on drums and falcons would kill them. Or perhaps they would go after herons or cranes. There were birds in the royal mews specially trained for crane-hawking. It took two of them working together to bring down their prey and a greyhound to subdue it once it was on the ground.

"They are not likely to return before evening," Meriall added.

George knew that, too, and settled down to wait.

He had plenty of warning when the hunting party was sighted. The entire castle turned out to welcome them. The king rode into the courtyard at the head of the party, his mood jovial. They'd bagged not only mallard and crane but also bustards, herons, partridges, and pheasants.

His Grace seemed delighted to find the cardinal waiting for him. When he turned to George, he was still beaming. After no more than a second's hesitation, the king flung an arm around George's shoulders, as if there had never been any dissension between them.

"Ah, Hastings, it is good to have you at court again," King Henry declared. "Your lady wife is somewhere in the party. She took a partridge with her sparrowhawk."

"I am delighted to be here, Your Grace," George said with a straight face. He backed away, bowing, as the king's attention shifted back to Cardinal Wolsey.

Despite the large number of riders dismounting in the courtyard, George had no difficulty locating Anne. She was still on horseback, riding alongside Tom Boleyn's wife and several other ladies. She was laughing and the setting sun bathed her in an amber glow. George stood for a moment just staring at her. Then he forged a path toward her through the milling courtiers.

He reached her side in time to help her dismount, sliding his hands along the curve of her hips to grasp her firmly by the waist. "Allow me, my lady."

"George!"

She slid from the horse into his arms, so that they were touching from shoulder to knees. Her eyes went wide. He stepped back in haste, since it would be unseemly to make a public spectacle of themselves, but he kept hold of one of her hands.

With fingers that trembled slightly, she reached up to touch his face with the other. "Are you real?" she asked.

"Very real. And I have the king's permission to return to court. And the cardinal's blessing, too."

"I . . . I am glad." Her words were hesitant but he sensed that she meant them. In truth, he was not surprised to find her unsure what to say to him. They had not parted on the best of terms. Later, in private, he would ask her forgiveness for that. At present, he played the role expected of him. "I am told your sparrowhawk took down a partridge."

Anne seemed grateful for the change in subject. She recounted one or two incidents from the long day and then dazzled him with a wide, delighted smile. "But I have not told you of the best moment. A tufted duck brought down by a tercel peregrine fell into the water. Ned Neville and Nick Carew tried to fish it out with their swords. There was a great deal of splashing but they had not a bit of success. And then Ned lost his balance and fell in. Since he was already soaked, he swam out after the duck and brought it back like the best retriever."

"In his mouth?" George started to ask if Compton had been in the hunting party but thought better of it before he spoke. His jealousy of the other man was unwarranted. He was sure of that now. He was determined not to make the mistake of reminding Anne of how foolishly he had behaved on the day of his departure from court.

It was late before George and Anne retired to Anne's lodgings, which were now also his, and sent the servants away. He took her hands in his.

"King and cardinal have granted me permission to stay," George said, "but I must have your forgiveness before I can do so. I had no business saying what I did to you before I left. Since we've been apart, I have come to realize that, for many years now, you have never given me the least reason not to trust you."

When she winced, he wished he could revise his words, but there was something in him that could not quite forget what had driven him from court the first time, at the very beginning of King Henry's reign.

A hint of desperation crept into his voice. "Anne, I would be reconciled with you. You are my wife. And . . . I love you."

She burst into tears but, when he wrapped his arms around her, she did not pull away. "I love you, too," she sobbed.

"Then come to bed, my sweet." He kissed away the dampness on her cheeks.

Slowly, gently, he divested Anne of her clothing and removed his own. Then, for the first time in far too long, he made love to his wife. She responded as she always had, with generosity and passion. He had just enough control of himself to make sure of her pleasure before he took his own.

48

*A*nne lay beside her gently snoring husband, unable to sleep as dawn crept ever closer. She kept reliving that moment in the courtyard when George had reached up and lifted her from her saddle. Caught off guard by his sudden reappearance, she had reacted without thought, reaching for him. More than that, when they'd touched, she'd felt a jolt of desire so powerful it had nearly knocked her off her feet.

How could that be? Only the day before she'd awakened in Will Compton's bed. They'd made lazy love in the predawn hours and risen to ride out with the king, spending the entire day together, even if a hundred other courtiers had been with them, too. But then, at one look, one touch from George, it had been *his* bed she'd longed to share, his hands she'd needed to feel on her body.

Anne had not been lying when she'd said she loved him. She had not realized how much until he'd been standing right before her. And when they'd lain together, here in this bed that still smelled of their passion, she'd discovered that the physical attraction between them was still as strong as it had been in the first days of their marriage.

It was as she'd feared when she'd first given in to her desire for Will Compton—she loved them both.

Dismay warred with guilt as Anne tried to decide what to do. She was a sinner. There was no question of that. A good Christian would confess to both her priest and her husband and do penance, but she was not that brave. The best she could do was make a choice, because no matter how sincere her feelings, she could not continue to go from one man's bed to the other's. She looked at George again. There was really no choice to make. George was her husband. And somehow, for all the fire of Will's passion, what she had with George was both more real and more enduring. She would not betray him again.

Resolved to remain faithful to one man from that day forward, Anne slept at last. When she awoke, George had gone, but she knew he would soon return. He had made it clear that he intended to remain at court and with her.

Anne sent Meriall to find Will Compton's man and arrange one last private meeting. Within the hour, they were together in the chamber Will had claimed for himself at Donnington. It was a most luxurious accommodation. Anne had to force herself to avert her eyes from the enormous bed with its soft feather mattress. A small sob escaped her.

"If he has hurt you, I will kill him," Will declared, taking her in his arms.

She pulled free, resolved to be strong. "George would never harm me, Will. He loves me."

"So do I." As if he knew what was to come, he sounded petulant.

Anne sighed. As ever, in Will's company, she wanted nothing more than to fling herself at him, to enjoy once more the delights of the flesh. But she had made her decision and, heart-wrenching as it might be for them both, she knew she must not waver from it.

"If you truly love me, Will, then you must do what I ask of you now. I can never lie with you again. I should never have betrayed my husband in the first place, nor you your wife."

"We could not help ourselves."

Although what he said was true, it did not make what they had done together right. "I wish it could be otherwise, Will, but it is not. I must think of my own immortal soul, and of my children, and of how devastated George would be if he ever found out what we have done."

"I cannot bear to lose you."

"I will still be here, Will. It is only that we can never again give in to the demands of the flesh."

"Am I to worship you from afar? Is that it?" There was a trace of anger in his voice now, and Anne was sorry for it.

"You may ignore me if you prefer, but I will not change my mind." She felt tears well in her eyes and knew that he saw them.

"I would do anything in my power to make you happy, Anne."

"Even leave me alone?"

"Even that, but it will tear me apart."

She bit her lips to hold back words of comfort. She did not dare reach out to him. Her emotions were too close to the surface, too volatile. Instead, she breathed deeply, taking in the full measure of his scent one last time before she left him.

A few hours later, Meriall brought Anne word that Sir William Compton had taken his leave of the progress and gone to pay a visit to his family seat at Compton Wynyates.

49

*B*y dint of hard riding, Will Compton reached his home in Warwickshire two days after he left Donnington. He cursed Thomas Wolsey for most of the journey and spent the rest of it trying to figure out what the cardinal was up to. Wolsey had deliberately brought George Hastings to Donnington. There had to be a reason for that. Wolsey did nothing that was not for his own benefit. And he knew entirely too much about the private affairs of every courtier close to the king.

Will had been eleven years old when he'd been torn away from Compton Wynyates. His father's death had made him a ward of the Crown and he'd been sent as a page to the household of the young Prince Henry. The future king had been but two years old at the time.

It had been Will's father who had begun building at Compton Wyn-yates, replacing the old manor house that had stood within the moat with a redbrick mansion. He'd planned four wings around a quadrangle, but building had stopped with his death. It had recommenced imme-diately following Will's marriage and the task of overseeing day-to-day construction had fallen to his new wife.

He was pleased with what he found on his return. He stopped on the stone bridge leading up to the drawbridge to look up at the entrance porch. There, newly carved in stone, were the Royal Arms of England supported by a dragon on one side and a greyhound on the other and surmounted by a Royal Crown. Around the crown were the words *Dom Rex Henricus Octav*—My Lord King Henry the Eighth. To the right of the portcullis was the badge of the Tudors and to the left the arms of Queen Catherine, including the castle of Castile, the pomegranate of Granada, and the sheaf of arrows of Aragon. Will had needed the king's permission to use these symbols to decorate his home. That it had been granted was a clear sign of just how high he stood in His Grace's favor.

Wolsey's machinations were an annoyance, he told himself. Nothing more. And he would win back Lady Anne. It only required patience and determination.

In the meantime, his wife waited for him in the courtyard. She was a little brown wren of a woman, capable and efficient, practical, and possessed of good taste when it came to furnishings and food. Unfortunately, she was utterly devoid of any interest in clothes or fashion. She wore a loose-bodied gown and a plain coif and her face was freckled from being out too long in the sun. She had taken it upon herself, so his steward had reported in weekly letters, to ride out over all the Compton holdings hereabout to oversee the welfare of his tenants. It had been a hot, dry summer and there was much suffering throughout the land. Lady Compton was attempting to alleviate what she could.

"Good day to you, husband," she greeted him, going up on tiptoe to kiss his cheek after he dismounted.

"Good day to you, wife," he replied. He felt no desire to kiss her back. She was not Lady Anne.

Her Christian name was Werburga, after one of England's native saints. It was old-fashioned, like Frideswide and Ethelreda, and Will did not much care for it. He preferred women to be called Catherine, Elizabeth, Mary, Margaret, Jane, or Anne. Especially Anne. Worse, St. Werburga had recently attained considerable notoriety, thanks to a monk at Chester Abbey who had written her life story. Every pregnant woman in England now seemed to have heard of St. Werburga's red girdle and want it in her possession to ease the pain of childbirth. That pain was punishment for Eve's sin, or so Will had always been told by learned ecclesiastics. It went against the teachings of the church to seek to avoid it.

Will accompanied his lady wife into the hall to inspect the changes she had wrought in his absence. He approved of what he saw. The timber ceiling and bay window he'd taken from the ruins of Fulbroke Castle, another of the king's gifts to him, had been installed there. A minstrel's gallery had been constructed. And the walls were now covered with linenfold paneling. Upon one hung two portraits he remembered from his father's day. They were painted on panels and represented the first Earl of Shrewsbury and his wife. Will was unsure why his father had owned these, but they were as old as any portraits he'd ever seen at court and he prized them greatly.

"I hope this will please you," his wife said. Her voice was soft but not at all tentative. Whatever "this" was, she was certain he would like it.

He looked where she pointed, then moved closer to peer at the scene carved on a panel. It showed both French and English soldiers and was clearly meant to represent the Battle of the Spurs.

"Since you were knighted for valor after the French were driven off," his wife said, "I thought it worthy of remembrance."

"You humble me, madam."

She continued to amaze him with the progress she had made in his absence. The new chapel was all but completed and their bedchamber had been furnished with a magnificently carved bed.

"For the king, when he comes to visit," she told him, "but in the meantime, I have felt free to sleep in it myself." She flashed an engaging smile that he could not help but answer with one of his own.

"I will have to try it out, to make certain it is comfortable enough for a king."

"I expected no less."

Momentarily in harmony, they next paid a visit to the nursery occupied by their two-year-old daughter, Catherine, and then returned to the great hall to sup. Will broached the subject of potential husbands for the girl, and found his wife in perfect agreement that young John St. Leger would make an excellent match for her.

"Unless I can find a better one," he said with a laugh, and settled in, content for the nonce, enjoying the good food, an excellent wine, and the promise of a warm and willing wife in a bed designed for a king.

50

hristmas at court with the king and all three queens—Catherine of England, Mary of France, and Margaret of Scotland—was an elaborate affair. Lady Anne wondered why she did not enjoy it more. She even had a part to play in the Twelfth Night revel, as one of six ladies walking in the "Garden of Esperance" with six knights. The garden was mounted on a huge pageant wagon and planted with banks of artificial flowers, everything from marigolds and daffodils to columbine and eglantine. Their leaves were made of green satin and the petals were of silk. In the center of the wagon was a wide plinth, six foot square, and on top of it, within an arch, was a bush full of red and white roses and a pomegranate tree, symbols for the king and queen.

Anne wore an elaborate headdress made of gold damask with ostrich feathers, hair laces, and jeweled pins, and a purple gown with cutwork lace over a kirtle of white and green sarcenet embroidered with yellow satin. Her under sleeves were of crimson satin. The knights were all in purple, except for black velvet bonnets and crimson velvet stocks.

When the playacting, mostly done by the king's players and children of the chapel, was complete, Anne descended with the others from the pageant wagon to dance before the king and the rest of the court. She supposed that was why she had been chosen to participate. She was as graceful a dancer as ever, despite her advancing years and numerous pregnancies. Afterward, they returned to the pageant wagon and it was towed from the great hall by a team of oxen. The wagon was too heavy for horses.

When the king moved on to a banquet that would last many hours, Anne was free of duties for the rest of the day. She thought longingly of sleep and soon slipped away. She was waylaid en route to her own lodgings by her husband.

"Are you ill, my love?"

She shook her head. "Only tired and seeking my bed." She smiled up at him. "Would you care to keep me company?"

"It would be my pleasure." He took her arm and together they made their way through the rabbit warren of rooms that made up the king's palace at Greenwich.

By the flickering torches that lit the passage, Anne saw a thoughtful expression come over her husband's face, but he did not speak again until after they had reached their lodgings, been divested of their clothing and prepared for bed by their servants, and sent those same servants away.

"I have done you a disservice, Anne," George said. "I should never have listened to your brother."

She blinked at him in surprise. "What are you talking about?"

"I refer to your banishment to Littlemore Priory. I should have known better than to doubt your honesty."

"Do you mean to say that now, only now, you have decided to believe me?" Anne did not know whether to be offended or simply astonished. "What caused this change of heart?"

"Compton's behavior these last few months." He shrugged and said no more, but he did not have to.

The way Will Compton had befriended her husband after his return from Compton Wynyates had worried Anne at first. Will had sought George's company instead of hers, making her wonder if he was playing some cruel game. So many of those she encountered at court, and in her family, too, had devious natures and only one ultimate goal—to do what was best for themselves. Still, the two men had been friends in their youth, before Anne had come to court, and it had not been impossible that they should be so again.

Anne told herself she was grateful that Will had listened when she'd told him that, henceforth, she would cleave only to her husband. He was helping George advance at court by bringing him closer to the king's inner circle. He no longer found occasion to be alone with her, although he did sometimes watch her with longing in his gaze. If only the wretched man did not appear so frequently in her dreams, she would be able to put her folly behind her once and for all time.

"Compton's wife's with child again," George said after a short silence during which he poured each of them a goblet of fine Rhenish wine.

"May God grant them a son." Anne accepted the wine and sipped. She wandered closer to the bed. "I have been thinking that I would like to leave court for a time."

"Leave court?" George looked profoundly shocked by the suggestion. "Leave the queen's service? But I thought you were happy here."

"I was. I am." Anne sighed and climbed the little steps that led to the featherbed. She doubted she could make him understand her restlessness, but she offered a reason that she hoped would make sense to him, one that had the added advantage of being true. "I miss our children."

"We can bring them to Stoke Poges, now that my mother has removed to Leicester, or even to the London house."

"But there I would still be at Queen Catherine's beck and call. Unlike you, George, she clings to old suspicions. She thinks, and rightly, that the king wished to make me his mistress all those years ago. It matters little to her that nothing came of it nor ever will."

George hoisted himself onto the bed beside her and arranged the bolster more comfortably behind his back. "At least your sojourn at Littlemore spared you that."

"I had already spared myself." Relieving him of his goblet and abandoning both it and her own on the small table on her side of the bed, Anne took George's hands in hers. They were good hands. Strong hands. Gentle hands. She gave them a squeeze. "I was with child myself at the time—our first child. I told Will Compton so after the king sent him to our chamber. The moment His Grace heard of my condition, he would have lost interest in me, but Edward's intervention prevented that from happening."

George blanched. Anne did not need to remind him that he'd doubted that child's paternity, or that the baby had been stillborn. Neither of them was ever likely to forget the harsh words they'd exchanged. But she could forgive. She shifted one hand to his face.

"I do not wish to dwell on the past. And I have discovered in this past year that life at court no longer holds the appeal for me that it once did."

"Then I will strive to free you from your duties here." George bent his head to seal the promise with a kiss.

Anne responded instantly. She gave herself to him willingly, taking as much pleasure as he in the carnal acts that followed. Later, when he was snoring softly beside her, she touched her fingertips to her belly and wondered if she might, once again, have caught a child. If she had, she vowed, she would not abandon her newborn babe to nurses and governesses. Not this time.

51

*N*othing was ever accomplished quickly at court—unless it was at the king's pleasure. They were still at Greenwich more than a month later. In spite of the cold weather, the king went hawking every day, leaving it to Cardinal Wolsey to manage the government of England on his behalf. His Eminence was not pleased by George's desire to return to Ashby de la Zouch.

"You are no use to me in the country," Wolsey informed him.

"I am little use to you at court. I will never be one of His Grace's intimates."

"You can keep me informed of what those intimates do, Compton in particular. I understand you have become passing close to your wife's lover."

"They were never lovers," George said through clenched teeth. "That was a false conclusion my esteemed brother-in-law leapt to years ago."

The cardinal's eyebrows shot up, but he did not contradict the statement. "The fact remains that you are useful to me here. You and your wife may visit Ashby de la Zouch if you must, but you will both return at the beginning of July."

Why July? George wondered, but he did not ask. The cardinal's orders, like the king's, were not something one disobeyed without consequences.

With a heavy heart, he returned to his lodgings to tell Anne the news. She would be glad to hear that they would soon be with their children, and deeply disappointed when she learned that the visit would be but a temporary respite from their duties at court. He would not, he decided, tell her that Wolsey seemed bent on orchestrating Will Compton's downfall.

52

Greenwich Palace, July 7, 1517

The court was at Greenwich again when Lady Anne returned from an all-too-brief sojourn at Stoke Poges with her children. A great joust was soon to be held at Greenwich to entertain foreign ambassadors and show off King Henry's newly completed tiltyard. Afterward, there would be a splendid banquet.

Anne's unpacked boxes and traveling trunks were still cluttering the lodgings she and George shared when she received an unexpected and unwelcome visit from her brother the duke. Edward was angry about something. His voice was sharp when he ordered Meriall and the other servants out of the inner chamber. Ignoring him, Anne calmly took over the task of placing satin cases lined with buckram into a wardrobe chest. The coverings protected the clothing inside both during travel and in storage.

"Are you pleased with yourself, Anne?" the duke demanded. "You have made me a laughingstock."

A glance over her shoulder showed her a red face and clenched fists. Whatever had upset him, it was no trifle, but she had no idea what it could have been. "I have done nothing to you, Edward. I rarely even think about you."

"You wrote to Wolsey."

Anne's hand stilled on one of the leather cases used to transport her jewelry. She had only ever written one letter to the cardinal. "That was years ago," she whispered.

"You should have made your complaints to me!" the Duke of Buckingham bellowed.

She whirled to face him, her temper flaring to match his. "You were the one who sent me to Littlemore Priory! You were the one who condemned me without a hearing. You, as much as Littlemore's wicked prioress, were responsible for the death of my first child!"

Taken aback by her heated attack, he went on the defensive. "How was I to know there was such evil there? Knyvett told me the prioress was very strict with her nuns. I thought that would be in your best interests."

"In my best interests to be put in the stocks like a common scold?" She shuddered at the memory.

Edward's face worked. He'd never taken insults to the family honor well. As she pondered his extreme reaction, Anne realized that he had not known about her punishment at the hands of Prioress Katherine Wells. It was the fact that she'd chosen Thomas Wolsey to confide in that had provoked his ire.

The two men had long been antagonists. Anne had not witnessed any incidents herself, but everyone at court had heard stories of their petty vindictiveness toward one another. Once, when Edward had been holding a basin of water for the king to wash his hands in, Wolsey had had the effrontery to wash with it after His Grace had finished. At once, Edward had tipped the ewer, so that the dirty water spilled all over Wolsey's shoes.

"Thanks to your complaint," Edward said, "there has been a visitation at the priory by agents of the local bishop."

"Only now?" It had been nearly seven years since she'd written that letter.

"Wolsey took great pleasure in informing me that numerous irregularities were uncovered," Edward continued, "along with the fact that I made several generous contributions to the place. Had I known how immoral the nuns there were, I would never have sent you to Little-more. Why, the prioress herself bore an illegitimate child!"

"That must have shocked you, Edward—a man who has at least three bastards of his own." Abandoning the unpacking, she sank onto a chair, her hands tightly clenched in her lap.

Ignoring her sarcasm, Edward blundered on. "One of the nuns has been sneaking out to go into Oxford to lie with a married man."

Juliana, Anne thought. She hoped the young nun had found some happiness in breaking her vows. She would surely know none now. She felt nothing but deep pity for Juliana and her sisters. If they had not been forced into taking the veil, they might have had husbands and families and homes of their own. Instead they stood condemned for taking what pleasure they could from the life they were forced to lead.

Dame Katherine was another matter.

"Has the prioress been removed from her post?" she asked, interrupting her brother's rant on the subject of priests who fathered children.

"She is being given a chance to atone for her sins and remains where she is."

"And her daughter?" Long ago, Anne remembered, she'd hoped that Dame Katherine would lose custody of the little girl as punishment for the death of her own child.

"Daughter?" Edward looked blank.

"The illegitimate child the prioress bore—what happened to her?"

"Oh. Dead these several years. But that does not mitigate the sin. While it was alive, both prioress and priest sold plate belonging to the priory to provide for their bastard."

How calmly he spoke of children dying! Anne did not regret the visitation she'd set in motion. Littlemore had needed reform. But she said a silent prayer for the soul of Dame Katherine's little daughter. And she found it in her heart to pity the prioress for her loss. In time, she might even forgive her.

As for Edward, Anne supposed her revenge against him had also, somewhat belatedly, been accomplished. She had written to Wolsey of her brother's contributions to Littlemore and Hinton, hoping to embarrass him when one or both were revealed to be unworthy of charity. Wolsey had indeed taken him to task. And apparently let word of his poor judgment leak out at court. Anne had expected to feel satisfaction at this moment. Instead she was ashamed of herself. Revenge was *not* sweet. It left a sour taste in her mouth. And she did not relish answering questions from curious courtiers about her own time at Littlemore.

"How much is generally known?" she asked.

"That I gave money to a whore!"

"But not that you sent me there?" Was it possible that could remain secret?

Without warning, Edward seized her wrist and jerked her to her feet, gripping her cuff so fiercely that one of the pins holding cuff to sleeve was driven deep into her skin. "I am the one Wolsey conspires against!" Edward shouted. "Not you!"

Anne held herself immobile, biting her lip to keep from crying out in pain. After a moment, Edward flung her away from him. She staggered and nearly fell, staying upright only because she was able to catch hold of the edge of a nearby table. She cradled her throbbing wrist. A trickle of bright red blood stained the cuff.

"Conditions at Littlemore can have no more than a passing effect on your reputation, Edward. You have no reason to be so wroth with me. You have no real connection to the place. And you did not father Dame Katherine's child."

Edward looked at her as if she'd lost her mind. "It takes very little to cause harm."

"As I know better than most."

Such impotent fury shone in her brother's eyes that Anne feared he might strike her. Instead, he leaned in close, until they were nose to nose. His voice came out as a low, threatening growl. "Never presume to meddle in my affairs again."

With that, he stalked out of her chamber. Because her legs could no longer hold her upright, she sank, trembling, back into the chair.

Her hand moved protectively to shield her belly. She had suspected for some weeks now that she might once again be with child. Her thoughts had been much on children of late, even before she'd learned the fate of Dame Katherine's daughter. Will Compton had just received a letter to inform him that his wife had given birth to a second daughter in distant Warwickshire, and to warn him that the infant was sickly and not expected to live.

Childbirth was always chancy, for both mother and infant. And in this particular year, there was also a dreadful contagion spreading throughout the land. It was called the sweating sickness. Some of those who contracted it were in good health one day and dead the next. Anne had been struck down by the sweat herself a few years before her marriage to George. She had been fortunate to survive, or so she had been told by the physicians Edward had sent for from Bristol to attend her at Thornbury.

For that kindness, Anne realized, she probably owed Edward her life. She sighed. She wished now that she had never written that letter to Thomas Wolsey. But who could have predicted how powerful the king's chaplain would become, or that he and Edward would develop such an enmity between them?

She cheered herself up with the thought that at least the worst was over. The cardinal had used the information she'd given him to deliver a blow to the Duke of Buckingham's pride. Edward would sulk. Then life would go on as it always had.

The king's great tournament was held as planned, but afterward the king and queen retired to the most healthful of their royal houses, well away from any risk of infection. They took with them only a much-reduced "riding" household. Anne's sister, Elizabeth, remained with the queen, but Anne and George were permitted to return to their children. Anne's brother Hal likewise departed for one of his country estates, expressing a desire to remain away from court. Like Anne, he'd grown tired of the constant catering to royal whims. The Duke of Buckingham retreated to Thornbury Castle in Gloucestershire, still fuming about his sister's lack of family loyalty and decrying King Henry's lack of judgment in placing England's government in the hands of an upstart commoner like Thomas Wolsey.

53

here will be a change before Christmas," the Duke of Buckingham said, "following which I will have the rule of all of England."

The monk's newest prediction both excited and alarmed Madge Geddings. This time Edward had sent Robert Gilbert to Hinton. The former chaplain was now the duke's chancellor.

"Perhaps the king will die of the sweat," Edward speculated, "despite his best efforts to avoid contagion by constantly moving from one palace to another." He lifted his goblet in a mocking salute to the large portrait of King Henry that hung on one wall, almost obscuring a painted mural depicting flowering plants on clumps of grass against a red and cream striped ground. Then he drained his drink to the dregs.

Madge, watching her lover from the other side of the small table set up in his privy chamber, only picked at her food. Even this light supper of freshwater fish and rabbit contained delicacies—a game pie stuffed with oranges and a bowl of aleberry, a bread pudding flavored with ale— but this evening she could not enjoy them.

She rose and went to stand by the fireplace. The screen placed in front of it in summer was carved with the duke's arms and its feet had been fashioned in the shapes of a lion, a dragon, a greyhound, and a griffin. The floor tiles that felt so blessedly cool beneath her slippered feet—the weather had been unseasonably hot since early June—also boasted heraldic patterns. The English royal arms and garter were surrounded by Stafford knots.

There were some who said that in summer disease killed faster. Madge supposed it was true. All over England, fairs had been canceled and shops closed. Large gatherings, both public and private, were forbidden, for fear of spreading the sickness. The court had been much reduced in size and everyone stayed as far away from London as they could.

The duchess and her ladies were at Bletchingly. The duke and his mistress, together with his unmarried children, remained at Thornbury. The bear Edward had kept for years had finally died, but they still had two monkeys, a ferret, and innumerable dogs and cats in the castle with them. The monkeys were useless, but the cats caught mice and rats. The greyhounds were excellent at otter hunting. The spaniels rooted out game and retrieved it, as did the ferret.

And the monk? He was as useless as the monkey, Madge thought. And like the monkey, made a mess that others would have to clean up. So far, the only one of his prophecies to come true had been the one about the Scots invading England, and anyone could have predicted that! But when Edward called to her and began to regale her with plans for his monarchy, she listened with rapt attention and never said a word to dissuade him from his firm belief that he would one day be king.

54

W e will call him William," George announced as he entered the chamber where an exhausted Lady Anne lay on the bed. Their newborn son had recently been fed by the wet nurse, but Anne cuddled him against her bosom. She'd have liked to nurse him herself. It was a pity that practice was frowned upon by physicians. And that she'd likely be obliged to return to court well before the baby was ready to be weaned.

"William," she repeated. It was a good name. Strong. But it was also Compton's name. George's choice seemed an odd one. "Why William?"

"It was my grandfather's name, and the name of my older brother, who died shortly before my father did."

Reason enough, Anne supposed, but she imagined there would be some at court who would speculate that the child had been named William because Compton, not George, was his father. She thanked God that George would no longer be one of them.

After their return to Leicestershire, time had passed quickly. Anne had felt well enough to continue hunting and hawking until nearly Christmas, and she'd taken pleasure in her children and her dogs. She had kept the pup Will Compton had given her. Dancer was an excellent hunting dog.

No sickness had touched them throughout the long summer and autumn, although they had heard that in the south of England it had reached epidemic proportions. The outbreak had largely subsided, as it was wont to do in winter, by the time Anne gave birth to little William.

The roads were poor and often icy that winter, but Anne and George continued to receive periodic news of the court after their son's birth. They knew that the king continued his travels, trying to avoid coming in contact with anyone who was ill. The cold had reduced the danger of contracting the sweat, but hard on its heels had come a new outbreak of the plague.

The king spent more than three weeks at Abingdon Abbey, fearful of infection, before moving on to Woodstock in early April. It was from Woodstock that Bess Boleyn wrote to Anne, a letter full of odds and ends of news that ended on a jarring note. The Duke of Buckingham, Bess wrote, was to join the king at Woodstock after St. George's Day. He had done something to earn the king's mistrust, Bess confided, and was therefore one of several noblemen on whom the king had ordered Cardinal Wolsey to keep a close watch.

It was just as well, Anne decided, that they need not leave Ashby de la Zouch until *all* danger of the plague was past. She had no idea what Edward had done to arouse the king's suspicions, but she thought it best to stay as far out of her brother's orbit as she could. She was still one of the queen's ladies of the privy chamber. She would have to go back sometime, but she would strive to delay their return as long as possible. For the present, the spread of the plague provided all the excuse she needed.

By Easter, few families remained unaffected. Although Anne and George and their children remained in good health, word came from Bletchingly that some of the ladies who attended Anne's sister-in-law, the Duchess of Buckingham, had fallen ill. One, Elizabeth Knyvett, half sister to Charles and therefore cousin by marriage to Lady Anne, did not survive.

55

his monk is the most remarkable fellow I have ever met," said the Duke of Buckingham.

Madge continued to make close herringbone stitches in her needle-work, creating a small blue bird. A French knot served for an eye. Keeping her hands busy concealed what a struggle it was to hide her doubts from her lover. After a moment, she was able to smile up at him.

Edward had gone to visit Hinton in person the day before. Now he was even more convinced that the seer-monk, Nicholas Hopkins, was a true prophet. Madge had her doubts. Hopkins had been wrong about "a change before Christmas." The king had not died. Nothing of import had happened that Madge knew of, not that Yuletide nor in the nearly fifteen months since.

She'd thought about that prediction many times during the last year. Hopkins had not promised that Edward would be king. He had said that the duke would rule England. Perhaps it would be Cardinal Wolsey who would die and Edward would be called upon to guide King Henry in his place. Or Edward might serve as regent for His Grace's daughter, young Mary Tudor.

Madge sighed. She doubted that Edward would consider the latter a possibility. He did not believe any woman capable of ruling in her own right. It was strange that he should think so, she mused, when Queen Catherine had been so successful during her brief tenure as regent. While the king fought in France, she had led troops out of London to repel King James's invasion from Scotland. And after his death at Flodden Field, she had negotiated with the defeated Scots to make Margaret Tudor regent for her baby son. But then, as if to prove Edward's point, Queen Margaret's tenure as regent had been a resounding failure.

"I *will* be king," Edward said now, his voice rife with self-satisfaction. "Hopkins has seen it."

And Hopkins had also said, Madge recalled, that King Henry would have no heirs of his own body. But Princess Mary was thriving. Moreover, the king's mistress, Bessie Blount, was reportedly expecting a child. Surely that was proof that His Grace could father more children. He was, after all, not yet twenty-eight years old.

"We have a king already," she said aloud, "one who does not appear to be at all sickly."

"That can change in an instant." Edward dismissed her comment with an impatient wave of one hand.

"Edward!" Surely he did not intend to do anything to cause the king's death!

Guessing her thoughts, he chuckled. "There is no cause for alarm, sweeting. I am a patient man. I can wait for fate to take its course."

Madge was not reassured. Even to imagine the king's death was treason, punishable by execution. She might not have been at court or have learned to read Latin and Greek, but people talked in her presence. She knew what was within the law and what was not.

"I could not bear for anything to happen to you, Edward. Are you sure the king knows nothing of your consultations with the monk or his prophecies?"

Absently patting her hand, he dismissed her fears as groundless. "Henry is fully occupied with his own pleasures. He does not concern himself with my doings."

"And the cardinal?" Edward had railed against him often enough for

Madge to know that Thomas Wolsey was a formidable foe. "You said once that he has a finger in every pie."

Turning fully toward her, he gripped her shoulders and looked her straight in the eye. "You must not worry, sweeting. We are safe. I take precautions. And the monk is cautious, too. Does he not always instruct my chaplain to keep these matters secret under the seal of the confessional? But you are right in one respect. If the cardinal knew I had listened to such predictions, he would use it against me. But he does not know, nor does the king, and so long as they never hear mention of my name in connection with Hinton Priory, they can do naught to harm me." He kissed her lightly on the forehead and might have done more had they not been interrupted by the arrival of Charles Knyvett.

Madge forced a smile as she watched them leave the gallery to deal with estate business. It faded when she noticed the contemptuous expression on Knyvett's face.

Pondering this anomaly, she sat with her embroidery in her lap but she did not pick up her needle. Charles Knyvett's blind obedience to the duke had undergone a change. It dated, she realized, to just after the death of his half sister, Bess, long one of the duchess's ladies-in-waiting. Bess Knyvett had died of the plague the previous spring, as had so many others. Her death had occurred shortly after she'd received her annual wages of twenty pounds and Edward had given Madge another fifteen pounds to oversee Bess's burial at Thornbury. Then, having been so generous, he'd seized the possessions Bess Knyvett had left behind. She'd owned several very fine gowns, some jewelry, and a few pieces of plate. Edward had refused to allow her brother to take any of them for himself or his wife or give any of them to Bess's other siblings. While it was true that Knyvett had not shown any overt anger at the time, the expression Madge had just glimpsed suggested that he'd been harboring a deep resentment ever since.

Madge's thoughts circled back to Edward's certainty that he would one day be king. He was deceiving himself about that. And he was deceiving himself if he thought everyone in this household was completely loyal to him. If Charles Knyvett ever found out about the prophecies of the monk at Hinton, he would not hesitate to use that information to force Edward to turn over Bess's possessions. And that was the least of what he might do with such dangerous knowledge.

56

Penshurst Place, Kent, August 9, 1519

Of all her brother's estates, Lady Anne had always liked Penshurst best. The manor house sat in the middle of green and lovely parkland in Kent, its crenellated curtain walls surrounding a sprawling mansion built of local sandstone. Towers rose from each corner of the walls and midway along each sat a smaller tower. Within these walls, well protected, was a building with large glazed windows and a sunny great hall. Its roof arched high over the octagonal hearth in the middle of the room and each of the huge supports holding it up had, at its base, a life-sized carved figure of a man.

Anne paused for a moment to study one of the figures, entranced by the detail with which the sculptor had imbued it. Wise stone eyes seemed to weigh her while the stone mouth quirked with what she hoped was approval.

"They are said to be satirical representations of workers on the estate at the time the hall was built." The voice was high and childish but, because she'd believed herself to be alone in the hall, it still made Anne jump.

She turned to find a young girl of perhaps eight years studying her with eyes much more solemn than those of the carved man. There was something familiar about those eyes. After a moment, Anne realized that they were identical to her brother's. This, then, must be Madge Geddings's daughter, young Margaret. The child had inherited her mother's prettiness.

"When I was younger," Anne said, "I liked to make up stories about them."

"They have real stories, too. My grandmother remembers when the last duke was alive. My grandfather was in his service. I think one of these statues represents him."

That could well be, Anne thought. Members of the Geddings family had been in service to the Staffords for generations. She smiled at the girl, and asked after her grandmother's health. Madge's mother, she recalled, had a life interest in a cottage on the Penshurst estate, a common reward for a loyal retainer.

"Mother and I live with her now," Margaret informed her. She took a step closer, peering up at Anne's face. "Are you Lady Anne?" At Anne's nod she looked pleased with herself. "I thought so. Mother hopes you will be able to visit us while you are here."

"Tell her I will try."

But even as she spoke, she caught sight of Bess Boleyn hurrying past the entrance to the great hall. The king was staying at Penshurst on his summer progress and the house was crowded with courtiers. Queen Catherine had become more demanding since she'd given birth to another daughter, one who'd lived only a few hours, instead of the much-hoped-for son and heir. Her Grace expected all her ladies to attend her when she took her morning stroll in the gardens. Reluctantly, Anne tore herself away from the stone men and the real girl.

Anne and George had returned to their duties at court earlier in the year, after the birth of their Dorothy, yet another healthy child to add to the Hastings nursery. Anne had been away nearly two years and had enjoyed her respite from the round of royal pageants, tournaments, disguisings, and hunts.

Not all of that time had been spent rusticating at Ashby de la Zouch or Stoke Poges with the children. There had been numerous family gatherings at Thornbury and Bletchingly and Penshurst, in particular to celebrate the weddings of her brother's son, Lord Stafford, and his daughter, Lady Mary. Anne's nephew had wed Lady Ursula Pole, daughter of the Countess of Salisbury. It had been a mark of royal favor that the Duke of Buckingham's son had made such a prestigious match. Like the Staffords, Lady Ursula had royal blood in her veins.

Further proof of the king's love had come in the form of generous "rewards" from the privy purse to Buckingham, Anne, George, and even Anne's sister, Elizabeth, and her husband, Lord Fitzwalter. Shortly thereafter, Lady Mary Stafford had made an advantageous match with Lord Bergavenny, Ned Neville's older brother, becoming Bergavenny's third wife.

Anne had encountered Madge Geddings at these events, and they had renewed the friendship that had begun when Madge came to Ashby de la Zouch to give birth to little Margaret. Odd as it might seem to someone who did not know both women, Anne felt closer to her brother's mistress than she did to his wife and exchanged more frequent letters with her. Although it took considerable effort to carve time out of the royal visit to Penshurst to slip away to Mistress Geddings's cottage, Anne managed it a few hours before the progress was scheduled to depart for the next stop on the itinerary.

"Lady Anne!" Madge cried in delight when she opened the cottage door. "We are honored."

"How could I come here and not seek you out?" The two women embraced and Madge drew her deeper inside, where Margaret sat at a table with her tutor and her lessons and Madge's aged mother occupied a wheeled chair drawn up close to the hearth, even though it was too warm a day for a fire. She stared at them through cloudy eyes that had long since lost the ability to see. Her hearing, however, was excellent.

"Is that little Lady Anne?" she demanded in a querulous voice. "Why, I remember you when you were a babe in swaddling clothes." She made a clucking noise. "Never knew your father, did you? What a terrible time that was. Him under arrest and executed and your brothers harried into hiding and your poor mother forced to remarry will she, nil she. Did you know Dame Delabere—well, she was not married to him yet, only the nursery maid when all this happened—protected the young duke by dressing him up in female clothing so the soldiers would not find him?"

"Lady Anne does not want to hear about the distant past, Mother," Madge interrupted. Her cheeks had turned a bright, embarrassed pink.

"On the contrary," Anne said with a laugh. "I am entranced by this particular tale. Female clothing, you say? Did he wear false hair, too?"

Goodwife Geddings's stories took up most of the rest of the visit, for she remembered a time Anne could not, as well as the mother Anne had barely known. It was only when Anne was about to take her leave that she realized how uncharacteristically quiet Madge had been throughout.

"Is something wrong?" she asked. "If Edward has reneged on his promises to you—"

"Oh, no! He would not."

Anne thought her naïve. The time would undoubtedly come when Edward would tire of Madge and send her away. Still, it would do Anne no good to warn her friend of the inevitable. Madge would not listen. For some inexplicable reason, she truly loved the Duke of Buckingham.

As if Madge had read Anne's thoughts, she launched into a catalog of Edward's virtues. "He has always been most kind and considerate. You know that, my lady. Has he not kept on all of Lady Mary's tutors to educate my Margaret? And he has promised to contract a great marriage for her. He has hopes of obtaining the wardship of a younger son of the late Earl of Kildare. If he does, he means to arrange their betrothal forthwith."

Anne's eyebrows lifted slightly at this news. Marrying a duke's bastard to an earl's son, even one of the younger ones, was reaching very high indeed. "That will be costly," she said.

Madge sighed. "So were the weddings of his legitimate children. Your brother has been thinking of selling off some of his manors to pay for them. He will need to raise even more money to meet the expenses of this royal visit."

"It is a great honor to have the king come to stay."

"And a great burden, as well. The duke is even desperate enough to deal with some of those he once despised."

"Never tell me he's sold land to Cardinal Wolsey?"

The suggestion coaxed a small smile from Madge. "No, but he borrowed money from Sir William Compton and is negotiating to sell him at least two manors, too."

"Extraordinary," Anne agreed.

Hearing Will's name gave her a start. She saw him often, since they were both at court. They had fallen easily back into their old habit of banter and flirtation, although she was never quite as relaxed around him as she once had been. That her brother had borrowed money from Will bothered her. That Will would lend money to his old enemy troubled her even more.

"Edward has never let his disdain for a man prevent him from making a profit," Madge said.

"That is true," Anne agreed. "My brother has always spent more time with his ledgers than most noblemen. But what about your future, Madge? Has Edward made provision for you?"

"He has been generous with both annuities and gifts of land." Madge's gaze shifted away from Anne, as if she had some thought she wished to hide.

Curious, Anne would have delved more deeply, but at just that moment the trumpets sounded to announce the departure of the royal progress. She left Penshurst without discovering why Madge had, of a sudden, become evasive. Amid the bustle and constant confusion of life on progress, she soon forgot the incident entirely.

57

*M*adge Geddings went down to the stables attached to the house the Duke of Buckingham leased in East Greenwich to check on her mare, Goody, who had returned from their last ride with a limp. For the past year and more, Edward had taken his mistress with him when he traveled. In the duchess's absence, Madge acted as his hostess and chatelaine. She liked having a horse close by, but it was not always possible. When they stayed in London, their mounts had to be stabled across the Thames in Lambeth at the Sign of the Bear, a great inconvenience. Sometimes Edward even sent his cattle straight back to Penshurst or Thornbury and hired hackneys for himself and his yeomen as needed.

When the court was at Richmond or Greenwich, the duke leased a manor house nearby—at Barnes for Richmond Palace and in East Greenwich for Greenwich Palace—and enjoyed the convenience of all the amenities in one place, although neither could compare to Thornbury, where there was stabling for over a hundred horses, everything from coursers and palfreys to cart horses and sumpters. As Madge fed Goody a carrot, she wondered if the dappled mare ever wished she were back in Gloucestershire.

Once she'd visited awhile with her horse, Madge sought out the duke's farrier. He assured her that Goody's trouble had been caused by a stone in her shoe, which had now been removed. Satisfied, she was about to return to the manor house when Charles Knyvett rode into the yard. Seeing her, he quickly dismounted, flung his reins to a stable boy, and hurried across the cobblestones to intercept her.

"The Duke of Buckingham is in disgrace," Knyvett announced as he fell into step beside her.

Madge thought he looked entirely too pleased to be delivering such news. She kept walking. "I know already that there was a misunderstanding between the duke and the king, and that, at the king's command, Cardinal Wolsey reprimanded our master for giving Sir William Bulmer, one of the king's servants, a Stafford livery badge to wear."

Edward had been in a temper about that. To be chastised by Wolsey, a butcher's son from Ipswich, was the worst sort of insult.

"I do not understand why this incident caused such a fuss," she continued. "Great men are expected to have great retinues. If they do not keep retainers, how else would it be possible to make a good showing at court?"

"Our *master* is too arrogant for his own good," Knyvett said bluntly. "He does more than dress extravagantly and put imported delicacies on his table. Any sympathy you feel for him is misplaced. It is Bulmer you should pity."

"Why? What happened to him?"

"Bulmer was hauled before the Privy Council in the Star Chamber and there the king himself took him to task for his misconduct."

Madge's eyes widened. She had glimpsed King Henry when the royal progress visited Penshurst. His Grace had a formidable presence and was not a man she'd ever want to anger. Edward in a temper was bad enough.

Knyvett's small, pale eyes lost focus as he imagined the scene. "He was terrified for his very life. The king told him that he would have none of his servants wear another man's badge on their sleeve and lectured him on the subject for a good quarter of an hour. Bulmer fell on his knees and pleaded for mercy, but by that time the king had worked himself into a rage. His Grace turned his back on Bulmer and called for the next case on the agenda. Bulmer remained there, still kneeling, until every other matter had been dealt with by the Privy Council. Not a single councilor dared look at him. Hours passed before the king deigned to notice him again. Then His Grace's glare had Bulmer convinced that he would end his life in the Tower. Instead the king forgave him and took him back into royal service. "

Madge frowned. "I still do not understand. Why was accepting the duke's badge so terrible? And how, simply by giving Bulmer livery, did the duke incur so much royal wrath?"

They had reached the house and entered by way of a side door that led through a storeroom. For the moment, it was empty, but Knyvett still lowered his voice. His color was even higher than was usual for a man with such a florid countenance. "It is against the law for a servant of the Crown to be retained by anyone else. For swearing allegiance to any other master while a man serves the king, he can be charged with treason. As for the rest, that should be obvious even to a female mind— the king and the cardinal suspect the duke of trying to raise a private army."

"But he is not," Madge protested. "And even if he were, why is that something to be spoken of only in whispers? When we went to war, the king demanded that all his noblemen raise troops to take with them into France."

"This is not wartime. Far from it. The king has just signed a treaty of universal peace with both France and Spain. There is even talk of a face-to-face meeting between King Henry and the new French king."

Madge felt more confused than ever. Why should the king believe Edward would rebel against the Crown? No one at court knew about the monk's predictions . . . did they?

She felt her chest contract with fear. Had someone betrayed the duke's secret? She could think of nothing else that would have turned the king against the duke. His Grace had been pleased with the entertainments at Penshurst in August. And less than a fortnight ago, Edward had still been high in the king's favor. He had been granted the wardship he'd so desired, the one that would mean a noble husband for Madge's little Margaret.

No, she told herself. She was in a panic over nothing. This matter of William Bulmer was all a misunderstanding, one that would soon be forgotten. The duke would return to favor. All would be well.

Gathering up her skirts, she hurried toward the stairs that led to Edward's privy apartments. Knyvett followed close behind her. Once the duke caught sight of him, it was as if Madge did not even exist.

"Is the Bulmer matter resolved?" he demanded.

"It seems to be, my lord." Knyvett's manner became subservient, almost obsequious.

"What of my appointment of Ned Neville as steward of my properties in Kent and Surrey? I am to pay him an annuity of five pounds. Surely as devious a mind as the cardinal's can misconstrue that as a bribe to turn him against the king."

"He is your new son-in-law's younger brother, my lord. No one questions the appointment."

"Nor should they have questioned Bulmer's wearing of my livery! The king and the cardinal conspire against me. They would send me to the Tower if they could."

Madge winced. Knyvett, solicitous, assured his master that no one wished him ill.

The duke's laugh was bitter. "How little *you* know." Even as both Knyvett and Madge tried to soothe him, his agitation increased. When she touched his arm, he shook her off with barely controlled violence. "If ever I believe I am about to be committed to the Tower of London, the king will have little joy of it!" He all but shouted the words. "I will do to King Henry what my father intended to do to King Richard at Salisbury, I swear it by the blood of our Lord!"

"And what is that, my lord?" A sly look came over Knyvett's face as he asked the question.

The duke did not notice, but Madge did. Her hands flew to her mouth, as if that muffling gesture might somehow silence her lover, too.

"When Father came into the king's presence," Buckingham

declared, "he intended to secret a knife upon his person and when he knelt before the king, he meant to rise up without warning and stab him." As he spoke, the duke gripped the handle of his own dagger, although he did not draw it from its sheath.

Madge could not bear to listen to any more. To contemplate regicide was a terrible sin, worse even than killing a father or a mother. She ran from the room, her anguish made all the worse by her certainty that the duke had not even noticed her abrupt departure.

58

Greenwich Palace, February 4, 1520

ess Boleyn's daughter, Mary, a maid of honor to the queen, was married in a quiet ceremony at court. The groom was Sir William Carey, one of the king's gentlemen. Neither the king nor the queen attended but the king made the same offering in honor of the day that he had when Anne and George were wed at Greenwich some ten years earlier.

It was a cold Saturday in the dead of winter. Those invited to the informal wedding feast were glad to have something new to distract them. Anne was a bit more distracted than she'd wished to be when she found herself seated between her husband and Will Compton.

"Is that the bitch I gave you?" Will asked when he noticed Dancer rooting in the rushes beneath the table for a discarded bone.

Anne acknowledged that she was, remembering too late that George had not known where the pup came from. She felt him stiffen at her right hand.

"She must be getting on in years. Perhaps I should present you with another."

"Is there some advantage to youth?" Anne quipped. "We are all getting older but, one hopes, wiser."

She sent a sideways glance in George's direction. His attention seemed to have returned to his food. They shared a trencher, as was the custom. Will was supposed to be partnered with the lady on his left, but so far he had ignored her very existence. She did not seem to mind. She was flirting with a gentleman farther down the table.

"There is nothing so faithful as a dog," Will commented, "nor as useful."

"That is true enough," Anne agreed.

"Cardinal Wolsey keeps a cat." He did not trouble to hide his contempt. "It even sleeps with him, dragging who knows what filth into the bed."

Anne had to smile, given that Dancer was now rolling in something spilled in the rushes, covering her fur with "who knew what filth." "Cats groom themselves," she pointed out.

"Would Lancelot own a cat, or give one to his Guinevere?" Will liked to compare himself to that legendary knight . . . the one who had cuckolded his king.

This was all meaningless conversation, Anne reminded herself. Nothing had changed in the last decade. Men and women at court still pretended to be the knights and ladies of the tales of chivalry. Gallants wrote poetry to idealized damsels, untouchable and pure. It was nonsense, especially when half of them were creeping into each other's bedchambers of a night! Anne had long since grown tired of the games, but so long as the queen commanded her presence, she was obliged to remain at court and at least such foolishness helped pass the time.

"Did you receive the silk flower I sent you?" Will asked.

"Oh, did that come from you?" She pretended surprise, although she'd known full well who had arranged for it to be left in her bedchamber.

"It is of a type called French fennel," he informed her, wiping his fingers on the napkin across his shoulder, "all things French being back in fashion."

She popped a slice of orange into her mouth to avoid having to answer. Oranges were also in fashion. Knowing she liked the flavor, George had purchased two hundred of them off a ship newly arrived from Spain. They had been delivered to Greenwich packed together with fifty quinces in a sugar case.

She turned toward her husband, meaning to thank him publicly for the gift, but the words stopped in her throat when she saw his face. He was quietly furious.

"What is it?" she whispered.

He only shook his head. "We will talk later."

"As you wish."

She was glad of it when it came time for the bride and groom to be carried off to their nuptial chamber. The festivities would be over soon. She could take her own husband off to bed and insist that he tell her why, after all this time, he was suddenly showing signs of renewed jealousy toward Will Compton.

In the meantime, she could not seem to rid herself of the other man. Will even held back when all the other courtiers escorted young Carey away to strip him of his wedding finery. That George also remained behind did not seem to inhibit him.

"Shall I tell you a secret?" He did not wait for a reply. "There's to be no consummation. Mary Boleyn's been married off for one reason and one reason only—she's the king's new mistress and he does not wish to risk getting another unmarried damsel with child."

It was no secret at court that King Henry's longtime mistress, Bessie Blount, had given birth to a son before she was married off to Lord Talboys's heir. The king had acknowledged the boy as his and decreed that he be known as Henry Fitzroy.

"I suppose you would know about such things, Will," George drawled, "being the one the king sends to escort innocent victims into the secret lodgings."

"Hardly innocent," Will said with a laugh. "I have it on good authority that Mistress Mary allowed herself to be tupped by the King of France before her father removed her from Queen Claude's service and brought her back to England."

"That is a terrible thing to say!" Anne protested.

Mary had been a mere girl when she first went to France with the king's sister. She'd stayed on to serve the new French queen because her father, Tom Boleyn, was King Henry's ambassador to the French court. The other Boleyn girl, Nan, was still in Queen Claude's service, which made it seem all the more unlikely to Anne that Mary should have become entangled with King Francis.

"The French king is said to have slept with every woman at his court," Will informed her.

"Just as King Henry is said to have slept with every woman at his?" George asked.

Will laughed. Anne did not. It was impossible not to see the similarities between the king's interest in Mary Boleyn and his desire, ten years before, to bed George Hastings's young wife. Anne did not wish to remember that time, nor did she wish her husband to be reminded of it.

The bedding ceremony went forward, and perforce Anne and George and Will joined all the other wedding guests to witness the removal of Mary's garter and the throwing of the stockings. As soon as she could, Anne fled to her own lodgings. She poured herself a cup of Xeres sack and, thus fortified, braced for George's arrival. It alarmed her that he'd become so heated over Will's remarks. It had been years since their rivalry over her had flared up that way. Something had changed, and she was determined to discover what it was.

George looked weary when he came into the room. He accepted the cup of sack she offered him and watched her over the brim as he sipped. "I owe you an apology, my love."

More relieved than words could express, Anne went up on tiptoe and kissed his cheek. Her hand came to rest on his chest, where she could feel the reassuringly steady beat of his heart beneath her palm. "What is it that troubled you, George? What made you so angry?"

"Not what. Who. The cardinal, as ever, sowing discord."

"What did he say?" She kept her gaze locked on his, willing him to tell her everything.

"He has implied, on more than one occasion of late, that you and Compton are lovers. I tell him every time that it is not so, but he insists that the rumors persist."

"He is lying. Trying to cause trouble for some convoluted reason of his own. You must believe me, George—it has been years since there was even the hint of anything more than casual flirtation in my dealings with Will Compton. And you know already how little basis there was for scandal before my brother involved himself."

She felt a twinge of guilt at directing George's thoughts to the time before her incarceration in Littlemore Priory. She wished to pretend, even to herself, that what had happened at The Vyne and for months afterward had never taken place. George meant too much to her to risk confessing the true circumstances of her adultery. Anne meant to take that secret with her to the grave.

59

*S*ix months after the incident involving William Bulmer, the Duke of Buckingham appeared to have regained the king's favor. There had been no more accusations of illegal retaining and the duke had made no further mention of regicide, nor had he spoken of the monk at Hinton in his mistress's presence. Madge had begun to hope her fears were groundless.

After a morning visiting London shops, she returned to the Manor of the Rose to find the duke walking in his gallery with Charles Knyvett. There was nothing particularly unusual in that, but for some reason the cadence of their lowered voices alarmed her. She set aside her basket, then hesitated. Knowing that the duke would not welcome an intrusion, she crept into the gallery by a back way and stood listening in the concealment of a convenient wall hanging.

"I have heard some of the general talk in London," the duke was saying as their steps brought them nearer the place where Madge was hidden, "but I would know what men think about the king's plan to travel to Calais."

He spoke of the king's coming visit, accompanied by most of the English court, to the King of France. It was to be a grand celebration, some two weeks of jousts and tourneys and revels. Duchess Eleanor was due in London any day now to accompany the queen. Madge was to go, too, as one of the duchess's four gentlewomen. But Edward had been railing against the expense of the enterprise for months. The cost for clothing and to caparison the horses and transport the whole, with provisions, across the Narrow Seas was enormous, especially since Edward had taken pains to make sure his entourage would be the most ostentatious in the company.

"Many have fears about the voyage," Knyvett answered. "They think the French mean some deceit."

"That is very likely," the duke said.

As they were moving away again, Madge missed their next exchange. She peeked around the side of the hanging, but all she had time to notice was how Knyvett's thinning hair stood up in wisps, disarrayed when he'd removed his cap. Then they were circling back and she was obliged to duck out of sight.

"Do you know something more of the matter?" Knyvett asked. "Have you agents in France?"

"I know what the future holds," Buckingham stated. Hearing the smirk in the duke's voice, Madge's insides clenched with dread.

"How?" Knyvett demanded.

Madge wanted to interrupt, to warn Edward not to trust his cousin, but she knew how useless it would be. She'd only provoke her lover's anger. He would not listen to advice from a mere woman.

She tried to convince herself that she had no real reason to be suspicious of Knyvett. He had never mentioned Edward's outburst in East Greenwich, not even to her. If he could keep secret the duke's threat to kill the king, then perhaps he *was* still loyal to his master, in spite of his irritation over Edward's seizure of his sister's possessions after Bess Knyvett's death.

"There is a certain holy monk in a certain charterhouse who has communicated with me diverse times," the duke said. "By the power of Almighty God, he has knowledge of the future. He has told me that neither the king nor his heirs shall prosper, and advised me that I should endeavor, to the best of my power, to obtain the love of the community of England because I and my blood *will* prosper and will one day have the rule of England."

Madge heard Knyvett's sharply indrawn breath and then a hesitant "My lord . . ."

"Speak freely, cousin," the duke commanded.

They had been standing still for some moments, making it easy for Madge to overhear. She held her breath, waiting for Knyvett's reply.

"Have you considered," he asked, "that this monk might be deluded by the devil? I have always been taught that it is evil to meddle in prophecy."

Sounding much offended, the duke rushed to the monk's defense. "His predictions can do *me* no harm. And only think how much I can accomplish when his words prove true." He gave a gleeful little chuckle. "I tell you true, had the king not recovered from his last illness, I would already sit on the throne of England. And you may be sure I would cheerfully have cut off the head of my lord cardinal by now, and others, too."

"What you say is treason, my lord," Knyvett whispered in an agitated voice. "You spoke once before to me of your fear of being sent to the Tower. To give credence to this monk's claims is a sure way to end there."

"I would rather die than continue to be ordered about as I have been of late. Why must I make this journey to meet with the French king? He is our enemy! And the whole is a wasteful expense! There will not be such extravagant spending when I am king."

When the two men resumed their perambulations, Madge slipped away. She had prayed nightly that Edward would abandon his grandiose dreams. What he had said and done already was dangerous enough, but until now only she and Gilbert and Delacourt knew about the monk's predictions. The duke's chaplain and chancellor were the men he trusted most. They would not betray him any more than Madge would. But now that Charles Knyvett knew . . .

She must, she decided, find a way to make Edward listen to common sense. He must not confide in anyone else. And he must give up the notion that he would ever succeed King Henry. Little Princess Mary was thriving. She would rule one day. Or else the king would legitimize his bastard son by Bess Blount, Henry Fitzroy, and Fitzroy would be king. It was even possible that the queen would have another child, the much-desired male heir.

Halfway down the stairway, one hand on the rail, Madge froze. What made her think that Edward would ever take *her* advice? Now that she thought about it, she realized that it had been weeks since Edward had talked to her of anything but the most mundane domestic matters. He did not even couple with her as often as he once had. More and more often, they simply slept together in the big ducal bed.

If she was to convince him to be more circumspect, she would need help. She thought at once of Lady Anne. Although the duke's sister was also a female, and the siblings had had their differences in the past, Edward respected Lady Anne far more than he did any other woman, probably because she was the only one who ever stood up to him.

Lady Anne was at court, for the moment out of Madge's reach. She did not dare put her concerns into a letter. But soon—in less than a month—Lady Anne and Madge would embark for France and the meeting of the two kings. Surely sometime during the two weeks of festivities there would be an opportunity to speak together privately. Madge could confide in the duke's sister and ask her advice. The burden of worry would not be lifted from her shoulders, but it would be lighter for being shared.

Much relieved in her mind, Madge retrieved her shopping basket and retreated to her own quarters to await the duke's pleasure.

60

A long with every other noblewoman who'd crossed the Narrow Seas with the king and queen, Lady Anne dressed in her finest clothing and prepared to cheer on the English knights who would tilt against the French. For once, the two countries were not at war. This was a peaceful gathering, planned for months in advance and running with the smoothness of a well-rehearsed play.

Over five thousand people had made the crossing to Calais on the last day of May, among them two duchesses, six countesses, Lady Anne and ten other baronesses, and a plethora of knights' wives and other gentlewomen. Each member of the queen's retinue had servants of her own. Baronesses, and those deemed to have equal precedence with baronesses—such as Bess Boleyn, as the daughter of a duke—were permitted two women, three menservants, and six horses apiece.

George Hastings was in attendance on the king and, like every other baron, had brought with him two chaplains, two gentlemen, eighteen servants, and twelve horses. That was nothing compared to the Duke of Buckingham's retinue. Anne's brother and the other duke present, the Duke of Suffolk—the Duke of Norfolk having remained behind to protect England in the king's absence—were each permitted five chaplains, ten gentlemen, forty servants, and thirty horses.

The English party took up residence within the English Pale, as the land that included Calais and Guines was called. Near the Castle of Guines, an enormous temporary structure, a "palace" on a stone foundation with a base of brick and the rest of the walls of timber painted to look like brick, had been erected to house court functions. The roof was made of canvas but had been decorated to give it the appearance of slate. The four ranges of the building had been constructed in England and reassembled in the Val d'Or. Huge glazed windows gleamed in the sun and tall towers rose at each corner. A moat surrounded the whole, as well as a barricade of brocade with two entrances. There was also a gatehouse.

Inside this mock palace, on the ground floor, the king's servants had their offices, just as they would in a real palace. On the first floor were lodgings for the king, the queen, the Duchess of Suffolk, and Cardinal Wolsey—three rooms for each. There were staircases and galleries, a great hall, a chapel, and a banqueting house. But luxurious as this mock palace was, the king did not sleep there. His Grace had more secure lodgings in the castle.

On this day of the first official meeting between the Queen of England and the Queen of France, Catherine of Aragon was carried in a litter of crimson satin embroidered in gold. The Duchess of Suffolk also rode in a litter, but hers was made of cloth of gold wrought with lilies. The letters *L* and *M*, joined together, and the porcupines in the design—the emblem of Mary's late husband, King Louis—marked it as a possession she'd retained from the brief period when she had been married to the present queen of France's aged father.

All the ladies of the court fell in behind the litters, some of them riding in wagons decked with cloth of gold and others on horseback. Eleanor, Duchess of Buckingham, and her two eldest daughters, the Countess of Surrey and the Countess of Westmorland, occupied one of the wagons together with George's sister, the Countess of Derby. Lady Anne rode between her sister, Lady Fitzwalter, and Buckingham's youngest daughter, Lady Bergavenny, who was expecting her first child.

Anne was well pleased to be mounted. She could see better from this high perch and, occasionally, find a breath of air. The crowding and confusion increased as their party approached the French queen's retinue. The noise was deafening. Anne's richly caparisoned palfrey shied when trumpets sounded a fanfare. It took all her skill as an equestrian to bring the animal back under control.

She shaded her eyes from the glare of the sun to get a better look at Queen Claude. The French queen's litter was cloth of silver decorated with gold knots and was drawn by two massive warhorses of the same type used in jousting. Her Grace of France was enthroned on a cloth of gold seat, dressed in a cloth of silver gown with an undergarment of cloth of gold. The precious stones in her necklace sparkled in the sunlight, but the most obvious fact about her was that she, like Anne's niece, was great with child.

Anne had heard that the queen was due to give birth in less than two months. Her condition had been the French king's excuse for insisting that this meeting take place no later than mid-June. King Francis had not been amused by King Henry's jocular proposal that Queen Claude give birth during the conclave, so that he and Queen Catherine could honor the French prince or princess with their presence at the christening.

The French queen's ladies traveled in three wagons covered with cloth of silver. Anne's interest sharpened as one particular dark-haired young woman sent a brilliant smile toward the ranks of English noblewomen. Bess Boleyn returned it with one nearly identical. Maternal pride shone in her eyes.

The arrival of another litter, this one covered in black velvet, pulled Anne's attention away from the Boleyns. It bore to the meeting the most important Frenchwoman in attendance—not the queen, but the queen mother. Louise of Savoy was reputed to have great influence over her son, even now that he was king. She was a straight-backed, stern-looking woman all in black, as befit a widow. Her ladies, however, wore crimson velvet with sleeves lined with cloth of gold. It was a fashion remarkable for its beauty.

The two queens left their litters and greeted each other. The French queen took precedence, by prior arrangement, because the lists that were their destination were on English soil. The entire party entered the royal chamber in the gallery to the right of the principal entry to the tiltyard. It was tiered and raised above ground level and the area where the queens and queen mother would sit was glazed and hung with rich tapestries. An exquisite piece of needlework, heavily embroidered and covered in pearls, hung over the railing in front of them.

Queen Catherine and the Duchess of Suffolk spoke enough French to converse with the French royal ladies as they waited for the competition to begin. Lady Anne was seated close by and could hear what they said, but she did not understand a word of it. Edward had always despised anything French. He had refused to allow the language to be taught to his sisters or his daughters.

Nan Boleyn, on the other hand, was fluent in French and, as Bess's daughter, was permitted to sit with the English ladies to watch the jousting. Nan was not a conventional beauty. Her skin was too sallow, her hair too dark, and her build too bony. But she had an appealing vivaciousness about her and she was happy to translate when Anne asked her what the queens were saying to each other.

The young woman listened for a moment, her huge dark eyes unfocused, then wrinkled her nose as if she'd encountered a bad smell. "Of needlework. Of flowers. Of mundane and boring matters." She gave a little laugh and caught her mother's hand. "Now tell me all the news of home. Is Mary pleased with her husband? I hear he is a most toothsome fellow."

The topic of Mary Carey, necessarily purged of any reference to her status as King Henry's mistress, held no more interest for Anne than the queens' talk of sewing. Nor did the tournament seem likely to enthrall her. The events had been so carefully orchestrated to avoid injury that they were devoid of excitement. The two kings were to participate, but not in any combat against each other. Against lesser mortals, both could be expected to emerge with high scores.

For a time, she found the display of color entertaining. The King of

France and his men wore purple satin embroidered with black ravens' feathers enhanced with gold. The King of England's coat featured a design of waves, wrought and friezed with damask gold. That was supposed to represent his mastery of the Narrow Seas, or so George had told her.

The expense of such a display was staggering, and the kings were not the only ones who had spent with abandon. The Earl of Northumberland's retainers, recognizable because they wore his badge with the Percy crescent and manacles, sported ostrich feathers in their caps. Anne's brother, the Duke of Buckingham, had silver bells sewn into his clothing.

Once the competition began, Anne had to fight to keep from yawning. She had seen similar displays so often at court that she'd grown jaded. When one of the forty or so gentlewomen crowded into the gallery handed her a flask, she put it to her lips and drank freely. Other flasks were also making the rounds, shared among the ladies. The one Anne had sampled had contained sweet Canary wine.

Mistress Nan Boleyn giggled. "The French noblewomen think this is most vulgar. They never share drinking cups, let alone flasks or bottles."

"And why," Anne's sister, Elizabeth, asked, "should we care what the French think?" She took a healthy swig of the Canary and passed it back to Anne. When she'd imbibed again, Anne handed the flask on to Bess Boleyn.

"It occurs to me," said a very plain little woman sitting behind them, "that it would be very easy to poison someone with a shared drinking cup."

Anne stared at her in shock. "What did you say?"

"I thought the same when I first saw the fountains in front of the king's canvas palace," the woman continued. Her voice was low and there was action on the field. Anne did not think anyone else had heard her outrageous comments.

"That is an alarming idea," she said. Those fountains ran constantly with wine. Silver cups had been provided for anyone to use.

"If someone possessed a vial of some deadly substance, it would take but a quick flick of the wrist and hundreds could die." When the woman smiled, the freckles dotting her complexion stood out in stark relief against her pale skin.

Anne was horrified by the notion and no less appalled by the audacity of this stranger in voicing it. "The king's guards—"

"Would never notice a thing, especially if the poison came from a woman's hand. But, in truth, I can see no advantage to killing so many, not when the object of the exercise is to eliminate only one person."

A cheer from the crowd momentarily drew Anne's attention back to the lists. When she looked behind her again, the woman had taken herself off to another part of the gallery. Anne caught Bess's sleeve. "Who is that woman? The one with the freckled face."

Bess had no difficulty picking her out. The mystery woman was glaring at them. If looks could shoot daggers, blood would have been pouring from a dozen wounds in Anne's body.

"That," Bess said, "is Lady Compton. Will's wife."

The rest of that day seemed endless. Anne did not understand the intensity of Lady Compton's enmity. The woman had no reason to be jealous now. It had been years since Anne had been her husband's mistress. Yet clearly, Lady Compton believed that Anne remained her rival. Anne wondered who had convinced her of that, and why. She was tempted to accost the other woman and ask, but no opportunity presented itself.

The contest in the tiltyard did not conclude until nearly seven that evening and only ended then because it began to rain. The heralds shouted "Disarm" in unison with trumpets sounding the call "to lodging" and the spectators fled to the shelter of the canvas palace. Even then, the day was far from over. The two kings and all those who had jousted changed their clothes and joined the queens and their retinues for a long evening of banqueting and dancing.

With everyone living in such close quarters, Anne thought it would be a simple matter to find Lady Compton again, but this was not the case. She did not even catch a glimpse of that gentlewoman until three days later, when the English contingent was once again gathered at the tiltyard.

This time Queen Catherine wore a Spanish headdress with her hair down over her shoulders and a cloth of gold gown. The king's costume was decorated with russet velvet and cloth of silver lozenges. Embroidered inside each lozenge was a golden branch of eglantine. In addition, the king wore one of the queen's sleeves in his headpiece instead of a plume, a fashion he'd picked up from the French. Anne thought it looked rather foolish, especially since the day was windy and the sleeve kept slapping His Grace in the face.

Catching sight of Lady Compton at the far side of the gallery, Anne began to ease through the crowd toward her. She had not gone very far before she was herself accosted by Madge Geddings.

"I must speak with you, Lady Anne," Madge said, clutching at Anne's sleeve.

"Come to me later in my tent." Anne tried to pull away, but Madge had a firm grip.

"It is important," she insisted.

"Not now, Madge." But she'd missed her chance. Lady Compton had seen her and taken flight. With a sigh, Anne shifted her focus to the woman still tugging at her sleeve. She did not trouble to hide her annoyance. "What is so important that it could not wait?"

Madge started to stammer an apology, but Anne waved it aside.

"You have my attention now. Tell me what it is that troubles you." She had not seen Madge in person since the king's visit to Penshurst, but they still exchanged letters with some regularity. Anne could not imagine that Madge had anything of earthshaking importance to say to her. Certainly nothing to compare to what Anne herself intended to say to an overwrought gentlewoman who'd all but threatened to poison her.

"Not *here*." Madge sent a fearful glance toward the Duchess of Buckingham, who was too intent upon watching the competition on the field to notice.

Exasperated, Anne was short with her friend. "Come to my tent later," she said again. The canvas house Anne and George had been assigned was one of the more elaborate in the encampment, though no match for the one housing the Duke of Buckingham.

"The duchess has rooms in the castle. It is not easy for me to come and go. There are guards."

Anne lost what little was left of her patience. She had missed her chance to confront Lady Compton and now Madge's behavior was attracting unwanted attention from both Queen Catherine and Anne's sister, Elizabeth.

"Do your best," she instructed.

Turning her back on Madge, Anne returned to her proper place in the stands. Once there, she brooded. Worrying what Will Compton's wife might do next effectively banished every other concern from her mind. She did not give her brother's mistress another thought.

61

George, Lord Hastings, ate heartily. "The king's cooks have once again outdone themselves," he remarked to Lord Fitzwalter, who sat beside him.

"I do not care for this sauce they have put on the beef," Fitzwalter complained. "Someone said it was made with clove gillyflowers."

George sipped a fine Malmsey wine and considered the issue. "It is not as satisfying as some sauces," he agreed. He was partial himself to the one his own cook served with roasts, a rich concoction made with the gravy of a roast capon, wine, mustard, and small shredded onions that had been fried in fat.

"And what is this?" Fitzwalter demanded, poking suspiciously with his eating knife at a bowl filled with green shoots.

"That is called asparagus," George told him. "It is an Italian herb." He'd been willing to sample it, but could not say he cared for the taste.

"Italian? That is as bad as French," Fitzwalter muttered.

Fitzwalter, George thought, became more like their mutual brother-in-law, the Duke of Buckingham, with each passing day. He mopped up more gravy with a piece of bread. By the time he'd polished off his wine, he felt remarkably content.

Three rooms were in use for eating on this second Sunday at what participants were now calling the Field of Cloth of Gold. In one, Queen Catherine shared a table with Cardinal Wolsey and the Queen Mother of France. The queen's ladies, including George's wife, were gathered in a second dining hall to eat while, here in this one, King Francis sat at the high table to share a meal with the nobility of England. He had brought his own royal musicians to provide fanfare when he was seated and when each new dish was carried in and to play background music throughout the meal. King Henry, who had gone to the French camp in Ardres to pay his respects to Queen Claude, had done likewise.

After they'd eaten, the three groups met in the great hall of the canvas palace. Ten French couples in long gowns of velvet and satin entered last, their faces covered with visors. The ladies wore horned headdresses of the sort George had seen in portraits from the last century. First they engaged in allegorical posturing, most of which George did not trouble to interpret, but later they removed their visors to reveal their identities. King Francis, to no one's surprise, had been the masked man in russet velvet bordered in white.

Free of the disguise, the king greeted Queen Catherine and the Duchess of Suffolk—who had once been his stepmother-in-law—and exchanged a few words with the cardinal and with his own mother. Then he led the dancing in the Italian fashion.

After King Francis danced with Lady Anne, George claimed her for himself. "His Grace has a reputation with the ladies," he warned her.

Anne laughed. "So I have heard, but I doubt he has any serious interest in a long-married matron like myself."

"You are as beautiful as you were as a young woman, and even more charming."

Obviously pleased by the compliment, she gave him a quick kiss on the cheek before she whirled away in the pattern of the dance.

His next partner was a mousy little woman with freckles, someone he could not recall having seen before. She approached him, which was unusual enough to have him halfway onto the dance floor before he realized he'd not actually agreed to dance with her. Nor did he know her name.

"You have the advantage of me, madam," he said as the music of tabor, pipe, and rebec began.

"I do," she said. "I believe I have knowledge that you lack."

"You intrigue me."

The steps parted them, but when they were face-to-face again, she smiled up at him and gave him her name at last. "I am Werburga Compton, Sir William's wife."

"Are you indeed?" Every muscle in his body tensed. In years past, the mere mention of Compton's name could evoke the bad blood between them. Then they had become friends again, after a fashion—a friendship that had been tested just lately with the advent of new whispers at court about a liaison between Compton and Lady Anne.

"We have something in common," Lady Compton said. "We have both been betrayed." She whirled away from him again before he could respond.

The next time the dance brought them face-to-face, he spoke quickly, keeping his voice low and level. "You are mistaken, Lady Compton."

"I do not believe so. My information comes from the highest authority."

"The king?" George let his skepticism show.

"The cardinal," she replied.

This time when they separated, he lost his place in the pattern. The lady he was supposed to bow to was obliged to strike him sharply on the arm with her fan to recall his attention to the steps.

George followed Lady Compton from the floor when the music stopped. She waited for him in a quiet corner, her face serene but her eyes dark with emotion. "Cardinal Wolsey himself sent word to me that your wife and my husband are lovers," she said bluntly. "He advised me to do something about it."

"He has said the same to me, but he is mistaken."

"I do not think so. Will speaks of Lady Anne often, and always with great . . . fondness. He has admired her for years." Bitterness leaked into her voice.

George felt sorry for the woman, but he still thought her suspicions unfounded. "Your husband is a friend of mine. A friend of *ours*. That is all there is to it."

"Fool," she said and, having planted the seeds of discord, she walked away, disappearing into the crowd.

All nonsense, George told himself. He must not listen to the fevered imaginings of a dissatisfied wife. He debated with himself whether to even mention the exchange to Anne when he returned to their tent that night, but in the end he had no choice. Anne had seen him dancing with Lady Compton and had recognized the gentlewoman.

"What did she say to you?" Anne demanded. "For a moment there on the dance floor you looked as if she'd stuck a knife into you."

After a brief hesitation, he repeated everything Lady Compton had said to him.

Anne glared at him. "Did you believe her?"

"No."

"Good. You have no cause for jealousy."

He was a fool, he told himself, to pursue this, but the question was out before he could stop it. "Did I ever?"

For just a moment, Anne's gaze wavered and, in that instant, he knew she was trying to hide something from him. He caught her by the upper arms and gave her a shake. "I will not tolerate lies, Anne. Did Compton bed you or not?"

Faced with a direct question, her face lost every vestige of color. Her lower lip quivered. He wondered if she was about to burst into tears but she got control of herself before a single drop of moisture could fall. Swallowing once, audibly, she lifted her head, stuck out that stubborn little chin of hers, and met his eyes.

"I thought to keep it from you. I have no wish to hurt you and less to drive you away."

"Are you his mistress even now?" The question was wrenched from him.

"No! Oh, no, George! *In the past,* I was briefly Will Compton's bedmate. It was a terrible mistake on my part. A sin I have much regretted in all the years since."

"Years?" he echoed, feeling a spurt of renewed hope.

"Yes. Years. I love you, George. Only you. And I will never be anything less than honest with you again."

Her words came from the heart. He could tell that. Confirmation that she had once been unfaithful to him wounded him deeply, but he clung to the rest of what she'd said. He set her gently from him, flexing his hands as he released her.

"We will speak no more of it," George said, and to make sure Anne knew she was forgiven, he made love to her with great tenderness.

He was capable of forgiving his wife. Absolving Compton of blame, however, was another matter entirely.

62

ighting at the barriers was just one more competition at the Field of Cloth of Gold. The barrier itself was about three feet high with a crossbar at either end and was set up within a stockade that allowed space for about twenty men. The contestants, chosen by lot, faced each other in teams of two. Several matches were completed without anything untoward happening. Then Sir William Compton and Sir Edward Neville took their places on one side of the barrier and George, Lord Hastings and Sir Richard Sacheverell approached the other.

Lady Anne barely contained her gasp. This was no chance pairing. No wonder George had been so careful to leave their bed before she was awake that morning. He'd planned this.

It would not be as if he came to blows with Will Compton at court. At the barriers, he could legally attack Will and do him bodily harm. Anne feared for Will's safety, but she was even more concerned for George, who was not the other man's equal at arms.

Even the most skilled combatants could be hurt in these contests, despite all the precautions and rules. No less a personage than King Francis of France had ended up with a black eye and a broken nose after one event and King Henry had been unable to compete on another occasion because of an injury to his hand.

All the competitors had years of training. They had been to war. But there had still been at least one death since the tournament began. Anne feared there was about to be one more.

Lady Compton was seated a short distance away from her. Bent slightly forward, her gaze was avid. Anne wanted to slap her. How could she find enjoyment in this? Did she want to see her own husband injured, even killed? Perhaps she did. Wicked woman!

Anne turned back to the barriers at the sound of a punchion spear shattering against armor. She bit back a cry of distress when she realized that George had struck the blow.

The sharp points of the spears were blunted. There had been no real damage done to Will's person, but he staggered back a few steps. Before he could regain his balance, George used the stump of his spear like a cudgel and began to strike Will about the head and shoulders.

Will responded with a heavy two-handed blow. When his spear also broke, he hurled the fragments at Sacheverell. George thrust both arms across the barrier, trying to catch hold of Will's throat with his bare hands. Heated words were exchanged, although they were inaudible to anyone but the two combatants, before Sacheverell hauled George back to their side.

The four men armed themselves again, this time with two-handed swords. These had "buttons" affixed to the points to blunt their deadly power but they still looked dangerous to Anne. The armor the men wore was for show, not true combat, and their headpieces, called armets, provided less protection than a regular helmet. The armet was naught but a globular cap with a visor over the eyes and a gorget to protect the throat. She closed her eyes and murmured a prayer for the safety of all four men. She did not want to see blood spilled here today, most especially when she was the cause of it.

She should never have confessed her infidelity to George. It had seemed the right thing to do at the time, and she'd hoped for the best. After all, George had believed her guilty of adultery once before and found it in his heart to forgive her. For a long time after he'd rescued her from the nuns, he'd remained convinced that she'd been Will Compton's mistress, and perhaps the king's, too. Yet he'd learned to care for her again, and he'd managed to deal with Will without attempting to revenge himself on the other man.

Since George had not asked her *when* she'd been unfaithful to him, Anne had taken care not to correct his assumption that her confession applied to those same early days, before she'd been sent to Littlemore Priory. The truth would have been much more hurtful to him. Or so she'd thought. She'd reasoned that he would let the matter drop, and abandon his renewed jealousy of Will Compton. It was difficult to hold on to a desire for revenge for so many years, as she well knew. But George, it appeared, was not as forgiving as she'd hoped. Or else he knew without her telling him that her infidelities had taken place more recently than she'd implied.

The sound of steel striking steel had her eyes flying open again. She sprang to her feet, but Bess Boleyn hauled her back down onto the bench they shared. "Do not make a spectacle of yourself," she warned in a whisper. "To everyone else, they simply look as if they have brought an excess of enthusiasm and high spirits to the competition."

Anne knew Bess was right, but she found it nearly impossible to sit still. The four men fought so hard that sparks flew up from their armor with each blow. Hands clutched in her lap so tightly that her knuckles showed white. Anne watched with her heart in her throat.

All four men at the barriers continued to fight until Neville's sword caught in Sacheverell's helmet and sliced into his ear. Even blunted, the sword was sharp enough to cause copious bleeding. The Earl of Essex, serving as the English marshal appointed to order the field, stepped in and, with startling suddenness, the match was over. No one had been maimed or killed.

Anne glanced again toward Lady Compton. The other woman's face wore a smug, satisfied smile. Why? Anne wondered. What had she gained by this combat? She was frankly astonished when the other woman approached her a short time later, as they were leaving the gallery for the great hall where the prizes would be awarded.

"A well-fought battle," Lady Compton said.

"If you call injuring an innocent party well done."

"A pity it was not my husband who was hurt," Lady Compton said, "but it is not his ear that needs clipping." Anne started to turn away in disgust, but the other woman caught her arm. "I wish you many years of loveless marriage, Lady Hastings. You will now know what I have been forced to endure."

Lady Compton walked away with a decided bounce to her step. The woman was mad, Anne decided. Not only did she believe the lies Cardinal Wolsey told her, but she thought that more than a decade of companionship and affection could be permanently undermined by such falsehoods.

Confident she had both George's forgiveness and his love, Anne returned to their tent to await her husband's return. She would not rail at him for risking his life. She would not criticize him for attempting to do harm to Will Compton. They would put behind them all that had happened, both today and in the past, and start anew.

But when George at last arrived, it was with a heavy step. The emotional turmoil that still seethed within him had a palpable presence. It seemed to Anne that it flowed toward her like an ocean wave the moment he glanced in her direction. It appeared that the matter was not settled, after all, nor could it be ignored.

"I feared for your life," she blurted out, and closed the distance between them to put her hands on his chest and lift herself onto her toes until they were eye to eye.

He just stood there, a bleak expression on his face.

"You listen to me, George Hastings," Anne said. "You are my husband. I pledged myself to love and obey you and I will do both. But I will also tell you the truth. You are as mad as Lady Compton if you let this groundless jealousy consume you. I cannot avoid Will Compton entirely, not while we both live at court, but I swear to you by all that is holy that it has been many long years since he could tempt me to be unfaithful to you. And even when he could, what was between us was never the equal of what you and I have together."

"He still desires you. He told me so at the barriers, after I said that I meant to pummel him to within an inch of his life for having had the effrontery to seduce you. He swore he would love you until the day that he died." George gave a short, humorless bark of laughter. "That day, I told him, had come. If Essex had not stopped the bout so soon, I might have succeeded in my quest."

"Or you might have been the one who died. I could not have borne that, George."

Anne loved her husband. In spite of his jealousy and his stubbornness. He had taught her the difference between mere infatuation and the enduring oneness of true love. George was the other half of herself, not only the father of her children, but also the one person she could not imagine living the rest of her life without.

The possibility of losing his love forever if she could not convince him of her honesty filled Anne with anxiety. What if the sins she *had* been guilty of had caught up with her? What if George knew exactly when she'd been Will's mistress and could not forgive her for trying to deceive him? What if he did not believe her declaration of love?

She wanted to shriek in frustration, but the tents of other noblemen had been pitched all around them and canvas walls did nothing to block sound. It would only make matters worse to let the rest of the court into their private business. Instead she buried her face in the front of his doublet, fighting to contain tears, struggling to keep control of her emotions and find the right words to convince her husband of her sincerity.

George's body was stiff with tension, but as she clung to him she felt him begin to unbend. His hand came up to caress her hair, making her glad she had removed her elaborate gable headdress while she was waiting for him to return. He ran his fingers through the thick brown strands as if he found the movement as soothing as she did. And then, at last, he bent his head and kissed her lightly on the cheek.

"I forgave you a long time ago, Anne."

She swallowed convulsively and steeled herself to meet his eyes. "But do you still love me?" she asked in a whisper.

"Always." Then he heaved a deep sigh. "Compton loves you, too. It may be misguided. It may be a sin. But he is as much in love with you as I am. I pity his wife."

"After all the trouble she's caused?"

"Even so, for as discontent as she may have been, this effort to create disharmony between us was not her idea. It came from Cardinal Wolsey."

Separating himself from her, he fetched a flagon of Canary wine and filled two goblets. She took the one he offered her and sipped, although she had no desire for drink. The worst was past. Or so she hoped. But it was not yet time to put aside the turmoil of the day and solace one another in their marital bed. First, it seemed, they must face an ugly truth—that the most powerful man in England had gone out of his way to cause trouble for them. From what Lady Compton herself had told George, and he had repeated to her afterward, it had been Cardinal Wolsey who had convinced her that Anne was still sharing Will Compton's bed.

"Why would Wolsey lie?" she asked, settling herself on one of the two stools pulled up to a small table. Their tent was luxurious, but too small to contain any other furniture save their bed and two wardrobe trunks.

"To cause dissension," George said, taking the opposite stool. "Why else?"

"But I thought you were on good terms with Wolsey these days. And my brother seems to be getting along with him, too."

"Perhaps it is Compton that Wolsey plots against." George pondered the possibility for a moment longer. "Wolsey has always been jealous of the influence King Henry's childhood friends have on His Grace. And as groom of the stool, Will is particularly close to the king. No few petitioners have given him generous gifts over the years to use his influence in the matter of pardons and grants of land and annuities. And he has control over the king's privy purse expenses. It would not surprise me to discover that he regularly skims some off the top."

"George! He's not dishonest."

"No, to be fair, he is not. That is simply one of the privileges he's earned by serving at the king's pleasure."

She winced at the choice of words, but George did not seem to notice. He cut two slices of cheese off the wedge his servant had left for them and passed one to her.

"I was under the impression that Wolsey already controlled almost every aspect of England's government."

"*Almost* every aspect. Some men can never have enough power."

"But that has nothing to do with us, not if we do not allow it to intrude upon our lives." Setting both wine and cheese aside, she removed George's goblet from his hand and drew him to his feet as she stood. "No one else's business need have any effect on us."

He allowed himself to be led to the bed and pleasurably distracted for the rest of the night. As for Anne, she tried very hard during the days leading up to the final celebrations at the Field of Cloth of Gold to convince herself that neither she nor George was Cardinal Wolsey's pawn in some diabolical game of chess. Unfortunately, she knew all too well that no one could live at court without becoming entangled in some scheme or intrigue.

On the last Sunday at Guines, Queen Catherine entertained King Francis in her tent. Anne's brother, the Duke of Buckingham, was also an honored guest. From her place among the ladies of the privy chamber, Anne was uncomfortably aware of his intense scrutiny. She wondered what he had heard, then realized that his interest could have been prompted by any number of things. Edward had *always* kept an eye on her.

In the hope of avoiding conversation with her brother, she fled immediately afterward to her own tent. She had no desire to run into Will or Lady Compton, either, having successfully kept her distance from them both since the day of the combat at the barriers.

Anne expected to find the tent empty, or perhaps inhabited by one or two servants. Instead Madge Geddings sat on one of the stools. Until that moment, Anne had completely forgotten that Madge had wanted to speak with her.

"My lady, forgive the intrusion." Madge rose and dipped into a curtsey.

"Sit down, Madge. I've candied fruit if you—"

"No. Nothing. Please. I just . . . that is . . ." Her voice trailed off and she seemed at a loss over what to say next.

"What has Edward done?" Anne asked.

Madge burst into tears. "That is just the problem. I do not know. He does not confide in me anymore. I no longer share his bed."

Anne had little patience for dramatics. She had her own worries. "I am sorry, Madge, but you must have known he would not keep you forever." She hesitated, then asked, "Is little Margaret provided for? You have no fears on her account?"

"I have fears aplenty, my lady." Her face worked as she struggled to get herself under control.

Anne felt sorry for Madge. She had truly loved Edward. Perhaps she still did. But there was nothing Anne could do to get him back for her. She made the only offer she could. "If you ever wish to leave the duke's household, you know you can always come to me, Madge. And Margaret, too."

Madge sniffled out her gratitude. "I have my post with the duchess still, and she does not treat me unkindly."

Eleanor, Anne thought, had probably been grateful to Madge for sparing her Edward's amorous interest all these years. Her sister-in-law had always struck Anne as a cold woman, uninterested in marital bliss. "The offer will remain open. You have my word on it."

"I will consider it, if there are . . . difficulties." Madge looked as if she wished to say more, but George chose that moment to return and so the chance was lost. Anne did not see Madge again before the English contingent left the Field of Cloth of Gold, nor did they meet on the journey back to England.

She returned to court in blissful ignorance of her brother's state of mind.

63

Bletchingly, Surrey, September 10, 1520

In the weeks that followed the Field of Cloth of Gold, Madge's misery increased. She wished more than ever that she'd been able to confide in Lady Anne. Edward's behavior grew more peculiar every day.

It had always been the Duke of Buckingham's custom to rise early and say Matins with his chaplain, break his fast, and then hear Low Mass in his chamber, followed by divine service in the chapel with the rest of the household. After that, aside from prayers before meals, the only other daily religious observance had been Evensong. Now, of a sudden, the entire household, all 150 or so, from the duchess's gentle-women through the duke's private physician to the youngest page and lowliest kitchen boy, was obliged to attend five services a day. They went to Matins before breakfast, Lady Mass after, a High Mass, Even-song, and Compline. The duke's chaplains—he had several of them, ruled over by Sir John Delacourt, his confessor—also began reading religious text during meals, putting an end to the cheerful chatter that usually accompanied food.

The duchess seemed pleased by the changes, even when the duke raised the possibility of making a pilgrimage to Jerusalem, a long, dan-gerous journey usually undertaken only by the most devout—or by those in particular need of forgiveness. When one of her ladies commented on the heightened piety at Bletchingly, the duchess reproved her gently for the hint of implied criticism in her remark.

"His Grace has acknowledged that he is a sinner," she added, "as are we all." Her placid gaze momentarily fixed on Madge.

There was no condemnation in it. There was no emotion at all. But Madge felt as if she'd been stripped to her shift and set to do penance by walking barefoot to church with a paper stuck to her forehead that proclaimed her guilty of fornication. Her fingers were suddenly too cold to wield her needle. Madge abandoned her embroidery, murmured an excuse about the need to visit the privy, and fled the duchess's chamber.

Seeking warmth, she sought the gallery with its abundance of tall, glazed windows. Because her legs felt wobbly by the time she got there, she plucked up one of the floor cushions, carried it to a corner, and settled herself there, half hidden by a pierced screen. She indulged in a good cry and afterward felt the better for it. She was just mopping her face when she heard someone come into the gallery. Before she could reveal her presence, she recognized Edward's voice.

No, not Edward, she reminded herself. The Duke of Buckingham. She must not think of His Grace in such familiar terms any longer. She did not have the right. But it was not easy to change how she felt about him. She had loved him for a long time and still cared for him. And they shared a child, even though the duke had recently made changes in his daughter's life, too. Young Margaret now lived permanently at Penshurst with her tutors and Madge's mother.

Indecision held Madge in place too long. Now she recognized the slow, measured speech of Lord Bergavenny, who was married to the duke's youngest daughter.

"I hear talk of your generosity to certain gentlemen at court," Bergavenny said. "Is that wise?" He was older than his father-in-law and not inclined to mince words with him.

"I gave a doublet of cloth of silver to your brother, Sir Edward Neville." The duke sounded testy. "I have Sir Edward's goodwill. No man shall take it from me."

Bergavenny made a dismissive sound in his throat. "Ned has no influence at court. If he did not possess skill at jousting, he'd have no place there at all."

"He has the king's ear." From the concealment of the screen, Madge saw Buckingham stroke his beard, a new adornment he'd begun to grow upon his return from Guines.

"Not so much as some." Bergavenny chuckled. "Not so much as Compton."

The baron was baiting the duke, Madge thought. He was either very brave or very foolish.

"I trust to see the time when Sir William Compton will be glad to give me back the land I sold him."

"*Give* it to you? That one never lets go of anything once he has it. Ask your lady sister."

"He's not had her for some time." Madge knew that tone of voice. Edward was barely keeping rein on his temper.

Egged on by Bergavenny, the familiar litany of complaints began slowly, with a mere murmuring against the Privy Council and others King Henry listened to at court. Before long, however, it built into a crescendo.

"By the Mass," the duke swore, "I have done as good service to the king as any man, but I have not been rewarded for it. His Grace gives fees and offices to lowborn boys rather than to noblemen. You know this as well as I do. But I tell you now that I will prevail." His voice rose suddenly, startling Bergavenny, and the baron stumbled as he backed away from the duke. "You speak of gifts. I have given away cloth of gold and cloth of silver and silks within this quarter year to many gentlemen. Your brother was not the only one. My generosity has found much favor within the royal guard. If the king should die tomorrow, I would have the rule of England, whoever might try to stay my hand."

"My lord!" Bergavenny protested. "I beg you, do not speak of such things in my hearing."

The duke's smile put Madge in mind of a wolf about to pounce upon its prey. "I have no fear of or for you, my friend, for if you speak of what has been said here today, I swear by St. George that you will be one of the first to feel my sword against your throat."

Considerably shaken, Bergavenny vowed to keep silent and a few minutes later the two men left the gallery.

Madge remained where she was, feeling miserable and alone. How many people, she wondered, had by now heard the Duke of Buckingham make similar treasonous statements? He was bound for disaster. Someone was sure to tell the king or the cardinal and then Edward would be charged with treason. She did not want to be present to witness his arrest.

The thought of losing Edward forever haunted her as the household prepared to move from Bletchingly to Thornbury Castle. Her fears increased tenfold when she heard that Charles Knyvett would not be going with them. He was leaving the duke's service.

"Why?" she asked the chamberer who told her the news.

The woman lowered her voice. "Still angry because the duke seized his sister's possessions, I warrant. What does His Grace need with kirtles and the like? That's what I'd like to know."

"That was more than two years ago," Madge objected.

But whatever Knyvett's reason, his departure was worrisome. He knew too much. The image of a rat abandoning a sinking ship popped into her mind and would not be dislodged.

Madge tried to concentrate on her duties, to pretend that nothing was wrong, but restless nights and constant fretting took their toll. She dropped a pitcher, spilling water all over the embroidered cushions where the other ladies-in-waiting sat and shattering the container into dozens of sharp pieces, one of which nicked another gentlewoman on the hand. The duchess, normally the most unemotional of women, abruptly lost patience.

"Perhaps, Mistress Geddings," she said in a cold, implacable tone, "you would like to visit your family at Penshurst instead of traveling to Thornbury. You seem overwrought of late. A respite from service might do you good."

It was not a suggestion. She wanted Madge gone.

"My lady, I—"

The duchess held a hand up for silence. "You have fine clothing, jewelry, and an annuity. My husband provided well for you and your . . . mother."

Was this dismissal meant to be permanent? Madge quailed at the thought but sensed that asking questions at this juncture would be a mistake. She curtseyed and backed out of the room. The full impact of the duchess's decision did not crash down on her until she was in her own quarters, attempting to pack her belongings. Then she simply sank down onto the floor and wept until she had no more tears left. She had never felt so confused. One moment she was relieved to be able to leave. The next she longed to stay close to Edward, as if she could somehow protect him from his own folly if she remained at his side.

Early the next morning, she finished packing and retrieved her money and jewelry from their hiding place beneath a floorboard. She arranged for her trunks and boxes to be sent to her mother's cottage on the Penshurst estate and then, taking only the necessities for a two-day journey, went to the stables.

Her plan was to order Goody to be saddled and to arrange to hire two of the duke's henchmen to accompany her. It was not safe for a woman to travel England's roads without some protection. But Charles Knyvett was there ahead of her, saddling his own horse, and he had already heard that she'd lost her post.

"I have business at Penshurst myself," he told her. "I'll take you there."

Madge accepted the offer. Knyvett had his own servants to provide protection on the journey. She'd be a fool not to take advantage of the escort. She made only one condition.

"I do not wish to speak of the duke during the journey. Or of the duchess."

Knyvett seemed to find this amusing, but he agreed.

A quarter of an hour later, they left Bletchingly. Madge kept her back straight and her resolution firm and did not look back.

64

*L*ady Anne returned from yet another evening of banquets and disguisings to find Madge Geddings waiting for her in her lodgings at Greenwich. Madge did not look well. She had lost her accustomed plumpness and her normally rosy cheeks were pale.

Although Anne had told Madge to come for her if she ever needed help, she had not really expected the other woman to appear without warning at court. The last she'd heard, nearly two months earlier, Madge was living with her mother at Penshurst, where Madge's daughter also resided.

When Anne realized that Madge had been weeping, she went to the wainscot cupboard, an impressive piece of furniture with two ambries and two tills, and fetched a flagon of wine and two goblets.

Madge accepted the cup and swallowed so much of the wine in one gulp that Anne suspected she was trying to fortify herself for a difficult interview. That did not bode well. Anne settled herself in a box-seated joined chair to wait until her friend was ready to confide in her, sliding her aching feet out of the slippers she'd worn to dance in.

Unlike Windsor Castle and Eltham Palace, where there were separate dancing chambers, Greenwich boasted no such amenity, but the king made up for the lack by clearing all the furniture out of the great watching chamber. Anne was still considered one of the best and most graceful dancers at court, but these days she could not perform pavane after pavane without later feeling the effects.

After a few minutes, Madge set aside her wine cup. Perched on the flat-topped trunk beneath the window, she drew her knees up to her chin, clasping them tightly to her chest. Anne leaned toward her.

"What is it that troubles you?" she asked in a gently coaxing tone of voice.

Madge opened her mouth but no sound came out. Afraid she was about to burst into tears again, Anne moved swiftly to her side and engulfed her in a comforting hug. When Madge shifted her legs to curl them beneath her and Anne did the same, they had just room enough to sit face-to-face atop the cushioned window seat.

Giving one final sniffle, Madge managed a watery smile. "I did not know where else to turn," she whispered. "I have been so afraid."

"Of Edward?" Anne asked. Had her brother objected to Madge's move to Penshurst?

"*For* Edward. I fear for his life."

Anne clutched Madge by the shoulders and stared hard into her eyes. She could feel the other woman trembling beneath her hands. "What has happened?"

"Did you know that Charles Knyvett has left the duke's service?" Madge asked. At Anne's nod, she went on. "He has no business at Penshurst any longer, or at any of the duke's estates, but I saw him there just three days ago. He was talking to Sir Robert Gilbert and another man, a man I recognized as one of Cardinal Wolsey's servants. I saw the fellow in attendance on the cardinal at the Field of Cloth of Gold."

The mere mention of Wolsey made Anne uneasy, but the depth of Madge's concern puzzled her. There could be any number of reasons why her cousin Charles might visit Penshurst, and Gilbert was her brother's chancellor.

"Why did this sighting alarm you, Madge?"

"Because Master Knyvett knows too much about the duke's business and Sir Robert knows even more."

"They have both been trusted family retainers for many years. It is only natural they should—"

"You do not understand!"

At the sudden urgency in Madge's voice, Anne let her hands drop into her lap, but she kept her gaze on the other woman's face. "Then tell me."

"I have been trying to order my thoughts," Madge began. "I have no idea why Sir Robert would turn on the duke, but Knyvett bears a grudge over Edward's refusal to give up his sister's goods after Bess Knyvett died. There is something more, too, but I do not know what it is, only that Knyvett was not happy about giving up his post as the duke's surveyor."

"Did Edward dismiss him?"

"That remains unclear, but however it came about, Knyvett was left with no source of income. What if he is selling information to the cardinal?"

"Even if he is, Madge, that does not mean he can do Edward any harm. Everyone who seeks advancement spies on everyone else. Nothing remains secret long at the Tudor court."

New tears welled up in Madge's light blue eyes. "Oh, Lady Anne—if the truth comes out your brother's life will be forfeit."

Anne's hands clenched in her velvet skirt so hard that her fingers left deep creases. Very carefully, she released the fabric and drew in a calming breath. Now they came to it. She should send Madge away. She should not listen to her confidences.

"What truth, Madge?"

"It is all the monk's fault," Madge blurted out. "His predictions have convinced your brother that it is his destiny to rule England. Edward has come to believe that no one can stand in his way. He had a scare, when Bulmer was taken to task by the king for wearing his livery. Edward genuinely feared arrest then, but even that experience did not persuade him to give up his ambition. Now he seems oblivious to his danger."

Monk? What monk? Anne knew who Bulmer was and that her brother had been reprimanded for giving livery to one of the king's servants, but she could not grasp the significance of the rest of what Madge was saying.

Then a faint glimmer of memory came back to her. Something about a priory Edward had supported years ago. Henton? No—Hinton. That was it.

She felt the color drain from her face as she remembered something else. Back then, desirous of revenge upon her brother for sending her to Littlemore Priory and costing her the life of her first child, she had written to Thomas Wolsey—he had not been a cardinal then, but simply the priest who had married Anne to George—to complain of her mistreatment by the prioress and to inform him of her brother's misguided support for that religious house and one other. She had mentioned Hinton by name, having learned about Edward's charitable gifts to the place from Madge.

Had she brought trouble down upon Edward's head? It was all too terribly possible. Wolsey sat on secrets like a spider, patiently spinning webs, letting his victims trap themselves before he struck. So long as he had a use for Edward, her brother was safe, but once Wolsey decided to act against him . . .

She clamped down hard on incipient panic and returned her attention to Madge. "Start at the beginning," she ordered. "Tell me everything that concerns you, most especially about this monk and his predictions."

Madge complied. It took her some time to tell the whole story, but by the end of it Anne knew that Edward believed that this Nicholas Hopkins, a monk at Hinton Priory, was a true prophet, especially when he predicted that Edward would one day be king.

"How can he have been such a fool?" she wondered aloud. "No one with any sense believes prophets can see the future. Prophecy is not based on sound principles. The only sure way to predict a person's fate is to cast a horoscope using the science of astrology and even then the signs are difficult to interpret. You must remember Edward telling us that King Henry the Seventh's court astrologer predicted that Queen Elizabeth's last child would be a boy and that she would live many years after giving birth to him. Instead, Elizabeth of York died in childbirth with a girl."

"There is worse to tell," Madge said in a small voice. "Edward threatened to take King Henry's life, and with his own hand, too."

Anne slumped against the window behind them. It would not matter if the words had been spoken in the heat of anger or with deliberate calm—such a threat constituted treason. "Who else heard him say this?"

"To my certain knowledge, Knyvett, but Sir Robert Gilbert, Sir John Delacourt, and Lord Bergavenny have also been his confidants."

Anne straightened abruptly, eyes wide in alarm. "Edward threatened to kill the king in *Bergavenny's* presence?" Surely Bergavenny was a greater threat than Knyvett. As a baron, he had access to the court. His younger brother was one of the king's boon companions.

Madge repeated the exchange she'd overheard in the gallery at Bletchingly. "Please, my lady—there must be something we can do to avert disaster."

"If there is, I do not know what it might be." Edward's own words had condemned him, but Anne herself had made matters worse for him with a few careless strokes of the pen.

A decade earlier, she had passed many hours plotting revenge upon the brother who had shamed and mistreated her, but even then she'd only wanted to cause him embarrassment, not send him to his death. Guilt and sorrow filled her heart as she contemplated how such a little thing could have such dire consequences.

Madge clutched her arm. "The king has forgiven Edward before for words spoken in anger."

"That was different. Less important." Her lips twisted into an ironic smile. Edward had been furious when he was banished from court for sending her to a nunnery. He had not minced words with the king and yet barely a month had passed before King Henry forgave him.

Sending her to Littlemore had not been a treasonable offense.

Anne might have said more to Madge, but George's return to their lodgings put an end to private conversation. Instead, she sent Madge off with Meriall to find a bed for the night and pasted a bright smile on her face for her husband. For the nonce, she would keep what she'd learned to herself. She saw no point in worrying anyone else.

The next day, in the queen's apartments, Anne deliberately sought her sister's company. Since Elizabeth was hemming shirts for the poor, Anne carried her embroidery frame over to the same bench. Her heart was not in her stitches. She suspected she'd have to rip them all out and start over again when she was in a calmer frame of mind. She hoped Elizabeth wouldn't notice how clumsy her fingers were.

In as casual a manner as she could manage, she asked for news of their brother. She knew Elizabeth heard from him on a regular basis. Edward even, on occasion, asked for her opinion.

"He regrets that he missed the christening of Mary's first child," Elizabeth said.

"Is there some particular reason he could not attend?" Anne wondered if Mary's husband, Lord Bergavenny, had told him to stay away in the hope of avoiding any contact with his traitor of a father-in-law.

"Edward did not say, but perhaps he simply had too much to do at Thornbury."

Elizabeth sent a sly, smug smile in Anne's direction and Anne obediently leaned closer, mutely encouraging her sister to share whatever secret she knew. Elizabeth was nothing if not predictable.

"Edward called a meeting of his council last week." Like the king, the duke had privy councilors to advise him. "He called attention to his beard—"

"Edward has grown a beard?" Madge had not told her that.

Elizabeth scowled at the interruption. "He called attention to his beard," she repeated, "and he told them that he has made a vow unto God not to be shaved again until he has seen Jerusalem."

Anne stared at her in shock. "Edward plans to make a pilgrimage to the Holy Land? *Edward?*"

Elizabeth set aside her sewing to give Anne her full attention. This time her smile was genuine. "He has given the matter much thought, even deciding which of his servants will manage his estates in his absence. He told his council that such a journey would give him more comfort than to receive a gift of land to the value of ten thousand pounds from the king."

Anne felt her eyebrows shoot up at this exaggeration. That did not sound like Edward at all.

"He expects to obtain a license to leave England from the king right shortly, although it may take some time yet, perhaps as much as two years, before all the travel arrangements can be made."

That Edward hoped to flee the country before his traitorous behavior was uncovered was the only explanation that made sense to Anne. Her brow furrowed in thought, wondering how she might help him do so. The sooner he left England, the better.

Anne considered what other persons she could approach without arousing undue suspicion. She wished her other brother, Hal, was at court, but he'd found country living to his liking and these days rarely ventured far from his rural estates. That left Will Compton.

To Anne's astonishment, the battle at the barriers between George and Will seemed to have cleared the air between the two men. They would never be close friends, but since their return from France they had been able to tolerate each other's company at court. Anne, too, had found herself more at ease with Will these days, although there were still occasions when she caught him staring at her with longing in his gaze. All three of them were grateful that Lady Compton was not at court. She had returned to Compton Wynyates and would likely remain there.

Anne chose her moment with care, intercepting Will as he crossed an empty courtyard on some errand for the king. She matched her pace to his and smiled up at him. The glance he sent her way in return was a wary one.

"To what do I owe the pleasure of your company, Lady Anne?"

"Curiosity," she replied. "I hear that my brother has requested leave to make a pilgrimage to Jerusalem. Is the king likely to grant permission?"

"His Grace is more likely to approve that request than he is to allow Buckingham to take hundreds of retainers with him into Wales."

"Does Edward desire to do so? Whatever for?" She stopped walking, obliging Will to come to a halt as well.

"To help him collect his rents, or so he claims."

Something in Will's tone warned Anne that the king, or perhaps the cardinal, did not believe this "claim." They stood near a bench shielded by an arbor. She sat. After a moment's hesitation, Will joined her.

"What is it you want to know, Anne?"

"I realize that there is no love lost between you and Edward, but have you some reason to believe he's lying about his need to collect his rents?"

"He wants to take a retinue of three or four hundred men with him. To have that many retainers smacks of gathering an army."

A sputter of laughter escaped her, in part because she was relieved that Will made no mention of monks or prophecies, but mostly because she understood why Edward wanted such a large escort. "My brother is not popular with his Welsh tenants," she explained. "He wants such a large escort for his own protection, and to compel his tenants to pay what they owe. Most of them are several years in arrears. I know this because Edward is steward for George's Welsh lands, as well, and our rents have likewise gone uncollected."

"Still, to ask to take four hundred men—other nobles have been charged with illegal retaining and thrown in prison for less."

"As I have reason to know!" She snapped out the words as her good humor evaporated. "And I also know that a charge of illegal retaining is nothing more than an excuse for the king to levy enormous fines on hapless noblemen—a convenient means to fill his own coffers—or banish unwanted courtiers from his presence. How, I wonder, does His Grace expect my brother to pay a fine if Edward is not allowed to collect the monies that are owed to him?"

She surged to her feet and let a wave of indignation carry her out of the courtyard. It had the added advantage of preventing Will from asking inconvenient questions. By the time she returned to her lodgings, she was smiling.

"Your concerns are valid," she told Madge later that day, "but at present no one suspects Edward of anything more than keeping too many men in livery. If they did, Will Compton would have known of it."

"Someone will find out," Madge fretted. "Too many people have heard about the prophecy."

"But Edward, I suspect, may already have had second thoughts about believing it." She told Madge about her brother's plans for a pilgrimage.

Madge nodded, looking thoughtful. "He has become more religious this past year."

"I can think of no reason why the king should not grant Edward permission to go. He will be safe once he leaves England."

"Except for the perils of the journey," Madge said.

"That is as God wills." If any harm came to her brother at the hands of the king, her conscience would trouble her, but that would not be the case if he met ill fortune while seeking to atone for his sins.

65

hree weeks after Lady Anne had reassured Madge as best she could, promised to keep an ear to the ground, and sent her back to Penshurst, she received a visit from Robert Gilbert. Although she'd heard nothing in the interim to alarm her, Anne regarded the Duke of Buckingham's chancellor with wary eyes.

Anne had made it a point to spend more time in Will Compton's company. She'd felt certain he would give her advance warning if he heard that Edward was in trouble with the king. When George had noticed, he'd accused her of encouraging the other man's interest in her but Anne had teased her husband out of his pique without confiding in him. She was loath to compromise his safety. In truth, she wished she were still in ignorance of her brother's machinations herself.

Gilbert's intense black gaze focused on her. He seemed to be hinting that *Madge* had done the duke some disservice. "I am aware that Mistress Geddings visited you, Lady Anne. What did she tell you?"

"We are old friends," Anne said in a noncommittal tone. She did not have to ask how he knew Madge had come at court. Anne had written to her brother and told him that they'd spent several days together. She had also warned Edward to be careful what persons he trusted because some of those he thought were trustworthy were not. She'd meant

Gilbert himself, and Knyvett. She wondered now if her letter had ever reached her brother. Gilbert might well have intercepted it. She was suddenly very glad that this meeting was taking place in a corner of the queen's watching chamber, a room well populated with yeomen of the guard who would respond instantly if she called for help.

Gilbert rubbed the bridge of his hawklike nose and sighed. "Let me begin again, Lady Anne. I mean your friend no harm. The duke is concerned about her."

"Then you may reassure my brother that Madge, and her daughter—*his* daughter—are surviving quite nicely without him."

"You mistake my meaning, Lady Anne. The duke is concerned because Mistress Geddings left Bletchingly in company with Charles Knyvett, and Knyvett parted with the duke on less than amiable terms. If these two have since formed an alliance, the duke would know of it."

"An . . . alliance? Do you mean a romantic attachment?" Amused by the thought that her brother might be jealous, Anne almost laughed in Gilbert's face.

"No, my lady. I mean that they may be part of a conspiracy against the duke."

Her smile vanished. Her chest tight with dread, Anne tried to think how best to respond. The idea that Madge Geddings would conspire against Edward was ludicrous, but Anne herself had tried to warn Edward that Knyvett might be bent on betrayal. And that *Gilbert* might be in league with him.

"Your brother," Gilbert continued, "has charged me to discover if Mistress Geddings has made any misreport of him to the cardinal."

"That is the last thing she would do."

Gilbert massaged the point where his nose met his forehead as if pain throbbed behind it. "May I be open with you, Lady Anne?" When she nodded, he went on. "The Duke of Buckingham has instructed me to determine whether Mistress Geddings is innocent of plotting against him. If she has done nothing to cause him harm, I am to ask Lady Elizabeth if she thinks the duchess will take Mistress Geddings back into her service."

Naturally, Anne thought, Edward would not care to hear the

opinion of his *younger* sister! Then again, Elizabeth wrote regularly to both Edward and Eleanor and Anne did not. "And if Lady Elizabeth says no?"

"Then I am to ask her to suggest some other gentlewoman to be the duchess's lady-in-waiting."

It would be best if Madge stayed where she was, Anne thought. "Perhaps I can name one or two suitable candidates myself," she said aloud.

Gilbert looked surprised by the offer.

"What other instructions did my brother give you?" Anne asked. "Perhaps I can be of further assistance."

Gilbert looked down his long nose at her. "I do much doubt it, my lady, unless you know the whereabouts of two chaplains who have abandoned their posts with the duke without his leave."

"Has he lost *more* servants? How careless of him. Is Master Delacourt one of them?" Anne held her breath waiting for Gilbert to answer. Delacourt was another who knew about the mad monk's predictions. Safety lay in his continued loyalty to her brother.

Gilbert's eyes narrowed. "Why would you think your brother's confessor would seek other employment? What have you heard?"

"About Delacourt? Not a thing."

She did not think he believed her, but he asked no more questions. Sketching a bow, he took his leave.

There was no reason, Anne told herself, to suspect that there was more going on here than the obvious. Her brother regretted letting Madge go. He was jealous of Charles Knyvett. He wanted reassurance that his mistress had not betrayed him with another man. Not even Edward could seriously believe Madge had been a spy in his household, or that she was part of a conspiracy to bring about his downfall.

Anne continued to keep her eyes peeled and her ears stretched. She communicated with Madge by letter, glad that her friend's father had seen the wisdom of having his daughter taught to read and write. Although Anne was not sure it was the best course for Madge to take, she eventually forwarded a message from her to the duke.

In early January, Madge returned to the duchess's service, traveling to Thornbury with young Margaret. She wrote to Anne after she arrived there. It was a bright, cheerful letter that spoke of the visit of a troupe of French players and of Edward's plans to spend the month of February visiting shrines—Prince Edward's tomb at Tewkesbury, Winchcombe, Gloucester Abbey, and the Holy Blood at Hailes Abbey—and to hunt all along the way.

With each passing week after that, Anne felt a lessening of her concern for her brother . . . until she chanced to see, in mid-February in an anteroom at Greenwich, two men in earnest conversation. One was Robert Gilbert. The other was Cardinal Wolsey.

She tried to tell herself that there was nothing out of the ordinary about this exchange. One of Gilbert's duties was to spend time at court, petitioning for favors and garnering news. But he had a furtive air about him that she could not like, and the more she thought about it the more uneasy she became.

She went for a walk in the extensive park adjacent to the palace in an attempt to clear her head. It was a cold afternoon. Her furs kept her body warm, but the direction of her thoughts sent chills through her blood. Somehow, without intentionally heading in that direction, she found herself standing in front of a small house in the midst of the parkland.

It belonged to Will Compton as keeper of Greenwich Palace. Although he more commonly occupied his lodgings in the palace, hard by the king's apartments, his servants kept the place ready for his use. Anne hesitated. Had fate brought her here? Did Will have the answers she sought? She could think of no one better suited to help her deal with the threat the cardinal posed. If Edward's troubles were as dire as she feared, Will might be the only one who *could* help.

She rapped lightly at the door and told the lad who answered that she wished to speak with his master. She was shown into a cozy parlor where the fire was lit and the seats were comfortably padded, but she almost went away again before Will arrived. Indecision had her pacing in front of the hearth while she waited.

Will's face was flushed when he strode into the room, as if he'd run all the way from the palace. "What is wrong?" he demanded.

Anne resisted the impulse to hurl herself into his arms. "Perhaps nothing. Perhaps everything. But I cannot say more unless you give me your word that you will repeat nothing of what I tell you."

"I would die before I'd betray you, Anne."

She did not doubt the sincerity she heard in his voice and saw in his clear hazel eyes. He still loved her and supposed she continued to love him, just a little. She knew better than to tell him so. What she would tell him would cause difficulties enough.

"I believe that Cardinal Wolsey is conspiring against my brother the duke," Anne began. "Edward has said and done one or two foolish things that Wolsey has learned of. Taken together, presented in a certain light, they make Edward seem a traitor."

"What things?" Will's eyes had gone hard and cold. Only the continued warmth of his hand over hers as they sat close together beside the hearth reassured her that he would keep her confidences to himself.

"He . . . he listened to the false prophecies of a monk at Hinton Priory. Predictions about the king."

Will sucked in a breath. "Are you telling me that this monk foresaw King Henry's death and that your brother knew of it?"

"Edward means the king no harm, Will. You know the way he is—quick-tempered and outspoken. That's all it was. But certain things he's said—they might be misinterpreted."

"If he said them, he meant them at the time. That is all that will matter."

"The king has forgiven his outbursts in the past."

"But it is not the king you fear, is it? It is the cardinal."

Heartsick, she nodded. "Why does he despise us so, Will—you, me, George, and Edward? You know he was behind the trouble your wife caused at the Field of Cloth of Gold. But what have any of us ever done to him?"

"We exist. Your brother has royal blood. I have the king's favor. You and George simply have the misfortune to have ties to us both. Thomas

Wolsey is jealous of anyone he perceives as a rival and is bent on bringing about our downfall."

"He cannot be allowed to do so. I know you do not like Edward, Will, but you two have a common enemy. You must find a way to help my brother."

Abruptly, Will released her hands and stood. "I would die for you, Anne. You know that. But there is nothing I can do for the Duke of Buckingham." He ran agitated fingers through his hair, leaving the golden brown locks in disarray.

Stunned, she stared at him. She had been so certain he would help her. "But you have influence with the king, Will. You are his closest personal servant. You have access to His Grace that no one else has." He could whisper suggestions in King Henry's ear in the privacy of the king's secret lodgings.

But Will was shaking his head. He avoided meeting her eyes. "I cannot act against the cardinal in any way. It is too dangerous. You do not understand just *how* dangerous."

"Then tell me. Let us work together to find a way around the danger."

His smile was bittersweet. "Ah, Anne—after so many years at court, how can you still be such an innocent?"

"You, more than most, know I am hardly that!"

"My love, even were you to offer me again what I desire most in this world, I would have to refuse to help you save your brother."

She rose in a rush, temper flaring at the insult. Will Compton had disappointed her yet again. She was as angry at herself as she was at him. She *had* been naïve. He was no chivalrous knight ready to ride to her rescue. How could she have forgotten the lesson she'd learned so many years ago at Littlemore? Face flaming, seething inside, she retrieved her fur cloak and fled.

Outside, she was surprised to discover that the sun had nearly set. The path leading back to the palace was wreathed in shadows. Half blinded by temper and her vision further obscured by the twilight, she did not realize that she was not alone among the trees until a large, dark figure stepped in front of her. She ran straight into his solid bulk.

Hard hands gripped her shoulders. Only at the last moment before she screamed did she recognize him and stifle the sound.

"George!" she gasped, breathless with surprise and confusion. "What are you doing here?"

"I should think that was obvious," her husband said in a cold voice rife with disgust. "I am fetching back my adulterous wife."

66

Greenwich Palace, February 12, 1521

he moment he spoke, George regretted his hasty words. Anne stiffened in his grasp and the muffled sound she made reminded him of the cry of a wounded bird. He wrapped his arms around her and hugged her close, wishing he could make the last few moments disappear.

"Christ aid, Anne!" he whispered as he stroked one hand down the back of her cloak. "You are married to a jealous fool. I know I had no reason to make such an accusation. Can you find it in your heart to forgive me for one single instant of doubt?"

She hesitated just long enough to have him in despair. "Your jealousy is unwarranted, George, but I *have* been keeping something secret from you. In that, I have been as foolish as you."

Keeping one arm around her shoulders, he started to walk back toward the palace. Darkness was almost complete. Only the torches burning in the distance showed them the way. "We will retire to our lodgings and send the servants away. Then we will have honesty between us."

When they were alone in their inner chamber, George sat on the side of their bed and patted the space beside him. Anne joined him there without hesitation, but she folded her lower limbs beneath her, tailor fashion, and faced him, rather than leaning against his side as he had expected. Then she told him everything she had been keeping from him. The whole story poured out, starting with a letter she'd written to Thomas Wolsey more than ten years earlier and ending with the return of Madge Geddings to the Duke of Buckingham's household.

"And Compton?" he prompted when she finally stopped speaking.

"At first I thought he might know something of what the king and the cardinal have planned. Then I hoped he'd be able to help Edward."

"Help him?" George looked at her askance. "Anne, your brother threatened to kill the king. He boasted of having men who would support an attempt to seize the Crown. Even if he never does more than that, he has already committed treason."

"But perhaps the king does not know it yet. Cardinal Wolsey has had his suspicions for a long time and yet he has done nothing. And once Edward leaves on pilgrimage, he will be safe."

"It's no good, Anne. Buckingham has brought disaster down upon himself. It is not a question of whether Wolsey will strike, but only when. Your brother will not be allowed to leave the country."

"I never meant this to happen. When I wrote that letter, I wanted to avenge the death of our son by revealing the prioress's sinful secrets." Her face was a mask of misery. "I did not even succeed in my first objective. I have made inquiries. In spite of the bishop's visitation—and that *years* after my complaint—nothing has changed at Littlemore. Dame Katherine still rules over her handful of nuns with an iron hand."

"I should never have taken you there."

"You could not have known what would happen."

"Nor could you guess that revealing your brother's support of a priory would have dire consequences."

She choked back a sob. "That careless addition to my letter could end up costing Edward his life!"

"Anne, Edward committed treason all on his own—you did not force him to listen to those prophecies, nor did you place his hand on his dagger and tell him he should threaten to stab the king."

"What are we to do, George?"

He hesitated, then plunged ahead. "What did Compton say?"

"He refused to help."

"How much did you tell him?"

"Not as much as I've told you. Just that Cardinal Wolsey is plotting to ruin my brother. And I swore him to secrecy. He'll not betray me."

"No," George agreed, "I do not think he will." He prayed they were right about that. Anne herself could be arrested for treason if the cardinal realized how much she knew. So could he. So could Compton.

"The past always seems to come back to haunt us," she murmured.

He wondered if she meant his jealousy or her letter, but it scarce mattered. The only thing that did was keeping Anne safe. They needed to distance themselves from the duke.

"Oh," she said suddenly, startling him. "I have just remembered something. The king once promised me a boon. We were hunting, during the summer following our return to court. His Grace sought me out to ride side by side for a bit. I do not recall exactly what he said to me, but it reminded me of how helpless I had been at Littlemore, with no resources of my own. I told King Henry that I thought it most unfair that everything a wife brings to her marriage becomes the property of her husband when they wed."

"You said that to the king?" George marveled at her boldness . . . or her foolishness. He could not decide which.

"I believe my outspokenness amused him. In any case, he offered me a loan from the privy purse, should I ever find myself in need of funds again. When I told him I did not wish to be in his debt, he asked if I would accept an outright gift. I fear I found his attitude condescending. To put an end to the discussion, I suggested that he permit me to ask a boon at some later date. His Grace agreed." Hope bloomed brightly in her dark eyes. "I have never collected that boon, George. King Henry owes it to me still."

"He has doubtless forgotten that he ever made such a promise."

"I am surprised that I remember it so well," Anne admitted. "I do not believe I gave the matter another thought after that day. But if I remind His Grace of the encounter, surely he will honor his word."

"And if he does—what will you ask for?"

"A pardon for Edward," she said at once.

Panic made his hands clammy. "Promise me you will say nothing yet, Anne. Do nothing yet."

"But Edward is in danger."

"We cannot be certain of that, and to speak too soon may make matters worse for him." *And for us,* he added silently. Anne must not put herself at risk. He had to find the words to convince her that there was no need for precipitous action. "I have heard not the slightest rumor of any action planned against your brother, nor a single hint that he is plotting against the Crown. I doubt Compton has, either. You know he would help you, no matter what he *said* and no matter the cost to him. The poor fool is still horribly in love with you."

"I do not understand why." That Anne sounded frustrated by Compton's continued devotion pleased George no end. "I give him no encouragement. I much regret that I ever did."

"You are no more responsible for Compton's obsession with you than you are for Buckingham's treason. But, between us, we may be able to think of a way to mitigate the damage. I will talk to him. To Compton, I mean."

Anne flung her arms around his neck and hugged him, banishing thoughts of anyone but her. "Oh, I do love you, George. And I swear I will never keep anything from you again."

For the rest of the night, they concentrated on each other and did not speak again of Will Compton, the Duke of Buckingham, Cardinal Wolsey, or the king.

67

rom behind a copse of trees, Sir William Compton and his companions watched the Duke of Buckingham set out for court. A summons from King Henry had been delivered by a royal messenger the previous day. Will's horse shifted restlessly, sensing his rider's tension.

"How far back must we stay?" asked his servant. The king had sent a party of a half-dozen men, several of them in royal livery, to keep a close eye on the duke's progress.

"Well out of sight," Will replied. "We are to follow Buckingham but not overtake him." Unless, he added silently, the duke made a run for the nearest port to take ship out of England.

It seemed more likely that Lady Anne's brother had no inkling of the fate that awaited him in London. He gave no evidence of concern. En route, he stopped at all the usual places to break his journey. He even took the time to visit the monastery of Reading and make an offering at the shrine there.

Long days in the saddle gave Will too much time to think. He brooded. Both the letter summoning the duke to court and Will's own orders to keep the ducal entourage in sight during the journey had ostensibly come from the king. Will knew better. Cardinal Wolsey was behind both. He could almost find it in his heart to pity Buckingham. The duke had railed too long, too loud, and too often against the cardinal. Even when the two men appeared to be allies, Buckingham had derided Wolsey for his humble origins. Now the butcher's son meant to have his revenge.

Since Lady Anne's visit to his house at Greenwich, Will had tried to stay out of the duke's troubles. George Hastings had made repeated overtures, seeking his assistance. Will had evaded every one. In the end, it had done him no good. *Wolsey* wanted him involved, and the cardinal had the means to compel Will's cooperation.

Will tried to avoid thinking of Lady Anne, but it was impossible. His heart ached, the pain as physical as a stab wound, with the knowledge that his refusal to help her brother had cost him whatever small hope he might have had of winning her back.

Still, he knew he had done the right thing. The only thing. By the time she'd come to him, it had already been too late to save Buckingham. Will hadn't known that then, but he had known that to go against the cardinal would have hurt Lady Anne. Barely a week before her visit to his little house in the park at Greenwich, Cardinal Wolsey had laid his cards on the table.

"I have a duty," Wolsey had said, "as a prelate of mother church, to bring charges against those who commit the sin of adultery, no matter how high their rank. Even a baroness can be brought before the church courts and made to suffer the full penalty under church law. A woman, even a noblewoman, can be forced to do penance in public in her shift, her crime written upon a paper affixed to her forehead."

Will had refused Anne's request and sent her away to spare her that fate. A man had to protect the woman he loved, even after she no longer loved him. He would not let Wolsey prosecute and humiliate her. He would go on protecting her as long as he had breath in his body. If that meant giving in to Wolsey's demands and helping him bring about the downfall of the Duke of Buckingham, so be it.

His decision did not make it any easier for Will to live with himself. On the day before he reached London, the duke stopped for the night at Windsor Castle. The next morning, after Mass, he made an offering at the shrine of Our Lady of Grace. It was there that he caught sight of Will's servant and recognized him.

"Why are you loitering about?" the duke demanded.

Will, who had been watching from the other side of the shrine, kept out of sight, but he was close enough to overhear his man's answer. He stood up to the duke, bristling with defiance. "My office lies here by the king's commandment."

He did not need to say more. Buckingham was not a stupid man. By his thunderstruck expression, Will knew he'd realized that the summons he'd received was no ordinary invitation to return to court.

Will questioned the duke's servants afterward. Buckingham went from the shrine to breakfast but was unable to eat. He'd pushed aside the platter filled with meat, ignored a fine, fresh loaf of manchet bread, and called for his barge to continue the journey downriver to London. He suspected trouble, but he knew there was no way to avoid it.

That day's traveling ended at the cardinal's palace in Westminster. Will and his companions no longer troubled to hide their pursuit. The Thames was full of river traffic, but not so crowded that sergeants at arms in the king's livery could go unnoticed.

Will was close behind the duke when he entered York Place and demanded to see Cardinal Wolsey.

"My master is ill," one of Wolsey's men informed them. "He will see no one today."

Whether it was true or not, Will could not say, but Buckingham's face drained of color. He recovered himself with an effort. "A pity," he said, "but you cannot deny me hospitality. I will drink of my lord's wine before I go."

While the duke refreshed himself from Wolsey's cellar, another of the cardinal's servants appeared at Will's elbow. "My master would speak with you, Sir William."

So much for Wolsey's illness!

From behind his desk, the cardinal stared hard at Will through narrow eyes sunk in rolls of flesh. He had been sick, after all, Will thought.

Instead of his scarlet robes and red hat, he wore a fur-lined night robe. His head, bald save for a few wisps of gray hair, was uncovered. One foot, afflicted by gout, was propped up on a stool.

"You need not follow the duke farther," Wolsey said. "When he lands at the Hay Wharf to disembark for the Manor of the Rose, his barge will be boarded by a contingent of armed men from the Tower. Buckingham will be arrested and taken off, then led down Thames Street to the Tower as a prisoner. He is to be indicted for high treason."

Will said nothing. He felt no exultation at the downfall of a some-time enemy, only pity.

Something of his thoughts must have shown in his expression. Instead of dismissing him, the cardinal leaned forward across the desk. The smell of strong liniment stung Will's nostrils. "When you return to your duties with the king, you will say nothing to soften His Grace's resolve in dealing with the duke. Remember that if the highest-ranking nobleman in the land can be brought low, how much easier it would be to destroy a mere knight."

"You need not threaten me, my lord. I have no intention of opposing your wishes."

Wolsey's smile did not reach his eyes. "I am pleased to hear it, for it would be the work of a moment to implicate others in the duke's treason. One of his sisters, perhaps?" His fat fingers toyed with the lid of a metal casket decorated in enamel in diamonds of red, green, and blue, as if to imply that he kept evidence within, to be taken out and used on a whim.

"I have no intention of opposing you, m'lord cardinal," Will repeated.

By the time Will returned to Greenwich, word of Buckingham's arrest had preceded him. He was not surprised to find Lady Anne and her husband waiting for him in his little house in the park.

"You betrayed me!" she accused him.

"I did not."

"I confided in you. You repeated what I said to the cardinal."

"I did not," he said again, and caught her hands to keep her from clawing his face. "Wolsey already knew what little you told me, and more. He suborned your cousin, Charles Knyvett, and Buckingham's chancellor, Robert Gilbert, and by now he has the duke's chaplain and the monk from Hinton in custody."

"Damn you, Will. There must have been something you could have done to prevent this!"

He just looked at her, then shifted his gaze to George. "Take her away from court," he advised. "No good can come of staying here."

"I will not abandon my brother!"

"God's bones!" he swore. "Buckingham has betrayed and berated you for most of your life! You owe him nothing!"

"What does the past matter now? Edward never sought my death. And he always *thought* he was doing what was best for the family."

Will wanted to throttle her at the same time he wanted to comfort her. He did not have the right to do either. Nor would he ever tell her how narrow her own escape had been or how precarious her position would continue to be so long as the cardinal lived. "Go to Leicester with your husband, Anne. You can do nothing to help the duke."

"I can ask the king to free him."

"Don't be a fool!" Will's restraint snapped and he lashed out at her. "The last thing you should do is call attention to yourself!"

But she was beyond reason. "I will speak with King Henry. If you ever cared for me, you will arrange a private audience. Is that too much to ask?"

George spoke quietly. "She is determined upon this course. You can smooth the way."

"If any harm should come to you," Will said in a choked voice, "I would never forgive myself." Bad enough that he would never be heart whole again.

George took his statement for assent. An arm around Anne's shoulders, he led his wife away. "Send word when the arrangements have been made," he said over his shoulder. "We will be waiting to hear from you."

68

The king looked impatient.

He was nearly thirty years old, Lady Anne thought, but he had not matured. Oh, his body had filled out since the early days of his reign, when he'd still been more boy than man, but his nature was the same—impulsive, as quick to laughter as to fury, and always overly sensitive about matters that touched upon his honor. He was, in fact, very like his distant cousin Edward.

She had not been granted her private audience. They were in the great hall at Greenwich, remarkable for its size and for having roof timbers that had been painted bright yellow. Dozens of people surrounded them, bearing witness as she prepared to humble herself and beg for Edward's life.

Anne knew she would have to be careful what she said. Both George and Will had warned her that one wrong word could send her to the Tower and a prison cell of her own. But Anne had a plan. She thought it was a good one.

She was dressed in her finest clothing, richly embroidered and bejeweled. She had rings on every finger, at least one of which would be slipped off and given to His Grace as a symbol of her submission to his will. She had taken care with her cosmetics, adding a delicate blush of pink to her cheeks and applying liberal amounts of her sweetest-smelling perfume. The time was long past when the king had any interest in bedding her—Bess Boleyn's daughter Mary was still his mistress—but King Henry still appreciated a woman with a pleasing appearance.

She curtseyed low, taking deep, calming breaths to still her trembling.

"Lady Anne," King Henry said.

"Your Majesty." Will had told her that the king liked that title better than the traditional "Your Grace" or "Your Highness."

"Come closer."

He sat in an ornate chair under a canopy. A footstool had been placed next to it and he gestured for Anne to seat herself there. From that awkward and markedly subservient position, she looked up at him, searching for some sign of compassion.

Small close-set blue-gray eyes stared back at her, studying her as if she were some exotic breed of bug. He had grown a beard again. He'd had one before, started in a sort of competition with King Francis before the Field of Cloth of Gold, but he'd shaved it off at the queen's insistence. Less than a year later, Queen Catherine did not have nearly as much influence over her husband as she'd once had.

The king leaned close enough for Anne to catch a whiff of his favorite scent, a blend of musk, rosewater, ambergris, and civet. "If you have something to propose," he said in a low voice, "speak now."

This was the greatest degree of privacy Anne could hope for. No one was nearby, not the king's councilors, not his guards, and not his personal servants. She reminded herself that His Grace was under no obligation to listen to her at all. He had granted her a few minutes of his time. Now it was up to her to make the best of them.

Mindful of the need to protect herself and George and their children, she began with a disclaimer. "I know not what sins my brother has committed against Your Grace, but it is my belief that he saw the error of his ways many months ago. Your Grace knows he asked permission to make a pilgrimage to the Holy Land. I beg you, my liege, to let him go."

She held her breath, expecting an explosion of anger. The king's eyes flashed but then, instead of a spate of harsh words, he let loose a booming laugh. "Exile over execution, eh?"

Anne went cold as the Thames in winter, and light-headed, too. If she had not been seated, she'd have swayed, perhaps even collapsed. Only strength of will kept her upright, her gaze fixed on King Henry's face. "Will you not consider it, Your Grace? It would not be the first time you have allowed an errant subject to visit Jerusalem."

The reminder sobered him. Pilgrimages were rare for Englishmen to undertake in this day and age, but Sir Richard Guildford, father of Sir Henry and Sir Edward, had set off on one such venture early in the reign, after he'd spent some time in prison on an unspecified charge. Rumor at the time had claimed he'd embezzled money from the Crown. Anne did not know the details and did not want to. The only thing that mattered was that the case provided a precedent. If King Henry had let Sir Richard escape punishment by the courts, then there was a possibility that he would do the same for the Duke of Buckingham.

Anne did not have to remind the king that Guildford had fallen ill and died in Jerusalem. There were many perils in such a journey, everything from pirates to plague. But there was also redemption. And a chance to avoid the public dishonor of a charge of treason. For a moment, Anne thought that the king might agree. Then he shook his head.

"Some sins are too great to be forgiven, Lady Anne."

She bowed her head. She wanted to argue, but irritating King Henry now would only make matters worse.

"What do you know of your brother's schemes?" he asked in the same voice he might use to soothe one of his horses.

"Nothing, Your Grace." Anne kept her head bent and prayed he did not mean to interrogate her.

"I am told that you received a visit some months back from the duke's mistress."

"If Your Grace means Margaret Geddings, she is an old friend, one of my sister-in-law's ladies-in-waiting." She did look up then, straight into royal eyes narrowed with suspicion. "She and the duchess had a falling-out, now mended. It had nothing to do with whatever Edward has done to offend Your Grace. It was a purely domestic matter." If she could not help Edward, Anne thought, the least she could do was try to protect Madge.

The king seemed to have a great interest in Edward's servants. He asked several more questions about the duke's household, but none that Anne was able to answer.

"I have not had a great deal to do with my brother since early in the reign," she reminded him, "when we had a falling-out of our own."

The reminder made the king look away. Anne wondered if he could possibly be embarrassed but decided that was doubtful. Then she worried that by mentioning the incident she'd hardened his resolve to punish the duke, adding that long-ago exchange of heated words to the list of offenses Edward had committed since Henry took the throne.

"Your Grace—"

An abrupt gesture of one beringed hand silenced her. "Your brother's fate is in the hands of the law, Lady Anne." His implacable tone convinced her that argument was futile.

Accepting failure, she rose from her stool, curtseyed again, and started to back out of the royal presence.

"Your husband's services will not be required to make up a jury of the duke's peers," the king said abruptly, "and you both have permission to absent yourselves from court for a time."

Her step faltered, although she knew that the king's words were kindly meant. It would have been sheer torture to remain while Edward was condemned to death and worse for George if he had to pass sentence on his brother-in-law. Difficult as it was to appear grateful to a man who seemed determined to kill her brother, Anne murmured appropriate words of thanks and retreated.

Just beyond the great hall, two noblewomen were waiting. Bess Boleyn embraced her. She could see by Anne's face that the interview had not yielded the hoped-for results.

The other was Anne's sister, Elizabeth. Anne was shocked by her appearance. She had a gaunt and haggard look, as if she had not slept since she'd heard the news about Edward's arrest. Perhaps she hadn't. They'd always been close. Anne turned to her, shaking her head.

"I tried, Elizabeth, but His Grace would not listen. The king is determined to put Edward on trial."

"But why? Edward is no threat to him."

"Perhaps His Grace *thinks* he is." It was possible. If the king had heard the monk's prophecy and believed it, then he acted to protect the Tudor dynasty.

She held her sister while Elizabeth sobbed. It took a long time for her to recover her composure. Once she did, she had a grimly determined look on her face. "I will persuade the queen to ask for Edward's life," she vowed. "Let Wolsey force this trial. Let him convict an innocent man. The king can still grant Edward a pardon, *and* restore all that the Crown has seized."

Anne did not correct her sister's assumption that their brother was innocent. She prayed that Queen Catherine would believe it, too. The king would not, but it might not matter. She pictured King Henry and King Francis at the Field of Cloth of Gold—enemies who'd tried to kill each other only a few years earlier embracing like the best of friends. As long as there was hope of a reprieve, Anne meant to cling to it.

69

gents of the king arrived at Thornbury before dawn. They had already been to Penshurst and Bletchingly and others of the Duke of Buckingham's houses to search for evidence to use against him. They had seized all of his property for the Crown.

Madge was newly risen from her bed and not yet dressed, nor was the duchess. Young Margaret, who had been reinstalled in the ducal nursery since January, was also rousted out of her chamber. All the women in the castle were herded together in the great hall. Amid much confusion and no few tears, they were informed of the duke's arrest for treason.

The duchess glared at the leader of the king's men. "Whatever my husband the duke has done, none of us here had any part in it." Her voice was as cold and haughty as ever. "I demand that you allow me to return to my chamber with my tiring maid to prepare for the day. I have not even heard Matins yet."

He was unmoved by her air of command. "You are in no position to make demands, my lady. You will remain here until I give you leave to go."

Then he turned his back on her and barked orders at his men. They were to bolt the gates and outer doors. Then they were to go through Thornbury Castle, room by room, seizing money, jewels, and papers. Madge thought of the hiding place under the floor in her bedchamber—she always created such a space in any room she occupied—and wondered if it would be safe from such a thorough search.

"What is happening?" the duchess wailed, for once losing her composure. "What are they doing?"

The duchess's gentlewomen seemed at a loss. None of them answered her, nor did they offer comfort. Only Madge, who in her heart of hearts had long feared this day, went to her mistress's side and led her to a window seat, taking the place beside her. She did not murmur consoling words. She had none to offer. But when the duchess calmed enough to listen, Madge began to speak quietly to her.

"The duke is charged with treason, my lady, as his father was long ago. My father was in the old duke's service then. I remember what he told me of the day the king's men came to seize his master's possessions."

The duchess swallowed hard, blinked away incipient tears, and clutched Madge's hands with clammy, clawlike fingers. "Tell me," she ordered. "What will happen to us now?"

Madge paused a moment to gather her thoughts. Her father had said that Lady Anne and Lady Elizabeth had been left behind at Brecon Castle, the family seat before Edward chose Thornbury for that honor, when their mother and brothers fled. Lady Anne had been but a babe in arms at the time, but Madge did not suppose the duchess cared about that.

"These men will make an inventory of everything the duke owns," she said, "from the finest golden candlesticks to the piece of moth-eaten tapestry stored in some forgotten chest. Then they will break up the household."

"Where will we go?" Alarm gave animation to her face. Her eyes widened, her mouth worked, and her color rose.

"That I do not know. Perhaps to London to be questioned."

"But we know nothing."

One of the king's men, overhearing and taking pity on the duchess, sidled closer. "You're to be sent to one of your dower houses, my lady. When the dust settles, the king will no doubt grant it to you and let you live out your widowhood in peace. And you"—he met Madge's worried gaze and winked—"if you are Mistress Geddings, you will be permitted to retire quietly to the lands the duke gave you. Being unmarried, you hold them in your own right and they cannot be taken from you unless evidence be found of your complicity in Buckingham's treason."

Neither woman was much comforted by this information, but Madge thanked him all the same. Only after he had moved away again did she realize that the duchess still held her hands with a viselike grip. She felt the shudder that ran through the other woman's body as if it racked her own.

"We will survive this," Madge whispered.

"Edward will not," the duchess said.

They sat in silence until the searchers returned, displaying a collection of treasures. The duchess bit her lip to keep from crying out in protest when she saw that they had seized her jewelry. Rings set with diamonds, rubies, emeralds, and white sapphires were tumbled into a pouch along with strings of pearls, gold brooches, and diamond-encrusted crosses. Silver spoons and silver and gold plate went the same way, along with wall hangings and books and even the cups and chalices from the duke's chapel.

At length, the women were permitted to return to their chambers and dress, although valuables such as jeweled girdles and pearl buttons had all been taken away. Madge found her hoard untouched and quickly secreted on her person one little pouch of money and another containing baubles. Then she rejoined the duchess.

Eleanor Stafford, née Percy, Duchess of Buckingham and daughter of an Earl of Northumberland, stood straight and tall, facing down the king's agents. "My ladies will accompany me," she announced, "and we will ride our own horses."

One of them started to object but the other sketched a bow. "The king bears you no ill will, my lady. We will not turn you out naked nor will we force you to walk to your new home."

Madge suspected sarcasm, but they were not in any position to sneer at small favors. The duchess had realized the same thing. She hustled her women out of the castle and onto their horses before the king's agents could change their minds. The house they were to be permitted to occupy was a hard afternoon's ride away, but if they encountered no delays they would arrive before nightfall.

The duchess turned in her saddle and held out a hand to Madge. Her gaze encompassed Margaret, who rode at her mother's side. "You have property of your own, but I would account it a great blessing if you would remain with me. I have always appreciated your good sense and your loyalty."

Madge hesitated, glancing at Margaret. The girl seemed shaken by the day's events, but Madge doubted she fully understood what her father's attainder for treason would mean for her. There would be no marriage now to an earl's younger son. Fitzgerald's wardship, along with everything else Edward had owned, was forfeit to the Crown.

Eleanor spoke softly. "He was the father of my children, too, Madge. For better or worse, we are family, and family should cling together in times of crisis."

"Yes," Madge agreed, her uncertainty dispelled like mist by the morning sun. "Yes, my lady, you have the right of it."

This household—the people in it, not the place—had been her home long before she'd become Edward's mistress and had remained her home after he turned her out of his bed. She would send for her mother to join them, since the cottage at Penshurst would doubtless be lost along with all the rest of the duke's property. The duchess would take her in. And if the duchess had need of it, as Madge supposed she might, Madge would share what money she had salvaged to put food on the table and wood in the hearth. She'd have income from the land Edward had given her. That, too, could go to support them.

Madge did not hold out any hope that Edward would be pardoned, although she was sure that Lady Anne and Lady Elizabeth would do all they could to save him. She found it easier than she'd thought to put Margaret's future ahead of the pain she felt at his loss. Those Edward had left behind would band together. They would survive. Filled with a new determination, she used her reins to urge Goody into motion and rode away from Thornbury Castle without a backward glance.

70

he Duke of Buckingham has been indicted for high treason," George announced, "charged with planning to depose and kill the king and take the throne for himself."

"He would never have rebelled against the Crown," Lady Anne objected. "At most he's guilty of speaking out in anger, and of being credulous enough to believe the predictions of a mad monk."

He'd listened to those prophecies for years. If he'd meant to act upon them, he'd have done so long ago. Anne had believed, for a time, that she'd be able to convince the king of that, but King Henry did not care that Edward would have been content to tend his garden at Thornbury, visit shrines, and plan a pilgrimage to the Holy Land. And the cardinal was determined upon a trial.

Anne took comfort in her husband's arms. His lips brushed lightly across her brow. She did not weep. She had run out of tears. But she allowed herself to cling to him, absorbing his solid strength. George had been her anchor since they'd left court, helping her learn to accept what she could not change.

"I still feel as if I abandoned Edward in his hour of need," she whispered.

"Any effort made now on his behalf can only bring harm to others," George murmured. "I will not risk losing you."

"Nor I, you," Anne replied.

The danger was very real. Her niece's husband, Lord Bergavenny, had been arrested for no greater crime than once listening to Edward rant at him at Bletchingly. For accepting the gift of a doublet of cloth of silver, Bergavenny's brother, Sir Edward Neville, long one of the king's boon companions and friends, had been banished from court.

Four days later, Cardinal Wolsey made a great display of his wealth and importance by leading a procession of bishops and ambassadors and members of the nobility through London, riding under a canopy like a king. When they reached St. Paul's, he gave a sermon against the Lutheran heresy. This was followed by the ritual burning of every Lutheran book his men had been able to confiscate. Some thirty thousand people gathered to watch the bonfire.

Edward's trial began the following day. George attended the proceedings, even though he would have no say in the outcome. There was little question about the verdict. The Duke of Buckingham was condemned to die by the headsman's ax on Tower Hill.

Anne's sister sent word from court that she had persuaded the queen to plead with King Henry for the duke's life and that Her Grace had been rebuffed. Queen Catherine's failure ended their hope for a reprieve. Edward's fate was sealed.

"I wish I could take back all the evil things I wished upon him when I was a prisoner at Littlemore," Anne said.

With gentle hands, George stroked her hair, her back. "Your curses were not the cause of the duke's downfall. They had as little effect as the monk's prophecies. Less."

Anne wanted to believe him, but she suspected she would always feel some guilt. The irony was that Edward had been right about one thing—the importance of family. These last trying weeks had shown her the true strength of her marriage. For the rest of her days, she knew she would have the courage to face whatever came her way—even her brother's execution—because she had George at her side and their children to go home to. There was to be another child in a few months. She drew even more strength and courage from that knowledge.

On the day Edward died, the seventeenth of May, the common folk of London protested the miscarriage of justice. A guard five hundred men strong had to be called out to escort the Duke of Buckingham from his cell to the scaffold on Tower Hill.

"He made a good death," Sir Richard Sacheverell reported several hours after the headsman's ax had fallen.

"Is there such a thing?" Anne asked. She sat with her head resting against George's shoulder, feeling more tired and despondent than she'd ever been before.

"He might have railed against the king or the cardinal. Or tried to escape. Instead he accepted his fate and chose to die with dignity."

"He was never so popular in his life," George observed, "as in his going out of it. There is much weeping and lamentation in London today."

"They believe Wolsey wronged the duke," Sacheverell said.

"As well they should." Anne dabbed at the moisture on her cheeks and forced a smile. "My lord cardinal will end up on a scaffold, too, one day. That is *my* prophecy, for death always seems to be the price for too much ambition."

"What is your ambition, my love?" George asked. "Shall we return to court, or go home to the children?"

"I have already set Meriall to packing for the trip to Leicestershire, but there is one thing I must do before we leave London. Do you know where Edward will be buried?"

"In the church of the Austin Friars," Sacheverell said.

"I would like to visit his grave." She had not been permitted to see her brother during his imprisonment in the Tower.

Two days later, George escorted her to the churchyard. There was no monument. Anne doubted there ever would be. She knelt beside the spot where her brother had been interred and spoke from her heart.

"I forgive you, Edward," she whispered, "and hope that you were able to forgive me for the part I played in your destruction. You did not deserve your fate. I would have all men know it."

She reached blindly for George's hand and drew strength from him when he clasped his fingers over hers.

"Here is my solemn vow," she continued as tears flowed freely down her cheeks. "We will name the child I carry in your honor, a living memorial neither king nor cardinal can deny you."

As soon as she spoke those words, Anne felt a weight lift from her heart. She did not know what the future would bring, but she walked toward it free of the burdens of the past.

A NOTE FROM THE AUTHOR

No one knows for certain if Lady Anne Stafford and Sir William Compton were lovers. What is known is that Lady Anne and her husband, George, Lord Hastings, had a long, harmonious marriage. He wrote affectionate letters to her when he was away and named her executor of his will. William Compton also had strong feelings for Lady Anne. In his will, written in 1522, he left money for prayers to be said for her soul, something that was not ordinarily done for anyone outside one's immediate family. In 1527, Compton was called before the Court of Arches at Cardinal Wolsey's instigation and made to swear under oath that he had not committed adultery with Lady Anne during his wife's lifetime.

You can find out what happened to many of the real people who appear in this novel in the "Who Was Who at Court 1509–1521" section that follows this note, but please be aware, if you haven't already finished reading *At the King's Pleasure,* that some of the entries contain spoilers. If you are looking for more information on the Tudors, especially Tudor women, I hope you will also visit my website at www.KateEmersonHistoricals.com.

Brereton, Werburga, Lady Compton (1487–1522+)

Werburga was the wealthy widow of Sir Francis Cheyney of Shurland when she married William Compton in 1512. As Lady Compton, she was at the Field of Cloth of Gold in 1520. A daughter named Margaret died in infancy on June 15, 1517. A daughter named Catherine died before her proposed marriage to John St. Leger, with a dowry of £2,346, could take place. Werburga was pregnant with a son, Peter, when Compton made his will in 1522. He never made a later one. Werburga died before 1527. Her effigy at Compton Wynyates, Warwickshire, was thrown in the moat during the Civil War. When it was retrieved, it was missing the head, shoulders, and praying hands. Her husband's effigy is missing the hands and lower legs.

Catherine of Aragon, Queen of England (1485–1536)

Catherine of Aragon was sent to England in 1501 to marry Henry VII's oldest son, Arthur, Prince of Wales, who died soon after their marriage. Catherine spent the next seven years on the fringes of the English court and in near poverty. When Henry VIII succeeded his father, one of his first acts was to marry his brother's widow. During the early years of Henry's reign it was a successful and harmonious marriage. When the king left England to make war on France, he named Catherine as regent. Although she had expert help from the Earl of Surrey and others, she was the one who ordered troops to defend England against the Scottish invasion that ended with the Battle of Flodden Field and she had a hand in negotiating the peace that followed. When she failed to give King Henry a son, he divorced her.

Compton, William (1482–1528)

A royal ward after his father's death in 1493, he was appointed as an attendant to Henry, Duke of York (later Henry VIII), who was some eight years his junior. When Henry became king, Compton was made groom of the stool. He was the king's go-between in an attempt to arrange a liaison with Anne Stafford, Lady Hastings, and may or may not have been romantically involved with her himself. He married a rich widow, Werburga Brereton, Lady Cheyney, and used her fortune to rebuild Compton Wynyates in Warwickshire, which still stands today. He was knighted after the Battle of the Spurs in 1513. In March 1522, he made a will leaving Lady Hastings a life interest in property in Leicestershire and founding a chantry where prayers would be said daily for her soul. The latter provision was one usually made only for one's self and close family members. Records of the Court of Arches (an ecclesiastical court) from 1527 indicate that he was required to take the sacrament to prove he had not committed adultery with Lady Hastings during his wife's lifetime. He remarried shortly before his death in an epidemic of the sweating sickness (possibly a form of influenza).

Geddings, Margaret (d. 1521+)

Margaret Geddings may have been the daughter of Nicholas Gedding, receiver general to the second Duke of Buckingham. By 1500, she was a waiting woman to Eleanor Percy, Duchess of Buckingham, and mistress of the nursery at Thornbury. In 1520, she was discharged from the duchess's service. In November 1520, her name comes up in connection with Charles Knyvett, another member of the duke's household, and it is possible that one or both of them were involved in a conspiracy that eventually led to the duke's arrest and execution for treason. The duke received a message from Margaret on January 4, 1521, and by March 26 she was back in his household. At the time of the duke's execution, Margaret held the lease on some of his lands in Gloucestershire. She was probably Buckingham's mistress and the mother of his daughter Margaret Stafford.

Gilbert, Robert (d. 1521+)

Robert Gilbert was the third Duke of Buckingham's chaplain in 1509 and later his chancellor. His testimony helped convict Buckingham of treason.

Hastings, Anne, Countess of Shrewsbury (c. 1471–c. 1512)

This Anne Hastings was Lord Hastings's aunt, married to George Talbot, fourth Earl of Shrewsbury, by whom she had eleven children. Anne was at court as one of Catherine of Aragon's ladies-in-waiting at the beginning of Henry VIII's reign.

Hastings, Anne, Countess of Derby (c. 1485–1550)

This second Anne Hastings was Lord Hastings's sister. She had been married to John Radcliffe, Lord Fitzwalter, as a child. In 1507, she remarried. Her second husband was Thomas Stanley, second Earl of Derby. Anne was at the court of Catherine of Aragon as the youngest of her ladies-in-waiting in 1509 and was at the Field of Cloth of Gold in 1520.

Hastings, Lady Anne, Lady Hastings—see Stafford, Lady Anne

Hastings, George, Baron Hastings (1486/7–1544)

He married Lady Anne Stafford at court on December 2, 1509, and reportedly took her to a nunnery the following May, on her brother's orders, when she was caught in a compromising situation with William Compton, the king's groom of the stool. Whatever the truth of that relationship, George and Anne had numerous children together and appear to have had a harmonious marriage. When George made his will, he named his wife as his executor. In 1529, he was elevated in the peerage to Earl of Huntingdon.

Henry VIII, King of England (1491–1547)

Henry married Catherine of Aragon right before their joint coronation in 1509, but as early as May 1510, a Spanish dispatch reported that he was carrying on with one of the Duke of Buckingham's sisters. The resulting quarrel with the duke ended with the duke and both his sisters leaving court.

Herbert, Sir Walter (d. 1507)

The identity of Anne Stafford's first husband is not really clear, but he may have been the second son of an Earl of Pembroke who died in 1469. They wed in 1500 and probably lived in Wales until his death. They had no children.

Hopkins, Nicholas (d. c. 1521)

Nicholas Hopkins was a monk at the Carthusian priory of Hinton, Somersetshire. He was believed to have prophetic powers and predicted that King Henry would have no heirs of his body and that the Duke of Buckingham would one day rule England. He was wrong.

Howard, Lady Elizabeth, Lady Boleyn (1476–1538)

Elizabeth Howard was the daughter of Thomas Howard, second Duke of Norfolk. She married Sir Thomas Boleyn in about 1499 and had by him three famous children, Mary, George, and Anne. She was at court as a lady-in-waiting to Catherine of Aragon and was Countess of Wiltshire during her daughter's time as queen. Her brother, the third Duke of Norfolk (who was married to the Duke of Buckingham's eldest daughter), became the most powerful nobleman in England and it is generally accepted that he controlled the rest of his family, including his sister's husband and children. It once was believed that Elizabeth Howard died early in the century and that her children were raised by a stepmother, but documentary evidence has since disproved this.

Hungerford, Mary, Lady Hungerford (c. 1468–before 1533)

Mary Hungerford was *suo jure* fifth Baroness Botreaux, and fourth Baroness Hungerford, and Baroness Moleyns. Described as a "wealthy West Country heiress," she married Edward, second Baron Hastings, around 1480. They had two children, Anne and George, third baron. On May 1, 1509, Mary wed her second husband, Sir Richard Sacheverell. By 1517, they lived in apartments within the College of St. Mary in the Newark, Leicester, where Lady Hungerford "let her dogs run free in the chapel" and "organized bear-baitings on the grounds."

Knyvett, Charles (d. before 1528)

Charles Knyvett was a grandson of the first Duke of Buckingham and spent most of his life in the household of the third duke, where his father served as chancellor. Charles held the position of surveyor. He left Buckingham's service in late 1520 and gave evidence against him to Cardinal Wolsey that was instrumental in Buckingham's downfall. On July 11, 1521, Charles Knyvett was granted protection for one year "from arrest and imprisonment for any offense whatsoever." On April 20, 1522, he entered the service of Lord Berners, Lord Deputy of Calais.

Knyvett, Elizabeth (d. 1518)

Elizabeth Knyvett was probably the daughter of William Knyvett, chamberlain of the second Duke of Buckingham's household, and his first wife. Knyvett left his daughter Elizabeth a marriage portion of £333 when he died in 1515. Elizabeth was definitely a lady-in-waiting to Eleanor Percy, Duchess of Buckingham. She appears on a list of the duke's servants as early as 1508 and was still there at Easter 1518, when she was paid the twenty pounds due to her on Lady Day. After her death, her possessions were "wrongfully withheld" by the duke. They were inventoried after his execution and included such things as satin and damask kirtles, a black velvet gown lined with yellow satin with gold buttons, a blue velvet gown lined with crimson tinsel, gold chains, a silver basin and ewer, and six silver spoons. These possessions indicate a woman of some wealth.

Neville, Edward (d. 1538)

Edward Neville was one of the king's boon companions and was said to resemble the king so closely in appearance that he could fill in as his double. He was the younger brother of Baron Bergavenny, one of the Duke of Buckingham's sons-in-law, and received a gift of a cloth of silver doublet from the duke. He was temporarily banished from court at the time of the duke's trial for treason.

Percy, Lady Anne, Dowager Lady Hungerford (1443–1522)

Lord Hastings's grandmother, she was the daughter of Henry Percy, third Earl of Northumberland. Her third husband, to whom she was married by December 1493, was Hugh Vaughan of Littleton, Middlesex, gentleman usher of the king's chamber. In 1492, Vaughan was at the center of a controversy because more nobly born competitors did not want to joust against someone of his humble origins. Henry VII insisted that he be permitted to enter the tournament, even though he was not knighted until several years later. Under Henry VIII, Vaughan was lieutenant of the Tower and a privy councilor.

Percy, Lady Eleanor, Duchess of Buckingham (1470–1530)
Eleanor or Alianor Percy was the daughter of Henry Percy, fourth Earl of Northumberland, who was murdered when she was a young girl. She was probably brought up in the household of Margaret Beaufort, Countess of Richmond, along with her future husband, Edward Stafford, third duke of Buckingham. They married on December 14, 1490. She was at the Field of Cloth of Gold in 1520 as the ranking peeress but the very next year her husband was attainted for treason and his titles and lands were forfeit to the Crown. She kept her jointure lands, which gave her an income of two thousand marks a year. Eleanor's second husband was John Audley of Hodnill, Warwickshire. Her will, written on June 24, 1528, requested that her heart be buried in the Church of the Grey Friars in London and her body in the Church of the White Friars in Bristol, "if I shall happen to decease in those parts."

Sacheverell, Richard (d. 1534)
Lord Hastings's stepfather, he was knighted after the Battle of the Spurs and made many of the travel arrangements for the Field of Cloth of Gold. His letter to the Earl of Shrewsbury provides many details of the meeting between Cardinal Wolsey and the Duke of Buckingham to discuss potential brides for Buckingham's son.

Stafford, Lady Anne, Lady Hastings (c. 1483–1544+)
Lady Anne Stafford was the daughter of Henry Stafford, second Duke of Buckingham. Her mother was Katherine Woodville, sister of Edward IV's queen. Lady Anne married Sir Walter Herbert on February 15, 1500, and, after his death, although she had jointure properties worth three hundred marks a year, lived in the household of her brother, Edward, third Duke of Buckingham, at Thornbury Castle, Penshurst Place, Bletchingly, and the Manor of the Rose, London. She wed for the second time on December 2, 1509, taking as her husband George, third Baron Hastings. Lady Hastings was at court as one of Queen Catherine

of Aragon's ladies. In May 1510, she was at the center of a scandal. Her own sister, Lady Fitzwalter, informed their brother that Anne's behavior was bringing shame on the Stafford family. Buckingham subsequently caught William Compton in Anne's chamber. After a heated exchange during which Buckingham is reported to have told the pair that "women of the Stafford family are no game for Comptons, no, nor for Tudors, either," the duke saw to it that Anne's husband spirited his wife away from court, initially transporting her to a convent some sixty miles distant. Speculation ran high that Compton had been soliciting Anne's favors on behalf of King Henry VIII, and that Anne was already the king's mistress, but whatever the truth of that relationship, William Compton was the one who developed a lifelong attachment to Lady Hastings. In spite of the scandal and Compton's continued interest in her, Anne seems to have had a strong and loving relationship with her husband, as evidenced by letters he later wrote to her. They lived primarily at Ashby de la Zouch, Leicestershire, and at Stoke Poges, Buckinghamshire, but both participated in court revels in the spring of 1515 and were present at the Field of Cloth of Gold in 1520. From the late 1530s, Anne was part of the household of Henry VIII's daughter, Mary Tudor. Anne and George had eight children—Mary, Henry, Francis, Thomas, Catherine, William, Dorothy, and Edward—but their dates and order of birth are unclear.

Stafford, Edward, Duke of Buckingham (1478–1521)

He was the only duke in England at the start of Henry VIII's reign and had a distant claim to the throne through his descent from two of the sons of Edward III. He arranged the dynastic marriages of his brother, his two sisters, his son, and his three daughters, and was in the process of arranging the betrothal of his illegitimate daughter to a younger son of the late Earl of Kildare when he was arrested for treason. He also acknowledged two illegitimate sons, Henry and George. He apparently believed the prophecies of Nicholas Hopkins and did make a number of treasonous statements in the privacy of his own home, but it is unlikely that he had any real intention of seizing the throne for himself. He was planning a pilgrimage to Jerusalem at the time of his arrest.

Stafford, Lady Elizabeth, Lady Fitzwalter (d. 1532)

Elizabeth Stafford was the elder sister of Edward, third Duke of Buckingham. She was at court as one of Elizabeth of York's ladies by 1494. On July 23, 1505, she married Robert Radcliffe, Lord Fitzwalter. As Lady Fitzwalter, she was at the court of Henry VIII in May 1510, when she informed her brother that their younger and newly married sister, Anne, was being courted by the king. When the king learned that Lady Anne had been sent away, he forced Queen Catherine to dismiss Elizabeth Fitzwalter from her service, as well. Elizabeth later returned to court and was in attendance at the Field of Cloth of Gold in 1520. Her husband was created Earl of Sussex in 1529.

Stafford, Lord Henry (c. 1479–1523)

His older brother, the Duke of Buckingham, arranged his marriage to Cecily Bonville, widow of Thomas Grey, Marquis of Dorset, and mother of fourteen children. She was nineteen years his senior but very wealthy. For reasons that have never been established, Lord Henry Stafford was arrested immediately following the death of Henry VII and held in the Tower of London for several months. Once he was freed, however, he was quickly restored to favor at court and shortly thereafter was created Earl of Wiltshire.

Stafford, Margaret (c. 1511–1537)

Sadly, Margaret Stafford, illegitimate daughter of the Duke of Buckingham, followed in the footsteps of her father and grandfather and was executed for treason. She took part in the Pilgrimage of Grace, but she was singled out for trial partly because she'd led such a scandalous life as the "untrue wife" of Sir John Bulmer, son of the William Bulmer who got into trouble with the king for accepting Buckingham's livery.

Wells, Katherine, Prioress of Littlemore (d. 1525+)

Katherine Wells was prioress at Littlemore in Oxfordshire by 1507. In around 1509, she gave birth to an illegitimate daughter. The father was Richard Hewes, chaplain of Littlemore. Katherine sold priory property to provide a dowry for the child and kept her daughter with her. She also gave priory plate to Hewes. The discovery of these irregularities in 1517 did not result in many changes. Katherine was deposed as prioress, but she was allowed to continue to perform the functions of that office, perhaps because there were only five nuns at Littlemore. She also continued her affair with Hewes. In 1524, Cardinal Wolsey recommended that the priory be dissolved and this was done in February 1525. Katherine Wells was pensioned off with an annuity of six pounds, thirteen shillings, and four pence. I have no proof that Anne Stafford was sent to Littlemore, but it is approximately the right distance from Greenwich.

Wolsey, Thomas (1470/1–1530)

In 1509, Thomas Wolsey, a priest, was the king's almoner and chaplain. In short order he advanced to Archbishop of York, a cardinal in the Roman Catholic Church, and King Henry's chancellor, controlling both the government and the church. He lived grandly, building Hampton Court and York Place (later renamed Whitehall Palace), and is generally held accountable for the downfall of the Duke of Buckingham, who had insulted him on numerous occasions. Wolsey incurred the hatred of Queen Anne Boleyn and might well have met the same fate as Buckingham had he not died of natural causes when he did.

Wynter, Juliana (d. 1518+)

Juliana Wynter, Joan Wynter, and Elizabeth Wynter were all nuns at Littlemore Priory in Oxfordshire prior to the Visitation of 1517. They were undoubtedly members of the same family and quite possibly were sisters. The Visitation revealed that Juliana had been sneaking into nearby Oxford to meet a married lover, John Wikisley, and had given birth to his child. It was after this that Elizabeth Wynter offended the prioress, Katherine Wells, by playing games in the cloister. Dame Katherine beat her and put her in the stocks. Together with Joan Wynter and Anna Willye, Juliana rescued Elizabeth, burnt the stocks, and broke a window to escape the priory. They stayed away for two or three weeks before returning.

Secrets of the Tudor Court:
At the King's Pleasure

KATE EMERSON

Introduction

Based on the historical life of Lady Anne Stafford—remembered as the woman who had an affair with both King Henry VIII and his companion, Sir William Compton—*At the King's Pleasure* takes readers on the incredible journey of her life at King Henry VIII's court. Accused by her brother Edward, the Duke of Buckingham, of cheating on her husband, Anne is sent to a convent to pay for sins she did not commit. While Anne eventually returns to court with her husband, she never fully forgives her brother for his false accusation. It isn't until Edward is brought under the scrutiny of the king that Anne realizes the importance and strength of family bonds.

Topics and Questions for Discussion

1. In the beginning Edward Stafford, the Duke of Buckingham, thinks, "In England . . . it paid to know what your enemies were thinking. It made even more sense to keep a close watch on your friends." In what ways did it "pay" for the characters to know what was happening at court? It what ways did it not? Did Edward take his own advice to keep a watch on his friends, as well as his enemies?

2. Discuss Anne's siblings. How would you characterize Edward, Elizabeth, and Hal? Can you name any similarities between Edward and Elizabeth? Between Anne and her siblings?

3. Consider Anne and her role at court. What does living at court represent for Anne? Arguably, the courtly life was both an escape and an entrapment—without the court Anne would not have been caught up in her affair with Will. But the court is also the setting where George and Anne first fall in love. Do you see the court as more of an escape or an entrapment for Anne?

4. The historical figure Lady Anne Stafford is said to have been mistress to both Will Compton *and* King Henry VIII. In the novel, Anne is able to avoid the advances of King Henry, but she does eventually fall in love with Will. Do you think Anne was in love with both George and Will? Is it possible to love two people at the same time? Did you think Anne loved George more than Will? Or did she choose to stay with George out of obligation? Why or why not?

5. Reflect on the title of this novel—*At the King's Pleasure*. Who, in your opinion, was most at the king's pleasure? How does the title

reflect the milieu of King Henry VIII's court? Do you think being at the king's pleasure was a positive or negative situation?

6. Revisit the scene when George takes Anne to the convent (pp. 96–101). Why do you think George is so quick to believe Edward over Anne? Why does George harden his heart against Anne? Do you think his pride overcomes his desire to believe in the woman he loves?

7. "She had nothing of her own, not land nor chattel nor ready money. Even if she sold her book of hours and all the gemstones decorating her clothing, she would lack the means to live for more than a few weeks" (p. 117). What is the role of women at court? Consider Anne, Queen Catherine, and Madge Geddings in your response. How does the author highlight the role of women at court?

8. Taking mistresses was a common practice among sixteenth-century English aristocracy. Why didn't Anne want to participate? Discuss Edward and Madge's affair, which was public knowledge to everyone including Edward's wife, Eleanor. Do you believe that Edward and Madge were truly in love? Why do you suppose Eleanor did not mind the affair?

9. Discuss the character of Cardinal Wolsey. Do you think he possesses any redeeming qualities? Why does King Henry give Wolsey so much power? Why are Will, Edward, and George all against Wolsey?

10. The desire for revenge is a central theme in the novel. Anne seeks revenge on her brother for forcing her to a convent and therefore losing her first child, while Edward seeks revenge on anyone who questions his authority. What are other examples of characters seeking revenge in the novel? How does revenge dominate the daily life and events at court?

11. On page 264, Edward declares: "I will do to King Henry what my father intended to do to King Richard at Salisbury, I swear it by the blood of Our Lord!" As the novel progresses, Edward makes several such declarations of regicide, a sin that was punishable by death. Why is Edward so obsessed with the monk's prophecy that he will be king? In the end, what is responsible for Edward's demise: his pride, his vanity, or his belief in the prophecy? Or was it some combination of all three?

12. How does Anne come to understand the importance of family? Was it only through Edward's execution that Anne realized how important her relationship with her brother truly was? Consider the transformation that occurs in Anne's relationships with her siblings and husband.

13. "Here is my solemn vow . . . We will name the child I carry in your honor, a living memorial neither king nor cardinal can deny you" (p. 338). Did Anne and George's decision to name their next child after Edward surprise you? In the end, what do you make of Edward? Did you forgive him, as Anne and George had? Why or why not?

Enhance Your Book Club

1. *At the King's Pleasure* is the fourth book in the *Secrets of the Tudor Court* series by Kate Emerson. If your group hasn't done so already, read the first three books in the series (*The Pleasure Palace*, *Between Two Queens*, and *By Royal Decree*). Compare and contrast the novels. What characters overlap? Does court life change with each book? Which book did your group like most?

2. Court life in England is a popular topic in contemporary film. Watch *The Other Boleyn Girl* (2008), *Elizabeth* (1998), or *Mary, Queen of Scots* (1971) with your group to further explore this time period.

3. Host a luncheon that Anne and the other ladies in waiting may have enjoyed. Have each member of your group research and make a recipe popular in sixteenth-century England. Visit www.gode cookery.com for some ideas. Over lunch, discuss the best and worst aspects of life in King Henry's court. Would you have wanted to live at court? Why or why not?

A Conversation with Kate Emerson

Q: **Kate Emerson is your pseudonym. As Kathy Lynn Emerson, you are the author of the *Face Down Mysteries* featuring Susanna Appleton. Why did you decide to write the *Secrets of the Tudor Court* series under a different name?**

A: I actually write under several names, and the reason is the same for all of them—to let readers know what kind of book they'll be getting. Although some of my mysteries are also set in the sixteenth century, the "voice" is different. And, of course, the novels in the *Secrets of the Tudor Court* series aren't mysteries, even though they may contain some elements of mystery, intrigue, and suspense.

Q: **You've written several other historical novels. Did any of your previous books inspire this story?**

A: Not really. I take most of my inspiration from the central character of each novel in the *Secrets of the Tudor Court* series and Lady Anne has never appeared in one of my books before.

Q: **Describe the research you had to do in order to correctly represent real-life characters such as Anne Stafford and King Henry VIII. In what instances did you make a choice between fact and fiction, and vice versa?**

A: In this case I started by reading an excellent biography of the Duke of Buckingham by Barbara J. Harris. My next step was to make a timeline, filling in all the specific dates and events I could find for the period of the novel. I have an extensive collection of books on sixteenth-century England and my file cabinet contains a great deal of information I've collected in notes over the years, so it's usually just a question of pulling together the details I may need on various people and places. I make a character sheet for anyone I think I'm likely to use. As for choosing between fact and fiction, for me there's no choice to make. I pick fact every time. Of course, some facts are debatable, which gives me some leeway in interpreting history. And when no one seems to know what really happened, I feel free, as a novelist, to extrapolate from the details that have come down through the centuries.

Q: Who is your favorite character in the story? Why?

A: I have to confess a fondness for Will Compton. He's always struck me as a charming rogue. I'm sure the real person was less appealing, but seeing him that way allowed me to understand why Lady Anne would be tempted by him.

Q: How did you come to be a writer?

A: I've been writing one thing or another since I was very young. My first literary efforts were newspapers for my dolls. I was an English/Drama major in college, but there were no creative writing courses offered at that time so I'd have to call myself self-taught as far as fiction is concerned. I finally made the commitment to write full-time when I decided I was not cut out to teach seventh-grade English.

Q: Do you have any interest in writing historical fiction set outside the Tudor era? If so, what other time period in history would you like to write about? Why?

A: I've actually written about several other historical periods under the name Kathy Lynn Emerson, specifically the 1880s in the United States, Colonial America, and the English/Scottish border in 1400. I also wrote an unpublished children's book set in New York State in the 1920s. My interest in genealogy has led me to most of those eras. I have to say, though, that the sixteenth century is my favorite, and there is still plenty to explore in that hundred-year stretch.

Q: According to your website, you live and write in rural western Maine. Are you originally from Maine? Have you lived elsewhere? Explain how the place(s) you call home have helped shape you as a writer.

A: I'm originally from the Sullivan County Catskills in New York State, a rural area very similar to the western Maine Mountains where I now live. In order to write, I need quiet and solitude, so a rural environment is perfect for me. I can always travel to do research if I need to.

Q: What would you name as the major theme(s) of the novel? Why did you choose to focus on these specific themes in *At the King's Pleasure*?

A: Revenge has been mentioned above, and it is certainly a factor, but most of my novels deal, in one way or another, with the difference between illusion and reality. Lady Anne and the heroines of the earlier novels come to realize that the gilded trappings of the court are tarnished. How they deal with this discovery affects how they deal with other characters and what they finally learn about themselves.

Q: Do you consider Anne something of a renegade? Unlike many women during her historical era, Anne is seemingly unafraid to stand up to her brother and to speak her mind. Is this part of Anne's character historical or fictional?

A: I'm not sure she's so unusual. Or a renegade. She married both of the men her brother picked out for her, apparently without a qualm. The occasions when she stands up to her brother come only after she has been gone from his household for several years. These scenes, of course, are fiction. We don't have any records of actual dialogue between brother and sister, nor do we know what Lady Anne's reaction was to being incarcerated in a nunnery. We don't even know which nunnery it was, or what happened there. The specifics in the novel, including the loss of her child, are my invention, used to motivate what happens next.

Q: **Who is your favorite author? Who are you reading now? What is next for you?**

A: I don't have any one favorite. In fiction I read primarily cozy mysteries, both contemporary and historical, and romantic suspense novels, with regular forays into the paranormal mystery genre. The book I've just finished reading, however, is Eric Ives's *The Life and Death of Anne Boleyn*, an excellent biography which is also research for my next historical novel, which will be set during Anne's time as Henry VIII's queen.